FRIENDSHIP ESTATE

LYNDA R EDWARDS

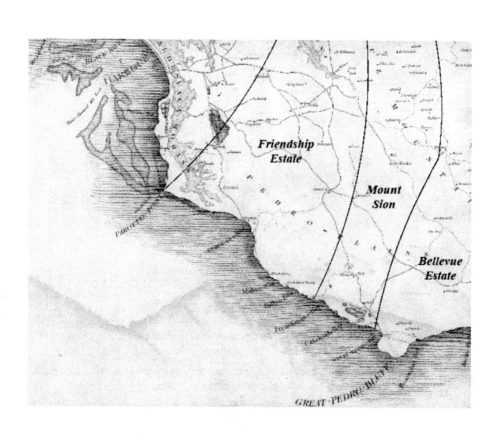

Friendship Estate
Copyright © 2020 by Lynda R. Edwards

All rights reserved

This is a work of fiction. Names, characters, places, and incidents are either products of the author's imagination or are used fictitiously.

The opinions expressed in this book are solely the author's opinions and do not represent the opinions or thoughts of the publisher.

The author has represented and warranted full ownership and/or legal right to publish all the materials in this book.

This book may not be reproduced, transmitted, or stored in whole or in part by any means, including graphic, electronic, or mechanical, without the author's express written consent except in the case of brief quotations embodied in critical articles and reviews.

First Edition
Printed in the United States

ISBN-978-1-7361633-0-6 Paperback
ISBN-978-1-7361633-1-3 eBook

www.lyndaredwards.com

This book is dedicated to

To my husband, Tim. He is my inspiration for every hero in my books, and our love is the inspiration for every love story I write. He reads my books just before I send them to print. He is and will always be my last word.

To the children of my heart:
Christopher, Ethan, McKenzie, Benjamin, Liam, Austin, and Blake.

Colonialism is the greatest transgression humanity has propagated on itself. But without it, we would not have the opportunity to create the greatest civilization humankind has ever known.

Table of Contents

Foreword		ix
Chapter 1	Friendship Estate	1
Chapter 2	Mount Sion	7
Chapter 3	Sabine Holborn	17
Chapter 4	Brixton Dunbarton	25
Chapter 5	Lady Margaret Dunbarton	35
Chapter 6	After the Storm	49
Chapter 7	Anne Holborn	65
Chapter 8	Spanish Town	81
Chapter 9	The Funeral	107
Chapter 10	Liam McKenzie	123
Chapter 11	The Dinner	137
Chapter 12	Lord Dunbarton	171
Chapter 13	Cockpit Country	193
Chapter 14	The Wedding	211
Chapter 15	Leaving Jamaica	223
Chapter 16	London Town	237
Chapter 17	William Wilberforce	267
Chapter 18	The House of Lords	293
Acknowledgements		318
Author Bio		319

Foreword

By George Graham
Author of Girlie, Hill an Gully Rider and Genevieve's Little Ways and many more wonderful books.

If only there had been a white boy named Brixton and a black boy named Dexter who had grown up as brothers, nursing at the same mother's breasts, celebrating their shared heritage and the dream of racial harmony. If only ancient spells could give power to the helpless and stem the brutality of oppressors. If only powerful men and women on that island could see the dawning of a new age and embrace the enlightenment, it would bring...

In the history books, Jamaica in the late 1700s and early 1800s was wracked by rebellions and reprisals. Plantations were set ablaze, and plantation owners were killed. The British government responded with hangings and extraditions. Emancipation came slowly and painfully, leaving a legacy of bitterness and resentment that poisoned the politics of future generations.

In Lynda Edwards' utopian fantasy, enlightened plantation owners take the torch of freedom into their own hands and join the abolition movement that is gathering force in Britain. Good hearted Lords and Ladies work behind the scenes to grease the wheels of progress.

From the plantations of Jamaica to the gilded halls of Georgian England, Lynda's magic carpet takes us on an enchanted journey. We witness the intricate romances and elegant customs of a bygone age, we meet a captivating array of characters, and we share their dreams, their passions, and their intimacy.

Lynda's book transcends history's oppressive grasp and conjures up a romantic age where anything is possible. We emerge from her dream world with renewed faith in the possibilities that lie ahead. By showing us what might have been, she points the way to what yet might be. If only...

CHAPTER 1

Friendship Estate

Lyndon Holborn, Master of Friendship Estate, lay on his deathbed on the 19th of August in the year of our Lord, 1786. Dawn was creeping over the mountains and would soon light up the Caribbean Sea. He could see the waves from his bed and tried to concentrate on breathing in with each incoming wave and out as it kissed the sandy shore and turned back toward the pull of the sea. He knew he was dying, but he still had things to do before he closed his eyes forever.

His second wife was much younger than he was. He had set aside his English wife and three children when he met her. Sent them back to England with enough money and a promise that he would never hear from them again. As the ship sailed out of the Jamaican harbor, he took for his wife, the love of his life, Anne Beauchamp. She was born in Haiti, and he met her there when he traveled to her father's estate to buy slaves. Her father was a Basque Prince from the Kingdom of Navarre. The small principality occupied lands on either side of the Western Pyrenees along the Atlantic Ocean between Spain and France.

Anne's mother was a slave, but when the Prince laid eyes on her, he married her the next day. He could have taken her without marrying her, as was his right as Master of the plantation, but he was so madly in love and out of his mind with lust for her that only the marriage bond would satisfy him and be acceptable to her. It was whispered that Anne and her mother practiced magic deep from the heart of Africa, so powerful they could bend the will of any man. Given how they were able to entice rich and powerful men to fall in love with them seemingly overnight, the rumor took flight as their fortunes improved. Anne bore Lyndon a daughter, she christened Sabine. Lyndon didn't think he could love anyone more than he loved Anne until he saw the perfect bundle the midwife laid in his arms with flawless mocha skin, a rosebud of a mouth, and beautiful dark eyes, the mirror of his own Anne's eyes. He fell in love all over again and vowed he would give this child everything he had. He spared no expense in bringing tutors to the island of Jamaica to ensure she could read, write, and speak English and French fluently, debate the history and politics of any nation, understand the science of crops, yields, harvests and manage her finances, which included the most abundant sugar plantation on the west coast of Jamaica. He worked to ensure that she would never have to rely on anyone for her livelihood. He raised her as he would have his only male heir.

Now, as he lay at death's door, he worried that he had failed her. His English breeding and enormous wealth had purchased her acceptance into Jamaican plantocracy society. But would it be enough to silence the whispers of 'half-caste' and 'browning' that occasionally floated to his ears? He had done the unthinkable in Jamaica's polite society; he had put aside his white family and made his life with his darkie family. He now worried that he would bring the life he had created crashing down around them with his death.

He had one card left to play, one given to him by his father-in-law, the Prince of Navarre. He asked his friend and confidante, Dr.

Richard Chapman, to attend him today so he could play his last hand in protecting the child he loved.

"Richard, thank you for coming," Lyndon was pulled from his reverie as his friend took the seat next to his bed. He tried to raise himself to shake his hand, but a coughing fit left him weak and spasming as he fell back against his pillow. Anne rushed to his side and gently propped him up against her so he could speak.

"I'm afraid I have little time left in this world, and I need to ask you a favor, my friend."

"Anything Lyndon, anything for you," Richard addressed the older man earnestly. Richard Chapman had arrived from England, battered and broken. He came from a good family in England, not royalty or gentry, but hard-working folk who had improved their lot from storekeeper to proprietors of a shipping fleet to learned doctors and lawyers. He had just finished his studies as a doctor and was to join a flourishing practice in London when his father was disgraced and died in a mysterious fire that killed his mother and young sisters.

His father lost a shipment of slaves at sea. He had undertaken the venture on the word of a nobleman who he later learned was penniless and needed the money from the sale of slaves he had procured off the coast of Africa. Richard's father sent all his ships without a deposit or guarantee from the nobleman and with great reluctance, because it was during the height of hurricane season. The vessels were all lost at sea along with their cargo, and the nobleman held his father responsible. He used his influence to get a judgment against his father, claiming all his assets except the family home. Richard could never prove it, but he knew it was the nobleman's lackeys who set the fire that killed his family.

Richard's society fiancé had refused to marry him after the scandal because he had nothing left in England. In disgrace, he had fled to Jamaica. His luck changed the day he met Lyndon Holborn, who asked nothing of him except friendship, until this day, the day he lay dying in his bed.

"Tell me, my friend, how may I help you?" Richard asked gently. He knew Lyndon was dying and was anxious to ease the anxiety he had seen on the old man's face as he attended him this past week. He moved into the Greathouse to be close to his friend in case he needed anything.

"Do you know the law of Primogeniture? What it entails?" Lyndon asked.

"I do, yes. According to English law, the firstborn legitimate son will inherit your entire estate," Richard started.

"Yes, correct, that is it," Lyndon cut him off.

"Are you worried that your son will come from England to claim your estate?" Richard asked.

"No, my firstborn son is dead, years past of dysentery and my English daughters have married well and have lives of their own. I suspect they have happily forgotten about me and about Jamaica years ago." Another coughing fit overcame Lyndon, and he stopped to take a drink from the cup Anne held to his lips.

"I want to talk to you about the law of Absolute Primogeniture; it is from the Basques, written in the laws that govern the Kingdom of Navarre. Anne's father was a Prince of Navarre. Absolute Primogeniture allows me to transfer the title of my property to any child of mine, regardless of their sex."

"Lyndon, all your property is in Jamaica, thus governed by the laws of England," Richard started.

But Lyndon interrupted him. "Anne, give him the document," Lyndon instructed. From behind her, Anne produced a long leather tube. Richard could see the insignia of the Kingdom of Navarre engraved into the leather. "Read this and let me know if you understand what it says," Lyndon instructed.

Chapter 1 | Friendship Estate

Richard carefully removed the fragile parchment and laid it out at the foot of the bed to see it better from the window's light. He read carefully, looking at Lyndon and Anne from time to time. Their eyes never left his face. When he finished reading, he walked to the window, but he saw nothing of the beautiful vista in front of him. He could not believe what he had just read.

Friendship Estate and all on it was the sole property of the Kingdom of Navarre and its heirs born in the colonies. As an only child, Anne owned it all, and as her sole heir, so would Sabine.

"There is no way this will hold up in an English court of law," Richard stated.

"It already has," Lyndon said. He was tired, and his energy was fading fast. "When I married Anne, her father petitioned King George to ratify that document, which he did. It does not have to go through the English courts; it is by royal decree."

"This will create a scandal that Anne and Sabine will never recover from. What have you done, Lyndon?" Richard asked.

"Anne is my other half, my equal, my better in many ways," he smiled and kissed his wife's hand as he said this. "My daughter is my only heir. She will inherit Friendship Estate and do wonderful things with it, I am sure. But I need your help."

"My help? How can I help?" Richard asked incredulously.

Lyndon took a deep breath before answering. "After a reasonable period following my death, I want you to marry Anne."

"What?" Anne and Richard exclaimed together.

"Anne, you have no family in Jamaica," Lyndon explained. "Your father turned his plantation over to your mother's family upon his death. That property is now a freehold, as it should be. Jamaica is a mixed-race island, Anne. We both know it. There are fewer pure Africans each year as they are fewer pure Englishmen. The abolition of slavery is around the corner, and I need you, Sabine and Richard, to prepare this plantation, hell! Prepare the island that bore our daughter for what is to come," Lyndon lay back, his energy spent. The resolve in his outburst had surprised them all.

Anne and Richard looked at each other. They were close in age, Richard being two years older than Anne. The only thing they had in common was their love for Lyndon, and they both understood why he wanted this marriage. Richard's name and white skin would protect Anne and Sabine. He would give them the legitimacy they needed to live life as they had, and no one in Jamaica would question them. It was the perfect solution for their bona fide continued existence. With tears in her eyes, Anne nodded her head in agreement. Richard followed suit as Lyndon hugged them both to him. Richard and Anne looked at each other over his head. What choice did they have but to grant the man they owed everything to his dying wish?

They were still looking at each other when Lyndon took his last breath.

CHAPTER 2

Mount Sion

Lord Harrington Dunbarton, the 6th Duke of Ergill, was not a happy man. He had a problem, and he had no idea how to solve it. It was a common problem for past Dukes of Ergill, so he was particularly annoyed that he could find no solution. In England, the Dunbarton name was associated with deceit, rape, theft, even murder. The final straw for the royal Crown came at the hands of the 4th Duke of Ergill, Gordon Dunbarton, Harington's grandfather. Coveting neighboring lands, he counted on the good manners of the Lord of said lands, even though there were generations of bad blood between the two families. He imposed himself and his fighting force on the reluctant Lord of the Manor to shelter them as they passed through his lands on a stormy night. As their hosts slept, he and his men slaughtered every man, woman, and child in their sleep. Unknowingly, they had left one witness alive.

Brimming with arrogance and self-satisfaction, Lord Gordon Dunbarton presented himself at King George's court, presuming to claim the lands based on the Lord's death along with all his heirs. Imagine his surprise when he walked into the throne room to find the youngest son of the murdered Lord, sitting at the King's feet. The King proclaimed him to be an unscrupulous reprobate, banishing him from court forever. As punishment for his crimes, the King levied a large fine on the Dunbarton Estate, taking all the income from their landholdings in England. In disgrace, Gordon left England for Jamaica to take possession of a coffee plantation he had won in a game of cards. By Jamaican standards, Bellevue was a small estate. Coffee barely made enough for him to live at the standard to which he was accustomed. In his opinion, the island of Jamaica only had one redeeming factor, slave girls that he could rape and abuse without recourse. Harrington's father, the 5th Duke of Ergill, Lord Harold Dunbarton, stayed in England, trying to reclaim the family's lost fortune.

Harold was a good-looking young man, with a glib tongue that earned him favor with young ladies whose only ambition was to improve their standing by becoming Lady of the Manor Ergill, humble as it may be. He snagged the beautiful and wealthy widow Camille Langley, whose husband had died, leaving her a sugar merchant's fortune. The marriage was a disaster from the start. Harold's disappointment in having to live in social exile, shunned by all his royal peers, manifested itself with intolerable cruelty toward Lady Dunbarton, exceeded only by the rapaciousness with which he went through her money. She died while giving birth to his only son, Harrington, the 6th Duke of Ergill. Her great friend, Lady Campbell, the King's consort, made such a stink over the depraved condition of Lady Ergill when she died that Harold was summoned to court, this time told to leave England once and for all. The court would no longer tolerate the dishonorable and disreputable behavior of the Dunbartons of Ergill. So, tail between his legs, he had fled to Jamaica with his infant son.

Gordon Dunbarton was barely eking out a living on the coffee estate and was none too happy to have any more mouths to feed until Harold drunkenly confessed to Gordon the details of the dwindling fortune he still had access to in England. In turn, Harrington had

Chapter 2 | Mount Sion

grown up at his father's knee, listening to his drunken ravings about the unfairness he was treated with by the English court, the Crown, and the woman he had married. The money was just running out when Harry, as Harrington was dubbed, went back to England, to the crumbling Ergill Manor to snag another rich wife. He had spent a year in his efforts; no one in England would have anything to do with a Dunbarton of Ergill, even two generations removed. Harry was forced to go to Scotland to find a bride. The stunning Margaret McKenzie, whose father was chief of the McKenzie clan. He, too, had lost favor with the English Crown. His family had been the fighting arm of the Jacobite army. Margaret's father was desperate to win back the good favor of the English Crown. Despite Margaret's warnings that the Duke of Ergill would not achieve that end, but quite the opposite, her father refused to listen to her when she begged him not to make her marry Harrington Dunbarton. Fooled by Harry's aristocratic looks, title, and estate in Jamaica, he demanded that she marry Harry. Against her wishes, Margaret married. Lord Harrington Dunbarton hastily dispatched himself and his wife back to Jamaica with a hefty dowry that Harry managed to get topped off regularly until now.

Therein lay his problem. He had just received word of his father-in-law's death. Margaret's older brother had taken his place as chief of the McKenzie clan and was no fan of Harry's. Shortly after the birth of their only son, Brixton, Margaret's brother had visited Jamaica to check on his favorite sibling and welcome her son into the clan McKenzie. What he found was a battered and bruised Margaret, the result of her husband's attention. Incensed by his sister's abuse, he gave Harry a proper thrashing and promised that as soon as he was chief, all financial support to Harry would stop, instead held in trust until his son came to claim it on his mother's behalf.

Margaret had happily presented him with the letter she received from Scotland that very day. So happy to hear the news of Harry's impending financial disaster, she could have cared less about mourning the death of the father, who she felt had sold her into hell. Harry would have loved to pummel her into submission as she tossed him the letter, laughing as he read it. His urge to hurt her was overwhelming, but some force beyond his ability to overcome stopped him. He could hear her laughing as he stomped out of the house, pacing up and down the long veranda as he yelled at the nearest slave to find his son and send him directly to Harry, without delay.

BRIXTON DUNBARTON WAS shirtless, his trouser cuffs turned up to his knees as he stood in the mud, barefoot. The only thing that differentiated him from the surrounding slaves was his skin color, deeply tanned as he was from days spent out in the Jamaican sun. Slung over his naked and muscled shoulders was a canvass bag. As he picked coffee beans and tossed them into the bag, he blew the blond hair that had escaped the ponytail at the nape of his neck out of his eyes. His hands never missing a beat as he quickly picked the precious coffee beans at their exact peak of readiness.

He looked to his right to find Dexter working as quickly as he was. They both knew they had to get the crop harvested today, or the estate would lose the only profit they would see this season. They were short of hands. Dexter had rallied all the slaves on the estate, even pulling them from the work details they sent to other smaller farms to supplement the estate's income. They all worked feverishly to harvest the crop before the angry dark clouds in the distance crashed ashore, taking their meager profit with the tearing winds. For the hundredth time, Brixton cursed his father. If the man did not have such a terrible drinking problem, coupled with a lousy gambling habit, they would not always be this hard up for funds. The man went through money like a waterfall went through water. So engrossed in his thoughts, he did not hear the little girl calling his name. When Dexter nudged him and pointed to her with his head, he focused his attention on her.

"Mas Brix, Mas Brix, yu papa calling fe yu," she yelled excitedly, tugging at his arm to follow her.

"I ca'an leave now, Pearly. You gwen have to tell my papa, to wait," Brixton answered, never taking his eyes from his work.

The little girl began to cry, "No, Mas Brix, you haffe come, or yu papa say he gwen beat me till me dead," she kept tugging at his arm.

Brixton looked at Dexter and sighed. They both knew it was no idle threat. He removed the bag from his shoulders and slung it over the girl's shoulders. "Tek me place, but just pick as far up as you can reach, when I come back, I will pick what you ca'an reach. Dex, you better come wid me," Brixton said as he patted the girl's head, wiping her tears, and set her to the task. Dexter nodded, taking his brimming bag and handing it off to the old slave who was placing the picked beans into the donkey-drawn cart that would take them to the sorting house.

"What fresh hell is this?" Dexter muttered as he followed Brixton to the house. Brixton stopped only to wash his feet and pull on a shirt. His father hated to see him dressed down as he was, and he wanted to get this interruption over with so he could get back to work. He found his father agitated, pacing up and down the long veranda.

As he saw Brixton, he started yelling at him. "Well, your feckless mother has done it again! She is the cause of our new woes."

Brixton's face hardened immediately. He knew his father was lying, but he was agitated enough for Brixton to realize something serious had happened. He stopped and rested one foot on the bottom step that led up to the veranda wrapped around the cut stone Greathouse. Dex stopped several feet behind him and waited. It wouldn't be the first time he would have to pull Brixton off his father. He danced on the balls of his feet, waiting.

"I am trying to save our crop. I don't have time for your hysterics now," Brixton was ready to turn on his heel and go back to harvesting.

"Your grandfather is dead, boy. Your mother got word today. Do you know what that means? Let me tell you what that means; there will be no more money coming from Scotland. Nothing for us to live on!" Harry was getting more worked up with each word.

"Good, with no money, there will be nothing to buy your rum and nothing for you to gamble with. All in all, I think this is good news," Brixton said. "Now, I have to get back to the one thing that may feed us through the next few months." Brixton turned to leave, but his father's next words stopped him.

"I'll sell some land, that's what I'll do! I'll sell Mount Sion," his father knew this would stop Brixton dead in his tracks.

Brixton turned slowly to face his father. Dexter moved closer to him. Mount Sion was the most beautiful property in Jamaica. The Santa Cruz mountain range, or the 'twins' as the slaves called them, because the ridges angled like two alligators facing each other, the tail of the ancient reptile resting on the edge of the six hundred acre property. The fertile hills gently slopped down to green fields that stopped at the edge of a flawless stretch of white sand beach. Mount Sion was part of the Bellevue Estate, but lay fallow because there was never enough money to do anything with it.

It was Brixton's favorite place in the world and the property his father put in trust for him. He and Dexter had talked endlessly about what they would do with Bellevue and Mount Sion after Harry died. "You wouldn't dare!" Brixton challenged him.

"Oh, but I would!" Harry exclaimed. "That Holborn bastard has wanted it for years. Even on his deathbed, he would give me a pretty price for it." Harry was always at his best when he was manipulating someone. Lyndon Holborn's massive estate bordered Mount Sion, and he had often asked about purchasing it. Margaret, the bitch, had made him put it in a trust for Brixton, but she had no money now, so she had no sway over him. Honestly, how he had agreed to do it in the first place still baffled him.

Dexter grabbed Brixton just as he started bounding up the steps. His father took a step back in dismay. "Don't do it, Brix; he's not worth it. We'll figure something out," Dexter whispered in his ear.

If looks could kill, Harry would have died on the spot, and he knew it. Brixton stopped his ascent but did not take his eyes off his father. He had never hated the man more than he did at that moment. "If you leave this veranda before I get back tonight, I will hunt you down and kill you with my bare hands. Lyndon Holborn is a good man, and he is dying. You will *not*, and I repeat *not*, bother him or his family during this troublesome time. Do you understand me, you hateful excuse of a man?"

Harry nodded; he felt genuine fear. Never had Brixton spoken to him in that manner, and he was actually frightened. Brixton's eyes shifted from his father long enough to nod his head, acknowledging his mother as she came out to see what all the commotion was about. She handed Harry the bottle of rum she had brought with her. She nodded at Brixton. She would make sure his father was too drunk to go anywhere, but that did not neutralize the threat he had made, and they both understood that.

Dusk was just beginning to set in as the last coffee bean was plucked from its branch and secured in the donkey cart. Brixton was physically and emotionally drained; his anger at his father had pushed him like never before, and by the grace of God, they had harvested the precious coffee. Angrily, he strode to the horse stable; still naked to the waist and barefoot, he jumped on his horse and galloped off toward Mount Sion. Dexter saw him leave and realized he needed time to cool down. Dexter was a slave born on the estate. His mother had been a slave and her mother before her. Harold Dunbarton was Master of the estate, and he had known no crueler man. Brixton Dunbarton would one day be Master. He waited patiently for that day because he knew no finer man than Brixton. He understood why Mount Sion was so important to Brixton. He knew why Brixton was so upset at his father's words.

Brixton pushed the horse to go faster. Born on Bellevue Estate, he had learned to ride without a saddle before learning to ride with one. He had grown to hate his father as much as he had grown to love his mother. From her and Nana, he had learned the value of women. They were always to be treated with dignity and respect. A lesson some of his ancestors had never known. Nana had been his father's nanny and the only person his father seemed to regard, albeit grudgingly. His great-grandfather had bought her before his grandfather had come to Jamaica. Nana had run the Greathouse for as long as he could remember. No one, not even Margaret, knew precisely how old Nana was, but nothing happened on the estate that she did not know about or sanction. It was because of her that Dexter lived in Greathouse. The boys, one a slave and one a master, had been raised as brothers from infancy. Never had either questioned their position on the estate. But times were changing, and they understood what that would eventually mean for both of them.

Brixton rode the horse into the sea and threw himself into the waves, kicked up by the storm offshore. He prayed the waves would wash away the anger that roiled inside him before he had to face his father again. He didn't know how much longer he could contain the hate and rage he felt toward him. He took off, diving into the waves, cutting deeply into them for the swim he hoped would silence the despair he was feeling. He was on his way back to shore when he looked up to see Dexter sitting on a horse; his foot casually slung across the saddle horn as he reached for Brixton's horse, who was getting more and more anxious as the churn of the waves grew. Brixton swam toward the beach, pulling himself out of the water, as Dexter backed out of the waves on his horse, leading Brixton's horse out. Exhausted, Brixton flung himself onto the sand. Eyes closed, he put one arm behind his head.

"Feeling better?" Dexter asked casually. Brixton opened one eye and looked at him. "I guess not," Dexter mumbled.

Brixton sat up, his arms on his knees, resting his head in his hands. "You know as well as I do why we cannot lose Mount Sion."

"I do," said Dexter.

"We are barely holding on as it is. Coffee does not make the same money sugar does. Your idea to hire out some of our workforce has brought in the cash flow we need, but we both know without that money from Scotland, we cannot afford to keep my father from looking at ways to supplement his income. If he finds out what we have been doing," Brixton's voice trailed off.

Dexter looked toward the mountain range; it held the secret to the real reason Brixton wanted to hold on to Mount Sion. "We will think of something Brix, we always do. The moon will not be out tonight, and the storm will be upon us by morning. Nana wants us to go over to Arcadia Plantation tonight. We both need to eat and get some rest before we can go. Avoid your father tonight. We will talk to Nana and figure this out. Don't worry," Dexter assured him.

Brixton stood up, shaking the sand off, and stretched. "You always tell me not to worry. You know it doesn't stop me from worrying, right?" Brixton responded before turning toward his horse, stopping as he noticed the lone figure on horseback. The horse and rider were on the hill that overlooked the beach. He couldn't see the rider's face, but from the way she sat in the saddle and the command she had of her horse, he recognized who it was immediately. Nodding his head toward the hill, he mounted the horse in one sweeping motion. "We have company," he said to Dex.

Looking in the direction Brixton had motioned with his head, he turned toward the lone figure on the hill. "Who would be crazy enough to be roaming the countryside as a storm approaches?" he asked Brix.

"Oh, she will make it home before the weather gets bad. She is the best rider in Jamaica; this is nothing for her," he said as he turned his horse toward home. "Race you," he challenged Dex as he took off.

Dex turned his gaze slowly from the figure on the hill. From Brixton's description, he knew who it was, and he understood why Brixton was not happy to see her on his land.

CHAPTER 3

Sabine Holborn

Sabine Holborn stood alone on the hill overlooking the white sand below her. She watched as the sea turned from turquoise to dark blue. The wind picked up the waves and crashed them against the shore, matching the anguish in her heart. Her father was dying. It was no longer if, but when and the unshed tears made the scene in front of her shimmer. The loud sobs that racked her body had subsided as she rode to her favorite spot overlooking the endless expanse of the Caribbean Sea. She loved Mount Sion, but it belonged to that hateful Brixton Dunbarton.

She had known Brixton Dunbarton all her life. A few years older than she was, she watched as he flirted his way through all the eligible girls on the island. All except her. She had listened as her friends prattled on about how handsome he was, his blond hair kissed by the sun, they romanticized. He was lean with long legs, hardened by years of riding and working his estate. No one seemed to care that his clothes were last year's fashions, slightly frayed and worn, or that his shoes were scuffed, and his dress stockings all had runs in them. He was so beautiful; everyone overlooked his financial shortcomings. As they grew older, a few girls had whispered of their romantic escapades with him. He was always polite but never flirted with her and had proposed no romantic assignations. It hadn't taken long for her friends to notice. They did not comment to her face, but she knew her standing with some of them had fallen, all because Brixton Dunbarton did not think she was important enough to flirt with her. She hated him for it.

Then she was angry with herself. She was better than this. Her father was dying, her champion, her protector, her mentor. They had said their goodbyes days ago. Her father had made it clear; he did not want her to remember him in death, but in life with all the joys and love they had shared. No man would ever love her the way her father did, and she feared losing that safety net.

She watched as Brixton frolicked in the waves, not a care in the world. He swam and splashed around, secure in his place in this world. She did not have that luxury now, and it shook her natural confidence to its core. She watched Brixton, and her resentment grew. Why was his hateful father still enjoying his life while hers clung to his? She watched as Dexter arrived. She knew Dexter too. He was always at Friendship Estate, sent on some errand, or with a message from Nana for her mother. He took the time to talk to her, smile, and shyly flirt with her, but none of her friends would ever notice Dexter or comment on how lucky she was to attract his attention.

Sabine sat up in her saddle, shaking herself. *Stop it! You are better than these thoughts. Brixton Dunbarton is not responsible for your troubles. Taking it out on him is beneath you!* She was angry at herself for her self-pitying and resentful thoughts. She looked back to the beach and realized that Brixton and Dexter had left. No doubt because of the droplets of rain that were falling. A storm was coming, and it was going to be a bad one.

She had to go home. She turned the horse reluctantly and headed toward the big wrought-iron gates of Friendship Estate. She didn't want to be outdoors when the rain pounded down. As she turned toward home, she saw it. Two forks of lightning converging above Friendship Estate. She couldn't see the Greathouse from her vantage point, but she knew what the lightning proclaimed. Her beloved father was dead. She urged the horse forward.

In addition to the lessons her father taught her, Sabine's mother had taught her the philosophies of her African ancestors. She repeated the ancient chant her mother had taught her to safely send her father across the plains of purgatory into his purification for his rise to eternal salvation in heaven.

"Wood feeds fire. Fire creates earth. Earth bears metal. Metal collects water. Water nourishes wood." In response, the wind howled, the rain whipped at her, thunder crashed around her as the lightning made her skin tingle. Her horse pushed itself to the limit as she gripped the saddle with her knees, opening her arms and her heart to the surrounding elements. Face skyward, she asked her ancestors to take her father into their arms. She asked the moon to watch over him. The sun to keep him warm and the Gods to make him happy. She, their servant, loved him and was willingly giving him into their eternal care. She grabbed the horse's reins, leaned forward until the horse's neck protected her face, and made it home before the earth kicked back the rain that pummeled it into submission.

She stabled the horse, taking off the saddle and drying him gently with a blanket. They were both breathing hard, heaving with the effort they had just spent. Sabine took a moment to collect herself. She knew what faced her in the Greathouse, and she wanted to present herself as the collected, mature Mistress of Friendship Estate. Her father's death deemed her so. They had talked about it many times; he had prepared her for this role, and she was ready for what would come next.

Calmly she walked into her home, the only one she had ever known. She knew she would find her mother in the great room, sitting in front of the fireplace. She went to her, knelt at her feet, and put her head in her mother's lap.

"You know?" her mother asked quietly.

Sabine nodded that she did. "I said the prayers. I prayed that he would be at peace."

Anne stroked her child's head. "How did it go in Black River? Is the sale of the land completed?"

Sabine took a deep breath and sat back, resting her arms on her knees. "The solicitor wanted to know why Papa was buying two hundred acres of land on the South Coast. He was skeptical of my answer that Papa liked the area because of its rugged beauty and crisp sea air," Sabine said, irritation in her voice. "I made him show me the original titles. I wouldn't put it past that cagey bastard to sell us land that wasn't for sale. He went on and on about how hard it was to find a title, and he should charge us twice the fee for all the extra work he had to do."

"What was your response to that? Anne asked.

"I told him to send the bill. He seemed happy to get the extra money but annoyed that the 'likes of us' had the money to pay him. We are now the proud owners of small patches of arable land beside long stretches of black sand beaches," Sabine said, parroting what the solicitor told her, derision in his voice. She was far more focused on how the solicitors dismissed her than her mother's response.

"There are no rivers, so navigation from the interior will be virtually impossible. The dry heat makes the cactus and bramble grow so thick you would have to hack at it for days to make one foot of headway. No one in their right mind would try to get to that land," Anne was saying.

"Mother, I don't want to know. Whatever you are doing there does not affect how I run Friendship Estate," Sabine said, waving her hand indifferently. She had more pressing problems to concern her and put the matter out of her mind.

Anne nodded at that. Those two hundred acres would suit her purpose well. Lyndon had searched endlessly for the perfect spot. He had disappeared for two and three days at a time, coming back with his clothes in shreds, torn at by the thick, thorny bushes he could not get through. If it had not been for the runaway slave looking for shelter and willing to trade the secret of the cave that led to a secluded beach, he would never have been able to find the hidden gem of land within. Now it belonged to Friendship Estate, and she had no time to waste.

Sabine was observing her mother. "If you plan to move all the runaway slaves you have hidden here on the estate, then you better move them out before the funeral."

Anne looked up at her daughter in surprise, a question in her eyes.

"Mama. I know how many people live on this property, down to the last child. If I noticed all the unfamiliar faces, others will, especially if they recognize them," Sabine warned her mother.

"How long have you known?" Anne asked.

Sabine did not answer her mother. Did it matter at this point? "Did Papa die peacefully?" Sabine asked, her voice small and concerned.

Anne took her daughter's hand in hers. "He did. He left nothing unsaid," Anne answered with tears in her eyes.

"Good, then I suggest you marry uncle Richard as soon as possible. The vultures are circling, Mother. The solicitor all but said so. Women will want you gone before you bewitch their husbands and send them back to England with disinherited children. Men will scheme to get their greedy hands on Friendship Estate, now in the sole possession of two 'black sorceresses'. We will need his white skin to protect us from the scavengers who will soon be at our door," Sabine said, wiping angrily at the tears in her eyes. Anne was taken aback at the bitterness in Sabine's voice.

"You know about your father's request?" A voice asked from the doorway, and they both turned to see Richard standing at the door. Nervously, Sabine looked at her mother; how much of their conversation had he heard?

Anne waved him in, and he came to stand beside her, resting his hand on her shoulder.

Sabine looked at the hand resting on her mother's shoulder. He removed it when she raised her eyes to meet his. "Yes, Papa and I discussed it. We will need your protection, Uncle Richard. Papa understood that; I understand it too."

"Sabine, you could pass for white in any English tea garden," Richard said, embarrassed by her words. No one could fail to notice that she was as enchanting a beauty as her mother was.

"Passing for white and being white are two completely different things. I don't expect you to understand Uncle Richard. I am a colored woman. You are a white man. Your superiority is guaranteed anywhere you go. I, on the other hand, need your protection just to cling to the only life and home I have ever known. Do you think that will ever change?"

"I hope so," Richard said, looking at his shoes.

"Well, it won't, and I am caught in the middle. If I were to marry poor, white trash like Brixton Dunbarton, society would call me a bewitching temptress who married up by devious means to secure a Duke who doesn't have a pot to piss in. If I married his slave, Dexter, I would be the one who married down. I would never be accepted into his world either. *What wrong wid the poor Master's daughter that she up and marry a darkie?* The people on this very estate, who have known me all my life, would say that behind my back. Black or white, being a mulatto as my mother is, or a quadroon as I am, makes me too good for one side and not good enough for the other. That is why I will consent to your marrying my mother, so soon after losing my beloved Papa. We both need the protection of your privilege." Sabine finished. She rose to stand in front of Richard. She put his hand back on his mother's shoulder.

"I will talk to the Vicar about an appropriate time to marry us," Anne said.

"But keep it quiet. We need to know who our enemies are, and they will show themselves as soon as Papa is in the ground. Once we know who is against us, we will know how to fight them," Sabine said as she left the room, stopping at the door and turning back to look at them both. She understood the closeness between Richard and her mother and what had brought them together. He was her partner in crime. "And get every one of those runaway slaves off Friendship Estate before Papa's funeral," she instructed.

Anne took Richards's hand in hers as she turned her attention to the fireplace. "The land we wanted on the South Coast now belongs to Friendship Estate. I would like to call it Treasure Beach. We can start moving the runaways tonight," she said distractedly.

"Anne, about Lyndon's request," Richard started.

"Richard, don't! He's correct; it's what needs to be done. We have been friends for years, I could not have gotten through Lyndon's illness without you, and I understand why I need you now, in his death. I only ask that you give me some time to mourn the man I love. I may not love you as a wife should, but I promise I will be a true wife to you. I just need time," Anne faltered on her words. She could no longer hold back the tears of grief that needed to fall. She knew she would never love Richard the way he deserved to be loved, but she would be a good and true wife to him. In time.

Richard held her as she cried. He understood why Lyndon had chosen him. When Anne had come to him, begging him to heal the runaway slaves that showed up in the dead of night, battered and broken from the abuse they suffered at the hands of his peers, he had not hesitated, and not only because he was in love with Anne, but because it was the right thing to do. Richard abhorred slavery; Lyndon knew that and had counted on it. He also relied on Richard's unrequited love for Anne. As he held Anne in her grief, Richard silently promised Lyndon he would love her enough for both of them, and that was a promise he intended to keep. Rocking her back and forth to soothe her, he said, "Treasure Beach, that is a very fitting name for the society you will create there, my love."

Anne raised her head, looking at him. Richard kissed her lightly on the forehead. He did not dare more, and she appreciated his compassion.

"I will send word to the Vicar at the Church and ask him to visit so we can plan the funeral and the wedding," Anne said, resignedly.

Richard nodded. "Hopefully, this storm will come and go without too much trouble, and we can give Lyndon the send-off he deserves. The rain is picking up. I have to leave now with Samuel if we are going to move twenty-five runaways to Treasure Beach," Richard said, turning toward the door.

"There will be more tonight; Nana says five more will come from Arcadia Plantation by morning light," Anne answered absently.

Richard wanted to caution her; too many runaways were showing up, someone would notice, sooner now than later. But he said nothing. He and Samuel had been working for days to secure provisions, including seed and small goats, everything the runaways would need to start their new life in Treasure Beach. It was all ready and waiting in the secret cave that led to freedom.

So, Richard turned away from Anne, now focused on finding Samuel and completing the task ahead before the weather worsened. The runaways could live and sleep in the cave until they built the huts they would need to live, not as free men yet, but not under the yoke and tyranny of slave life on a Jamaican plantation.

CHAPTER 4

Brixton Dunbarton

Brixton and Dexter hurried toward the Bellevue Greathouse. They wanted to be on their way as soon as it was dark enough. The rain would make their task even harder, leaving prints in the muddy ground that any tracker could follow. They entered the kitchen through the slave entrance at the back. Brixton could not remember the last time he entered the house through the front door.

Nana was waiting for them, with hot bowls of stewed peas and rice. They each kissed her on the cheek as they walked in. Quietly, they sat on the floor and started eating. "You boys going to have to be very careful tonight, cover your tracks or pray dis storm is big enough to wipe them away clean." She said.

Both men nodded but kept eating. There was no time to waste. They would have to be even more cautious tonight. "How many we picking up tonight?" Dexter asked, swallowing quickly.

"Five, two so severely beaten, they can't walk. Dat wicked Backra who run de place beat dem nearly to death. You gwen have to get two dead body to tek with you. Dat man gwen want proof, him two slave dead," Nana explained.

Brixton choked on his food upon hearing that. He hated having to take dead bodies with them. The bloated corpses with the fixed, staring eyes always made his skin crawl. But as slaves started disappearing, more masters wanted proof of their death. There was never a shortage of dead slaves in nearby graveyards packed into shallow graves to provide the evidence they needed. Nana had an arrangement with the gravediggers, slaves who had earned their free papers. They carted off dead slaves from the plantations and buried them for a small fee. It was always a risk switching bodies, and one Master had walked away from the corpse presented to him, muttering that he did not realize he had beaten the poor bastard so severely. Dexter and Brixton had shared a chuckle when hearing that story.

"When you pass de graveyard on the way to Arcadia Plantation, you will find two bodies ready fey yu," Nana continued.

Brixton couldn't help himself; he shivered at the thought but said nothing.

"One more ting, and Brixton, you gwen have to behave yuself. Remember what you are there to do, save life. De Backra tek a likkle gal fe himself, she is about ten years old. Him rape and beat her so bad, she ca'an lift up herself. Yu gwen haffe carry her Brix, but she fraid a white man, so you ca'an let yu temper flare when you see her so you frighten her even more," Nana stood next to Brixton.

He put down his bowl and wiped his mouth with the back of his hand. His eyes were hard as he looked at Nana. "She ca'an walk?" He asked as his face tightened.

"No, she will, maybe over time. But him mash her up bad, and they have to pack her wid cloth to slow the bleeding. I don't know if Mas Richard can save her, but right now, it don't look good," Nana answered.

Brixton couldn't eat anymore and put his bowl aside. The cruelty with which some masters treated their slaves was not new to him, but the barbarism he had witnessed since the rescue operations began made his stomach turn. He and Dexter had been rescuing slaves for the past five years. Nana had started the effort. The first rescues were her youngest daughter and granddaughter on their own estate after Harry had led his dinner guests on a late-night raid through the slave quarters. Their debauchery had led to the rape and mutilation of Nana's daughter and the rape of her thirteen-year-old granddaughter. Brixton and Dexter were in Black River overnight and came back to discover the destruction Harry and his friends had wrought.

As Harry slept off the night's excesses, Brixton and Dexter had taken the girls to Friendship Estate into Mistress Anne and Doctor Chapman's care. They had come back to find Harry crawling around in the mud, retching so violently he vomited blood. They left him where they found him, despite his pleas for help. For two days, whenever he seemed to stop puking and begin to fall asleep, Nana would go to him, forcing him to drink a concoction that started the entire process over again. He slept in the mud and his vomit until he had lost twenty pounds and was delirious. Brixton carried him to his room after dunking him in a nearby pond to clean him off, where he lay motionless for the two weeks it took him to recover enough to walk gingerly downstairs.

Brixton and Margaret were seated at the dining table, having dinner, and fell silent when he appeared at the door. They watched him as he took his seat at the head of the table. Ignoring his presence, they continued their conversation as if he were not even there. Nana's daughter and granddaughter never returned to Bellevue, and Harry didn't even notice they were missing. Brixton was livid. His father, in his wickedness and depravity, never recognized who he and his friends were hurting. It was the last time Harry ever led a dinner party raid on the slave quarters, but his actions had mobilized Nana, and it opened the floodgates to the freedom pipeline. Brixton and Dexter had no idea how she knew who needed rescuing, but she always seemed to know exactly where they were to go on a given night and what they would find waiting for them. They had been her willing accomplices when she had come to them with her plan.

Brixton would never forget the condition he found May, Nana's granddaughter, in. He still remembered the smell of all that blood, the feel of her in his arms as he rode to Friendship Estate. He was drenched in her blood by the time they got there and watched in dismay as Mistress Anne tore up a bedsheet and wadded it tightly between the girl's legs. In no time, it too was covered in blood, and she had to start the process all over again. He held May's head in his lap, trying to comfort her as fat tears fell from his eyes onto her face. It was not the last time he had spirited away a female slave in that condition, and it never got easier for him. The last time he had done so, the young girl had died. Brixton was so angry; he destroyed Nana's pantry. Dexter had to sit on him while Nana poured rum down his throat until he passed out. He was always tasked with carrying the slaves who could not walk because they wouldn't fight him in their battered and terrified state. While the slaves trusted Dexter because of his blackness, they feared Brixton because of his whiteness. Many saw him as the devil come for them and ran away from him in fear.

Nana had spread the story of the White Spirit, sent by African ancestors to free them from bondage, hoping that her people would fear his presence less. It did not take all the fear away, and he saw in the eyes of the ones he carried, their resignation along with the hope that death would find them quickly and release them from their chains forever. Brixton dreaded what he would see in this young girl's eyes, but it did not break his resolve. He lay down across from Dexter on the cool veranda, getting some much-needed sleep. Nana woke them close to midnight; their horses were saddled and ready to go. Dexter grabbed the lead rope for the donkey cart as Nana covered Brixton's face and hands in mud. She rubbed dirt in his hair to darken it.

"Your beautiful hair is the halo God give you when you born," Nana said lovingly as she finished with him. Brixton smiled at her, kissed her on the cheek, and mounted his horse. There was no moon to show them the way. Thick clouds hid it as the rain fell intermittently. They waited for the sound that wafted along the wind to guide them. Soon they heard it; the voices joined in song.

"By the rivers of Babylon
Where he sat down
And there he wept
When he remembered Zion

They crept forward, silently into the night, following the voices lifted in a chorus, leading them to their destination.

But the wicked carried us away in captivity
Required from us a song
How can we sing King Alpha song in a strange land?
'Cause the wicked carried us away in captivity
Required from us a song
How can we sing King Alpha song in a strange land?

Sing it out loud
Sing a song of freedom, sister
Sing a song of freedom, brother
We gotta sing and shout it
We gotta jump and shout it

Shout the song of freedom now
So let the words of our mouth

And the meditation of our heart
Be acceptable in Thy sight, oh Far I

So let the words of our mouth
And the meditation of our heart
Be acceptable in Thy sight, oh Far I

They stopped briefly at the cemetery to pick up the two bodies, wrapped in rough crocus bags. Thankfully, Brixton could not see their eyes as he and Dexter lifted them into the donkey cart. The voices were growing louder, and they could see the bonfire at the edge of the tree line. They made their way forward, stopping in the trees on the east side of the blaze, so they would not be cast in the shadows of the singers dancing around the fire. Lined up like sentries, lying on a bed of leaves, were five bodies also wrapped in rough-cut crocus. The rise and fall of chests were imperceptible to anyone glancing in their direction. Quietly, they lifted the bodies and put them in the donkey cart, leaving the bodies they brought in their place. The smallest crocus bag, Brixton picked up carefully and carried it to his horse. Dexter held the girl as Brixton mounted his horse and took the girl from him. She weighed almost nothing in his arms; he looked down and could see the blood beginning to seep through the rough cloth covering her from head to toe. He hugged her closer to him as he cradled her, gently opening the bag so she could take a breath of fresh air. She looked at him with dead eyes. She was breathing, but he could tell her soul was gone. She was catatonic. He cursed softly and moved his horse forward. The wind was picking up, and the raindrops fell more angrily, matching Brixton's mood.

They followed the path closest to the brush and trees around them. They moved quickly but carefully. They prayed no one would be out in this weather, but you never knew who you could encounter on a dark road in Jamaica. Thankfully, they were not out in the open for long. The girl in his arms whimpered once. Brixton hummed softly, trying to calm her. He kept his horse at a steady gait, hoping the rhythmic movement would soothe her. The rain was just beginning to fall steadily when they saw the wrought-iron gates of Friendship Estate in the distance. They bypassed the welcoming entrance and headed toward the back of the estate, where a secret path led them through the brush behind the slave huts. As they passed below the main house, a bolt of lightning illuminated the way ahead and frightened the terrified girl in his arms. Brixton looked down, cradling her closer, trying to soothe her. They came to a halt behind the cabin from which the faintest glow of light emanated. Brixton jumped from his horse, falling lightly to the ground with the girl still in his arms. Dexter moved ahead of him and knocked at the door softly. Mistress Anne opened the door and ushered them in. Gently, Brixton lay the girl on the long table as Doctor Richard turned around from the smaller table where he was laying out his instruments. Mistress Anne and Dexter left the room to attend to the four other runaways in the cart.

As Brixton turned to follow them, the young girl grabbed his hand. Surprised, both Brixton and Doctor Richard looked at the girl, whose eyes were firmly fixed on Brixton's face. "Don't leave me," she whispered.

Brixton knelt at her side, cradling her head in one hand and holding her hand to his heart with the other. "I won't leave you, little one, not until you feel safe."

Brixton held her as Doctor Richard removed the wadding between her legs. She arched her back in pain as a fresh wave of blood fell from her onto the floor. Brixton never let go of her hand, trying to calm her and keep her still through the pain as Doctor Richard stitched her up and replaced the padding. He held her as she drank the sugar water laced with rum he fed her. Brixton stayed by her side until she fell into a deep sleep.

"The beatings are getting worse, Mistress Anne. The masters are worried about another rebellion. They are moving to stamp out the resistance they feel in the air. More and more slaves are escaping from Jamaican plantations every year; we are only responsible for a fraction of them. Runaways are not safe here, Mistress Anne, not any longer," Dexter said to Anne as they waited outside.

"I know, Dex. There are whispers in every grand salon on the island that Jamaica has had more rebellions than all the other Caribbean islands combined. Their concern is genuine. Samuel moved all the runaways we had here to the cave. Friendship Estate owns two hundred acres of land on the South Coast now. They will be safe there; it is impregnable, and only a handful of people know how to find the entrance, and now one of them is dead," Anne was as concerned as Dexter was. All five of these runaways had been beaten severely, two nearly to death.

"Mas Lyndon dead Mistress?" Brixton asked Anne as he bowed before her. He had left the sleeping girl with Doctor Richard and stepped outside.

"He is Brixton, this very day. We are waiting until the storm passes to send out the announcement and post the banns," Anne answered.

"We are so very sorry for your loss," Dexter said.

"Mas Lyndon was a good man. I will miss his kind council," Brixton said.

"He was very fond of you, Brix, fond of both of you," Anne said, the words catching in her throat.

Richard came out then and put his arm around Anne, pulling her close as Brixton and Dexter looked away. Too many good men were dying in Jamaica.

"You boys had better head out before this storm gets any worse. It is going to be a bad one, and I am sure they will need you at home," Richard said.

Both men bowed to Anne before they turned to leave. Brixton led the way as Dexter followed behind him on his horse, holding tight to the donkey cart's lead. The animals were becoming skittish as they instinctively felt the danger of the coming storm. They rode hard until they came to the entrance of the tunnel that would take them back to Bellevue Estate.

Brixton and Dexter were young boys when they accidentally found the tunnel entrance that led them to the caves. They had spent their teenage years disappearing for days as they systematically explored the full length and breadth of the cave system. They mapped out passages, inspected pathways, rooms, and waterfalls, discovering every mile of the web of caves underneath Mount Sion's fertile fields.

They had fled through these caves with May and her mother the day after Harry had attacked them. The day Nana had begged them to get her children to safety, and they fled through the labyrinth of caves that had led to the birth of the freedom pipeline.

Not only did Brixton love Mount Sion for its beauty, but he loved it for the secret it held. The secret that allowed him to fight against the evil of slavery and the misery it brought to the people he loved. He loved Mount Sion for the salvation it brought him.

CHAPTER 5

Lady Margaret Dunbarton

Lady Margaret fingered the amulet around her neck as she waited for Brixton and Dexter to return. Dawn was breaking over the horizon, and she could see the angry bands of rain scurrying in with each crashing wave the sea threw to shore, ready to slash and tear at everything they touched. She wanted her boys home with her, safe and sound.

She stood at the door that led to the large veranda at the back of the house. Harry, firmly ensconced in the large planter's chair, was snoring loudly. He was too drunk to feel the brace of the wind or the raindrops that would eventually find him in the sheeting rain that would come when the storm intensified. He could stay there and drown for all she cared. She turned her stern gaze from him and looked toward the stables, looking for any sign of movement.

Nothing yet. She continued to rub the amulet at her neck, praying it would bring her boys the safety it had brought her. She tried not to think of the night she received it, but she could not help herself on nights like this. Married to Harry for just under a year, she was gripped in her living nightmare. On their wedding night, he had taken her by force, with devastating brutality. She was so surprised she could do nothing but whimper, scampering to the other side of the bed and away from him, as soon as he was finished with her. The next day they left for London, and the abuse only worsened. At first, she tried to fight back, kicking, punching, and biting; but it only seemed to excite him more, and he did unspeakable things to her. By the time they got to Jamaica, he had broken her. Margaret didn't know about the slave girl he had in Jamaica. He moved her into the house as Margaret's maid, but the abuse he meted out to them collectively forged a bond between them.

One night, he had come to Margaret, as she lay by herself. She begged him to leave her alone; she was still bleeding and sore from the night before. He laughed at her as he raped her again and again until she passed out. She awoke in a panic, kicking and screaming, as Nana tended to her wounds.

"I can't take it anymore, Nana. I will kill myself. I will climb up to the roof of this horrible place and jump off, or I will drown myself in the sea! I swear, I will! I can't take it anymore."

"I know, Miss Mags, I know! You poor body ca'an tek no more, especially now. I send fe help fe yu. I send Cotton to go get help fe yu."

Margaret could not stop the sobs that wracked her body. Cotton was Margaret's maid. Harry had never even taken the time to give her a name. He called her Cotton because he said her hair felt like cotton waiting to be plucked from its thorny bulb. Margaret had no idea who Nana had sent for. She understood there was no one to help her. She was as much a slave as Nana and Cotton were. No one in Jamaica would go against her husband to help her. Nana turned her to face the wall so she could treat the wounds on Margaret's back. He had clawed and scratched at her back as he bent her to his will.

"Dear God! That man is a beast!" Margaret heard the words but did not know who said them; her face buried in her pillow, shame enveloping her.

Chapter 5 | Lady Margaret Dunbarton

"It bad, Miss Anne, it bad! She not bleeding, but if he keep do her like dis, she gwen lose de baby," Nana addressed the voice.

Nana turned her over. Too humiliated to look into the eyes of her visitor, but she recognized Anne Holborn's voice.

"Mags, it is Anne Holborn. I need to examine you, dear."

Margaret closed her eyes as Anne examined every inch of her. Margaret could not help herself when Anne touched a spot that hurt. She grunted in pain.

"Mags, you are four months pregnant. Did you know that?" Anne asked softly.

Margaret shook her head, no. She did not even know what month it was or how long she had been in Jamaica.

"Margaret, look at me. I need to know if you want to keep this baby. If you don't, I will make it go away, and I will give you something that will stop Harry from coming to you in this way, ever again. But, if you want to keep this baby, you need to promise me you will fight, Mags. Fight for your life so that you can bring this baby into the world," Anne's voice was insistent.

Pregnant? I'm pregnant? Margaret thought. *I'm going to have a baby?* She fought to clear the fog in her mind. Someone she could pour her heart and soul into! Yes, she would fight for that.

"Are you strong enough to fight for your child's life?" Anne asked persistently.

Margaret looked at Anne and nodded, trying to sit up.

"Miss Anne, you gwen have to give her something to set dat man mind against her. If he keep doing her as he is, he will kill de baby." Nana whispered.

"Put a magic poon him, Mistress Anne. Magic him against Mistress Mags so him will leffe her alone, please ma'am," Cotton begged.

"Cotton, if I put the Master's mind against Miss Mags, he will do you worse than ever before. Can you take that?" Anne asked Cotton.

Cotton looked at Mags lying on the bed. She was curled up in a ball, her eyes vacant. The Master had been abusing Cotton since she was eight years old. She was now sixteen. Cotton had tried to teach Mags the trick of leaving her body and going somewhere else with her mind when the Master was on them, but Mags couldn't do it. She felt everything. Cotton knew she would lose Mags if the Master continued to abuse her the way he was. "Do what you have to and save Miss Mags, I can tek it. I can tek whatever de Master do me," Cotton said with conviction.

Nana and Anne nodded. Anne moved toward Margaret, shaking her so she would focus her attention on Anne. "Margaret! Margaret, look at me and listen to me carefully. I am going to give you this necklace. Look at it! In the amulet is powerful magic. It will make Harry stay away from you. No matter how much he may want to hurt you, he won't be able to touch you as long as this amulet is around your neck. You must never take it off," Anne instructed as she put the necklace around her frail neck.

"Thank you, Anne. Do you have one for Cotton too?" Margaret asked, her voice hoarse and broken.

"No, I can only protect one of you from him. I'm sorry. You must never take it off your person. The minute you do, it loses its power," Anne explained. "This amulet holds the darkest magic I know. It is powerful, Mags! Strong enough to turn his vile intentions from you, but the evil in his soul is too much for even the darkest magic to expel."

"Can I make him do my will?" Margaret asked.

"Your resolve has to be very strong, and you will have to say an incantation before, during, and after you make him do what you want. It will only work once, so use it wisely. Please be very careful. Bending evil comes at a high price," Anne cautioned.

"Thank you, Anne; I will never forget your kindness toward me," Margaret said. She fell into a deep sleep, with Cotton by her side.

Chapter 5 | Lady Margaret Dunbarton

"He is even wickeder than his father before him," Nana said as she walked Anne downstairs.

Anne said nothing, but shot a glance at Nana's face from the corner of her eye. She knew Nana bore the scars of living with Harry's father and grandfather. Nana had done everything she could to cure Harry of the evil in his blood, but it was no use. His father and grandfather held more influence over him than she ever would.

"If history repeats itself, it will not go well for Cotton, Nana. We both know these men will find an outlet for their perversions, and whoever they turn their attention to will suffer for it," Anne cautioned.

Nana knew only too well what Anne was referring to. Absently she fingered the amulet around her neck. The charm Anne had given her for protection. One night long years ago, after being sorely used by Harry's father and grandfather for days on end, she ran away. Beaten and bleeding, Nana had made it as far as the water well that separated Bellevue estate from Friendship estate. After nursing her back to health, Anne had asked her to go back to Bellevue Estate. Someone had to control the evil that hung like a cloud over the Dunbarton men.

But Harry was a special kind of evil; there was no controlling his appetites, which he exercised with malicious abandon. Only Nana was safe from his wickedness. Now Anne would be, but the cost of their protection endangered everyone around them.

Harry approached Margaret's room that very afternoon. All day he had relived the humiliation and pain he had subjected his wife to the night before and could barely contain his desire to continue the pleasure of it. He took the stairs two at a time, grinning as he touched the doorknob to open the door. But he could not open it. Try as he might, his hand would not turn the knob to open the door. He tried to raise his hand to pound on the door, but he couldn't. He tried to shout at Margaret to open the door. He opened his mouth, but no sound came out. In frustration, he stepped back until his back was against the wall, across from the door. He roared in defeat; the sound startling Margaret and Cotton from their sleep. He stood at the wall, screaming for Cotton. He started throwing furniture around, destroying everything in the hallway.

"Me haffe go, Miss Mags. I fraid a what he will do if I doan go," Cotton said fearfully.

"He will kill you, Cotton!" Mags grabbed her arm fearfully.

"I will be all right Mags, I likkle, but talawah," she answered as she stepped outside the door. Harry lunged at her, pulling her away from the door before she could close it. Bending her over the railing, he tore her clothes off until she was naked from the waist down. He yanked open his fly and entered her violently, pumping viciously as he pulled her hair, forcing her head back to claw at her breast. His eyes never left Margaret's, who sat up, clutching a pillow to her breast as she watched in horror. When it was over, he turned Cotton around and beat her until she couldn't stand anymore.

"I will do this to her every day, every night, right here as you watch. You may be safe for now, but she never will be," Harry said to Margaret, his eyes never leaving hers. He stepped over Cotton, crumpled on the floor, and went downstairs, calling for Nana to bring him a bottle of rum.

He was true to his word. Every day, he went after Cotton. As soon as he left, Margaret would run to Cotton, helping her up and bringing her into the room they shared. She did everything she could to ease Cotton's suffering, but it only made it worse. As soon as Harry realized how fond Margaret was of Cotton, the abuse intensified, and he made sure Margaret watched every minute of Cotton's misuse.

Cotton lost weight; she couldn't keep anything down. Half the time, Cotton wasn't even conscious, but Harry's abuse did not let up. He had discovered a unique way to torture them both, and he missed no opportunity.

He could never lay a hand on Margaret, God he wanted to, but he could not bring himself to do it. He took it all out on Cotton, doing unthinkable things to her, all the while wanting to do them to Margaret. He did not even notice as Margaret's belly swelled with pregnancy. Margaret was far along in her pregnancy when Harry announced he was going to Black River to meet with his solicitors; he petitioned her father for more money and would be away from the estate for two days. He wanted Cotton to go with him, but Nana put her foot down. "Golong wid yu bad self, Harry, but you gwen leave Cotton to dead in peace," Nana said as Margaret and Nana held a barely conscious Cotton between them. Harry had dragged her down the steps, intending to tie her to the back of his horse.

Harry bellowed in anger, powerless when faced with the combined forces of Margaret and Nana. He kicked the horse viciously, screaming like a madman as he left. It was then, Nana and Margaret heard the whoosh as Cotton's water broke, and hot liquid splashed on them both. They looked at each other in surprise; they had no idea Cotton was pregnant.

It was a long and difficult labor. Cotton's body was at its limit. Margaret fed her sugar water as Nana tried to coax the baby out of her. Cotton finally pushed the baby out, entirely undone by the effort it took.

"It's a boy," Nana revealed as she laid the little body on Cotton's stomach, who didn't even have the strength to hold him.

Cotton smiled weakly and looked at Margaret. "I give him to you, Mags, love him as you have loved me, tek care of him, and raise him as your own."

Tears flowing, Margaret held Cotton to her, putting her arm around the child that still lay on her stomach. "I promise Cotton, your son will want for nothing, and he will be loved," Margaret promised her.

Cotton spent her last breath kissing her son goodbye. It was then Margaret felt her water break. Her son would come into this world in the wee hours of the next morning. The boys were born precisely six hours apart.

Margaret named her sons Dexter and Brixton. Nana summoned Dr. Richard to attend to Margaret. If it surprised him to see a black baby attached to her left breast as she gave birth to her white baby, he said nothing. Dr. Richard affixed his name and seal to her son's birth paper. Before he left, Margaret asked Dr. Richard for one amendment.

"Are you sure, Margaret? It won't even be legal until it is notarized and filed in Black River. I highly doubt your husband will agree to this," Dr. Richard advised her.

"Don't worry about my husband, Dr. Richard. I have my sons; he is no match for me now," Margaret answered.

Richard looked at the woman in front of him. The woman standing before him was no shrinking English rose, a steadfast Scottish thorn had replaced her, and if Harry Dunbarton was worthy of pity, Richard might have pitied him.

Harry came home that night. He started screaming for Cotton the minute he walked through the door. Nana led him to the dining room, where Margaret had insisted that Cotton's body be laid out for viewing before her burial. Margaret sat next to Cotton, holding her hand as Harry came through the door.

Harry looked from Margaret to the body and back again. "You killed her? Did you kill her to thwart me?" Harry asked.

"No, I did not kill her, you did," Margaret answered. He finally noticed the bassinet next to her. Walking over, he looked inside, then back to Margaret.

Chapter 5 | Lady Margaret Dunbarton

"Cotton's gift to me before she died. I gave birth shortly after she did," Margaret offered an answer to the question in his eyes.

"That darkie is not staying in my house," Harry responded.

Margaret stood up, lifting Dexter in her arms. "Nana and I will raise my sons in this home, my home. You are but a tolerated guest here, and you would do well to remember that. You will sign the documents over there, and then you will go upstairs to your room. A bottle of rum is next to your bed. Make sure you drink every drop of it."

"The hell I will! You forget yourself, Margaret!" Harry bellowed.

"The Light of the Moon – surround us.

The Love of the Sun – enfold us.

The Power of our ancestors – protect us.

The Presence of God – watch over us.

The Mind of Justice – guide us.

The Law of Nature – direct us.

Wherever we are – God, be our strength and harbor against evil."

Margaret and Nana whispered the incantation, each holding their protective amulet forward in front of them. Margaret held Dexter with one arm as Nana led Harry to the table to sign the documents already affixed with the witnesses' signatures. Docile as a lamb, Harry signed the papers, then turned on his heel and went upstairs. It was only when he got to his room, bone-tired and still hungover, he wondered how he got there. Then he saw the bottle of rum waiting for him. Taking a long pull of the bottle, he kicked off his boots and lay across the bed, cradling the bottle with his head on the pillow.

Nana dispatched the documents to Black River, with a note from Harry to his solicitors asking that they file them with the courthouse and send the notarized paperwork back to him for safekeeping.

His solicitor wondered why Harry didn't bring the documents himself, but looking at the date and time on the birth paper, he realized that the child was born while Harry was already in Black River. The birth paper was on top of other documents, but he did not see the need to examine any of the other papers included in the packet. It was the end of the day, and he was in a hurry to get them to the courthouse before it closed for the day. Harry's gift of a young, nubile twelve-year-old darkie waited for him at his home. He dropped off the papers, instructing the clerk to send the notarized documents to Bellevue Estate at his earliest convenience. Then he promptly forgot about the paperwork as he hurried home in anticipation of the night's depravity.

Those notarized documents were now safely tucked away from prying eyes. She looked again toward the stables. It was difficult to hear anything with the rain pounding on the metal shingles of the roof. The Bellevue Greathouse was typical of the time, built of cut stone on the first two levels and stucco on the third and uppermost level. At the front of the Greathouse was a grand staircase, also crafted from cut stone that led to the second level stately entrance. She stood on the back veranda on the seaward side of the building. Only Harry and his cronies ever used the front entrance. It was much easier to access the house from the back veranda that stood directly in line with the stables and processing factory, which was the hub of the estate. Margaret did not take her eyes off the path that led to the veranda from the stables. It was a small dirt track, worn from years of use and framed on each side by colorful hibiscus plants that grew in wild abandon all over the island.

She let out the breath she was holding as she saw Dexter and Brixton coming down the pathway. Her father always said the McKenzie blood was mixed with wild Norse men, pillaging up and down Scotland and England's Atlantic coast. In her son, she saw that it was true. He was tall and lithe, nimble on his feet and graceful. His blond hair was the color of the sun as it grew long and untamed. Brixton could easily pass for any Viking God, with his good looks and quick wit. Dexter looked exactly like his father, but with a darker complexion. He was a studious man with a stocky build—the brain to Brixton's brawn. Dexter's resemblance to Harry was uncanny. Dexter had Harry's straight nose, full mouth, and piercing eyes, albeit without the evil that emanated from them. Harry was quick to throw out any guest who dared to remark on the similarity in their looks. The only person who did not see the likeness was Harry.

Dexter smiled and waved at her as they drew closer. She and Nana had raised them as the brothers they were, with every advantage they could squeeze out of Harry for them. Both had suckled at her breast, and she loved them equally. Brixton stopped under the rain run-off pipe before he approached his mother. The rain had not washed away the mud and dirt Nana had covered him in, so he stood under the cascading water, washing the remnants of the night's activities off. Dexter walked ahead to kiss Margaret on the cheek.

"Mother, it's late, and the weather is getting worse. You shouldn't be out here. You will catch your death," Dexter said.

Margaret reached up to caress his face lovingly as she smiled at him. "Don't worry about me, I am likkle, but I talawah."

Dexter smiled as he took her arm to lead her inside. He knew how fond his mother was of that Jamaican saying. "You may be small in stature, but you're a strong-willed and determined woman. I admire you for that. However, even you are no match for the elements."

Brixton bounded up the stairs, grabbed her around the waist, lifting her, and carried her through the door. She couldn't help but laugh at his antics. Nana met them with a bottle of white rum as they came into the kitchen. Brixton immediately grabbed it and put it to his lips, swallowing deeply.

Nana grabbed the bottle from him. "It is not to drink! It is to rub in yu head, so yu don't catch yu death," Nana admonished him, but Brixton just laughed and kissed her. She had brought both boys warmed towels and dry clothes. They changed clothes as she asked them how the night went.

"The slave population outnumbers the white population by twenty to one, and the masters are in fear of their lives, afraid of rebellion. The beatings are getting worse, and they are killing any slave they feel will rise up against them," Dexter said, concern in his voice.

"Mistress Anne tell me the estates are paying the Maroon slave trackers by the head, and they can bring dem back dead or alive. She say two Maroons come by Friendship Estate offering dem services to Mas Lyndon, and she run dem," Nana said. The Maroons were African slaves brought in by the Spanish when they ruled Jamaica. These fierce men and women did not take to slavery willingly. They ran away to the mountains. When England captured the island, they fought valiantly against the English. They were so feared, the English Governor signed a treaty with the Maroons, giving them freedom and autonomy on the condition that they return any runaway slaves they encountered.

"That won't win her any friends around here now that Mas Lyndon is dead,' Dexter said.

"Lyndon Holborn is dead?" Margaret asked.

"He died yesterday. Mistress Anne says they are waiting for the storm to pass before they post the bans and make the announcement," Brixton explained.

"Oh, dear, poor Anne. Lyndon and Anne shared a true love story; she must be broken-hearted. I have to go to her," Margaret exclaimed, upset at the news.

"Not tonight, Mother, I will take you there myself when the storm passes, but tonight, we are all going indoors and far away from the windows," Dexter instructed.

"What about your father?" Nana asked. Neither of the boys had noticed him in the chair on the veranda. But Nana has been watching him from the window.

"What about him?" Brixton asked. "Do you think we are that lucky, and the storm will take him with it when it leaves? I wouldn't count on it, but just in case, leave his sorry ass where it is," Brixton took his mother and Nana's arm and led them out of the kitchen.

Dexter watched them go. He understood Brixton's anger toward his father, but he did not understand his lack of empathy. Quietly he went to his father, pulling the chair under the roof overhang's protection and covering him with a rain slicker. Harry turned away from Dexter and vomited. Dexter followed his brother inside. He knew this storm would wear itself out quickly. Hopefully, it would blow away the winds of tension that had invaded the island and stirred up so much trepidation and cruelty.

CHAPTER 6

After the Storm

Harry had stumbled in late the next morning. He barely glanced at Dexter, Brixton, Margaret, and Nana seated at the dining table, having a late breakfast. He grabbed a bottle of rum from the breakfront and headed to his room. His presence interrupted their conversation, only for a moment.

"There was one more bit of news in my brother's letter that I wanted to share with you. He is arriving within the fortnight, on the Halifax, sailing out of London. Dexter, I would ask you to meet them in Black River and escort them home to us," Margaret had announced before Harry walked in unexpectedly.

"Of course, it will be a pleasure to make his acquaintance. Why is your brother coming to Jamaica?" Dexter asked.

"Hopefully, to give Harry another proper thrashing," Brixton mumbled under his breath.

Margaret ignored him. "On his twenty-fifth birthday, the 7th Duke of Ergill will inherit lands in Scotland given to him by my father, and he will be eligible to take his seat at the House of Lords in the British parliament," Margaret explained. "You will have access to the greatest minds in England and to the library and faculty that accompanies the House of Lords. It is an important prospect."

"Not for me, it's not!" Brixton exploded. "I'm not leaving Jamaica; I was born here, and this is the only home I've ever known. I know nothing about England, except that it's cold, rainy, and the sun never shines."

"It is the opportunity we have been waiting for, Brix," Dexter said. "With your seat in the House of Lords, you can add your voice to the calls for the abolition of slavery that grow louder in England each day."

"Dex, Bellevue Estate is a little over two thousand acres if you include Mount Sion, it is not even enough to feed us, and it is certainly of no significance to the Lords of England. I am a colonial in their eyes. They will never see me as their equal," Brixton argued.

"It is your birthright Brix, they can't take that away from you, and it will give you a voice where one is desperately needed. How can you not see this for the gift that it is?" Dexter countered.

"No Dunbarton has been accepted at court in three generations. What makes you think they will welcome *me* back with open arms?" Brix said.

Margaret answered his question. "My brother Liam has no children, and he has no intention of marrying and having any. Liam is coming here to die, Brix. He wants to bestow upon Lord Dunbarton, the 7th Duke of Ergill, the title of Chief of Clan McKenzie along with the wealth and lands that come with the title," Margaret expounded. "Through the McKenzie's, the Dunbarton name will finally regain some respect in England."

"Dying?" Dexter asked.

"He has consumption. He has made his wishes known to the clan and my brothers. They are all in agreement. I was born after him, so my son is the next true heir. I want him to spend the few days he has left with me. I have missed him so," Margaret's voice broke as she said this.

Chapter 6 | After the Storm

Brixton and Dexter looked at each other. This turn of events meant a lot to their mother, they could see that, but Brixton did not want to leave Jamaica, so her news didn't sit well with him. He sat back in his chair, hands behind his head, staring at the ceiling; his desolation evident on his face.

Dexter watched his brother. Brixton's inability to see the bigger picture was due to his privilege, an impediment Brixton did not realize held him back. Dexter understood the significance of what Margaret was telling them and wondered how she had lobbied to make it happen so far away from Scotland. Dexter was the beneficiary of unheard of advantages for a slave, raised in the Manor house, with access to all the educational opportunities afforded to Brixton. While Brixton took his education for granted, Dexter had been attentive and absorbed every lesson like a sponge. He overcame his tutor's objections to educating a slave with the interest he took in their lessons and the intuitive questions that had his tutors up well into the night, looking for the answers. Dexter was a thinker; Brixton was a doer.

While Dexter analyzed a situation, looking for solutions in his education, Brixton would cock his head to one side, looking at the problem from that angle, and confidently suggest a solution. Their different approaches complemented each other, and they learned to work together at an early age. Brixton had discovered the cave system under Mount Sion by riding headlong and recklessly into the tunnel. Dexter had approached it more cautiously, finally convincing Brixton to wait until they could get some lanterns and rope to take with them so they could find a way out if they became lost. They had returned the next day, Brixton bouncing on his heels with excitement, Dexter begging him to be patient as he staked the rope at the entrance of the tunnel, pulling it behind him as Brixton rushed headlong into the darkness.

He had patiently mapped out the cave system as Brixton rushed back and forth, exploring each room with wild abandon. It was Brixton who had discovered the underground hot springs. Dexter had found Brixton staring in wonder, drawn by the sound of rushing water and the glimmer of light in the distance. Brixton moved toward his discovery fearlessly until he found the luminous gleam of the emerald water in a lagoon fed by the waterfall above it. The water reflected on the roof of the cave from the phosphorus covering the bottom of the pool, creating a shimmering effect that took their breath away. Brixton had wandered to the edge of the lagoon in a daze and fallen headlong into the water. Dexter rushed to the side, scanning the pool for Brixton, who had resurfaced seconds later.

"Dex, I have found my paradise," Brixton exhaled, floating on his back as he watched the lights dancing on the cave's roof above him.

"Brix, be careful! You don't know what is living in that water," Dexter cautioned.

But Brixton ignored Dexter, completely mesmerized. "I want to live right here for the rest of my life," he had announced.

Dexter remembered those words as he looked at his brother's sad face. Dexter had always admired Brixton's self-confidence; he knew his place in the world and embraced it. Dexter did not have that luxury. But Dexter could see that Brixton's confidence was shaken with the news of his uncle's arrival and what it would mean for him.

Brixton was still in a foul mood when they sat down for dinner that evening. Harry's appearance in the dining room only served to put a scowl on Brixton's face.

"Why all the long faces, aren't you happy to see the Master of the Manor?" Harry asked from the doorway. The smell of food had drawn his attention. "I thought it only fit that I partake of the

Chapter 6 | After the Storm

food I have provided for this table," he said as he sat down and reached for the bowl of rice and peas in front of him.

"You provide? Oh God, no! I can't handle Harry's delusions. On top of the days' bad news!" Brixton snarled as he pushed his chair back and stomped out of the room.

"What bad news?" Harry asked, ignoring Brixton's outburst and reaching for the roast chicken.

Nana and Margaret looked at each other. Dexter pushed his chair back and left the room before he was told to by Harry. It angered Harry to no end to see Dexter seated at the dining table.

"Lyndon Holborn died," Margaret said.

"Really? The old bastard is dead, you say?" Harry put down the bowl of chicken and sat back in his chair.

"Yes, they are waiting for the storm to pass before they post the announcement of his death," Margaret said.

"Well, this is indeed an interesting development," Harry muttered to himself. His mind was working furiously, his hunger forgotten. Lyndon Holborn's estate encompassed three profitable plantations, Friendship, Greenwich, and Mesopotamia, totaling three thousand, four hundred and fifty acres. Harry and Lyndon used the same solicitor, who had mentioned to Harry that Lyndon was finalizing the purchase of Appleton Estate, which encompassed over eleven thousand acres of land. Lyndon Holborn owned nearly fifteen thousand acres of land in the parishes of Westmoreland and Saint Elizabeth, the two largest parishes in the county of Cornwall. *Quite the inheritance for a darkie girl,* Harry thought to himself.

Nana knew that look on Harry's face. She had seen it on three generations of Dunbarton men, and it usually meant a world of trouble. She nudged Margaret, pointing with her lips, for her to look at Harry. A knowing look passed between Margaret and Nana. He was up to something, and they suspected it involved Anne and Sabine Holborn.

Turning back to the chicken on his plate, "I will have to go into Black River as soon as this damnable rain is over. I have important business to discuss with my solicitor," Harry declared.

Margaret stood up irately, flinging her napkin on the table. Without a word, she turned and left the room. Harry took no notice of her departure, consumed with his plans. Margaret stormed past Dexter, who was sitting on the steps leading to the upper rooms, reading a book. Nana followed shortly after.

"Dat man covet what another man have instead of working for it himself," Nana said.

Dexter closed the book and looked up at her. He had found Brixton standing on the veranda, looking out toward Mount Sion. Brixton hated being cooped up inside. As soon as there was a break in the rain, Dexter knew Brixton would make a run for the stables, finding some excuse to get away from Harry.

"I'm more worried about Brixton than I am about Harry," Dexter said.

Nana looked at him. "You don't worry about Brixton. Brixton is a child of this island, a Jamaican through and through. Dese tings have a way of working out the way they should. What is fe yu, is fe yu. Brix know dat."

Dexter wasn't so sure. Brixton was willful and headstrong. As long as things were going his way, all was well in his world. Brixton did not react well to change; he was steadfast and constant, just like the land he loved to work. His surly attitude would undermine all the opportunities he would have access to in England, all because he didn't want to be there. Dexter loved his brother, and he understood his limitations. He was Brixton Dunbarton, the 7th Duke of Ergill, and like his forefathers, no matter his intentions, he did nothing unless he wanted to do it.

He wandered out to the veranda. As he suspected, he saw Brixton sprinting toward the stables. Dexter envied Brixton's natural confidence as he watched him go. Dexter was a student of history. He wanted to understand why the white man was so good at invading and conquering civilizations, especially of color. Even Harry, with his multitude of failings, had the same assurance that his place in the world was secure. As a slave, even one as educated and loved as he was by Margaret and Brixton, could never be sure of his place in the Greathouse or even on the estate. It was within Harry's power to kick him out of his room in the house, sell him to another estate, or even kill him if the mood struck. He had made it clear to Dexter, on many occasions, that he was not welcome, going as far as hitting or kicking him when he was angry at Brixton. He never laid a hand on Brixton, but Dexter had no escape from Harry's abuse. After one particularly harsh beating, Dexter had asked Margaret why Harry hated him so.

"Your mother was a slave on the estate. When I came to live here, she became my maid. I was young and unsure of myself, so afraid of Harry. I couldn't take any more of his abuse, and I was going to kill myself. Then I found out I was pregnant with Brixton. Your mother lay down her life for me, and in that act of selflessness, I found the strength I needed to stand up to Harry. She died giving birth to you, and I owe her a debt I can never repay. I promised to love and care for you, a promise easy to keep, for you are as dear to me as Brixton is. But for Harry, you remind him of losses. The loss of my fear of him and the outlet for his anger and disappointment, your mother. He will never truly hurt you as long as Nana and I live. Brixton loves you like the brother you are; he will also protect you."

"But Mother, why do I need protection. If I am Brixton's brother, why am I treated differently?" Dexter had been eight years old when he asked Margaret that question, bloodied and beaten by Harry because Brixton had called him a drunken fool. Harry had tried to grab Brixton, but Brixton pushed him back, and he had fallen, hitting his head on the floor. Brixton had stood over him, wanting to do more, but Dexter had stepped in and sent him to Nana. Harry was livid, roaring as he sprang to his feet, grabbing Dexter, hitting and kicking him until Dexter squirmed away and ran to his mother.

"Because you are a black man in a white man's world. Until that changes, you will need our protection," Margaret had answered, taking him into her arms and kissing his forehead.

That was the most profound lesson of Dexter's life, and he had vowed to find out why it was a white man's world. He wanted to understand where his brother's natural sureness came from, his security in the place God had granted him in this world. He wanted to know how he could achieve that level of self-assurance and self-confidence. Dexter wanted to understand why Brixton would even think of walking away from an opportunity to change the world just because it inconvenienced him. Brixton had the one luxury in life Dexter longed for, the ability to make decisions that directly affected how he could live his life.

Dexter sighed heavily; the rain was letting up. He was not surprised to see Brix ride off toward Mount Sion. With a heavy heart, Dexter turned and headed for the kitchen. He could read quietly there until the storm passed, and life returned to normal on the estate.

BRIXTON RODE OUT of the stables, hell-bent on getting to the caves on Mount Sion before the rain started pelting again. He needed time to think, and being around Harry was not conducive to deep, meaningful thought. His mother had upended his life today, and he needed to figure out how to correct it.

He cobbled his horse at the entrance of the cave. He and Dexter had built a stable of a sort, with a rough-hewn log, attached to two poles, that served as a hitching post for their horses. Nearby was a bucket for water that he filled from the rain and put it next to another bucket of oats he had brought for the horse. Once his horse was taken care of, Brixton made his way to the lagoon. He jumped into the warm waters, diving deep as he allowed the water to relax the tense muscles in his shoulders and back.

Lyndon Holborn came to mind. He would miss the old man who had become a mentor to him. Brixton surfaced, floating on his back, as he remembered the first time they had ever spoken. Brixton had been riding toward Mount Sion after a fight with his father. It was the first time he had pushed his father, who had fallen back and hit his head on the hard floor. Brixton stood over the fallen man, but Dexter had intervened, instructing him to go to Nana. Brixton was horrified at what he had done and even more surprised by how empowered the act had made him feel. For a boy of eight years old, it was a terrifying feeling.

Lyndon had found Brixton sitting on the beach, his knees drawn to his chest and his head on his folded arms. At first, Lyndon thought he was crying, but when the boy raised his head to look at him, he saw nothing but anger and defiance in his eyes.

"What are you doing out here by yourself? You shouldn't be this far from home," Lyndon said.

"Why not? I'm perfectly safe on my land, and I can take care of myself," Brixton had answered politely but abruptly.

Lyndon sat back in the saddle and looked at the boy. His first instinct was to leave the boy where he found him. He wanted nothing to do with a Dunbarton, but Anne had told him the boy was nothing like his father, and there was obviously something bothering him. "Mind if I join you?" Lyndon asked and jumped off his horse. Brixton shrugged noncommittally but scooted over so Lyndon could sit next to him. "You do know that this is the most beautiful beach in Jamaica, don't you? This is heaven, right here on earth. Your Mount Sion," Lyndon said, trying to draw the boy out.

Brixton nodded slowly and looked around him. He loved Mount Sion with all his heart. "Yes, sir. I do know that. My mother says it will be mine one day; she made my father sign a paper saying so," Brixton said.

"She did, did she? Smart woman, your mother," Lyndon responded, his dislike for Harry evident in his tone. He looked at Brixton and could see the hardness in the boy's eyes. "Your father is a difficult man to like; I'm sorry, Brixton."

"Don't be. He is even harder to love," Brixton responded.

"Ahh, so today's troubles are with your father, are they?" Lyndon pushed gently.

"Yes, sir. But I am afraid to tell you, lest you have a poor impression of me, sir," Brixton answered nervously.

"I doubt that can happen, Brixton. From what I have heard, you are a hard worker who loves his mother, his brother, his Nana, and his home. I think you will find that you and I are very similar, indeed," Lyndon responded, resting back on his arms with his legs stretched out in front of him. His relaxed posture had the desired effect. It put Brixton at ease, even more than his words did.

Brixton looked at Lyndon, then back out to sea. "My father and I had words today. He made me so angry that I pushed him. He fell back and hit his head. I was standing over him, and all I wanted to do was lean over and punch him until his face was blooded and swollen."

"Well, that is serious. But I have to ask, what did you and your father have words about?" Lyndon asked.

"Does it matter? The Bible says you should honor your father. At least that is what my father says. He said God would smite me for even pushing him down," Brixton responded miserably.

"So that is what you are worried about, God's wrath?" Lyndon asked. He watched as Brixton nodded. "I see. Well, supposedly, God has said a great many things, including that it is his will that white men rule over black men. You disagree with that, don't you?" Lyndon asked.

Brixton knew what Lyndon was referring to. After the last rebellion in Jamaica, the parish priest was particularly dismayed at the damage to his church when slaves armed with machetes, axes, and picks engaged the small regiment of soldiers sequestered on the church grounds. He had stirred his parishioners' ire by vehemently preaching that God himself sanctioned slavery of the black man. It was incumbent on Jamaica's white population to assert their dominance over their slaves and regain control. Brixton was offended by the sermon and refused to go back to his services, deciding instead to go to the black church services with Nana, where the music was much better, and he could play with the children.

"My brother is black, so is my Nana," Brixton responded.

"My wife and daughter are black," Lyndon said. "The point I am making is this. Yes, you should not have pushed your father, but sometimes there are extenuating circumstances."

"Extenuating circumstances? What are those?" Brixton asked.

"Well, if you hurt someone because you are protecting yourself or someone you love from that person, then the act of defending yourself is an extenuating circumstance. Do you understand my meaning?" Lyndon asked.

"I think so," Brixton responded cautiously.

"English law says that if you kill someone in self-defense, that's an extenuating circumstance which makes the act different from murder. Why did you push your father?" Lyndon asked.

Now Brixton looked embarrassed; he was ashamed at what his father had done, what he had done. "I was watching a girl take a bath in the pond by the stables. I don't know why, but my peanywally stiffened like I needed to pee, but I didn't. I was touching it, and my father came up to me. If I had a need, he said, then I should take the girl and do what I had to. I didn't know what he meant, so he pulled her out of the pond, threw her to the ground, and, well, he did a horrible thing to her. She was crying and begging him not to do what he was doing to her, but he just kept doing it. When he was done, he started hitting her, and I told him to leave her alone. She was my friend, and he was hurting her." The memory of it made him shiver, and he took a moment to compose himself. "I followed him to the house, yelling that he was a drunken fool; he just turned around and smiled at me. He said what he did was the master's right. I was so angry that I pushed him."

"Brixton, if it is any consolation, I would have done the same thing; hell, I may have killed your father. What he did was wrong, very wrong. A man must never force a woman to have sex with him, even if he owns her," Lyndon said. The look on Brixton's face stopped him. "Brixton, do you know what your father was doing to her?"

No one had ever explained to Brixton what happened between a man and a woman. He lived on an estate with animals, so he knew what the sex act entailed. He had accompanied his father once, when he insisted, to the slave quarters. His father had coupled slaves demanding that they have sex so he could breed them. He made them do the act in front of him to ensure the men completed the impregnation process. His father ran wild eyed between the couples until he fell to the ground next to them, heaving alongside them. The entire process had disgusted Brixton, and he refused to discuss it with anyone, not even Dexter. Brixton was now putting two and two together.

"When my peanywally gets hard, I have to put it inside a girl?" Brixton asked in horror. "Like an animal?"

Lyndon sat up in dismay. This is not what he had expected to face when he rode out that afternoon, and he was botching it badly. "No, Brix, it is not always like that. When you are older, much older, you will find a woman you will fall in love with. She will be the reason you were born, and you will want to hold her, to kiss her, to sleep next to her every night. With that love will come the desire to be with her, and it will be the most beautiful experience of your life."

Brixton jumped up in dismay, "I will never put my peanywally inside a girl. I could never hurt someone like that. That is disgusting, sir," Brixton was beside himself.

"Brixton, do you love Mount Sion? Do you love this beach? The sea?" Lyndon asked. He waited for Brixton's nodding confirmation. "One day, you will love a woman the way you love Mount Sion, the way you love this beach and the sea beyond. That love will fill your heart with joy because it means you have found your partner, your missing piece. Together you will build a beautiful life, and you will bring new life into the world to share your joy. When you lie with her, it will not be like what you see the animals do, or even your father. That is not love. That is a baser, more carnal instinct that will have no place in the life you create with the woman you love, respect, and cherish. Hold out for that, my boy. It will be worth the wait."

Brixton was not sure what Lyndon was talking about, but he trusted him, and he took his words to heart. They had been fast friends after that. It had been Brixton who had ridden out with Lyndon, in search of the cave that led to the place Anne named Treasure Beach. Lyndon nurtured Brixton's love for the island and encouraged him to think of it as an independent nation. Lyndon taught Brixton that Jamaica would prosper and grow only with the abolition of slavery and freedom from colonialism. Lyndon led Brixton to believe that colonialism and slavery would one day be in Jamaica's past. Those who loved the island would forge Jamaica's future, building a society out of many, so one people would emerge, with liberty and equality for all.

Brixton lay on his back, floating in the soothing waters, and watched the light show above him. Lyndon had given him something to aspire to, a dream for what Jamaica could and should be. Now, he was forced to go to England to assume a title he hated and give up on an idea he held dear. He wished Lyndon was here so he could discuss this development with him. Brixton rolled over onto his stomach and started swimming around the lagoon. He smiled when he thought of that conversation with Lyndon all those years ago. He had learned what to do when his peanywally stiffened, but he had never taken a woman by force. Women came to him willingly, drawn in by his charisma and charm, but he always made sure their needs were met before his own. A fact that had made the rounds in Jamaica, so fulfilling his sexual needs had never been an issue for him. He knew they credited more amorous adventures to his name than he had actually engaged in, but he kept his counsel with his 'Les Histoires de Coeur.' The great love of his life had yet to reveal herself to him.

One thing is for sure; she is not in bloody England; he thought to himself. He pulled himself out of the lagoon and sat down to dry off. It was warm and comforting in his hideaway, and he was soon fast asleep. He woke up many hours later and went to find his horse. He could see that the storm had passed; the sky was a bright blue with hardly a cloud threaded through it. As he rode toward the Greathouse, he marveled at the beautiful rainbow that followed him home. He hoped it was a good omen for him.

His eyes teared up thinking of Lyndon; it would be hard for Brixton to say goodbye to his mentor and friend. He stabled his horse and walked to the back of the Greathouse. Nana was sitting on the veranda picking peas as Dexter read to her from the book he was holding. They both looked up as Brixton walked toward them.

"Glad to see you back," Nana said casually.

"Glad to be home, Nana," He replied as he bent to kiss her cheek.

"Brixton, you're home," his mother said as she came out, putting on her gloves, parasol firmly in hand. "Dex and I are on our way to Friendship Estate. Please clean yourself up and dress properly. I don't want dear Anne to go through this by herself. You boys will help to bring Sabine's spirits up. Poor thing, she was so close to her father, her heart must be quite broken," Margaret prattled on as Dexter rose to escort her to the little carriage that stood waiting. He helped her to climb in and then jumped into the driver's seat.

"I will follow directly, Mother, don't worry," Brixton replied dutifully. He watched as they drove off, then noticed his father riding out like the devil was after him. "Where is he going?" Brixton asked Nana.

"Nowhere good, to do nothing good," Nana commented dryly. "Yu never mind about him, Brix, go do as your mudder say. Today gwen be a hard day for everybody." Brix nodded sadly, turning to enter the house. Nana grabbed his hand and kissed it. "Yu is a good boy Brix, blessed by God himself, don't worry, tings have a way of working themselves out."

"Can he get me out of being the 7th Duke of Ergill? Of having to leave Jamaica?" Brixton asked, his anguish not far from the surface.

"He will do what is best for yu, Brix, for dose yu love and for all what yu love. Trust in God, my child. He will deliver yu," Nana said passionately.

Brixton wished his faith was as strong as his Nana's.

CHAPTER 7

Anne Holborn

In the Jamaican tradition, the body is believed to have three parts, the body, the spirit, and the ghost, known as the duppy. The duppy would not leave Lyndon's body until the ninth night of his death, where it is dispatched with a rousing send-off so he wouldn't linger but ascend happily to his eternal rest.

Since his death, the people of Friendship estate lit candles every night to show their respect for Lyndon. Anne looked out as she lit the lamp in the drawing-room and saw the estate aglow with bright flames in each window. The funeral would not occur until the nine-night ritual was over, and everyone on the estate had their chance to speak, sing, and dance for the Master they esteemed and adored, one final time.

She would have liked more time to grieve and say goodbye, but time was not a luxury she had. The storm had come and gone, and with its passing, she was both happy that the damage had been minimal and sad that the cleanup process to make the roads and bridges passable would buy her two more days. Five more nights and word of Lyndon's passing would spread. She rose from her seat at the dining table. They lay Lyndon out on it since his death. She had cleaned the body and prepared it herself.

Anne had sat by his side, holding his hand, telling him of her undying love. She had fallen asleep each night, with her head on the table next to his. Now, she kissed Lyndon gently on the forehead and stood by the window. If she missed him this much as she held his hand each night, how would she survive without him? The thought plagued her. Something attracted her attention, and she focused on what had caught her eye in the distance. She recognized Margaret Dunbarton's carriage as it made the turn toward the gates of Friendship Estate. A sad smile made her hang her head. *Of course, dearest Mags would be here to help me through this difficult time*, she thought. She had a few minutes to wash her face and change her dress. If she had to receive condolences, this would be the best one to begin with, she surmised as she ran to complete her toiletries so she could greet Margaret.

Richard watched Anne hurry upstairs from the door of the drawing-room. He understood she needed time to grieve and did not intrude on her time with Lyndon. The storm had given them some respite, but he knew the wolves would soon be at the door. Lyndon had given him a copy of his Will years ago; it was waiting with his things in the room he currently occupied in the Greathouse. As soon as he could, he would take it to Black River to Lyndon's solicitor for the probate process to begin. Richard greeted Margaret and Dexter at the door and showed them into the dining room to pay their last respects to Lyndon before Anne came downstairs.

"Oh, dear! It is so hard to see such a vibrant man laid out in death," Margaret said, dabbing at her eyes.

"He was a great man who will be missed," Dexter added softly.

"Indeed, he will," Richard agreed.

"My dearest Mags," Anne said, coming into the room, walking into Margaret's open arms.

Chapter 7 | Anne Holborn

"My darling Anne, I feel his loss so deeply, along with you," Margaret said, folding Anne into her arms. Dexter and Richard stood and waited.

"Let's retire to the drawing-room, shall we?" Anne asked, clutching Margaret's hand and pulling her along as she walked out of the room. Dexter and Richard followed.

"Anne, I hate to have to bring this up," Margaret said as they settled in chairs facing the fire. Fireplaces were rarely used in Jamaica, but the storm left behind a dampness that only the fire blazing brightly in the room seemed to dispel. Richard stood by the fireplace as Dexter excused himself, saying he had left something in the carriage.

Margaret continued. "As soon as word of Lyndon's death gets out, every estate owner in Jamaica will try to get their hands on Friendship Estate. It is the most profitable estate on the island, and I am afraid you and Sabine are most vulnerable."

Anne looked at Richard; they understood what Margaret was trying to say. "We know. Lyndon has made provisions, I have his Will, and I will go directly to Black River to submit it for probate this very day," Richard said.

"I hope it is enough to protect you, Anne. The British courts will not allow a woman to own anything, much less an estate of this magnitude, and being a woman of color," Margaret stopped short. The embarrassment of having to issue the warning caused her cheeks to turn pink.

"I know, Mags. So did Lyndon. He has made Richard his executor, and in doing so, well, let's say he ensured that Richard's position would not be challenged," Anne answered.

"How so?" Margaret asked.

Again, Richard and Anne looked at each other. "Lyndon asked that Richard and I be married as soon after his death as is appropriate," Anne responded.

"Brilliant! Absolutely brilliant!" Margaret said. "But I don't think you should wait, get married today if you can."

"That may be the best course of action," Dexter said as he entered the room. All eyes turned to him and the large envelope he held in his hand. "I beg your pardon, Mistress Anne, but I have Mas Lyndon's Last Will and Testament right here."

"What?" Richard asked.

"What Will?" Anne asked, confused.

"What are you talking about, Dexter?" Margaret asked.

"Begging all your pardons. When Mas Lyndon became ill, he asked me to find a solicitor in Jamaica who could petition the Privy council in England," Dexter began.

"Petition the Privy council for what?" Anne asked.

"For Sabine to take ownership of Mas Lyndon's estate," Dexter said. "The document of Absolute Primogeniture grants Sabine his estate by royal decree only. If someone has a mind to, they could challenge it with the Privy council in England and most likely win. This estate is worth making that challenge. Mas Lyndon knew that. So, this Will stipulates that the petition to grant Sabine's Absolute Primogeniture is to be submitted to the Privy council for ratification upon his death. Sabine Holborn will not only be the first woman, but the first woman of color to own land and property in the British empire," Dexter said.

"Then why the request for Anne and I to marry?" Richard asked.

"To make sure there are no challenges to the ratification. Mas Lyndon's solicitors in Jamaica have been working with the English Privy council, in secret. It has to remain secret until the process is complete. With Dr. Richard married to Mistress Anne, there will be no need for anyone in Jamaica to petition the Privy council for ownership of Friendship Estate, thus ensuring there would be no challenges to the Privy council to dismiss the approval. Mas Lyndon is asking the Privy council to make legal, with no basis for a future challenge, what they see as a king's whim. The Privy council is taking this matter very seriously and moving with extreme caution. The precedent this will set, well, it opens the door for black ownership of land and property throughout the British empire, including its colonies. It sanctions families of mixed race to inherit and share wealth, titles, and lands the same way white families do. Dr. Richard is the bandage until the wound has healed," Dexter added.

"Liberté par la loi," Anne whispered.

"Oui, Madame," Dexter answered. "Liberty by law."

Anne was in shock. "Lyndon and I spoke about doing this so many times. Whispered it into the dead of night, where it is safe to dream the impossible. I had no idea he would try to make it a reality for me, for Sabine."

"In the dead of night, where dreams are born, Mistress Anne. Mas Lyndon did not see color; he just saw love. He is doing this for all of us," Dexter said gently.

"Dear God! Anne, you have to get married right now, this very day!" Margaret said. "Dexter, go St. George's Anglican Church in Savanna-la-Mar, ask for Vicar Collins and only Vicar Collins. He preaches at the black church. Explain to him that this marriage has to take place today, and bring him back with you."

"Yes, mother," Dexter said and headed for the door.

"Margaret, are you mad? I haven't yet buried my husband. This is most inappropriate," Anne voiced her objection.

Margaret turned to Anne, grabbing her by the shoulders and shaking her to get her attention. "Harry knows that Lyndon is dead. He rode out this morning like the devil was on his tail. I am quite sure he is sitting down with that maggot in Black River, trying to figure out how to get his hands on Friendship Estate. If he succeeds, all that Lyndon has worked for is for naught."

"Dear God!" Richard exclaimed, his hand moved to his forehead, and he started pacing the room.

"You need not tell anyone when you remarried, Anne, for propriety's sake, but you do need to get married right away," Margaret insisted.

Anne nodded; she understood. She sat down on the window seat, facing the sea beyond. Margaret sat next to her and took her hand. Anne didn't even have five nights left with Lyndon; as of tonight, she would be another man's wife.

BRIXTON WAS ON his way to meet Margaret and Dexter at Friendship Estate, totally unaware of what was transpiring. As Lyndon and Brixton's friendship grew, they had spent a lot of time together, mostly at Mount Sion. Early on, Brixton found a path from the Dunbarton Estate that took him to the back gates of Friendship Estate. He pointed his horse in the direction of the secret path, his last goodbye to his old friend. Brixton nudged his horse into a full gallop along the beach that connected Bellevue Estate with Mount Sion. Before the beach ended at a rocky limestone outcrop that began the mountain ridge behind the property, he turned and headed inland, toward the hill that continued to Friendship Estate. He brought his horse to a full stop when he suddenly spied the lone figure on horseback at the top of the hill.

Brixton trotted up to Sabine as she studied the land below her. He patted his horse's head to calm the excited horse and waited for Sabine to speak. She had yet to acknowledge his presence.

"I love the view from here; it looks like the entire island is laid out at my feet, ringed by the blue hue of the Caribbean Sea. Nowhere brings me the peace I feel when I sit right here, in this spot." Sabine breathed, the wonder of it clear in her voice.

Brixton said nothing; he tried to quiet his restless horse, sensing that Sabine needed the calm to settle her nerves. He could not

Chapter 7 | Anne Holborn

imagine what she must be going through. Lyndon had told him many times of the special bond he had with his daughter and how much he loved and cherished her.

"Why are you out here? There doesn't seem to be much damage from the storm," Sabine asked. Brixton, just sitting there, not saying anything, unnerved her.

"I was on my way over to pay my respects to you and your mother. I'm sorry for your loss, Sabine. Your father was a good man," Brixton said softly

"My father? We haven't announced his death; how could you possibly know he's dead?" Sabine asked.

He was surprised at her reaction, confused by the harshness of it. "One of your slaves came over and spoke to Nana this morning."

"We don't have slaves on Friendship Estate. Everyone living there is free, including my mother and me," Sabine answered sharply. She turned her horse around, sawing at the reins, and rode off brusquely toward Friendship Estate. The wolves were already at her door.

Brixton shook his head, baffled. He knew Sabine Holborn didn't like him, but for the life of him, he didn't understand why. He never seemed to say the right thing when he was in her presence; he was sure that contributed to her disdain of him. He turned his horse and followed at a distance that did not allow for any further conversation. It surprised him to see that she followed the footpath that took them to the back of the estate, the same path he had discovered so many years ago. He wondered if she knew where it led to or how many people had run to safety using the trail he had worn into the ground. *She seems to spend a lot of time at Mount Sion*, he thought spitefully.

He jumped from his horse first, handing the reins to the stable boy who appeared at his side. He walked over to help Sabine from her horse, but she didn't see him and jumped into his arms instead, unbalancing them both. "Oh, you oaf! Are you trying to maim me?" Sabine asked, exasperation in her voice.

"For the love of God, Sabine. I was trying to be a gentleman and help you with your horse," Brixton responded, equally annoyed.

"I am perfectly capable of getting off my horse on my own!" She shouted back at him.

"Fine! I was merely offering my help, as I would to any other woman getting off her horse in my presence," Brixton answered through gritted teeth.

"I am not any other woman," Sabine said, equally angry.

"Mademoiselle, you are definitely not like any other woman I have ever known," Brixton said cuttingly.

Sabine's sharp intake of breath was her only response to his words. His words wounded her deeply. She watched as he turned on his heel and walked toward the house. He did not look behind to see if she followed. Brixton had only been in the Greathouse on the rare occasion the Holborn's had thrown a party. His meetings with Lyndon had been at Mount Sion or out touring the island together. As Lyndon's sickness progressed, Brixton would pick him up in the small open-air racing carriage Lyndon had gifted Brixton with after losing a carriage race as a young man. Brixton had been winning the race until his old and disheveled racing carriage fell to pieces turning a corner. It was only Brixton's agility that saved him and his horse from a devastating injury. Brixton's embarrassment over the shabbiness of the carriage had wounded him more than the accident could have. Harry had refused to buy him a new one, even though he bet heavily on the outcome of the races the young gentry of the island liked to engage in at parties and picnics. His winnings went to rum and gambling, not to a new carriage for Brixton. Lyndon had quietly left the new carriage on Mount Sion's beach with a note to enjoy it and keep it in good repair. It was Brixton's most prized possession, and he lovingly polished and waxed it, taking care to do any repairs it needed himself.

As Brixton mounted the steps at the back of the Greathouse, righteous indignation fueled every step. Suddenly, he realized he had no idea which door would lead him into the common rooms. He tried to remember the house's layout as he looked at the two closed doors in front of him.

When Sabine caught up with him, she realized his dilemma. Both still angry at the other, they stood awkwardly for a moment until Brixton's words broke the tension. "After you, Mademoiselle," he said, bowing deeply and sweeping his arm, indicating that she should lead the way. Sabine tossed her head and pranced in front of him, opening the door that led to a side entrance. He followed her through the hallways until they found Margaret, Richard, and Anne sitting solemnly in the drawing-room.

Her mother's stricken face drew Sabine's attention, and she went to her mother's side. "Mother, what's wrong?"

Anne took Sabine's face into her hands, "It would appear the wolves are at the door sooner than we had hoped," Anne answered. As Sabine hugged her mother, her eyes found Brixton. They hardened as she understood her mother's words.

Brixton went straight to his mother's side. "Mother, what's going on?" he whispered as he knelt beside her chair.

"Your father," Margaret said softly. "We believe he is trying to steal Friendship Estate."

"But Mas Lyndon made provisions to avoid just that?" Brixton answered.

"You know what Mas Lyndon was doing?" Margaret asked.

"I took him to Spanish Town for the initial meeting with the solicitor Dexter found. I fully support what he is trying to do," Brixton answered quietly.

"Dexter has gone to fetch the Vicar. Lyndon asked Doctor Richard to marry Anne, to forestall such an occurrence. We are awaiting his arrival," Margaret explained. It was then that Dexter walked through the door, the Vicar fast on his heels. Dexter nodded in Brixton's direction and went to his mother's side.

"This is most unusual," the Vicar was saying to Richard. "There has been no posting of the banns."

"But not unheard of?" Richard asked.

"I can perform the marriage, but I don't know how legal it will be without the posting of the banns," The Vicar said. "By law, a marriage cannot take place until the banns, announcing the intention of the union, are read from the church pulpit or posted on the church door for two consecutive weeks.

"If I may, Vicar," Dexter cut in. "The Marriage Act of 1753 stipulates that a marriage is valid with the posting of the banns *or* with a legal marriage license acquired before the ceremony takes place."

"I am aware of that young man, but I do not possess such a license, they are issued in Spanish Town," The Vicar responded impatiently.

From the large document holder Dexter carried, he pulled out a certified document with a seal affixed to the top and bottom of the parchment. "I think you will find this in order, Vicar."

The Vicar took the marriage license from Dexter, looking at him in surprise as he perused it. "Yes, yes. I think this will work nicely." Dexter nodded and stood back.

Margaret took over. "Anne stand in front of the fireplace; Richard stand next to her. Vicar, proceed."

"Madam, a marriage license requires two witnesses," the Vicar admonished.

"Dear God, you are insufferable, Vicar," Margaret said irritably. "Sabine, stand next to your mother. Brixton, stand next to Richard. I will see you properly wed Anne."

Chapter 7 | Anne Holborn

"But Madam," the Vicar interrupted.

Margaret had enough of the Vicar and shot him a look so severe, he shut his mount instantly. "Brixton, take Sabine's hand and lead her to her mother's side," Margaret instructed, ignoring the Vicar.

Brixton crossed the room to take Sabine's hand. Sabine had remained behind the chair her mother was seated in when Sabine arrived. She had her back turned to everyone as she tried to wrap her head around what was happening. Her poor father lay in the next room as her mother married another man to protect her. Brixton could see the turmoil on her face and gently moved to take her hand. She tensed at his touch. "Sabine, take my hand," he instructed.

Sabine could not move; she was afraid if she touched him, it would be to tear his eyes out. She blamed Brixton for all of this.

Brixton had no idea what she was thinking. He certainly had no idea she held him responsible for the day's events. "Sabine, for God's sake, take my hand! Now!" he commanded.

Sabine did not move. He gently but firmly turned her around to face her mother. "Take my hand!" he commanded. She couldn't do it. He grabbed her hand and did not let go. "Walk!" he hissed in her ear. She held her head up, blinking back tears as she walked to her mother's side.

It was the most solemn marriage ceremony the Vicar had ever presided over. The entire event took less than ten minutes, leaving everyone in attendance feeling disheartened, especially the bride and groom. Richard did not want to start his life with Anne this way, and Anne didn't want to marry another man with her husband's body lying in the next room. But their lives were not yet theirs to command, and this was one small sacrifice for the sake of the greater good. As Richard leaned over to kiss his wife on the cheek, Sabine looked away. As was the custom, Brixton leaned over to kiss Sabine, as her mother's maid of honor. She turned her face away from him, refusing to look him in the eye. The harshness in his voice was still ringing in her ears.

Sabine was the last to sign the license. Brixton handed it to the Vicar.

"Make sure this license is secure in the church's possession. I don't want to hear it has gone missing," Margaret ordered, looking in the Vicar's direction.

Before the Vicar could offer a retort, Dexter stepped in. "There are two copies, Mother. I suggest Doctor Richard hold on to one. The church does not need a copy because I will take the original to Spanish Town and give it into the keeping of the solicitors there. No one will question the legality of this marriage."

"But they may question the haste of it," Brixton murmured. The marriage did not sit well with him. He was also fully aware that his friend's body lay in the next room.

"Which brings me to your next task," Margaret pulled the boys to the side out of earshot. "Whatever your father and his cronies are up to, they will have to send it to Spanish Town. I want you boys to make sure it never gets there."

"I know the courier they use; he's a young Irish man. Never says no to whoever is buying drinks," Dexter said.

"Brixton, make sure you are buying the drinks," Margaret said.

"But Mother, that means I have to wait in Black River for him to leave for Spanish Town. I will miss Mas Lyndon's nine nights and his funeral. I have to pay my respects," Brixton started.

"You are paying your respects! By protecting his family," Margaret hissed at him. At Brixton's crestfallen face, she softened her tone. "Go now, take the time you need with him, then you and Dexter make your excuses and leave."

Dexter went over to Sabine, who was standing by herself, to offer his condolences. Anne was off to make sure the Vicar had something to eat and drink. Then she and Richard sat with him to complete the plans for the funeral.

Brixton left the room and headed into the dining room, taking Lyndon's hand in his as he sat down next to Lyndon's head. "My dear friend, I will miss your guidance, your counsel, and your wisdom. You have taught me so much about life and love. I am the better man for knowing you, and I will never forget you," Brixton said as tears rolled down his face. He laid his head in his arms, holding Lyndon's hand to his heart, and sobbed.

That was how Anne found him, and her heart went out to the young man. She knew the role Lyndon had played in his life. She had encouraged Lyndon to take the boy under his wing. They were so proud of the man he had become. Quietly she went to Brixton, rubbing his head softly.

Brixton sat up immediately, wiping the back of his hand across his eyes. Jumping to his feet as he apologized. "I'm sorry, Mistress Anne. I didn't mean to lose my composure like that."

"No one should ever apologize for mourning the loss of someone they cared about, Brixton. I know how loved you were by Lyndon; if you loved him half as much, then I am grateful for the tears you shed for him," Anne commented.

"I loved him, Mistress Anne. I always will. He was the father I wish I had," Brixton said, the words catching in his throat.

"And you are the son he wished he had. I know you want to be here to mourn his passing. Your mother has explained why you cannot. I understand, and I appreciate the sacrifice you are making in not being here to say goodbye to Lyndon. He understands too, and will forever appreciate what you have done for Sabine, for me and Jamaica's future," Anne said, taking Brixton in her arms as a fresh wave of tears engulfed him. "Take as much time as you need to say goodbye; I will make sure no one disturbs you."

Anne went back into the drawing-room. Richard had taken the Vicar outside, where his carriage waited to take him back to the vicarage. They had completed all the arrangements for Lyndon's funeral. The last goodbye would take place in six days, the day after the nine nights ended. Both the African and Anglo-Saxon traditions would play their role in sending Lyndon off to the afterlife. She made her way to Dexter and Sabine.

"Dexter, thank you for all you have done today and for being a true friend to the Holborn family," Anne pressed Dexter's hand in hers.

"There is no need for thanks. We all owe Mas Lyndon a debt we can never repay," Dexter answered modestly.

"If there is anything Sabine and I can do for you, please do not hesitate to ask. Isn't that right, Sabine?" Anne directed her gaze at Sabine.

Sabine heard nothing anyone said to her since Brixton's cold kiss upon her cheek. She had nodded at Dexter's kind words of condolence, consumed with anguish. Now she smiled at him and then her mother. "Yes, of course. Dexter, anything at all. Now, if you will excuse me, it has been a very tiring day." Dexter and Anne watched her go. Sabine noticed the door to the dining room closed but did not dwell on it. Her need to give in to the tears of anger and sorrow that had threatened to fall a hundred times that day was too great. She rushed to her room, flinging herself onto the bed, burying her face in the pillow to hide her screams of rage. She pounded the pillow with her fists, wishing it was Brixton Dunbarton who felt the blows. She felt it deep in her bones; she knew without a shred of doubt, the wolf at Friendship Estate's door was none other than Brixton Dunbarton.

Dexter watched Sabine leave before he turned his attention back to Anne. "Mistress Anne, there is something else in this envelope you should be aware of. Mas Lyndon has left a sealed letter for Sabine," Dexter started.

"Dex, why didn't you give it to her? It might be the comfort she needs," Anne asked.

"I can't, Mistress Anne. Mas Lyndon told me to tell you she can only open it on her wedding day," Dexter explained.

"Her wedding day?" Anne asked.

"I am to give it to you for safekeeping. Mas Lyndon says you are to give it to her on the day she gets married and only then. He was explicit about that instruction," Dexter said as he removed the small, sealed envelope from the larger one he was still holding, handing it to Anne. He assumed from Anne's reaction that Lyndon had never discussed the contents of his letter with her.

"I'm sorry this is a bit of a surprise. Lyndon never mentioned a letter to Sabine to me. I will take it and put it in safekeeping to give to her on her wedding day," Anne said, taking the letter from Dexter.

Out of the corner of his eye, he saw Brixton emerge from the dining room, wiping his eyes and heading for the outdoors. Dexter headed over to his mother. "Mother, I think it is time we take our leave. Brixton and I have to leave first thing in the morning for Black River. Brixton is waiting outside for us."

"Yes, yes. Anne, I am sorry for what you had to do today," Margaret said as she hugged her friend. "I know Nana will want to spend a few days with you, so I will send her to you within the next two days if that is acceptable to you."

Anne nodded that it would be. Margaret turned her attention to Richard, who had seen the Vicar off and returned to the drawing-room.

"Dear Richard," Margaret said, taking his hands in hers. "I know this is not the wedding day you wanted to have with Anne, but I admire you for what you have done, what you are doing. You are both in my prayers," she said, squeezing his hands before she let them go. It was a secret to no one who spent time with Richard and Anne that Richard was in love with Anne. He looked at Anne, the way every woman dreams a man will look at her. As Anne followed her out, Margaret stopped her. "No, darling, you must be dead on your feet. Dex and I will see ourselves out."

Just like that, they left Anne and Richard alone on their wedding night. Richard wanted nothing more than to take Anne into his arms to comfort her. He took a step toward her, but she held up her hand to stop him. The other hand stifled the cry on her lips. As her tears fell, she turned and went into the dining room, closing the door behind her. Richard followed, standing guard at the door as he listened to his wife cry throughout the night. He felt her pain and could not hold back the anguish he felt, not only for losing his friend but also for not being able to comfort the woman he loved in her sorrow and loss. He slid to the floor, his knees to his chest and his head in his hands as he cried unabashedly. "I promise you, Lyndon, I will love her enough for you and for me," he whispered.

CHAPTER 8

Spanish Town

Dexter and Brixton were on the road to Black River as dawn lit the mountains over the horizon. Harry had not come back last night, which they took as a good sign. Either he was still working on his devious plan, or he was too drunk to ride back to the estate. Whichever one it was, it meant the Irishman had not left for Spanish Town, and that was good news for them.

Brixton did not sleep well. Saying goodbye to Lyndon was much harder than he thought it would be. He would miss the old man. Sabine's attitude toward him was maddening. He had done nothing to deserve her scorn. He understood that she knew nothing of Lyndon's plans. Lyndon had told him as much. Sabine was an educated woman, more than capable of running a plantation. So, Lyndon turned the running of the Estate over to her on her seventeenth birthday. He replayed the days' events over and over in his head, trying to figure out what he could have done differently to ease the tension between them. Her obstinate behavior irritated him, but he could not bring himself to find any fault with himself. However, it bothered him enough to disturb his sleep.

In the wee hours of the morning, Brixton found himself on the back veranda; sleep still eluded him. He loved the weather after a storm. The land was once again in harmony with itself, cleansed by the deluge it had endured. The air was sweet, and a gentle breeze blew all around, calming nerves and lulling everyone back into the island routine that had been upended by nature's temper tantrum. Brixton settled into his hammock at the corner of the veranda. From there, he had a beautiful view of the estate and the sea off in the distance. His eyes were drawn to the silhouette of the mountain range that surrounded Mount Sion. As he focused on that comforting view, his eyes fluttered closed. Before he knew it, Dexter was shaking him awake. It was time to leave for Black River.

"What do you think Harry is up to?" Brixton asked as he and Dexter rode out to the main road that would take them to Black River. It would be hard riding once they hit that road, to get to the town in three hours, so they took the time to formulate a plan of action.

"My guess is that he is going to petition the Privy Council for ownership based on Mas Lyndon dying with no legitimate heirs," Dexter answered.

"What about the Absolute Primogeniture thingy? Doesn't that document give Sabine the legal right to own the property?" Brixton asked.

Dexter smiled at Brixton. "The thingy?" Brixton shrugged his shoulders in response. "The thingy gives her the property by royal decree, but that doesn't mean the Privy Council cannot overturn that. In any case, Harry won't have a claim as soon as Mas Lyndon's Will is probated. His Will leaves everything in trust, administered by Dr. Richard, who is now legally wed to Mistress Anne, so that avenue is closed to Harry. Harry can try to question the legality of Dr. Richard and Mistress Anne's marriage, but such a marriage is settled precedent."

"In short, Harry can continue to be the pain in the ass he has always been," Brixton said.

Chapter 8 | Spanish Town

Dexter nodded, "If his request gets to England, it would be the excuse like-minded men on the Privy Council have been looking for to deny liberty by law to the colonies."

"How do you want to handle this?" Brixton asked.

"We get the document Harry's solicitors have prepared, destroy it, and then go to Spanish Town to see Mas Lyndon's wishes through and register Doctor Richard and Mistress Anne's marriage license," Dexter answered.

Brixton nodded. They had arrived at the main road and kicked their horses into a thunderous gallop. They would get to Black River just as the town opened for the day's business. Brixton allowed his thoughts to turn to Lyndon. As Lyndon's illness progressed, Brixton had taken him to the mineral baths in the cave on Mount Sion. Lyndon had looked around in wonder at Brixton's secret hideaway. The curative waters eased the pain in Lyndon's joints, but he remembered the day he had had to carry Lyndon to the pool because he could no longer walk without help.

"I'm not long for this world, Brix. There are still so many things I need to do before I die," Lyndon had confided in Brixton.

"Don't speak like that, Mas Lyndon, an hour in the pool, and you will be right as rain," Brixton had said, gently lowering him into the water.

"Ahh, the optimism of youth. I miss that," Lyndon said, settling down into the water. "Thanks to Anne's father, I may have a way to protect Sabine, a way to stop anyone who may want to take what she should legally be entitled to inherit from me. I want to protect her from the avarice of men."

"Mas Lyndon, Sabine is a white woman, no one in Jamaica would ever question that she is white," Brixton assured him.

"It is not Jamaica I am worried about, Brix," Lyndon said seriously. "I admire the way you Jamaicans think. You embrace the shared yoke of colonialism as your bond, rejecting what it was meant to do, create irreparable divisions based on class and color."

Brixton looked at Mas Lyndon. "I will never apologize for being white, Mas Lyndon. I had no control over that, and I do understand that the white man is not history's sympathetic figure, but I am painfully aware that the only history I can change is my own," he said solemnly.

Lyndon looked down, understanding the tone in Brixton's voice. "So, you consider yourself a Jamaican? Born and bred albeit of British ancestry, but very much a child of these shores. Your brother, Dex, is also Jamaican, born of African descent. Two women raised you as brothers, one white and one black. Jamaica is your birthright, as it is Dex's, as it is Sabine's," Lyndon mused.

"I could not agree more," Brixton said.

"You understand that one cannot be truly loyal to the land of their birth if they hold fast to a history and ancestry that they can no longer identify with. You owe it to the future to build a society that looks past the color of a man's skin to the character within. To judge his actions and his patriotic duty to the island that bore him," Lyndon said passionately, warming to the subject.

"How can you build the firm foundation of a society if you identify as something else first? I am a Jamaican of British stock, but first and foremost, a Jamaican. I have never even been to England," Brix said dismissively.

"That is the Jamaica I want for my Sabine. But, I want the world to see her as I do, a beautiful but capable woman, able to take charge of her destiny without permission from a King, a government, or even a husband," Lyndon said quietly.

"Is that what you still have to do? You want to leave a place for her in Jamaica?" Brixton asked.

"I do, but not just Jamaica. More than anything, I want to secure her place in this world," Lyndon answered.

Chapter 8 | Spanish Town

"How would you do it?" Brixton asked. Lyndon turned a questioning gaze to him. "You want to secure her place, her property in Jamaica. What do you need to do to achieve that? Surely you must have thought about it?"

"I only know how Anne's father did it in the Kingdom of Navarre. He made the king's decree, law. It is not so easy to do in England. There is a House of Lords, Parliament, and Privy Council that all need to agree that what King George sanctioned should become law. I don't see the resolve for that in England. Their hold on the colonies is tenuous at best; they will never willingly hasten the divide."

"Maybe you should ask Dex," Brixton offered.

"Dexter? Why, Dexter?" Lyndon asked.

"He would probably have an answer for you. If not, he will know where to find one," Brixton said.

"How? He can't go into the courthouse in Black River; he is not even supposed to know how to read," Lyndon said.

Brixton tried not to show his resentment to Mas Lyndon's comment out of the deep respect he felt for the man. "Dexter is clever, much more intelligent than I. We have a system. Dex goes anywhere I go."

"Pray tell, how do you manage that?" Lyndon asked.

Brixton looked at Lyndon; there was genuine interest on his face. Brixton realized that. This was a sensitive topic for Brixton. Many of their tutors had objected to educating a black child which offended Brixton to no end. Frequently Brixton had refused to attend their classes until they did. There wasn't much need for tutors in Jamaica. Those who would come to the Dunbarton Estate came because of Lord Dunbarton's reputation for decadence. Brixton's refusal to allow them to teach him would deprive them of Lord Dunbarton's rum stocks and slave quarters. Brixton and Dexter had learned early on how to manipulate that desire. They had perfected their system with 'Lame James.'

"Lame James was the last tutor we had. He lasted for five years but refused to answer any of Dexter's questions. So, Dexter and I convinced him to give us a lesson plan, and we would study on our own. Then we, and by we, I mean Dexter, would submit written questions to him based on our lessons. He would answer our questions the next day. It worked beautifully, and thanks to Dexter, I am sure I received a better education than I would have listening to Lame James for six hours each day. Now, if Dexter needs a book from the library or the courthouse, he writes down what he needs, and I get it. No one is any the wiser."

Lyndon chuckled to himself. That was a good plan. "Do you think Dexter could help me figure this out? I need a solicitor, preferably a King's council, who can approach the Privy Council with an argument that would sway them to our cause."

As soon as Brixton returned home that evening, he took Dexter aside and explained what Mas Lyndon needed. Dexter lay into the project, accepting the assignment with tenacity. After two weeks of thrice-weekly trips to Black River, Brixton had had enough.

"Jesus, Dex, anyone who knows me will not believe I read five books in two days. You are going to have to space this out more, man. You're killing me, not to mention my ass has more blisters on it than a whore's backside," Brixton complained as he handed Dexter a stack of legal briefs.

"Brix, I don't think you understand the implications of what I am doing or what it will mean for Jamaica's future," Dexter explained excitedly.

"You're damn right. I don't. I opened the last book to make sure it was the book you wanted and nearly fell asleep reading the bloody title. Stop rushing through these books. You need not rewrite the whole bloody book in a notebook, then read it back, searching for an answer. Trust me; no one is coming looking for these books. Take your time, and give my ass a break. Please," Brixton pleaded.

Chapter 8 | Spanish Town

Dexter and Mas Lyndon would meet each week in the cave as Mas Lyndon lay in the mineral waters. Living with Harry, Dexter had learned to read people. Each week, Dexter saw a deterioration in Mas Lyndon's health, and his pace hastened. He found a solicitor in Spanish Town and went with Mas Lyndon and Brixton to the first meeting, taking copious notes. Dexter wrote many of the instructions and arguments Mas Lyndon presented to the solicitor. The solicitor was so impressed that he used them all, then offered Brixton a job as his law clerk. Dexter should have been offended, but that was not in his nature. Besides, the look of utter panic on Brixton's face was so comical; Dexter barely managed to contain his laughter. Mas Lyndon saved the day by saying he could not lose such a valuable asset as Brixton was to their cause. To Brixton's chagrin, Mas Lyndon and Dexter laughed uproariously, well into the night.

That was the only time Mas Lyndon had visited the Spanish Town solicitors. Dexter and Brixton traveled to Spanish Town to meet with the solicitors on three separate occasions over the last year of Lyndon's life. Brixton lost interest in the project but dutifully came along to make sure the solicitors presented and accepted Dexter's briefs as his own and with the approval of Mas Lyndon.

Dexter's arguments had been an education in pure logic. He first needed to prove that the black man was on equal footing with a white man, that the black man was a man. In 1776, Thomas Jefferson had written the first draft of the United States Declaration of Independence. Dexter had focused on one statement in the declaration. "We hold these truths to be self-evident, that all men are created equal, that they are endowed by their creator with certain unalienable rights, that among these are life, liberty and the pursuit of happiness." As the American Revolution raged, Dexter had looked to the abolitionist movement for further support. The

Society for the Abolition of the Slave Trade was founded in 1787 by Granville Sharp and Thomas Clarkson. To move hearts and minds, they had come up with the slogan, 'am I not a man and a brother?'

Dexter had thought about this in great depth. Three generations removed from Africa, Dexter first had to define himself. He was not the only educated black man in the British colonies, not even in Jamaica. His birth mother was dead. Dexter was her only child, but his brother was white, and his father was white. His only biological family was white. Dexter did not think of himself as a slave, but by no means was he equal to his brother Brixton in colonial Britain's eyes. Dexter lived in the Greathouse; he valued education and embraced it. He was afforded the opportunity to study the law and saw that rules had already begun to change to accommodate the love white parents had for their mixed children. Some went as far as to proclaim them 'white by law" so they would be free from the confines of slavery and be able to inherit. Dexter was a highly intelligent man, able to live between two worlds. It was clear to him what needed to be done to reconcile them both.

His briefs and papers had to be submitted to solicitors as Brixton's work for them to be accepted. He did not have the freedom of movement and acceptance that his brother did. Dexter realized that he straddled both worlds of slave and master, and what he had to do was create one society of equivalents. The question was how. So, he tried to answer the first question, "If I am a man and a brother, am I not entitled to be treated as a peer and allowed the individual pursuit of happiness with liberty by law?"

Like the Europeans, Africa was a continent with a civilization that its citizens had created. Like Europeans, Africans had created distinct countries based on the culture and language of their people. Like Europeans, they had their Gods, their way of life. They bled, died, loved, and lived on in their offspring. They learned from their mistakes, thus improving the lives of the generations that came after them. They read, wrote their language in a recorded history, and the only difference between the black man and the white man was their skin pigment. This singular truth was evident to everyone and one accepted by the solicitors.

Once the privy council accepted the black man as an equal, the next question concerned the custom of slavery itself. "Slaves are criminals sold into slavery as payment of their debt to society or prisoners of war between the tribes of Africa," the slave traders argued. Dexter countered with the history of Britain itself. The Romans had conquered Britannia and ruled it from afar because tribalism was so ingrained in the Celtic tribes of the land that their hate for each other was stronger than their own self-preservation. It was a fact that Africans took prisoners during wars between tribes, but not at the rate accounting for the millions of Africans enslaved and sold into bondage outside of Africa. Just as the Romans did to the British, Europeans stoked tribalism in Africa, stirring up conflicts to secure slaves, driven by their own quest for profit.

When Roman rule ended after hundreds of years, the Romans and the tribes of Britannia had intermingled so much that no one knew where Rome ended and Britain began. Roman influence was in the architecture of buildings all over Britain and Scotland. Latin was taught in schools, and the Romans invented the form of government that Britain and its colonies use to this day. So, the Romans did not leave Britannia; they laid the foundations that Britannia built upon and assimilated as a culture and a people. The solicitors were very excited about this premise and felt the reasoning was relevant to Jamaica's current situation. Black and white had so intermingled in Jamaica over the generations that brown was more prevalent and, in many cases, beloved by both their white and black progenitors. So, the desire to protect and nurture this offspring was growing all around the West Indies.

Then came the argument Dexter had been waiting for; God sanctioned slavery. The bible is rife with stories and references to the legality of slavery. Harry had unwittingly provided the counter argument for this during a heated debate with Brixton regarding the abolition of slavery, which he vehemently opposed. "You are telling me that we are not to go to Africa, where they enslave each other, turn every infringement into a reason for kidnapping, then sell their own, half-starved, hard-labored, and ill-treated when the very Bible these wretches turn to for salvation, sanctions it?"

Brixton's answer to his father had been one he and Dexter had discussed many times. Dexter held fast and true to Christian beliefs. He believed that God had blessed him and would show him the path he would walk with God by his side. Brixton did not have the same depth of faith Dexter did, but he knew enough of bible teachings to use the story of the Tower of Babel to support his argument. "Harry, Genesis 11:6-7 clearly shows God's displeasure with the descendants of Noah, who all spoke one language and decided to build a tower that would reach to the heavens. God took objection to this and made the people speak many different languages so they couldn't work together on building the tower. Then he scattered them to the four corners of the earth, where they created new civilizations and cultivated new beliefs, including new Gods. If a man is created in God's image, then this is proof that He created all the men of the earth, then gave them free will to decide their own fate."

Harry sat gaping at Brixton, his mouth working, but no words came out. Margaret and Nana's laughter had driven Harry from the room in anger. Dexter had presented this argument to the solicitors by making Brixton repeat what he had said to his father, and the solicitors had included it verbatim in their written case.

The last card to play in the deck was their ace. But, as Brixton pointed out, it was more of a queen of hearts than an ace because it came with a timing issue. They had the signed and sealed Absolute Primogeniture from King George to Anne Holborn's father, giving Anne title to the property in Jamaica. Herein lay the last obstacle to success. King George was still alive, and he still ruled. His anger at America and their revolutionary war had hardened his heart to granting his colonies any freedoms from his rule. If he had a mind to, he could rescind the Absolute Primogeniture. He also had two sons, one of whom would take the throne upon his death. Not only was the Absolute Primogeniture a threat to succession by birth order, but Lyndon only had one heir, a female, thus posing a threat to male supremacy. Dexter had no way of knowing that King George's surviving heir to his throne would be a woman. A woman named Victoria was crowned Queen at the age of eighteen after the death of her father's three older brothers. All who died without a surviving heir, making Victoria the last reigning monarch of the House of Hanover.

But Dexter was a progressive and had to take into consideration that one day, a woman would be Queen of England. Anne Holborn was the only child of the Prince of Navarre, second in line to the throne. Anne's uncle was the King of Navarre. If her uncle had died without an heir, Anne's father would have become the King of Navarre by the laws of succession. Should that have happened, as his only child, Anne would succeed him as Queen of Navarre, the ultimate in land ownership. Sabine Holborn was the only child of Anne Holborn, thus a Princess of Navarre. By creating a line of succession based on the rules of legitimacy, Dexter presented the crown with the real possibility that a Queen would one day have to rule England and her colonies or risk losing the power and position the throne of England brought with it. It was the foretelling of a future that neither King George nor the Privy Council had considered.

Brixton and Dexter had stopped to water their horses at a small waterfall on Black River's outskirts. "This would be much easier if Sabine Holborn were Lyndon Holborn II," Dexter said to Brixton.

"Sabine Holborn is very much a woman," Brixton answered as he tied the horses to a rock and sat down on it.

"I didn't think you had noticed," Dexter commented.

"No, I have noticed, for some years now. But she has a tongue as sharp as a sword and can cut a man in two with a look. I would sooner take on road bandits than verbally spar with Sabine Holborn. Besides, she hates me," Brixton responded.

"Why is that?" Dexter asked.

"No idea. I can't imagine what I have ever done to offend her," Brixton answered.

"Do you think it may have to do with the fact that you have never turned your attention to her?" Dexter teased.

"My attention? Sabine Holborn is far more educated than I am. She is more intelligent than I, and she is not looking for a cheap title of Lady from a Lord who has nothing more to offer. You know that as well as I do," Brixton said with a mischievous smile.

"Yes, it was well-timed that I overheard young Mistress Eve's maid discussing the lady's plan to have you deflower her and then pretend to be pregnant to force you to marry her," Dexter laughed.

"Dex. I will say, your well-placed ear has saved my backside more than once. But, where Sabine Holborn is concerned, I have a great deal of respect for her, maybe because I loved and respected her father as much as I did, as I still do," Brixton said. The reminder of Lyndon's death sobered them both.

"I know, she is not one of the girls whose only worth is to while away a few romantic hours," Dexter said as he mounted his horse.

"No, she is not," Brixton said as he mounted his. "But if you are worried that a woman is not good enough to inherit and improve upon what she has inherited, then Sabine Holborn is the

Chapter 8 | Spanish Town

one to prove that assumption wrong. Since she has been running Friendship Estate, the lands and profits have grown considerably. Mas Lyndon was very proud of that."

"I think time will show that women are not our equals, but our betters," Dexter said. That had certainly been their experience with the women in their life.

Brixton looked at him and nodded. "Time longer than rope, Dex. Time longer than rope."

They were half an hour away outside of Black River. Already they had passed several carts loaded down with produce to sell at the local market. It was time to find the Irishman. Brixton strode into the solicitor's offices on the premise of needing to find his father. Only the Irishman was in the building, busily stuffing leather-bound documents into his messenger bag.

"Your father is not here," he answered Brixton's inquiry to his father's whereabouts. "I left them late last night at the Sir's house. I don't expect to see them before I leave," he commented distractedly.

"My father was to meet me here, so we could head to Mandeville to purchase some coffee beans. If we are to be the first to arrive at the auction house, we need to leave now," Brixton explained, concern creasing his brow.

The Irishman looked at him as he headed toward the door. "Don't know what to tell you, mate. You best leave without him. From what I saw last evening, he won't be in any condition to ride a day and a half, anytime soon."

Brixton followed him outside. Dexter was just unwrapping one of the johnnycakes Nana had made for them. It was dripping with butter and honey and caught the man's attention.

"I, myself, am off to Spanish Town on important business, but I wouldn't mind the company to Mandeville if you are willing to share those johnnycakes with me," he said, nodding in Dexter's direction.

Brixton smiled brightly. "We would be happy for the company; we have plenty of food and rum to spare," he said as he mounted his horse.

The Irishman smiled brightly at the mention of rum. He nodded his thanks to Dexter as he took the johnnycake from him. Brixton and Dexter shot each other a smile as they kicked their horses into a gallop and followed the Irishman out of Black River. At around noon, they stopped for a cold lunch of tongue sandwiches and lemonade. They gave the horses water and a chance to rest. The Irishman was impatient and anxious to get back on the road.

"What's the rush, friend. Spanish Town is not going anywhere," Brixton said.

"The Halifax is sailing back to London in four days from Passage Fort, and my master has documents for the Privy Council to address with great haste. I must get to the harbor before the ship sails," the Irishman answered distractedly. During Spain's possession of the island, an English Buccaneer dropped anchor in the port of Passage Fort, then marched six miles inland to Spanish Town, plundering it without opposition. Passage Fort became the port that landlocked Spanish Town, Jamaica's political capital, used from thereon.

Dexter shot Brixton a look. They planned to get the man drunk, steal the document, and ride out before he awoke. But now, the Irishman had confirmed that he had what they wanted in his possession. Technically, they would be culpable and open to accusations if the document went missing. As the Irishman excused himself to go into the bushes, Dexter approached Brixton.

"Brix, we can't openly steal that document. He has all but admitted he has it. If it goes missing, we will face accusation for it," Dexter whispered.

"Well, what's our other option? We have to get that document," Brixton whispered back.

Chapter 8 | Spanish Town

"I don't know. When we stop for the night, I will think of something. Let's avoid stopping at an Inn. Best if it is just the three of us," Dexter said as the Irishman appeared out of the bush, buttoning his pants.

As they mounted and rode off, Dexter tried to think of something. The Irish had just started coming to Jamaica, fleeing a famine in Ireland that showed no signs of ending. Like the new flood of Asian emigres from China and India, they came as indentured servants. Indentured servitude was the latest manifestation of slave labor. The Irishman had sold himself to his master in exchange for passage to Jamaica, a bed to sleep in, food in his belly, and a few coins to buy rum. Indentured servitude was just as brutal as institutionalized slavery, with most dying before their bond contract expired. This Irishman was better off than most. He held a job that gave him a modicum of dignity and respect. Dexter could not help thinking about the poor white woman who roamed the streets of Black River. It was heartbreaking watching her, dirty and unkempt, as she wandered absentmindedly in search of a handout. She arrived from Ireland as a mail-order bride, hoping to build a life with her new husband in Jamaica. Instead, she found nothing but derision and abuse from the man, who refused to marry 'white Irish trash.' Finally, the man had relocated to Kingston, leaving her behind. Abandoned and alone, she slept under the bridge that led into the town. Taking pity on her, Dexter had run off the children who thought it amusing to pelt her with stones and rotten food. He took her to the hospital in the hopes they would take her in. Dexter explained that she was insane and had no one to care for her. He had left her in their care, but the next time he came to Black River, she was under the bridge, sucking the last drops out of an old rum bottle she had found. The sight of her always left Dexter feeling hopeless.

Dexter explained his plan to Brixton when they stopped for the evening. By midmorning the next day, they would be in Mandeville and would part company with the Irishman, so anything they were going to do had to be accomplished while he slept. As Dexter prepared dinner, he watched the man's every move. Brixton had offered to hobble his horse as the man headed toward the bushes to relieve himself. Dexter noticed the messenger bag, still attached to the saddle, and motioned for Brixton to hobble the horse, so the bag was hidden from view of the camp. Dexter served dinner and hung back in the shadows as Brixton poured the Irishman drink after drink. Between the hard horse ride, his full belly, and the rum, the man was fast asleep as dark settled around them. Brixton pretended to sleep as he watched Dexter out of one eye.

Dexter moved in and out of the shadows, guided by the light of the fire. Moving stealthily, gently stroking the horses, so they were not startled by his movements. He stood at the head of the Irishman's horse, feeding him a handful of sugar cubes so he would keep his head raised and Dexter sheltered from view. Dexter reached for the messenger bag. Opening it, he riffled through the contents, careful to put everything back the way he found it. Halfway through, he found what he was looking for in a leather, cylindrical tube. He pulled out the rolled parchment and looked it over. As he suspected, Harry was petitioning the privy council to award him ownership of Friendship Estate and all its contents on the basis that it was abandoned due to the death of its owner with no legitimate heirs. Shaking his head at the audacity of the man, Dexter folded the parchment and put it under his shirt, secured in the waistband of his pants, and put the empty tube back in the bag. He nodded to Brixton as he settled down to get some sleep, his back to the Irishman. Brixton closed his eyes.

The next morning, they awoke, the Irishman a little worse for wear but ready to go. They arrived in Mandeville just as the

Chapter 8 | Spanish Town

auction house was opening and parted ways with the Irishman as he headed toward Melrose Hill. He would have to travel down the hill through the island's interior, passing through May Pen and Old Harbor before turning toward Spanish Town.

Dexter and Brixton headed south, toward Alligator Pond and the lesser-known south coast route that would get them to Spanish Town two hours before the Irishman. They rode hard, arriving at a small inn on the outskirts of Spanish Town just as night fell two days later. They secured a room, taking a bath in the nearby river. Bright and early the next morning, they presented themselves at the offices of Enos Knowles Esquire and King's Council.

To their surprise, they were ushered into the offices of Mr. Knowles himself. During all the meetings with his law firm, Brixton and Dexter had only ever met with the solicitors under his direction, never the man himself. Silently, they stood and waited for him to finish reading the legal book in front of him. Brixton and Dexter exchanged nervous looks.

"Are you here to tell me of the death of Master Lyndon Holborn?" Mr. Knowles asked quietly. For such a tall and authoritarian figure, it surprised them how soft-spoken he was. As they both nodded their heads, he continued. "I am saddened to hear that. I was quite hoping he would be around to see this undertaking to fruition."

Overcome with emotion, Brixton realized that tomorrow was Lyndon's funeral, and he would not be there. He asked to be excused, rushing from the room, leaving Dexter standing alone, staring after him. Slowly Dexter turned to face Mr. Knowles, who was staring at him intently.

"Dexter, is it?" Mr. Knowles asked him, motioning for him to take a seat. "I leave for England tomorrow. What needs to be completed before I depart?"

Dexter looked behind him, hoping that Brixton would return. Brixton was the spokesperson. Dexter felt entirely out of place. "Umm, I'm not sure how to answer that, sir," he stumbled.

"Well, that's surprising. I am familiar with all the briefs prepared to argue this case. I am familiar with the meetings you have both attended with members of my firm. I believe, young man, that you are exactly who I need to be speaking to," Mr. Knowles said as he sat back, folding his arms in front of him and steepling his fingers in front of his nose.

Enos Knowles was a learned man. He was the only King's council on the entire island of Jamaica, appointed by King George himself to his majesty's council. Enos' position as a legal scholar recognized not only by the English court but by the Privy Council was intimidating. Dexter had never addressed a man of such prestige and had no idea what to say or do.

"Well, sir, I have Mas Lyndon's Last Will and Testament here. I am sure you are familiar with it since your firm prepared it," Dex started.

"I am, what of it?" Mr. Knowles pressed.

"Well, sir. I think it needs to be submitted for probate immediately, sir," Dexter stammered.

"What's the rush? The poor man has only just passed," Mr. Knowles asked.

"Sir, I believe there will be a challenge to the estate. The sooner Mas Lyndon's Will is probated, the easier it will be to present the case for liberty by law for the colonies to the Crown and the Privy Council."

"Do you know of a challenge to his Will?" Mr. Knowles asked, sitting forward in his chair.

"Yes, I do, sir. But I also know that the threat is neutralized, at least for the foreseeable future," Dexter explained as he sat in the chair across from Mr. Knowles.

Chapter 8 | Spanish Town

"Keep that knowledge to yourself," Mr. Knowles counseled. "And any proof you may have of such a challenge, destroy it immediately if it is in your possession. I will start the probation process today. Anything else?" Mr. Knowles asked.

"Yes sir, I have the marriage license of Doctor Richard Chapman and Mistress Anne Holborn that has to be submitted to the registrar's office, also immediately," Dexter said as he handed the document to Mr. Knowles.

Mr. Knowles called for his assistant to come to his office. Dexter listened as Mr. Knowles explained that Mas Lyndon had died, instructing that probating his Will was to start immediately. Mr. Knowles also handed him the marriage license telling him to make sure he registered it without delay.

It was then that Mr. Knowles turned his full attention to Dexter. "I have much to do today and would appreciate it if you would attend me. I have some guests arriving on the Halifax, and I would like to greet them at my home, make them welcome and then send them on their way before I leave for London tomorrow."

"I will have to check with Lord Dunbarton," Dexter started.

"I extend the offer to young Brixton, but I would like some time to speak with you, young man," Mr. Knowles said as he stood, taking his hat and cane from the stand next to him.

"Me, sir? Why me?" Dexter said, uncomfortable with the request.

Mr. Knowles turned to look at Dexter. "Am I correct in my assumption it was you who drafted all the arguments Mr. Holborn presented me with for his case before the Privy Council?" He asked.

Dexter considered his answer carefully. "That would depend, sir."

"On what?" Mr. Knowles asked.

"On whether my answer will influence your decision to use them with the Privy Council, sir," Dexter responded, not looking the man in the eye.

"I have already used them, young man. They are well thought out and pertinent without being emotional. What I would like to do is enhance my presentation by knowing the motivation behind such beautifully articulated arguments against a system that desperately needs to change," Mr. Knowles said, then turned and walked out the door.

Dexter, following dutifully, whispered, "I think I can help you with that." Dexter missed the smile on Mr. Knowles's face as he followed the older man to his home.

Mr. Knowles's home was a flurry of activity as he prepared to meet his guests that afternoon. As his wife barked orders to the battalion of servants, Mr. Knowles asked Dexter to follow him to his library to pack what he would need to take with him. The extent of the man's library amazed Dexter and said as much to him.

"I am an avid reader. I love books. In these pages are the thoughts of minds greater than mine—men who have changed the world with their vision of a better one. I have learned more from reading one book than sitting in a lecture hall for hours on end," Mr. Knowles said. Dexter smiled but said nothing. "If you wish, I will leave instructions with my housekeeper so you may stay here when you visit Spanish Town. You will have full use of my library at your leisure," Mr. Knowles offered.

"You would do that? For me?" Dexter asked.

Mr. Knowles stopped packing and looked Dexter in the eye. "I would, happily. Great thinkers should always have access to profound minds," he said.

"You honor me, sir," Dexter responded humbly.

It was then that Brixton made his grand entrance, tripping over the rug and falling headlong at Dexter's feet. "Hello, brother," Brixton said tipsily.

"Seriously, Brix, there are more gracious ways to enter a room. Had a liquid lunch, did we?" Dexter teased, laughing at his brother's escapades.

"No, sir! Not all liquid," Brixton answered, jumping to his feet. Dexter patted Brixton fondly on his back. He had never seen Brixton drunk to the extent Harry would get fall down drunk. Brixton had too much self-control, but he understood how hard losing Mas Lyndon was for Brixton.

Mr. Knowles smiled at the exchange. "Brixton, thank you for joining us. If I may be so bold, I would impose on you to go with my valet to collect my guests at the Passage Fort harbor. They should disembark within the next hour or so, and I am sure they will be eager for a hot meal and fresh bed after such a taxing voyage."

"It will be my pleasure to be at your service, sir," Brixton answered.

"Wonderful, my valet has all the details; he should be down by the stables, waiting for you," Mr. Knowles said.

"Then I am off to do your bidding, sir. Brother, I will see you later," Brixton smiled mischievously as he bowed his way out of the room.

"He calls you brother?" Mr. Knowles asked Dexter after Brixton's departure.

"We have the same father, and I was born six hours before Brix. My mother, well, our mother, raised us both. Although she is technically Brixton's mother. It is all rather complicated," Dexter tried to explain.

Mr. Knowles nodded. "Your arguments to the Privy Council are well reasoned and thought out. Would you mind explaining to me, in your words, how you arrived at your conclusions? I think it would help me to understand the black man's perspective of his own history and will help to determine his future."

Dexter, still dazzled by the books in the library and the kindness Enos Knowles extended to him, lowered his guard. He answered the question with the intelligence and acumen he usually kept hidden from men like Enos Knowles. "I like to think I am a student of history, and from looking at the road already traveled, we can see what the road ahead may hold for us," he began. "The Spanish defeated the Aztecs with the help of their rivals by exploiting the ethnic antagonisms already firmly entrenched between the tribes. Hernán Cortés de Monroy y Pizarro Altamirano could not have defeated the superior fighting force of the Aztecs, who numbered two hundred thousand warriors with only the thirteen hundred soldiers he had, were it not for the help of the native auxiliary fighting forces he manipulated into fighting for him," Dexter said. "Right here in the Caribbean, the Arawak tribes turned the Spanish invaders' attention toward the southern Caribbean islands where the Carib tribes lived. The warring Caribs had terrorized the Arawak tribes on the islands, including the Taino here in Jamaica, for years, so they thought they could use these invaders with their deadly diseases of smallpox and measles to conquer their enemies once and for all. They felt empowered by the 'them or us' mentality. But their failure to see the dangers in that mentality was their downfall when they became the 'them' with no immunity to the invader's diseases or greed. History is rife with examples of tribalism, leading to the extinction of entire cultures. If one can't see the inherent dangers in those examples, then one will never learn from their cautionary tales, the only thing left of those civilizations," Dexter explained as he looked through the books in Mr. Knowles's library.

Mr. Knowles sat enthralled as he listened to Dexter. The young man had an excellent understanding of history and philosophy. "If you stood before the Privy Council, what would you say to sway their minds?" he asked.

Dexter turned to look at him. "Rome fell, the Aztecs fell, the Caribs fell; even Spain's dominance in the new world failed when their empire grew too costly for them to govern effectively. The fall of these empires teaches the same lesson. Right now, the British Empire is at a crossroads in history. One road will lead them down an already well-traveled path of domination and enslavement of people they feel they have conquered. History shows that this road will eventually lead to ruin. But the road less traveled, the other fork in the road, where we live with inclusion and acceptance, will ensure the longevity of life and liberty for all who chose to live in harmony with this world."

"The road less traveled," Mr. Knowles said softly, captivated by Dexter's words.

"Yes, sir. The same sun shines on all people; the same rain falls on us, and the same moon guides the tides of all sentient beings. We seek shelter, food, protection like all God's creatures do. What makes us human, what makes us equals, is our capacity to love and care for one another by celebrating our common humanity and ignoring our baser instincts of divisiveness. It is the road less traveled because it is the harder road to navigate," Dexter said.

Mr. Knowles looked at Dexter in awe. He did not see the color of Dexter's skin or the threadbare clothes he wore. He saw a prophet in front of him, come to deliver a message that would free the world from the scourge of slavery and point the way toward a better life of love, liberty, and justice for all.

At that moment, Enos Knowles understood how vital his petition to the Privy Council was and what it would mean for the world he would leave for his children and grandchildren. Deep in thought, he didn't hear his wife enter; she had to shake him to get his attention. His guests had arrived, and he needed to greet them. He took one last look at Dexter, who stood engrossed in his reading. A book in each hand, he did not notice Mr. Knowles leaving the room.

"My old friend! It has been too long," Mr. Knowles said as he greeted his guest. Enos was shocked at the man's appearance. Just over fifty years of age, the poor man was stooped and bent over, relying on the cane he held in one hand and the young man at his side for support.

"Dear Enos, I thought it was time I visited you on your side of the pond instead of you always coming to my side," the man answered weakly. Enos noticed how grey the poor man's skin was and how brittle to the touch it felt when he took his hand. "I am glad we have this time together before you leave tomorrow. We have much to discuss before your departure," the man said quietly.

Enos nodded as he gently escorted the man inside and helped him to a seat in the parlor by the door. "We do, but you must rest. You look exhausted."

"Frankly, I am feeling better than I have for some time. The air on your island suits me. It is the coughing that tires me more than anything else. But where are my manners? Please allow me to introduce my youngest brother, Declan. He has spent most of his formative years in King George's court, so he has not been with me on the occasions you visited."

The young man turned to shake Enos's hand. "It is my distinct pleasure to meet you, sir," he said.

Brixton came in, asking Enos which room he wanted their luggage to go to. It was Declan who answered. "We have an overnight bag; the trunks and cases will stay on the carriage for our journey inland tomorrow. I will come with you and get it sorted."

Enos and the man watched them go. "I see you have met Brixton," Enos said as he sat on the bench next to the man.

"He looks so much like his mother," the man mused.

"Did you tell him who you are?" Enos asked.

"I did not, no. I wanted to observe first," the man said.

"Understandable," Enos said and stopped talking as the two men came back in. Declan was carrying a valise. "Brixton, Dexter is in the library. We can all join him there and make the introductions," Enos said, helping the older man to his feet. They all walked slowly to the library, where they found Dexter.

"Declan, this is my brother, Dexter," Brixton said. He had taken an instant liking to Declan. A few years older than Brixton, Declan was handsome and quick to smile. His proper English accent was in contrast to the older man's deep brogue that Brixton found challenging to follow. Declan and Dexter shook hands as Enos found a seat for his friend but remained standing.

"Brixton, Dexter. Allow me to introduce you to Liam McKenzie, Chief of Clan McKenzie," Enos announced formally. The smile vanished from Brixton's face, but Dexter was happy to see the man and rushed to his side as Brixton stood rooted in his spot.

"Dear Sir, my brother and I are happy to make your acquaintance. Our mother has been awaiting your arrival with great anticipation. I apologize, sir; we expected to collect you at the port in Black River. This is not the greeting our mother would have arranged for you," Dexter said, embarrassed.

Liam smiled at Dexter. His resemblance to Harrington Dunbarton was uncanny and a little off-putting. But Liam could see none of Harrington in the young man's demeanor. "Having never traveled to Jamaica before, I was not sure where I would end up or when. Thankfully, Enos made most of the arrangements, and I am glad for the happenstance that allows us to meet here in Spanish Town and travel together to meet my sister," Liam said as he took the seat Enos offered him.

"I look forward to spending time with you and Brixton. Declan, my younger brother, already seems to get along well with your Brixton," Liam continued, pointing to Declan and Brixton standing next to each other. Now that the family ties were revealed, it was apparent that the two tall, slender, blond men were related to each other.

"Well, now that I have made the introductions, I am sure Liam needs a well-deserved rest before suppertime. Brixton, Dexter, why don't you show young Declan around Spanish Town. We can all meet back here for dinner at around six if that is in agreement with everyone?" Enos asked.

Dismissed, the young men turned to leave, Brixton trailing behind, his head down, his reaction to Liam's arrival not lost on the two men as they waited for the younger men to be out of hearing range.

"Brixton does not seem happy to see me," Liam remarked.

"Well, Dexter is, and your sister is anxiously awaiting your arrival. I suggest you have Dexter ride with you in the carriage. Declan and Brixton can ride alongside, giving them time to get to know each other. I think you will find Dexter to be a fascinating young man," Enos said mysteriously.

"Declan has been the one laying the groundwork for the 7th Duke of Ergill's return to England, hopefully, back to King George's court. It is probably a good idea for them to spend some time together. Is there anything else I need to know before you depart for England?" Liam asked as he stretched out on the sofa.

"Yes, I want to spend a few moments bringing you up to speed on some developments," Enos began as he closed the door leading to the library.

CHAPTER 9

The Funeral

Harrington Dunbarton awoke bright and early on the day of Lyndon Holborn's funeral. He had arrived at the Bellevue Estate late yesterday afternoon from Black River and gone straight to his study. He had not had a drop of rum to drink. His mind was clear. Aside from a slight case of the shakes, he was ready for the day ahead.

He went in search of breakfast. Upon his arrival yesterday, he was advised that Nana and Margaret were attending to Anne Holborn in her time of grief, so there was no one in the Greathouse. He did not think to ask where Brixton was, and he never gave Dexter a thought. He was happy to have the place to himself so that he could think and dream in peace.

His visit to his solicitors had been very productive. Both men were receptive to his idea of taking the Holborn Estate, and they looked forward to a generous reward when it was in Harrington Dunbarton's hands. Harry's excitement had nearly overcome him when he thought of what he would do to Anne Holborn once he had her in his bed. The very thought now made his blood run hot, and he grabbed at his crotch in anticipation.

The funeral was to begin at ten o'clock in the morning. Before the heat of the day became too much for the attendees. His solicitors had advised him to wait until after the ceremony to approach Anne. She would be highly emotional and too grief-stricken to put up much of a fight, not that there was anything she could do to prevent what he was planning. By now, the document he had signed would be in Spanish Town, waiting to board the Halifax for its journey to London, where Anne's fate would be sealed. He would never have to worry about money again. The respect he would gain from owning the most profitable estate on the island would silence his detractors forever. He scowled as he remembered a comment said under the breath but loud enough for all to hear when his father died. "He lived despised and died unmourned." That would not be Harry's fate now. Why, he may even be welcome back at court, now that he was *'as rich as a West Indian planter.'* Harry was happier than he could ever remember being.

He tugged at the formal coat, trying to pull it across his stomach as he called for his horse. In anticipation of today's successful venture, he had dressed in the most elegant clothes he possessed, from the wardrobe he had acquired on his journey to England, over twenty-five years ago. The pants squeezed his knees as he tried to mount his horse, trying desperately not to rip the seat of his pants, which hugged his backside more tightly than he would have liked. The silk and brocade overcoat was too heavy for the tropics, and he was dripping with sweat before he even turned onto the main road. But appearances were everything, and today, he had to make a grand impression on all who saw him.

Nana was advised of Harry's arrival back from Black River as soon as he turned onto the road that led to Bellevue estate the day before. So, the morning of the funeral, Nana had posted her lookout to await Harry's arrival at Friendship Estate, with

Chapter 9 | The Funeral

instructions to let her know as soon as he saw him. Nana and Margaret had been with Anne for two days. They had helped her with the funeral preparations and held her as she cried late into the night. Nana felt for poor Richard Chapman. It was evident that he was in love with Anne and wanted to help ease her pain even as he dealt with his own. Anne would not let Richard near her. Nana and Margaret understood that and provided the buffer she needed. But after today, they would not be there, and Anne would have to face Richard and his love for her.

As Nana stood by the window, she saw her lookout running toward the house. Harry was near; she left her post to find Margaret. They would meet Harry together. As they waited at the top of the Friendship Estate Greathouse's steep stone staircase, they watched Harry approach. He was sweating buckets and looked like he would fall from his horse at any moment. They couldn't help themselves and started to laugh as the full picture of his ostentatious attire came into view.

"You look like the fatted goose, trussed and dressed for the Christmas table," Margaret laughed as he pulled his horse next to the lowest step.

"God's tooth, you hateful woman! Come down here and get me off this damnable horse," Harry panted in response.

"And how would you suggest I do that?" Margaret said as she doubled over with laughter.

"You and Nana come to the bottom step. Catch me as a slide off the horse. Pray, I don't split the seams of my pants," Harry ordered.

Nana and Margaret descended the steps and waited as Harry slid sideways off the horse. Their peals of laughter, rendering them helpless as he fell in a tangle on the steps.

"Dear God, you are no use to man or God!" he said to the two women bent over with laughter as he picked himself up. "Nana, go ahead and meet me with a wet cloth doused in rose water and a tall glass of lime water to drink. Margaret, help me up these blasted steps. I can barely feel my feet in these shoes."

Nana hurried up the steps, her laughter putting a scowl on Harry's face. He tried to cuff Margaret across the face but missed, catching himself before he tumbled backward down the steps. Her laughter intensified as he grabbed her arm and dragged her up the steps with him. Nana met them at the door. As Harry drank the water and wiped himself off, he looked around.

"Has anyone else arrived?" He asked.

"No, you are the first. Not even the Vicar is here yet," Margaret answered.

"Good," he responded. "I should like to look around, get the lay of the land, so to speak."

Margaret stopped laughing. "You will do no such thing, you hateful man! The viewing of the body is in the dining room. The least you can do is go in there and pay your respects to the kind of man you will never be. Then you will wait in the drawing-room for the service to begin. The burial will be for close friends and family, neither of which you qualify to be," Margaret spat at him.

"I have no intention of viewing the body. I also have no respect to pay. Lyndon Holborn hated me, and the feeling is quite mutual. I am here to support the grieving widow," Harry said.

"Do not go anywhere near Anne Holborn today, do you hear me?" Nana said, her voice low and menacing. He moved away from her as fear ran down his spine. "Go sit in the drawing-room, and wait for the service to begin. One word out of you, and I will have you tossed out on your ample ass."

Harry scurried away, following behind the young boy who had served as Nana's lookout. Nana made it clear to the young man that his only job today was to escort and watch Harry. As Harry settled himself in an oversized chair at the back of the room, he started

Chapter 9 | The Funeral

to feel more himself. The room was magnificent, the epitome of a great room, with high floor to ceiling windows offering stunning views of the bountiful grounds and the sea beyond. Harry reclined in the comfortable chair, ordering the young man to bring him a glass of rum and fan him as he drank. The young man dutifully did his bidding. He understood that his job was to make sure Harry had no reason to leave the room.

So, Harry sat quietly, biding his time. He nodded hello to the people he knew, desperately trying to give the impression that he was an honored guest who had been received and welcomed before they were, seated in a place of honor while they milled about, waiting for the service to begin. The glass of rum had stilled the shaking of his hands. He told the young boy to bring him lime and water. The heat was unbearable in the heavy clothing, even with the boy standing over him, dutifully fanning him. Harry watched and waited. He saw Anne enter with the Vicar, she was even more beautiful than he remembered, but when Sabine walked in behind her, he sat up. The skinny little girl he vaguely remembered had grown into a beautiful and voluptuous enchantress. His pants tightened uncomfortably, and he shifted to ease the discomfort. His anticipation was almost more than he could stand. His focus was solely on Anne and Sabine; he heard nothing of the service. The kind words, the speeches of admiration, and the palpable loss in the room meant nothing to him. He was there to take what was his right to take, and nothing else mattered to him. He remained in his seat, watching as Anne and Sabine accepted their guests' condolences and bade them goodbye.

At last, the Vicar left with Richard Chapman, Sabine kissed her mother on the cheek and departed. Anne turned to look out the window. Finally, alone, or so she thought. Quietly, Harry told the boy to leave and waited until he left the room. Anne did not notice. Harry stood, steadied himself, and walked to the window, standing slightly behind Anne. It was all he could do to stop himself from grabbing at her.

"No one can ever say you don't know how the gentry does things. Lyndon taught you well," Harry said.

Startled, Anne turned to see Harrington Dunbarton step forward, so he was directly in front of her, trapping her between his bulk and the picture window she stood in front of. She could tell the fear on her face pleased him from the slow, languid smile that spread across his face.

"Lord Dunbarton! You startled me; I was not expecting you to attend Lyndon's funeral," Anne stammered.

"I'm not here for Lyndon's funeral. I am here to survey my property, including you," Harry sneered as he took a step closer to her.

"Your property?" Anne asked, trying to take a step backward, but there was nowhere to go.

"Now that Lyndon has died without a legal heir, I have petitioned the Privy Council to give me possession of his estate and all its property, including you and your darkie daughter," Harry chuckled, reaching with his fat hand to grab a stray lock of Anne's hair that had fallen to frame her face.

"A legal heir? I'm afraid you are mistaken, Lord Dunbarton. I am Lyndon's lawful wife. We have a daughter," Anne stated, not understanding what he was talking about.

"You are a darkie and a woman. Your daughter is a darkie and a beautiful woman. Neither of you has rights according to British law. Whereas I do," Harry said, his tone menacing. "I had thought to take you to my bed first, but seeing your little vixen of a daughter, I think I will enjoy her first, then you," Harry said as he grabbed at Anne, pulling her to him.

"I don't think that will be necessary, Lord Dunbarton!" Harry spun around to see Richard Chapman in the doorway, the young

Chapter 9 | The Funeral

man attending Harry standing behind him. "Anne, please come to me," Richard said, his voice hard, broking no disobedience. Anne hurried to his side as he moved into the room, dismissing the young boy. He put an arm protectively around Anne.

"Doctor Chapman," Harry said, straightening his coat and drawing himself up to his full height. "I don't believe you have business here. Friendship Estate belongs to me now, and I think it best you leave," Harry said, hoping to sound authoritative.

"Does it? That is news to me! Isn't it news to you, Anne?" He asked, looking at Anne, who nodded. "I'm not sure you can acquire something that already legally belongs to someone else."

"My solicitors in Black River are petitioning the Privy Council to grant me ownership of Lyndon's estate because he died intestate and has no legal heirs," Harry said, now unsure of himself in light of Richard's challenge.

"Intestate, you say? I'm afraid you have been misled, sir. Lyndon Holborn did indeed have a Will, which has been submitted for probate by now, don't you think Anne?" Richard said, his voice low and menacing.

"My solicitors are Lyndon's solicitors. They have assured me there is no Will, sir," Harry stumbled.

"Your solicitors in Black River? Now I see the confusion. Enos Knowles prepared Lyndon Holborn's last Will and Testament. I'm sure you have heard of him, the only King's council on the island, based in Spanish Town," Richard said.

Just then, Margaret and the Vicar returned, stopping at the entrance of the room as they saw the tableau in front of them, tension thick in the air. The Vicar started to back away, but Richard's words stopped him.

"I sent word of Lyndon's death to Master Knowles shortly after he died. The same day I married Anne, in fact. The Vicar here will confirm the marriage. He performed the service," Richard said as all eyes turned to the Vicar, who nodded and stammered a confirmation. "Lyndon Holborn left his estate to me, by British law, I have every right of inheritance, wouldn't you agree?"

All eyes turned back to Harry. "Of course. But you will understand if I chose to verify all you have said," he stumbled a response. "Before I make my claim."

"I would expect nothing less. But in the meantime, I ask you to get off my property and never return. If you so much as attempt to lay a hand on my wife or my stepdaughter, I will kill you with my bare hands," Richard took a menacing step toward Harry, who jumped back in fright.

"Margaret, I think it is time we leave," Harry said quickly, putting chairs between himself and Richard as he made his way to the door.

"I'm not going anywhere with you. I will find my own way home in my own time with Nana. I can no longer stand the sight of you, Harry," Margaret hissed at him as she moved to the side, allowing him to pass. She watched as he dashed out of the house.

Anne sagged against Richard. "How does one fight evil, such as that?" She asked, drained.

"There is no magic strong enough to fight evil so deeply ingrained," Sabine said bitterly. No one had noticed her standing at the back of the room. She had entered from a small servant's door in the corner of the room and had heard everything. She seethed with anger.

Margaret stepped in, "Richard, take Anne up to her room; she is positively faint with exhaustion. Vicar, I will show you to your quarters. Tomorrow, we will bury Lyndon. I think we have all had quite enough for one day," Richard picked Anne up and carried her out of the room as Sabine watched them go.

Margaret and the Vicar left as well, leaving Sabine standing alone, her hate and rage roiling like a hurricane inside her, all

Chapter 9 | The Funeral

directed at Brixton Dunbarton. Who else would Harrington Dunbarton have tried to get his hands on her property for?

Richard took the steps two at a time, hurrying to Anne's room. She and Lyndon had separate bedrooms with a door that connected the two rooms. He placed Anne on the bed and closed the door to Lyndon's room. It was then Anne started to cry. Richard lay next to her, taking her in his arms.

"Oh, God, Richard. I have never been so terrified in my life; what that horrible man threatened to do! He can't do it, can he, Richard? He can't rape me, rape my daughter?" Anne was frantic.

"No, my love! No! He cannot make good on any of his threats. You are protected. Sabine is protected. Lyndon saw to it, and I will make sure you are never at the mercy of that hateful man," Richard said, rocking her in his arms as he tried to soothe her fears.

"Are you in love with me, Richard?" Anne asked.

"I have always loved you!" Richard answered fiercely.

"Then show me! Make me feel something other than this heartbreaking grief that threatens to crush me," Anne begged, raising her face to his.

Richard understood. It was not the way he wanted to take her for the first time, but he realized she needed to feel a desire so intense it sapped her strength and rendered her body helpless to anything but a deep, encompassing sleep. He undid her bodice as she tore at his clothes. Their lips found each other, and fought an impassioned duel. Anne loosened the lacings of his pants as his hands pushed her skirts up. His fingers found her, gauging her readiness to receive him. She was ready, so he entered her as she threw her head back, teeth bared as urgency overcame her. He turned over so she was on top of him and could feel the full force of his longing for her. She ground into him, again and again, until her pleasure poured out of her, making him hot and wet as he emptied himself into her. She collapsed on top of him, asleep before her head hit the pillow.

He laid her gently down, taking her clothes off so she could sleep unhindered. He lay down beside her, joyous as she found him in her sleep and folded into his arms. His head next to hers, they slept.

It had been a long day for everyone. Sabine had not moved from the spot in the drawing-room she seemed rooted to. Brixton had not been at her father's funeral service. She assumed he was on his way to Spanish Town to do his father's bidding in taking her land and her freedom. Tomorrow she would bury her father, and in his name, she would exact her revenge.

Harry had retreated to his home to lick his wounds. He was not ready to concede defeat in his quest to take what he did not deserve, so his mind continued to plot and twist. Tomorrow, he would go to Black River and have his solicitors look into all Richard Chapman had told him, but in his heart of hearts, he knew it to be true, and he had lost, again. He slunk to his study, a bottle of rum in his hands, barking orders to send two slave girls from their quarters to attend to him. He sat back in his chair as they arrived, losing himself in the degradation he visited upon them.

Margaret and Nana entertained the Vicar. After a late lunch, everyone was ready for the day to end. Margaret and Nana retired to the room they shared and discussed the hope that Brixton and Dexter had been successful in their endeavors. Harry would be a beast to live with once thwarted, but they could handle him. The inhabitants of Friendship Estate were exhausted; losing their master was almost too much for them to comprehend. Tomorrow would begin the journey to his final resting place. No one knew what the day after that would look like.

Anne was the first to wake, just as the sun rose and encompassed the island in its warm embrace. As she looked at Richard, passion rose in her again. She understood she did not love him, but she knew that would come because of her body's reaction to him. She looked at his physique, her eyes taking in the firm, muscular length of him. He was much younger than Lyndon had been, and his body excited her in ways she had never experienced before. Her eyes traveled back to his face. He was awake and looking at her, passion blazing in his eyes. Slowly he kissed her. She moved closer to him. He made love to her tenderly until she was begging him to take her and ease the sweet ache inside her. When it was over, she lay satiated in his arms and raised her eyes to look at him.

"I want you to move into this room with me," she said softly. "I don't want what is between us," Her voice trailed off.

"I understand, my love," Richard said, licking at the nipple of her breast. "The door between the two rooms will stay closed. I don't want to sleep in that room. I want to spend my nights here, beside you. Inside you," He breathed. She kissed him then.

"Today, we let the dead bury the dead?" she asked.

"Yes, today, we let the dead bury the dead. You and I have a lot of living left to do," Richard said gently. They lay together, not saying anything until the house awakened and they detected movement. Richard helped her to wash and dress. With a final kiss, she left him to his ablutions as she went in search of Sabine. She knocked on her daughter's bedroom door but did not wait for a response before opening the door and entering. Sabine was sitting in a chair, looking out the window toward the sea. Anne noticed her daughter's bed wasn't slept in, and she was in the same dress she was wearing yesterday.

"Sabine, you are not dressed? Did you get any sleep last night?" Anne asked, concern in her voice.

Her daughter's tight smile confirmed her suspicions. "I'm fine, Mother."

"If it is too much, you don't have to attend the burial service," Anne offered.

Sabine stood up and moved behind her privacy screen to change. "I said, I'm fine. I am now mistress of Friendship Estate, am I not? I will see my father buried and then attend to the running of this estate. I still have an estate to run, don't I?" Sabine asked, coming out from behind the screen in her undergarments and moving toward her wardrobe for a clean dress. She looked at her mother, her eyes hard.

"Of course, you do. That hateful man has no idea what he is talking about. It was an empty threat. It means nothing; he means nothing," Anne answered, surprised at the rigidity she saw in her daughter. Sabine moved in fits and starts that concerned Anne. Her daughter had not come to her once in her grief, had not once looked to her for comfort. This was not like Sabine, and her behavior worried Anne. "Sabine, nothing has changed."

"Oh no, Mother, don't fool yourself! Everything has changed! We now need to look behind us at every turn to see if someone is there trying to take what they believe we should not have because of the color of our skin and because we are women. We are no longer secure in our future. We will have to fight just to keep what is ours," Sabine said. The bitterness in her voice startled her mother.

"Sabine, you're wrong. Richard," Anne started.

"A white man whom you have had to take to your bed to bind him to your cause," Sabine interrupted angrily.

"No, that's not true. Richard loves me. In time, well, maybe," Anne did not know how to explain to her daughter how she felt about Richard.

"In time? Maybe? Yet he is in your bed. Can you honestly say he is in your bed because you want him there?" Sabine turned on her mother.

Chapter 9 | The Funeral

"Sabine, stop it! Yes, I do want Richard in my bed. Right now, that is where I need him to be. I know you can't understand," Anne tried to explain.

"No, Mother, I can't understand it, nor do I want to. I have other pressing matters to attend to. What you do or do not do with Richard Chapman is not one of my concerns," Sabine said harshly as she flung the dress over her head and stormed out of her bedroom, leaving her mother looking after her in surprise.

Richard looked through the door, shock on his face. The ladies were too engrossed in their heated discussion to see him as he approached the door, but he had heard everything they said. "Anne, I'm so sorry! I'll speak to her," Richard offered.

"And say what, Richard, your mother seduced me so she could stop grieving for your father for a moment? What explanation would you give for what we shared last night, this morning?" Anne barked at him.

Taken aback, Richard stammered, "Anne! It's not like that. You cannot characterize what we have shared so bleakly."

The hurt in his voice melted Anne's anger, and she moved into his arms. "You're right, Richard. I am sorry, I didn't mean those harsh words. What we have is complicated."

"Anne, I have loved you, I think, from the moment I laid eyes on you. Lyndon knew that, he counted on it, and he trusted me to take care of you and Sabine. I have pledged my life to this end. Take whatever time you need; I will always be here. In whatever capacity you need me to be," Richard said, holding her close.

Anne turned her face to Richard and kissed him. "When we get back, I will help you move your things into our room," Anne said.

The argument with Sabine had upset her. She understood Sabine was grieving for her father, dead but not yet buried, as she watched her mother take another man as her husband. She realized Sabine was worried about what the future might hold for both of them and how tenuous their position was because of their skin color and sex. Sabine was an accomplished and intelligent woman. It was understandable that she resented having to hide behind Richard to keep what was rightfully hers.

Richard looked at her, love shining in his eyes, and nodded. Together they descended the steps. Sabine had already left the house for the stables. They walked into the drawing-room together, where Margaret and Nana were seated. Margaret was reading to Nana from a note she had just received.

"Brixton and Dexter were successful in their acquisition. They have met with Enos Knowles, who departs for England today. Brixton and Dexter will leave Spanish Town as well, this very day with my brothers Liam and Declan!" Margaret said excitedly. "They should all arrive by the end of the week. Dexter says Liam is very ill, so it will be slow going to accommodate his health."

"Liam and Declan? That will not be welcome news for Harry," Nana laughed at the thought.

"Why not for Harry?" Richard asked.

"The last time Harry and Liam were in the same room, Liam beat the daylights out of Harry because of the condition he found his sister in. Harry has lived in fear of him ever since," Nana said, chuckling at the memory.

"Then I should like to meet your Liam and buy him a drink," Richard said.

"Mags, why are they both here? Did you tell me they were coming, and I forgot?" Anne asked, worried that she had slighted her friend's good news.

"Darling Anne, no! With everything going on, I didn't want to mention it. Liam is dying of consumption. He is here to spend the last of his days with me. Declan will be returning to England with the 7th Duke of Ergill. It is time Lord Dunbarton returned to England and claimed his seat in the House of Lords."

Chapter 9 | The Funeral

"Lord Dunbarton?" Richard asked.

The Vicar came into the room then, to tell them it was time to bury Lyndon. The small procession left the house, following the cart carrying Lyndon's body. He had asked to be buried on a hill overlooking the sea, pointed toward Mount Sion. Sabine was already there when the procession arrived, followed by all the free folk living on Friendship Estate. They stood listening to the prayers the Vicar offered up. Sabine threw the first handful of dirt on the coffin, then left, headed toward Mount Sion. The Vicar departed after the simple service escorted by Margaret and Richard. Anne and Nana stayed behind with the free folk. Together they sent Lyndon to the hereafter in the tradition of their ancestors.

Every day, Sabine rode to her perch overlooking the beach of Mount Sion, but it would be three days before Sabine would confront her nemesis, Brixton Dunbarton.

CHAPTER 10
Liam McKenzie

Enos and Liam had concluded their discussions just as Brixton, Dexter, and Declan had returned from their outing. Brixton was polite, but Liam noticed he avoided him as much as he could. As they all sat down to dinner, Liam carefully observed the interaction between Dexter and Brixton. They loved each other; that was clear. It was a comfortable relationship; they were relaxed with each other, fast to share a joke, ready to laugh, and quick to challenge each other in a friendly debate. Declan had asked them their thoughts on the abolition of slavery. Britain's decision to abolish slavery throughout its colonies would immediately impact the Bellevue Estate.

Liam did not miss the look passed between Dexter and Brixton or the slight nod of Dexter's head, giving Brixton consent to expound on the topic. They listened as Brixton laid out a well reasoned and concise argument supporting the abolition of slavery.

"Dexter, you are quiet. As someone directly affected by the abolition of slavery, I'm curious to hear your thoughts on the topic?" Liam asked.

The table fell silent. Brixton's jaw tightened, and he sat forward in his seat, ready to defend his brother. Dexter sat back in his chair, wiped his mouth with his napkin, and crossed his legs.

"The abolition of slavery is very nuanced, just like the institution of slavery itself. When men and women were taken from the only home they had ever known, taken across an ocean, and dropped into an utterly foreign setting, it challenged them to adapt or die. Those who were willing and able not only survived, they thrived, and, in doing so, created a new identity and culture all their own," Dexter said.

"We could say something similar for the English men and women, who left England to find their fortune in the West Indies," Liam said.

"Precisely, sir. Their journey may have been different, but we all ended up here. We had to build a life, create a civilization, and develop a culture together. So, I will answer you thus, I talked when I should have listened, I was harsh when I should have been tender. I judged as I was being judged. The abolition of slavery is not the end, sir. It is the beginning. The question then becomes, when will the hate end? And the answer is simple when there is no longer a 'they' or 'them', just an 'us'. We are beginning to have that here in Jamaica, a result of how we have had to live together for generations. But in the rest of the world, it will not happen for years after you, I, and our grandchildren have departed this world. The culture of hate and degradation human beings have nurtured for generations will not be stamped out quickly as long as it benefits one over the other," Dexter said.

Liam looked from Dexter to Brixton. The same fire of conviction burned in Brixton's eyes. Dexter calmly took a sip of wine, put the glass back on the table, and met Liam's gaze.

"And Brixton, what say you to your brother's words?" Liam asked.

Brixton pushed his chair back, raised his glass of wine, and answered, "To that I say, every hand to the task, quick's the word and sharp's the action," he drained his glass of wine and left the room.

Chapter 10 | Liam McKenzie

Liam looked back to Dexter, a question in his eyes. Dexter spoke deliberately. "Brixton is a child of this island. He knows no other life. He doesn't want another life, but for the love of his brother, he will pick up the mantle of the 7th Duke of Ergill and fight for my freedom, for my right to live as he does. Lord Dunbarton will lend his voice to the abolition of slavery and, in doing so, will lose everything he has ever known, but he will shoulder that burden because it is his calling," Dexter said.

"Dexter, Liam will need your help on the arduous journey across the island to Bellevue Estate. I think it best you attend him in the carriage. Would you be so kind?" Enos asked, changing the subject.

"Of course, it would be my honor, sir," Dexter said, getting to his feet to help Liam to his. Dinner was officially over.

"Oh, well, thank you. I should like to hear how my sister has fared," Liam said. Declan and Enos looked at each other but said nothing as they listened to Dexter's loving description of his mother.

"My mother is the most beautiful woman I have ever known. She is strong, she is gentle, she is quick to smile and just as quick to anger," Dexter said, his love for his mother shining through in his words.

"Yes, I do remember the quick to anger," Liam said, smiling. Their voices drifted down the hallway as Dexter helped Liam to his room. They continued to talk as Dexter helped Liam to bed.

Declan and Enos remained at the table as Dexter and Liam departed. They had a few things left to finalize. Declan turned to Enos, "Sir, everything is ready for you in England. We would be honored if you would avail yourself of the comforts of the Dunbarton house in London. Should you need repose in the English or Scottish countryside, the Dunbarton lands and castle are at your disposal."

"I accept with gratitude, sir. I had no idea they were," Enos did not know what to say without insulting the McKenzies and looked at Declan, who was smiling.

"That they had been restored? The Duke of Ergill will find his land and properties restored to his possession and renovated to a grandeur his ancestors could never envision. All is ready for his triumphant return to England. We desperately need his voice at this time in our nation's history," Declan answered.

Enos smiled. "I look forward to meeting Lord Dunbarton in his home when he returns to England."

"A joyous homecoming it will be," Declan said as he stood and bid the older gentleman goodnight.

ENOS' HOUSE WAS a bevy of activity the following morning, as everyone prepared for their various departures. Enos said his goodbyes. As his guests readied to leave, Enos took Dexter aside. "Dex, take the time with Liam to get to know him. He is a man wise beyond his years and has taken quite a shine to you."

"I will, sir. Thank you for your kind hospitality," Dexter said, taking his hand and shaking it vigorously.

"Don't forget, my home and my library are always at your disposal," Enos said.

"That is the greatest gift; thank you again," Dexter bowed as he turned away to climb into the carriage where Liam was already in repose.

"Mr. Knowles, thank you for your hospitality, sir," Brixton said as he leaned down from his horse to shake the man's hand. "God's speed on your journey to England."

"And on yours, Lord Dunbarton," Enos replied.

Brixton looked at Enos but said nothing. He kicked his horse into a gallop, motioning for the carriage driver to follow him as he thundered down the lane, Declan by his side.

Chapter 10 | Liam McKenzie

Liam settled into the carriage as it rumbled down the rutted lane, away from Enos' home; he liked Jamaica. The climate agreed with him, and he felt invigorated. He enjoyed Dexter's company, and his companionship eased the arduous journey. Liam told Dexter the history of the McKenzie clan in Scotland. Longshanks, King Edward the first, had been a ruthless king and conquered Scotland in 1296, instituting harsh and cruel laws designed to break the Scottish clans' spirit. The McKenzie clan had fought hard against his occupation and stood with Richard the Bruce during the signing of the Treaty of Edinburgh, giving Scotland their freedom and Richard the Scottish throne. The McKenzie clan had been the fighting force of the Scottish throne from then on.

"What is Scotland's stance on the abolition of slavery?" Dexter asked.

"Have you read about the law of Primo Nocta?" Liam asked. As Dexter shook his head no, Liam continued. "That law gave English lords the right to take a Scottish woman's virginity on her wedding night. It was a law designed to subdue Scottish men. Not even their wife's honor was theirs to take. The Scots know oppression, maybe not on the same scale the Africans do, but we understand the treatment of being less than. Scots will always fight on the side of freedom."

Dexter looked down. He had known this history; his mother had taught it to him as a child. "Why are you here, sir?" He asked, his eyes boring into Liam.

"Please call me Uncle Liam," Liam asked, unsure of how to answer.

"Fine. Uncle Liam, why are you here?" Dexter asked again.

"I am here to pass on the mantle of Chief of Clan McKenzie to the 7th Duke of Ergill. I will hand over the wealth, the power, the influence, and the army of the McKenzie clan to Lord Dunbarton," Liam answered.

"Why?" Dexter asked. Brixton would need good men around him to steel his resolve. Dexter wanted to make sure Liam's dedication to ending slavery would be strong enough to support Brixton as he fulfilled his destiny.

Liam looked out the window of the carriage for a long time before he answered. "The 7th Duke of Ergill is in a unique position. Lord Dunbarton can influence the course of history because of how he has lived his life on the tiny island of Jamaica."

As Liam dosed off, Dexter thought about what his uncle had said. It is not that he didn't trust a white man's intentions, but he knew enough of them to feel the need to question their resolve, especially in the face of what they would consider a loss for their side. Liam understood subjugation; he hadn't experienced it first-hand, but it had influenced the Scottish spirit so much that it still resonated generations after they had successfully fought against it. This fight was not white against black; it was a freedom fight against tyranny and oppression. Tapping into that shared experience, no matter how far they had to go back in time to remember it, would be the key to winning the war of 'them' and 'us'.

The three days it took to journey from Spanish Town to the Bellevue Estate took its toll on everyone. Brixton's trepidation about his future was palpable, and Dexter did all he could to ease the tension in his brother. Declan observed without comment, Liam watched with growing unease.

Dexter could tell they were close to Bellevue Estate. Liam awoke with a start as the carriage came to a jolting stop, and he heard Declan's shout of excitement.

"My darlin' Mags! What a beautiful sight for these sore eyes!" Declan yelled.

"Little Declan? My little man! You are now one of the biggest men I have ever seen. My God, how I have missed you!" Margaret exclaimed as Declan swept her up into his arms, spinning her around.

Chapter 10 | Liam McKenzie

Dexter stood back after helping Liam from the carriage. Brixton was still on his horse, watching the joyful reunion. On seeing Liam, Margaret tapped Declan on the shoulder, indicating she wanted to be put down. Slowly she walked to her brother. Her hand over her mouth, tears flowed freely down her face.

"Ah Mags," Liam said, as he took her in his arms. "Are those tears for me? Don't cry, my Mags. Just the sight of your beautiful face lifts my spirits," he said, trying to soothe her.

Margaret cried as she hugged her brother to her. The powerful arms that had once swung her over his head could barely hold her now. She drew back to look at him. His smile! His dazzling smile was still the same, and she laughed through her tears. "This is the happiest day of my life since the birth of my sons. I cannot tell you how much I have missed you, my darling brother."

It was more than Brixton could take. Brixton moved his horse so he could speak privately to Dexter. "Dex, do you mind making sure everyone is settled? I need to check on Mount Sion. I haven't been there since the storm."

Dexter understood. This was the beginning of the end for Brixton. "I'll take care of everything. Go, Brix. I understand," Dexter said, laying a hand on his brother's leg and patting it.

Without a backward glance, Brixton kicked the horse forward and headed toward Mount Sion. He rode his horse along the beach connecting Bellevue with Mount Sion, turning inland as soon as the mountain range came into view.

Sabine Holborn was waiting for Brixton, positioning her horse behind the rocky outcropping that would shield her from Brixton's view as he rode along the beach. It surprised her to see him turn inland, so she watched until she could follow him without being detected.

Brixton had no idea anyone was following him. His thoughts crashed into one another, and he lost focus. Concentrating on getting to the cave took all the will he could muster. Automatically he tied his horse to the hitching post. He removed his riding boots, so he was barefoot.

Sabine arrived at the entrance of the cave and saw Brixton's horse tied up. She jumped off her horse, led it into the cave, and tied it off next to Brixton's horse. Sabine spied Brixton just as he turned to go deeper into the cave. She followed at a distance. She had seen nothing like this cave before. There was a rope guide along one side, held off the ground by iron stakes about two feet tall with a circle at the top it threaded the rope through. She turned a corner and saw the mysterious glow of light ahead; the sound of rushing water grew stronger as she moved toward the dancing light. At the entrance, she stopped, her mouth falling open in awe at the sight in front of her. The light played off the ceiling, framing Brixton as he stood naked, ready to dive headlong into the pool in front of him.

Something made him turn around. Brixton did not recognize Sabine at first. She was dressed in britches, with a white linen shirt open at the collar exposing the swell of her breasts. The tight pants hugged her legs and clung to her hips, highlighting her curves. Their eyes met as his opened in surprise, hers narrowed in anger, and she flew at him. He caught her, staggering back in shock as her hands pummeled him.

"You bastard, you evil bastard. I will kill you before you take what is mine," Sabine shouted at Brixton.

"Dear God, Sabine? What are you doing? Have you gone mad?" Brixton did not understand what was happening.

Sabine pulled a dagger from her waist, kicking at his shins so he would release her. She brandished the blade in front of her. "Your father came into my home. My home, Brixton! Threatening to take my inheritance, threatening to take me to his bed by force. Threatened my mother!" Sabine screamed at him.

Brixton backed away. "Sabine, I have no idea what you are talking about. Please put that knife down so we can discuss this. You are obviously upset," Brixton said.

"Upset? Upset you entitled prick! You think I am upset?" she screamed

"Sabine, please! I have been away for the past week; I have no idea what you are talking about," Brixton tried to calm her.

"I know where you have been—traveling to Spanish Town with your father's petition to take Friendship Estate. Tell me, were you successful? Is it only a matter of time before I am forced to your father's bed, then yours?" Sabine shouted.

"What! What are you talking about?" Brixton asked. The look on his face gave Sabine pause. He genuinely did not know what she was referring to.

"Your father came to Friendship Estate on the day of my father's funeral to advise my mother that he had petitioned the Privy Council to give him ownership of Friendship Estate and once successful, he would take my mother to his bed and then me, by force," Sabine said.

"My father did what? There is no way he can do that. Dexter and I intercepted the petition. Dex burned it! Besides, Mas Lyndon protected you and Mistress Anne by asking Doctor Richard to marry her. He can do nothing of the sort, Sabine. Believe me, Mas Lyndon, Dexter, and I made sure of it!" Brixton was having a hard time understanding what Sabine was telling him.

Sabine stood back, her mind working to understand his words. Nothing he said made sense. Yes, Brixton had been there when Richard married her mother, but that was just a coincidence, wasn't it? He spoke of her father as if he knew him. Her father had never mentioned Brixton to her or any conspiracy they were involved in. "You're lying!" She said.

"Lying about what?" he asked, exasperated. "Nothing you have said makes any sense," Brixton said, dropping his hands and letting his guard down.

Sabine lunged at him, nicking him with the knife on his side, just above his thigh. He jumped back, shocked. He turned his head to look at the cut, wiping at the blood with his hand. The light the phosphorus omitted bounced off the wall behind him, framing the profile of his face. For a moment, he seemed illuminated as he looked down at the wound. It struck a memory in Sabine, and she cried out.

"My God! You are the White Spirit the free folk whisper about!" she said as Brixton looked up. Sabine's face was ashen. "I saw you! The night of the storm from my window. You were on your horse, the lightning struck, and I saw your face! You were looking down at the girl you carried. I saw the kindness, the caring. How could it be you?" Sabine dropped the knife and looked away. She could not believe what she was saying.

Brixton was sure she had lost her mind; the grief of losing her father had to be the cause. Slowly he went to her side, silent as she cried. Finally, she stopped crying and looked at Brixton.

"I'm sorry," she mumbled.

"No, I'm the one who should be sorry. I understand nothing that has happened here. Why don't you start from the beginning, and let's talk this through, shall we?" Brixton said. As she nodded, Brixton continued. "Start with my father's visit to your home."

As Sabine told him of his father's conduct, Brixton's anger grew. He tried to control his rage as she ended her story. He would deal with Harry soon enough.

"Harry is no threat to you, your mother, or Friendship Estate. He tried to petition the Privy Council, but Dexter saw that coming, and we stole the document from the Irishman before it could get to Spanish Town. Before your father died, we," Brixton stopped as Sabine cut him off.

"We?" She asked.

"Yes, your father, Dexter, and I have been working with Enos Knowles, the King's council in Spanish Town. Your father is petitioning the court of King George and the Privy Council to uphold your right to inherit based on Absolute Primogeniture," Brixton said as Sabine interrupted him again.

"Absolute Primogeniture? You know about that?" Sabine asked in surprise.

"Yes, I do. Next to Dex, your father was my best friend, Sabine. He was my mentor, my teacher, my guide ever since I was a boy. I learned so much from him, and I miss him. One of the hardest things I ever had to do was miss his funeral. But it was the least I could do to protect the people he held dearest to him. You and your mother," Brixton said, his voice catching.

Sabine turned to look at him. "How could I not know any of this? Why would my father keep his friendship with you from me?" Sabine asked, still skeptical.

"I have no idea. Your father was an enigma," Brixton started.

"Wrapped in a puzzle," Sabine completed his sentence. "My mother always said that."

"She did; it was she who taught it to me," Brixton smiled at the memory.

"And you are the White Spirit? The man from the mist come to free slaves from bondage?" Sabine asked.

"Well, it is not so romantic as that," he said, smiling ruefully. "Dex and I help runaway slaves, but we are only one part of a much larger tapestry," Brixton explained.

Sabine walked away from Brixton. He did not follow her. "All these years, I have thought you to be a selfish brute, cut from the same cloth your father is."

"Is that why you have always hated me? Because you thought I was like my father?" Brixton asked.

"No, well, not really," Sabine stammered.

"Why then?" Brixton asked, staring at her intently.

"Well, you never seemed interested in me. I thought you, well, I thought you disliked me," Sabine explained, embarrassed.

Brixton looked at her as if seeing her for the first time. Her flawless complexion kissed by the sun. Her beautiful face, with big ackee seed eyes, was framed by her long, ebony hair. Brixton's eyes traveled down her body to breasts straining against the damp shirt, her nipples hard. The britches she wore hugged her legs enticingly. His eyes traveled back to her face, to pouting lips that begged to be kissed. "I loved and respected your father, Sabine. You are a beautiful woman, but you will never be a casual tryst for me. You are much more than that," he said as he approached her. "It is true; I did not fully realize it until now, but that does not take away from the fact that I am quite taken by you."

Sabine looked at Brixton. He was still as naked as the day he was born. His body looked like the drawings of Greek Gods she had seen in her schoolbooks. She looked away. "You are still bleeding," she commented, breathlessly. She had no idea why her body was responding to him the way it was.

Brixton stopped his advance and looked down. "A few minutes in the pool will stop it," he said as he turned and jumped headlong into the shimmering water. He surfaced just as she came to the edge of the pool. He stared at her, his eyes just above the water.

Sabine wanted him. She did not understand why. A few moments ago, she had hated him, wanted him dead. Now she was drawn to him like a moth to a flame. Slowly she removed her clothes and dove into the pool, surfacing just close enough to Brixton that all he had to do was reach out and pull her to him. Slowly he extended his hand and touched her face, caressing it. Their eyes held. He put one hand on her shoulder as the other arm circled her waist. A gentle tug moved her toward him as her lips parted and her eyes closed of their own volition, anticipating his kiss. They felt the kiss reverberate through their bodies, tingling their toes. Still kissing her, he swam to the edge of the pool, letting her go long enough to pull himself out of the water, then turned to drew her up and into his arms.

Slowly Brixton lowered her to the ground, kissing her from head to toe, taking her to dizzying heights of pleasure she had no idea existed before this moment. She reached for Brixton, exploring him as he had her, with his guidance. His body ignited her, making her feel like she was on fire from within. Brixton braced himself above her, looking into eyes that implored him for something she did not know she wanted.

It was then Brixton stopped. He could not have her, not like this. Never, not the way she deserved. He rolled away from her, sitting next to her, his knees to his chest and his head in his hands. He would soon leave Jamaica to take up a post he had no desire to. He would be miserable in England, he knew that, but he also understood the importance of why he had to go. Lyndon had taught him about duty and honor, about loving others more than he loved himself. He could not subject Sabine to his misery. Brixton could not take her away from the home she loved, the people who counted on her, and the island that needed her, so she could provide him with a few moments of comfort. She would hate him for doing that to her as he would hate himself.

"Leave now, Sabine! Please, before we do something, we will both regret," he said, anguish in his voice.

"What? Why? Brixton, I want this, I want you," Sabine said, confused.

Brixton stood up, picked up her clothes, and threw them at her. "Go, Sabine; I can't give you the life you want, I can't marry you, so I will not take your virtue," Brixton said, turning away from her.

Sabine grabbed her clothes and started putting them on, anger fueling her movements. "Oh, I see. The great Duke of Ergill cannot be seen consorting with a darkie. Is that it? I'm not the sort a Lord marries, right? You are the bastard I thought you were, Brixton Dunbarton. No matter the good you think you may have done, you are still the entitled, selfish ass I have always known you to be."

Brixton's back was to Sabine. He could say nothing in his defense, his body tense from the conflict that coursed through him. Sabine screamed in frustration as she brushed past him, hurrying before Brixton saw the tears in her eyes. Brixton did not move. Finally, he gathered his clothes, dressed, and walked to the entrance of the cave. Mount Sion had not brought him the peace of mind it always did before today. Now, he had to have dinner with an uncle he resented, an uncle who would tear him away from the only life Brixton had ever known to a life they pledged him to, but he did not want.

But first, he would deal with Harry. He would punish Harry for being the son of a bitch he was and for creating the asshole his son would become because of his actions. His step quickened as he anticipated the satisfaction thrashing Harry would give him. The pleasure that would replace the pain of letting Sabine Holborn out of his arms. He kicked his horse into a gallop, sand flying behind its hooves as Brixton raced home, his mouth hardened into a thin, angry line. The realization that he was in love with Sabine Holborn was yet another burden he would have to shoulder.

CHAPTER 11

The Dinner

Margret and Nana arrived home after Lyndon Holborn's funeral to find Harry drunk, face down in his own vomit on the floor of his study. They had closed the door and left him where they found him. When Harry surfaced late that afternoon, he found his home in turmoil. Margaret and Nana were busy cleaning the house in preparation for her brothers' arrival. Grumbling and cursing as he banged into furniture that wasn't there before, Harry tried to navigate his way out of the house. Everyone was moving at such a speed; his head spun, so he made his way to the back veranda, gratefully falling into his planter's chair.

He called for Margaret to no avail. He then tried calling for Nana, who finally sent a young man to find out what he wanted.

"I want the strongest cup of coffee you can make, then bring me some johnnycakes with honey," he demanded, holding his head in agony as the furniture in the room behind him scraped the floor as it was shoved into a new position. "Dear God, what the hell is going on in my home!" he roared.

Margaret came out, the apron over her dress dusty, as she wiped her hands on a towel. "We are expecting guests by the end of the week, so we are preparing the house," she explained happily.

Harry looked at her; he didn't like to see her happy. "I have not been asked to allow guests into my home, woman. No one stays in my home without my approval."

Margaret sauntered over to his chair, picking up the broom leaning against the wall by the door as she advanced toward him. Harry sat up in his chair and leaned away from her. "This is not your home, Harry. Your very presence takes away its homeliness. You are the cockroach that keeps flying in through the window and will not die," she said, her voice low and menacing. She held the broom in front of her like a cudgel.

Harry tried to move the heavy chair away from her, but the scraping noise it made rattled through his head and made him wince in pain. He looked up at her, squinting as he held his head. "Bring me my damn coffee! I don't care what you do or with whom, just don't expect me to be social, and don't let them get in my way," he ordered as false bravado filled him.

Margaret advanced toward him, slapping the broom handle with one hand. Harry refused to meet her gaze, which made her laugh. "Oh, and stay out of your study. I am turning that into a bedroom."

"Woman, you will not!" he bellowed. Turning away from her, "That is where I work and run this estate. I am still Lord of this estate," he muttered gruffly.

"It's cute that you think you still run this estate," Margaret sneered. Then, turning to go back inside, "You can be Lord of your chair, right here on this veranda. At least the vomit will wash off with the rainfall," she said as she turned to go back inside.

Margaret turned to see Nana standing in the doorway, smiling at her. "The Scottish rose has her thorns out today, I see. It's good to see yu happy, Mags."

"Oh, Nana, only happy days ahead, I pray," she said. "We will put Liam in the study. That way, he won't have to go up and down the stairs."

Chapter 11 | The Dinner

They set off to tackle the study as Harry's breakfast was brought to him. After the first cup of coffee, his head began to clear. He should be atop his horse on his way to authenticate what that bastard Richard Chapman had told him, but in his heart, he already knew his words were true. Furniture continued to scrape against the wood floors of the house. Gritting his teeth, he went to his bedroom and packed an overnight bag. Maybe, Black River was where he needed to be until this madness was over. His solicitors would gladly put him up for a couple of nights. Within an hour, he was on the road to Black River.

All was ready when Margaret greeted her brothers and welcomed them into her home two days later. Harry had not returned yet, and no one seemed interested in his whereabouts. It was an unfortunate turn of events when Harry did return later that evening to find his wife's guests seated at his dining table. The laughter and animated conversation ceased as Harry walked into the room. He recognized Liam immediately, and fear paralyzed him. It took him a moment to realize that it was not the Liam he remembered. The man now seated at the head of the table was a jaundiced ghost of the man he once knew. Harry could not help it; a smile spread across his face. That is until Declan rose from his chair, understanding precisely what had made Harry smile. So focused on Declan, Harry did not see Brixton storm down the hallway, his fist raised. Before Harry could react, he flew into the dining room, crashing into the hutch and falling at Liam's feet.

"You bastard! You shitty bastard! You've gone too far this time. I am going to kill you, Harry!" Brixton advanced as Harry scurried behind the chair Liam was sitting in. Declan was too shocked to move, but Dexter had seen this before and rushed to Brixton's side.

"Brix! Brix! Stop man, think about this," Dexter counseled, latching onto Brixton's raised arm.

"Dex, he went to Mas Lyndon's funeral. He accosted Anne Holborn. He told her he was going to take Friendship Estate and rape her! Rape Sabine! He threatened Sabine!" Brixton shouted, advancing. Declan jumped into action and grabbed Brixton from behind as he roared in rage.

"Mother?" Dexter asked.

"It's true! Every word," she answered. All eyes turned to Harry as he cowered on the floor.

"You unconscionable bastard. You haven't changed one bit," Liam spat at him as he moved the chair, exposing Harry to Brixton's wrath. Declan and Dexter released their hold on Brixton as he lunged for Harry, dragging him to his feet and holding him against the dining table.

"Rape the woman I love? Her mother? I will show you rape, you piece of shit," Brixton yelled as he turned Harry over so he was face down on the dining table. Holding Harry down by the neck, Brixton kicked his legs open and looked around for something to assault him with, but it was Nana who stepped in.

"Brix, that is enough," she said softly, reaching for his arm. He let go of Harry, who jumped up and hid behind her. He couldn't leave the room because Dexter and Declan blocked his escape.

Big tears fell from Brixton's eyes. "Nana, I can't live in a world in which he draws breath."

"I know me bwoy. I know," Nana said as she held Brixton to her. His frustration was evident in his loud sobs, the only sound in the room.

Dexter and Margaret looked at each other. "The woman he loves?" Dexter mouthed the question to his mother, who shrugged her shoulders, as perplexed as he was by Brixton's admission. Harry moved, catching Dexter and Declan's attention. They moved to the side so he could pass between them. Neither Dexter nor Declan took their eyes off Brixton, but Brixton took no notice of

Chapter 11 | The Dinner

Harry's hasty departure. His heart was breaking as Nana held him in her arms.

Dexter tapped Declan's arm, indicating that he should follow him. They found Harry on the veranda, sucking in deep breaths of air, trying to calm his nerves. Harry started to back away as he saw them.

"I've no argument with you! Whomever you are," he said, pointing at Declan.

"No one is going to argue with you, Lord Dunbarton," Dexter assured him. "The missive you and your sordid lawyers sent to Spanish Town never made it. Never made it to the ship bound for London. I burned it myself. You will never lay claim to Friendship Estate or anyone residing on it. And, now I am sure you will never be able to show your face there. You are running out of places that will welcome you, sir," Dexter said.

Harry's mouth worked as he realized what Dexter was telling him. "You spiteful little darkie! You stole a legal document, and you burned it? I will have you flogged within an inch of your miserable life!" he shouted as he moved toward Dexter, who stood his ground unfazed by Harry's outburst. It was Declan who stepped forward, grabbing Harry by the throat and lifting him off the ground as Harry sputtered, and his feet flayed in thin air.

"You are fortunate that I am the man my mother raised me to be. I believe in the power of forgiveness. I believe it builds character in men. Your petty mentality of retaliation extinguishes a man's soul and turns him into something less than human, turns him into you," Dexter said as he walked up to Harry, looking him in the eye. Declan released his hold. As Harry staggered back, he looked at a black man with real fear in his eyes for the first time.

Declan and Dexter returned to the dining room. Nana was still in there with Brixton, so they went in search of Liam and Margaret, who were in the study. It was now a comfortable bedroom for

Liam, who was reclining on the bed, Margaret next to him. Declan sat on the edge of the bed, as Dexter sat in the chair by the door.

"Dinner is always an adventure when Brixton and Harry are at the table," Dexter said, trying to lighten the mood.

"Who is this girl Brixton is in love with?" Liam asked, concern on his face.

"Sabine Holborn, her family owns Friendship Estate, Brixton was very close to her father. I am not sure how long Brix has known he is in love with her," Dexter said, shaking his head at this new turn of the night's events. "But I am not surprised," Dexter answered.

"Not surprised?" Margaret said. "Well, I certainly am. Last I heard, Sabine Holborn hated Brixton, and those were her exact words, according to Nana."

"There is a fine line between love and hate. Besides, they have been dancing around each other for years," Dexter said.

"Brixton being in love may complicate things," Declan said quietly.

"No, it won't. Brixton will always do the right thing. He may not like it, but he will do the right thing," Dexter said. He missed the look of concern that passed between Liam and Declan.

Nana was sitting on the floor, her back against the hutch as Brixton's head lay in her lap. His body curled up next to her legs as he had done when he was a child in need of her comforting. He listened to Nana's calm humming as she rubbed his head. Nana heard him sigh. "Yu want to tell me what happen between yu and Sabine?" she asked gently.

Brixton sat up, moving to sit next to her with his back against the hutch. He raised a knee and lay his arm on it, wiping at his face. "She must have been waiting for me. She followed me into the cave and found me at the pool. She was mad as hell. God, Nana, I have never seen a more beautiful woman. We talked, really talked, for the first time. There were so many misconceptions between us, misunderstandings that had festered for years. I have never wanted a woman as much as I wanted her. My arms ached when she left them. I have never felt that before," Brixton said, wonder in his voice. Nana took his hand as he continued. "I would have married her then and there, taken her as my own forever, but I couldn't do it. I wanted to so badly, but I couldn't," Brixton said, his voice catching.

"What stopped you, Brix?" Nana asked.

Brixton ran his hand through his hair. "I don't want to go to England, Nana. I don't want to be Lord Dunbarton, the 7th Duke of Ergill. I want to be Brixton Dunbarton of Jamaica. A simple coffee farmer in love with the most intriguing and challenging woman I have ever met. I want to spend the rest of my life lost in her eyes. But a higher duty calls me; I have to lend my voice to the fight against slavery for the people I love. Dexter, you and Sabine. For your sakes, I cannot let anything make me doubt my destiny."

"Why do you think she would not be a true partner to you and help you in your cause?" Nana asked.

Brixton looked at Nana. "It's not her I doubt Nana. It's me. I am my father's son. I don't *want* to fulfill my duty; I don't *want* to honor my path. I will resent every minute of being in England. I will be angry, and I will be bitter. In time, she will hate me as much as my mother hates my father. And that will be my undoing. I would fall into a bottle of rum and never find my way out if that were to happen."

"Brixton, you listen to me. I know you from before yu born. Yu are nothing like your father. Yu are a good man, a man deserving of great love. You underestimate yourself, and you underestimate the path God has laid out for you," Nana said, conviction strong in her voice.

Brixton smiled sadly. "You may be a little biased, Nana."

"Brixton, it is no secret I love yu above all others. Yu were born in my hand, and my sun has risen in yu every mawning and set wid yu every night. I pray for yu always. I pray for yu to be happy. God gwen give me dat for you, Brix. Yu just have to have faith in him, have faith in me," Nana said.

Brixton smiled at her, hugging her to him. He hoped Nana's faith was strong; right now, his was non-existent. He helped her to her feet, and they went looking for the others. All eyes turned to them as they stood in the doorway of Liam's room.

"Feeling better?" Margaret asked. Brixton smiled and nodded, his arm still around Nana. Silence enveloped the room. No one knew what to say.

"So, Sabine Holborn, huh? When did you figure that one out?" Dexter asked.

Brixton laughed, and the tension in the room broke. "Cut like a knife," Brixton said, raising his shirt and showing Dexter the cut Sabine had given him in her anger.

"Sabine did that?" Dexter asked, astounded. Brixton nodded. "And that's when you realized you were in love with her?" Dexter asked incredulously.

Brixton shrugged, and the room again erupted in laughter. "That girl has some Scots blood in her," Declan laughed.

"Brix, that looks like it needs a salve," Margaret said, jumping up from the bed. "I'm not so sure I approve of this match if she is going to cut my baby like that. Nana, let's get this taken care of, then off to bed with everyone. We have a big day tomorrow, and Liam needs his rest," Margaret said, pushing everyone out of the room. Only Declan and Liam remained in the room as she turned and blew them a kiss from the doorway.

"Harry?" Brixton asked Dexter, his voice hard.

"Harry is nothing for you to be concerned about now," Nana said curtly.

Chapter 11 | The Dinner

"Why?" Dexter asked as Nana rubbed salve on Brixton's cut.

"Your mother is having a dinner party tomorrow," she answered. "Your attendance is mandatory. And you are required to dress well and wear shoes," Nana said as she kissed the spot above the cut and sent them on their way.

Groans of misery escaped as Nana shooed them down the hallway and up the stairs to their beds. Nana stood at the foot of the steps, watching them go up to the room they had shared since infancy. Dexter had his arm around Brixton, their heads together as they whispered to each other. Nana had seen them like this a hundred times. But tonight, she wiped a tear from her eye as she turned to go to her room.

Brixton slept fitfully. He dreamt of making love to Sabine, and the pleasure was more than he could stand. He awoke with a most painful erection. Frustrated, he punched at his pillow, trying to find a comfortable position to lie down in. "That girl is going to be the death of me," he muttered.

As Dexter snickered, giving up the pretense of not enjoying Brixton's torment, Brixton jumped out of bed.

"Damn you straight to hell, Dexter Dunbarton!" Brixton said as he turned Dexter's mattress over, dumping him on the ground. Dexter's laughter followed Brixton as he ran down the stairs, out the house, and jumped right into the cold pond by the house.

"What the hell?" Liam asked as he heard Brixton's shout as the cold water hit him. He and Margaret were on the back veranda and had been surprised by a naked Brixton running past them to jump into the pond.

"He had a hard night," Dexter said from the door, pointing to his penis as Liam nodded in understanding. Nana pushed Dexter out of the way, running down to the pond with a warm towel for Brixton. Brixton and Nana arrived minutes later, the towel wrapped around Brixton's waist.

"Did that soften the blow?" Dexter asked, laughing.

"Go to hell," Brixton answered, shaking the water out of his hair as Nana fussed over him. "Nana, I'm fine. Stop brushing at me like that. You are going to make the towel fall," Brixton tried to push her hands away.

"Lawd God Brix. Yu don't know what live ina dat pond. Me haffe check yu for leeches. And, I dun see you likkle peanywally since yu was a baby, it na nuttin," Nana said.

Brixton grabbed her hands to stop her. "Nana, it is not a likkle peanywally anymore. Leff me, please."

Nana threw up her hands in defeat and walked into the kitchen, muttering to herself. Margaret was all business.

"Brixton, I need you to go to the butcher down the road and pick up some mutton and beef for me. Dex, I have a note I need you to deliver for me. Lots to do today, boys, let's have at it," Margaret ordered.

"Mother, who is coming for dinner tonight?" Brixton asked, annoyance in his voice.

"What time is dinner? Mother, we have been away for a week, we have a lot to do around here," Dexter added.

Margaret turned to Liam, "Quite the pair I have here, don't you think?" He nodded, agreeing with her.

"Now listen to me. Nana and I are perfectly capable of running this property without you two. Everything you could possibly think to be done has been done. Your uncle Liam has not been here in years. This is the first visit your uncle Declan has ever made to Jamaica. Their visit has brought me great happiness, and I want to show them off to my friends. I shouldn't have to explain this to you," Margaret said through gritted teeth.

Heads hung, looking at their feet, both men responded. "Yes, Ma'am." Dutifully, they turned to hurry upstairs and dress. Margaret watched as Brixton left for the butcher. Then she called Dexter to her.

Chapter 11 | The Dinner

"Take this note to Friendship Estate. Explain to Mistress Anne what has happened between Brixton and Sabine," his mother ordered.

Dexter's eyes widened. "Mother, you invited the Holborns and Doctor Chapman for dinner? Brixton is going to shit his britches."

"Watch your mouth. They have to be here tonight. They cannot back out. It is your job to make sure they don't. Give the note to Doctor Richard," Margaret ordered. Dexter nodded and took the note. "And for God's sake, don't tell your brother," Margaret added.

Dexter did not like keeping a secret from Brixton, but completely forgot about it when he walked into the drawing-room of Friendship Estate to find a loud standoff taking place between Sabine and her mother. Dexter stood next to Doctor Richard, who was watching with great dismay.

"I am not going to the Dunbartons for dinner tonight, Mother. It is not happening!" Sabine stood across from her mother, pacing back and forth with her arms folded in front of her.

"Margaret Dunbarton is my dearest friend, and this dinner means a great deal to her. She is welcoming her brothers, and she wants our support. I will not deny her," Anne argued.

"Then you and Richard go! Why is my presence required? I cannot promise you I will behave myself when I see the Lords Dunbarton," Sabine threatened, her voice loud.

Without taking his eyes from the drama in front of him, Dexter handed Richard the note. He read it and tried to get Anne's attention.

"What?" Both women turned and yelled at him at the same time.

Taken aback, he hurried toward Anne and handed her the note. She read it; then, she advanced on her daughter. "Sabine Holborn, you will attend this dinner tonight. I don't care if you end up swinging from the chandeliers, but you will be there. Do I make myself clear?"

In a huff, Sabine nodded. Screaming in frustration, she left the room, slamming the door behind her.

"What the hell has gotten into her?" Anne asked in exasperation as she threw the note to the ground.

"I may be able to help you with that," Dexter said, cautiously advancing into the room.

Both Richard and Anne turned their attention to Dexter. As he thought about what to say, Anne asked. "And?"

"Well, Brixton and Sabine seemed to have had a slight run-in yesterday. It would appear that Brixton is in love with your Sabine. Maybe she doesn't share his feelings?" Dexter asked, unsure of himself.

Anne looked at Richard, who shrugged his shoulders. Her finger to her mouth Anne, was lost in thought. Sabine's reaction was too visceral. If she did not share Brixton's feelings, she would relish the opportunity to torment him with them. Sabine has never thought much of Brixton and had never hidden her low opinion from Anne or Lyndon. But, if she shared his feelings, then why such animosity? "Dex, did something happen between Sabine and Brixton that I need to know about? Did one of them act inappropriately?"

Dexter understood what Anne was asking, had Brixton offended Sabine in some way? He was quick to defend his brother. "No, mistress. Brixton did nothing wrong. As far as I can tell, he was a gentleman, but Sabine did cut him with a dagger..." His voice trailed off as he realized he did not know what happened between them.

"Dear God," Anne said.

"Anne, we have to go. You know what the note says. We all have to be there tonight," Richard said as they turned away from Dexter.

Chapter 11 | The Dinner

Now Dexter was curious. What could be so important that they had to come to dinner? As their backs turned to him, he inched closer to read the note on the floor. *We are going to tell them tonight*, was all it said. He jumped back as Anne turned around to address him.

"Please assure your mother; we will be there tonight," Anne said, dismissing him.

"Yes, Mistress Anne, I will, Ma'am," Dexter said as he turned and left the room.

The rest of the day was a flurry of activity. Dexter did not have time to think about the note or what it could mean. He completely forgot about the message when he and Brixton arrived in the drawing-room to find Harry holding court with Liam looking bored and Declan looking like he wanted to be anywhere else but where he was.

"Do you think a boatload of pasty white men went into Equatorial Africa and stole a million Africans by themselves? They had help. Their own people sold them into slavery. Abolish slavery in Africa, and then maybe we can talk about abolishing it in the colonies," Harry held forth.

"Harry, can you just not speak?" Brixton implored, reaching for a glass of wine.

Harry turned to Brixton, "My boy, it is you who don't know what you are talking about. You want to set these people free to do what? The sable race are savages, instinctively driven by generations of giving in to their baser needs. They kill their own for the mere pleasure of it. The white man did not go into Africa and pluck them out of the bushes. Africans sold their own into slavery and made a damn fine living doing it, I might add. If you ask me, we saved their lives. At least here, they live in peace. Left to me, I would pack them all up and send them back to Africa. Let them live off the overflowing coffers of the tribes who sold them into slavery in the first place."

"They are no more African than I am British. Like me, they are two and three generations removed from their motherland, from their culture. Like it or not, we are all Jamaicans, and it is in our best interest to live and prosper here, as one people," Brixton yelled at his father.

"Pish posh. Our estates can prosper just as well with indentured servants from Asia, India, and the damnable Irish," Harry sneered.

"This from a man who had been to England once in his miserable life. Once, so he could bring despair to everyone he met. If you are the epitome of the English gentry, then I want no part of it. I will stand with my brother, with my Nana, with my island, to fight against the tyranny of any man, be he white or black. I will stand against any man who refuses to judge a man by his character instead of the color of his skin. I will stand against you, Harry. My brother Dexter is the finest man I have ever known. He has no hate or acrimony in him. It is an amazement to me! He should hate you more than I ever could, but he doesn't. You have two sons, but only one who refuses to hate you. That makes him a better man than you or me."

Sabine Holborn quietly stepped into the room. Her back to the wall, she listened to Brixton as he stood over his father.

"But I, the lesser man, will take my place in the House of Lords, and I, the lesser man, will fight against you until my dying breath. I will fight to make sure every man, woman, and child is free. Free of bigotry and the power men like you wield. I will fight until we are all valued by the content of our hearts and our actions toward our fellow man. I will fight until the color of one's skin or the sex between their legs is no more important than the color of their eyes. I will fight to undo everything that you hold dear. And I will do it all the while being the lesser man," Brixton finished, his eyes so full of contempt that Harry was the first to look away.

Chapter 11 | The Dinner

Brixton did not turn from his father until he felt Dexter's hand on his shoulder. He was shocked to find all eyes on him, including those of Richard and Anne Chapman.

Liam stood, and everyone's attention turned to him. "I have come to Jamaica to send my nephew back to England, to send him on the most important duty of his life. Declan and I have been working for years to cast the shame associated with the Dunbarton name into the shadows. We have used our wealth, power, and influence to secure the 7th Duke of Ergill his seat in a house of power and authority that desperately needs his voice. We are at a crossroads in history. We have the chance to eradicate the scourge of bigotry and prejudice from this world once and for all. My sister suffered greatly for this day. She is the architect of this new world—an idea born in the depth of despair. A plan brought to fruition tonight," Liam drew from his side a sword with the McKenzie crest emblazoned on the handle, a stag with a snake in its mouth. "Margaret present to me the 7th Duke of Ergill. Present to me, your firstborn son."

Margaret Dunbarton moved to stand between her sons. She kissed them both. "I present to the Clan McKenzie, your new Chief. I present my firstborn son," Margaret took her son's arm and led him to stand before her brother. "I present to you, the 7th Duke of Ergill, Lord Dexter Dunbarton."

"Mother?" Dexter turned to his mother, unsure of what was happening.

Margaret laid a hand gently on his arm. "Kneel, my son." Dexter knelt as Liam performed the centuries-old ritual that would anoint Dexter.

"NO!" Harry howled, lunging at Dexter. "This is an abomination; he is not my son!"

Brixton stood up and grabbed his father so he could go no further. "Margaret, he has no right, no claim," Harry screamed as he strained against Brixton.

"He has every right. His birth paper proves his claim. It has Dexter's name on it, signed by me, Margaret and you, yourself. A birth paper accepted and ratified by the English crown." Dr. Richard Chapman came forward from the back of the room.

Harry bellowed. "Margaret, you tricked me! This is a sham! Once I explain it in England, they will not allow it; the crown will strike this down."

"No, they won't. Lyndon Holborn and Enos Knowles saw to that. As your legal firstborn son, Dexter inherits the title. The law of primogeniture makes it so," Richard answered.

"And you will not be going anywhere near England. You are banished forever from Britain. One of the terms I negotiated with the crown when I petitioned for Dexter's seat in the House of Lords," Declan explained. "By royal decree, you will be jailed and hanged the moment you set foot on English soil," Declan stepped forward and bowed to Dexter. "Let me be the first to pledge my fealty to you, Lord Dunbarton, 7th Duke of Ergill."

"My Lord," the room echoed as everyone bowed, except Brixton, who stood staring at Dexter, a slow smile spreading across his face as he realized what this meant. He pushed Harry into the closest chair and went to hug his stunned brother, picking Dexter up and whirling him around the room. It was then he spotted Sabine standing in the corner.

"Sabine!" he called out as she turned and fled the room. "Sabine, wait! Please!" he implored before turning to look at Dexter, who motioned for him to go after her. They would deal with what had transpired later. Dexter understood what Sabine meant to Brixton. He now understood the meaning of the note his mother had sent him with this morning. It was a lot to take in.

Brixton ran after Sabine, who fled out the back door and was headed toward the beach leading toward Mount Sion. Brixton stopped only long enough to tear the shoes from his feet. Then he took off after her.

Chapter 11 | The Dinner

"Sabine, please stop so we can talk," he begged. He finally caught up with her, sweeping her into his arms to stop her from running away from him, but she did not stop fighting. He held her down on the sand and kissed her. The fight left her then.

"Why, Brixton? I'm not good enough for you, remember?" she said when he released her.

Brixton looked down at her and smiled. "You are a Princess of Navarre. Those sycophants at court would worship you like a God. But I would have been miserable in England, and I love you too much to subject you to that. I would have become my father, and losing you would have been the end of me," he kissed her again, and she melted against them. "No more misunderstandings, no more miscommunications. I love you, Sabine Holborn, I think I always have, and I want you to be my wife. No, I need you to be my wife. I don't want another day to pass that I don't wake up next to you," Sabine kissed him then, and they stopped talking.

It was Dexter who found them, locked in an embrace. He sat down next to them and looked out to the sea. "Well, this has been a hell of a dinner party."

Brixton smiled at him and sat up, pulling Sabine onto his lap. The brothers shared a moment, and Sabine sat still so as not to intrude.

"Now what?" Dexter asked.

"Now, we hear the rest of Mother's grand plan, but first things first, I need to marry this one. Tonight, if possible," Brixton said, leering at Sabine and making her laugh.

"Brix, you cannot legally be married for two weeks. I don't have another marriage license lying around, so you will have to post the bans and wait two weeks," Dexter started listing the requirements.

"We can do that, but I am not waiting. There must be another way. I can't wait two weeks," Brixton said as he and Dexter looked at each other, remembering how the day had started for them.

"Does my opinion matter? You haven't asked me for my hand in marriage. You just told me we were getting married. With that pretty speech you made back there about equality of the sexes, shouldn't I have a say in this?" Sabine asked. Given all the miscommunications between them, Brixton was not sure if she was serious or not.

"Sabine, I am so sorry. Of course, your opinion matters. I didn't mean to minimize…" Brixton began worriedly.

"Oh, shut up, Brixton, I was just joking. I have every intention of marrying you!" Sabine answered as she pulled him to his feet. "Let's go figure this out."

As the three of them walked back into the house, everyone was seated at the dining table. The conversation stopped when they walked in, and all eyes turned to the three. Brixton and Sabine turned to Dexter, who rolled his eyes before he spoke.

"Brixton and Sabine want to get married. Mistress Anne, Brixton, is asking for your blessing to marry Sabine. The catch is, they want to get married tonight," Dexter said. No one moved, and all eyes remained on the three young people.

Finally, Liam spoke. "As Chief of the McKenzie clan, you can perform a binding ceremony. It is not a legal ceremony, mind you, but if they have to be married tonight, and by the looks of them, they do, then you can perform the ceremony."

"Me?" Dexter asked.

"My ancestors had that too. I will agree to that," Anne said, smiling at her daughter.

"Well, let's prepare for a wedding then, shall we?" Margaret said as everyone stood up. "Dexter, take the groom and get him dressed appropriately, make sure he washes his feet. Then come down to Liam so he can teach you the ceremony. Anne, Nana, come with me, and we will get Sabine ready. Richard, Declan, find a place suitable to perform the ceremony."

Chapter 11 | The Dinner

Dexter pulled Brixton away from Sabine and pushed him up the stairs. Brixton lay on his bed in the room they shared, looking at Dexter, who was searching through his trunk for something. "I know today was a surprise, a wonderful one for me, but how do you feel about being named the 7th Duke of Ergill?" Brixton asked.

Dexter found what he was looking for and sat across from Brixton as they had when they were boys. "I don't know. I'm a black man that has just been given something only a white man has ever inherited."

"I've never seen you as a black man, only as my brother," Brixton said.

"I know, and that is probably the best gift you could have given me in preparing me for this role. I am secure in the knowledge that I am loved as your brother. But, how do I get others to see me as a brother and not a black man come to take what is theirs?" Dexter asked.

"Dex, you are not taking anything away from anyone, certainly not from me! You have earned everything you were given tonight with your dedication to family and your unwavering commitment to righting a terrible wrong. With your birthright, you will change the course of history!" Brixton said, earnestly.

"I've never met a challenge without you by my side. I don't know if I can do it without you," Dexter said, voicing his real fear.

"Aww, Dex, man, I will be with you for as long as you need me. But my life is not in England, and your life is no longer in Jamaica. At some point, we will both have to stand on our own, in the soil we are meant to occupy. But I will always be your brother, and I will always be your most loyal champion," Brixton said, grabbing his brother's hand.

"That is why I want you to have this," Dexter said, holding out a ring of polished gold, diamonds all around it. "This ring belonged to our mother's mother. Do you remember it?" Dexter asked.

"I do, yes. I remember the night Mother showed it to us. How old were we, seven or eight?" Brixton said.

"We had just turned eight. Mother took it out to show us, saying it would go to whichever of us married first. But I wanted it, Brix. At that moment, I had never wanted anything more than I wanted this ring. For the life of me, I can't tell you why I did it, but when you and Mother left the room, I took it. Harry found me with it the next morning. He accused me of stealing it, which I did," Dexter said, smiling sadly.

"I remember hearing him shouting. I came out to see what all the commotion was. He raised his hand to hit you. I jumped on his arm to stop him," Brixton said, looking down.

"Yes, you did. You have always protected me from Harry, from anyone who tried to make me feel less than. I will never find the words to explain to you the confidence your love has given me, the freedom to soar when others would have chained me. I am in awe of the purity with which you love, the selflessness of it. You love without condition. You have never treated me as anything other than your cherished brother. That is why I want you to give Sabine this ring. Let it be a reminder of the priceless treasure being loved by you is."

"But I told you to keep it, Dex. I had never seen you take anything without permission. I knew you would not have taken that ring unless it held great significance for you," Brixton said, looking at his brother.

"It did have significance. It signified love. To me, if I could just hold onto this ring, I would always be loved by you and by our mother. I don't need the ring to symbolize that love anymore," Dexter said.

"You are the best of me, brother," Brixton whispered as he hugged Dexter.

Wiping tears from his eyes, Dexter handed Brixton the ring. "As you are the best of me, brother." Nana had taught them that

Chapter 11 | The Dinner

goodnight blessing as children and they said it to each other every night before they fell asleep.

"You will not be getting married wid all dat sand pon your foot, Brixton Dunbarton," Nana warned from the door. "Come, mek your Nana wash yu like I did when yu was a young boy, not a big married man," Nana said as she started to cry.

Dexter kissed Nana, "I will leave Brix in your gentle care, Nana. Today must be a hard day for you, letting your likkle bwoy become a man," Dexter teased.

"Get yourself downstairs, Lord or no Lord, I can still tek yu over me knee and buss yu backside," Nana threatened as Dexter ran out in mock fear.

"Come here, Brix, mek me brush yu hair and wash yu foot," Nana said as Brix walked over and sat on the floor in front of her. "I tell yu God will tek care of yu. I tell yu God will give yu happiness. He never give one man more dan he can stand."

"You know about dis, Nana? You know what was going to happen tonight?" Brixton asked.

"I did. Your mother, she change the night Dex born, the morning yu born. When yu came out, all the strength she did use to bring yu into dis world never left her; it went right into her backbone. When she call us together, me, Mistress Anne, Mas Lyndon, and Doctor Richard, and tell us what she gwen do, we never doubt she would do it. She tell Mas Liam what she do as soon as she see him. Together they find Mas Enos, and they put it all together. She neva change her mind; she neva doubt it, not one time as yu two boys grow," Nana said.

"I never want to live anywhere but in Jamaica. This is my home. It is where I want to build a life with my wife, on the hill on Mount Sion. I want to raise our children there. I want them to be Jamaican," Brixton said.

"Yu, born in the sun, my child, yu will die in the sun. Dat is what I ask God to give yu, dis love, dis happiness, and him answer my prayers," Nana said as she brushed Brixton's hair.

"I am happy, but I don't want to be happy at the expense of my brother's happiness," Brixton worried.

"Yu don't worry bout Dex," Nana said confidently. "Your mother, she prepare him for what she know he have to do. Every time yu fight for your brudder to go to school, to learn, to grow, every time yu and he put your head together, yu give him the armor he need. Is yu and she prepare Dex for dis life, don't ever forget dat."

"I love you, Nana," Brixton said.

"And I love yu, me golden bwoy. Now, let's get yu married to that likkle she-devil yu say yu love. But I tell yu bwoy if she ever cut yu again – she and me! She and me!" Nana cautioned as they headed downstairs.

Dexter was huddled with Liam in the drawing-room when they came down. Declan and Richard had found a little spot by the beach, where the grass met the sand. A large Blue Mahoe tree grew on a grassy knoll, providing a canopy of leaves, the perfect covering for a wedding. It was a full moon, so the glow beautifully lit the area. Richard was busy putting together a crew to light torches leading down to the spot and setting up chairs for the guests. Word had traveled of the impending marriage, and people were arriving from Friendship Estate to watch their Mistress marry as they did from Bellevue Estate to watch their beloved Master marry. The mood was festive and joyous.

As Declan came in, he smiled at Brixton. "I can see you are delighted with tonight's events. Congratulations, Brix. I must admit, Liam and I were not sure what your reaction would be, but your mother and Nana assured us it would be precisely what we witnessed tonight."

Chapter 11 | The Dinner

"Yes, I do have a concern, though. I have always had Dexter's back. I will do that as much as I can, but our circumstances have changed. Who is going to protect him now? I have a genuine concern for his safety and well-being in England," Brixton said, the worry unmistakable in his tone.

"I admire the relationship you two have. You always seem to put each other first. The first thing your brother did as Chief was to reinstate your annual stipend from the clan coffers, but it goes to you now, not your father," Declan said.

Brixton looked over at Dexter, his head bent toward Liam as he listened intently to his instruction. "If he needs that money, I won't take it. I can manage without it," Brixton said.

Declan chuckled, "Dex said you would say that. He wants you to use it to build your house on Mount Sion."

Brixton nodded, overwhelmed. Only Dex knew how much Mount Sion meant to him. "About his protection?" Brixton asked.

"Don't worry, Brix. His brothers in arms will be with him at all times. Clansmen who have dedicated their lives to this cause and to our chief. They know who he is, we have prepared them, and they are all pledged to protect him with their lives. I will never leave his side. That I can promise you," Declan said, resting a reassuring arm on Brixton's shoulder.

Brixton nodded his thanks as Dexter joined them. "As for your wedding gift," Dexter started, but Brixton interrupted him.

"Declan told me; it is far too generous. The ring was enough. You, making this happen tonight, is enough," Brixton said.

Dexter put one arm around Brixton and the other around Declan, their heads together, they enjoyed the moment of just being. "Tonight, our lives change. I pray it brings us what we have been seeking, that it makes our lives meaningful, and that we will always remember that we live in the service of others," Dexter whispered.

"Spoken like a true chief," Declan answered.

Margaret found Liam sitting in a chair, looking out the window. She came to sit next to him. He took her hand. "Harry just left, hightailed it out of here on his horse."

Margaret nodded. "Most likely on his way to Black River to find out if he can do anything to undo the night's revelations."

"Probably. That is why I had Declan paper the town with the notice of Harry's impending arrest should he try to go back to England. For good measure, he hand-delivered the official declaration to his solicitors." Liam said, turning to smile at Margaret. "Everything you suffered through, everything you worked for, it is happening, Margaret. You did it, and you will change the world."

"We did it. Everyone who helped to raise my boys, who saw in them what I did, who saw our cause as just and right; we all did it," Margaret said, overcome.

"Come, come now; let's get young Brixton married. Please remember, they are getting married by the sea. We don't need to be washed out to the briny depths by yours and Nana's tears," Liam said, taking her arm and making her laugh.

Nana joined them, and together they walked toward the wedding location. A crowd had gathered, and they parted as the three came forward.

In Margaret's room, Anne covered her daughter's face with a veil. Margaret had found a simple shift dress, made of white organza. To it, they added Margaret's wedding veil, made of gossamer; it trailed behind the dress as if floating on air. Both Brixton and Sabine had decided not to wear shoes.

"You look beautiful. Your father would be happy today," Anne said, tears making her eyes shimmer.

"It's all happening so fast, Mother. But I know I am doing the right thing. I know Brixton is the man I love," Sabine said.

Chapter 11 | The Dinner

"I believe you," Anne laughed. "I knew for sure this morning. You were so adamant about not coming here to dinner, and then Dexter told me Brixton was in love with you, and I just knew you were in love with him. Whatever came between you before, don't ever let it in again, Sabine. Never!" Anne said earnestly, clasping Sabine's hands in hers and looking deep into her eyes.

Richard opened the door, "It's time," he said.

"Richard," Sabine's words stopped him as he turned to go. "Would you walk with me? With my mother?"

Richard looked at Anne, then smiled at Sabine. "I would be honored," he said, his voice catching with emotion.

A hush came over the crowd as they parted to let Sabine walk to her groom, Anne on one arm, Richard on the other. Low drum beats started in the distance, and the chanting in an ancient tongue set the mood. Brixton was sure an angel danced toward him; he had eyes for no one but Sabine. As Dexter placed her hand in his, he felt as if he were in a dream.

"Handfasting is a Celtic and African tradition. It binds two souls to one heart. When Brixton and I were five, we were playing on this very beach, and we found two shells. They looked exactly alike, two pieces of one whole. We took them to Nana, and she made them into necklaces, one for each of us. We wore those necklaces until they no longer fit over our heads. I gave them to Nana. All these years, she kept them. Tonight, she bound the leather as one, the two shells weighing each side down. Tonight, I use this to bind Brixton to Sabine and Sabine to Brixton. Repeat after me. I, Brixton, take Sabine to be my wife and thereto plight thee my troth," Dexter said. Brixton repeated the words, his eyes on Sabine.

Dexter turned to Sabine. "Sabine, repeat after me. I, Sabine, take Brixton to be my husband and thereto plight thee my troth," Sabine repeated her vows, smiling as Brixton smiled back at her.

"Brixton, give her the ring," Dexter prodded. Brixton pulled out the ring Dexter had given him and placed it on Sabine's finger. "I now pronounce you man and wife, in the eyes of God and in the tradition of our Celtic and African ancestors. Brixton, kiss your wife."

As cheers and hollers erupted from the crowd, Brixton took Sabine in his arms and kissed his wife. It seemed to take forever for them to get back to the Greathouse as they waded through the throng of well-wishers. Just as they arrived, three donkey-drawn carts were coming down the lane, toward the back of the house.

"What's all this?" Brixton asked. Sabine had no idea.

"I knew today would be a celebration; I just did not know what kind of celebration," Anne said. "We have been cooking at Friendship Estate since Dexter left this morning. Richard and I thought, well, maybe we could all celebrate as one," Anne was worried that she might have overstepped her bounds.

"Anne, you are a lifesaver! I had no idea how I was going to feed all these people. Thank you for thinking of this," Margaret gushed as she saw the bounty on the carts. Hand in hand, they rushed off to oversee the unpacking and set up of the celebration to come. Dexter grabbed Declan's arm, and off they went. Brixton and Sabine breaking into a run to catch up. Richard and Liam held Nana's hand and followed. The party went on late into the night. Brixton and Sabine were the last to return to the Greathouse, where they found Dexter, Declan, Liam, Margaret, Nana, Anne, and Richard reliving the day's events.

"Um, I think Sabine and I will be off for the evening," Brixton said, unsure of what one said in such a situation.

"Oh dear, where are you off to? I have no bridal suite ready for you! How could I have forgotten that?" Margaret said, looking at Anne in a panic.

Chapter 11 | The Dinner

Anne looked equally stricken. "They could spend the night at Friendship Estate in Sabine's room," Anne offered.

"If you don't mind, I would like to spend the first night with my wife in the place where we will one day make our home," Brixton said, looking at Sabine. She knew where he was referring to, and she nodded her head in agreement.

Anne and Margaret looked at each other, completely confused. Dexter answered the question, "Mount Sion, Mother. They will go to Mount Sion."

"Anne, the letter," Richard prodded.

"Oh, dear me, yes. Sabine, your father left a letter that I am to give to you on your wedding day," Anne said, pulling it out of her pocket.

"Papa left me a letter?" Sabine asked, going to her mother and taking it from her. She put a hand to her mouth. "That is his handwriting. Brixton, would you read it?" She asked.

"If I can." Brixton took the letter from her and opened it as she came into his arms, her face buried in his chest. "My darling Sabine, it is my fervent hope that I have walked you down the aisle today. If I did not, then I pray this letter will suffice. I did not think I could love anyone more than I loved your mother until I met you. When your mother put you in my hands, you looked at me and smiled. Then you fell asleep, right there in my arms. My love for you grew as you grew. You are the woman I dreamed you would be, and more than I had dared to hope, me being your very flawed father. My proudest day, next to the day you were born, will be the day you walk down the aisle to start your life with Brixton Dunbarton," Brixton stopped speaking. Sabine hugged him and started crying. Brixton could not continue. Dexter stood and took the letter from him.

"My proudest day, next to the day you were born, will be the day you walk down the aisle to start your life with Brixton

Dunbarton. I have watched him grow from a boy to a man, and he is a good man, my love. He will love you with his whole heart, and he will be a true and loyal husband to you. Know that I have loved and admired him, and I pray you find your way to each other. Have a happy life together, build it on the foundation of Mount Sion, and create the world you want to live in. I have faith that your love will change the world. Your loving Father," Dexter finished.

Brixton held Sabine. He kissed the top of her head. "I will, you know," he said as she turned to look at him. "I will love you with everything I am because I am nothing without you."

Dexter gave the letter back to Anne. "Mistress Anne, maybe you better hold onto this for safekeeping. Brix, your horse is outside. Everything is waiting for you at Mount Sion."

"Dex, we still have a lot to talk about," Brixton started.

"We do, brother, we do. But it can wait until tomorrow night. Enjoy your honeymoon," Dexter said.

Sabine hugged her mother, tears still falling. Brixton hugged Dexter. "You are the best of me, brother."

"As you are the best of me, brother," Dexter answered.

Everyone walked outside to see them off. Brixton lifted Sabine and put her on the horse, jumping up to sit behind her. Taking the reins, Brixton turned the horse as Sabine blew kisses to everyone. Brixton held her tight as they rode to the cave. Lyndon's words had moved him; he missed his mentor. He could only imagine how difficult that letter had been for Sabine, and his arms tightened around her.

Brixton took Sabine's hand after he tied the horse to the post, putting the buckets of food and water close to it. Together they walked to the grotto with the waterfall and hidden pool. Dexter had taken care of everything. Hurricane lanterns surrounded a wooden frame that would serve as their bed. Satin sheets covered

Chapter 11 | The Dinner

the mattress, and a table stood behind the bed, laden with food, water, and wine. Brixton felt the change in Sabine immediately. Her body tensed, and she pulled her hand from his. He pretended not to notice and moved to inspect the bed, giving her space. Finally, he looked at her. "We don't have to consummate our marriage tonight if you're tired. We can just go to sleep."

Sabine looked at him. "Have you done it much?" She asked.

Brixton understood what she was asking and thought carefully before he answered. "I understand the mechanics of the sex act, and I know what to do. But I have never made love to the woman I love. I expect it will be very different from anything I have experienced before tonight."

She came to him then, kissing him. "Show me," she said. More than anything, Brixton did not want to frighten her. He took her gently in his arms and kissed her softly until she begged him for more. He undressed her and lay her down on the bed so she could watch him undress. She opened her arms to him, and he sunk beside her, half-covering her with his body. He kissed and caressed her until she was shaking. Gently, he took her hand and guided it to him. He tried to control his passion as she wrapped her fingers around him.

"I don't know what to do," she whispered.

"Lie back, open your legs to me, and guide me to you. I will take it from there, but keep looking at me, concentrate on my face," he said.

Sabine did as he instructed and lay back as Brixton entered her gently. She focused on his face until a sharp pinch of pain surprised her. Her eyes grew wide, and her mouth opened.

Brixton kissed her. "The hard part is over. Now I will make you feel pleasure beyond your wildest imagination," he said as he started to move inside her. Sabine felt the tidal wave begin to build. Her hips moved with Brixton as her pleasure grew. She cried out as she crested the wave and held tight to Brixton. His release came soon after, and they fell back in a tangle of limbs.

"Dear God! Is it always like that?" Sabine asked.

"For us, my darling. It will be," Brixton said as he kissed her. She curled into his body, her head on his chest, and fell asleep. It took several minutes for Brixton to stop shaking and fall asleep.

In the early hours of the morning, Sabine awoke, not quite sure where she was. Then she saw Brixton asleep next to her and remembered her wedding day. Her eyes traveled down his body as she remembered her wedding night. Her hand moved to his manhood, and she was amazed at how it jumped when she touched it. As she moved her hand along the shaft, it grew hard in her hands.

"Good morning, wife! Is there something you need from me?" Brixton asked huskily.

Sabine looked at him and smiled shyly. Her hand never stopping its caress. She enjoyed the effect she was having on Brixton.

"Would you like to go riding this morning?" Brixton asked as he reached behind her and grabbed her around the waist. He picked her up and held her above him. He was hard and ready. Gently he brought her down on him, guiding her hips. "It's just like riding a horse," he said.

Sabine flung her head back as her desire grew, and she started moving. Brixton was inflamed by her abandon and how glorious she was as her newfound passion burgeoned. He held her as she collapsed on him, spent. He moved her to his side and kissed her. Would he ever get enough of her?

"Your father said it would be like this," Brixton said. Sabine looked at him, a question in her eyes. "I was young, just a boy. My father had awakened an anger in me I was afraid I would never be able to control. Your father found me on the beach here. He told

Chapter 11 | The Dinner

me that one day I would find a woman that I would fall in love with. She would be the reason for everything I would accomplish, and I would want to hold her, to kiss her, to sleep next to her every night. He said the desire I would feel for her would be the most beautiful experience of my life, and it is."

Sabine sat up, wanting to know more about Brixton and her father's relationship, but the soreness between her legs made her wince. Brixton noticed.

"Are you alright? Did I hurt you?" He sat up, trying to examine her.

"No, not at all. Please stop touching me like that. Your very touch ignites my blood," Sabine said, reassuring him. "I'm just a little sore," she explained.

"I know how to fix that," Brixton declared. He picked her up in his arms and carried her to the mineral pool, sliding down into it, still holding her in his arms. "Open your legs," he said, looking down to make sure she did as he instructed.

"How did you find this place?" she asked, looking around.

"Dex and I found it when we were boys. You have only seen a small section of the cave system. It goes on for miles. We have been using it to smuggle runaways from plantations across the island, hiding them at Friendship Estate until we move them to Treasure Beach," Brixton explained.

"Treasure Beach?" Sabine asked as she felt the curative waters start to work their magic.

"A place your father and I found on the Southwestern tip of the island," Brixton answered. "It is surrounded by almost impenetrable bramble, but we found a cave that leads to beautiful acreage alongside a black sand beach. Your mother has created a free town there."

She had suspected her mother's use of the land, but Brixton's role in finding the acreage was surprising. "How do you know the water in this pool is curative?" she quizzed as another thought crossed her mind.

Brixton turned her to face him, wrapping her legs around his waist. "That was by accident. I fell off my horse not far from here. Again, angry with my father, I rode out in a thunderstorm. The horse shied and threw me against the rocks. I was able to make it to this pool and fell in. The stones had shredded my skin, but the next morning, when Dex found me. I was floating in the pool, and all the cuts had healed. I used to bring your father here every week for a full year before he died."

"Every Friday?" she asked.

"Yes, how did you know that?" Brixton asked, surprised.

"Because every Friday night, he would join us for dinner. He was his old self," she said as tears formed in her eyes. "At first, it lasted for a few days, and then it started to get shorter and shorter. But every Friday night, at dinner, my papa was there, smiling and laughing with me. I lived for those dinners as his illness progressed. I had no idea they were because of you, Brix."

Brixton kissed her. "I loved your father," he said. "He was the kind of man I aspire to be."

"Brix, why would my father keep his relationship with you from me?" she asked, shaking her head in wonder.

Brixton looked at her before answering. "I suspect it's because he wanted us to find our way to each other without his influence," Brixton replied. "He knew us better than most, Sabine. Would his opinion of me have changed how you saw me?"

Sabine did not answer. They both knew it would not have. Brixton was right; her father understood them both and realized they needed to find each other in their own time.

Sabine kicked her legs, moving them closer to the edge of the pool, grabbing hold of the rim as she pushed Brixton's back against the wall.

Chapter 11 | The Dinner

Brixton laughed, "Sabine, we can take a break."

But Sabine just looked at him through hooded eyes. She wrapped her legs around his waist as she guided herself onto him. "We can stop anytime you want, Brix," she said, her voice hoarse with desire.

"Dear God, no. Please!" Brixton said as she kissed him.

CHAPTER 12

Lord Dunbarton

Brixton knew that dinner was promptly at seven each night at Bellevue estate. Reluctantly they dressed and prepared to leave.

"Brix, can we come back after dinner and spend the night here?" Sabine asked, looking around.

"We can spend as many nights here as you want, but we both have estates to run. At some point, we will have to figure out where we will live, at least until our house is built.

"Our house? Here on Mount Sion?" Sabine asked.

"Yes, your father and I drew up the plans for the home. I didn't know it would be *our* home, but now I am happy he talked me into doing it with him. It will be on that little hill you like to spy on me from," Brixton said, grabbing her around the waist.

"I do not, did not spy on you," Sabine said, embarrassed and defensive.

"Of course, you did. I would recognize you atop a horse from ten miles away and in a crowd," Brixton said softly.

Sabine smiled and kissed him then. Hand in hand, they walked out of the hidden cave and headed back to Bellevue Estate. They arrived to find everyone in the drawing-room, Richard and Declan amusing them with the story of the day's events. Declan was a gifted storyteller. Richard, caught up in the excitement, was just as animated.

"So, there we are, standing in front of the Vicar, explaining to him that the groom, not present, and the bride, also not present, would like to post the bans to get married," Richard said.

"The Vicar just kept looking at us, as if we had three heads, nodding and saying uhuh, uhuh," Declan said, warming to the story. "He then turns to me and says, "It is highly unusual for the bride and groom not to be present and not to make the petition for the marriage in person." So, I say, "Father, trust me, they want to get married." The Vicar turns to me and says, "young man, the last time I saw Sabine Holborn and Brixton Dunbarton in the same room, they were trying to kill each other, *with their eyes!*" Declan concluded as the room erupted in laughter.

"Please tell me you were able to post the bans," Brixton said as all heads turned to him and Sabine. Shouts of welcome and applause ushered them into the room.

"We were, we were," Richard assured them. "You will be 'officially' married in two weeks, in the drawing-room at Friendship Estate with a grand reception to follow."

"And shoes will be required this time," Margaret said as she hugged her son. Anne went to hug Sabine.

She took her daughter's hands in her face, "You look happy, my love," she whispered.

"I am happy, Mother. Very happy," Sabine smiled back, returning her mother's kiss.

"Dinner will be slightly delayed tonight, we had a late lunch, but if you're both hungry, I can fix something for you," Margaret offered.

"No, Mother. We're fine, thank you. Dex made sure we had plenty of food and wine," Brixton explained as he nodded to his brother, who lifted his glass of wine in acknowledgment. Brixton took the seat next to Dexter, pulling Sabine onto his lap.

"You both look well-rested," Dexter said. Brixton kissed Sabine on the cheek, and they both smiled at Dexter.

"I think the time has come for you to know how last night's events came to be," Liam said. "Not the lovely surprise of Brixton and Sabine's marriage, but of how we welcomed Lord Dexter Dunbarton as the 7th Duke of Ergill," Liam said.

"Let me make sure Harry is not in earshot," Declan said.

"Harry's back?" Brixton asked, his voice hard.

"Richard and I found him walking back from Black River this morning. It seems the solicitors had taken his horse as payment for a past debt. He was none too happy to see us but more worried about having to walk all the way. We brought him back, and he headed upstairs to his room with a bottle of rum. No one has seen him since," Declan explained as he left the room.

"Too bad, I wanted to kick him out of that room and give it to Dexter so Brixton and Sabine could have their own room, Margaret said dryly.

"No, mother, we will not add insult to injury. He is still our father. Brixton and Sabine can have our room; I will make a pallet for myself in the kitchen," Dexter said.

"You will do no such thing," Margaret erupted.

"You are more than welcome at Friendship Estate," Anne offered.

"No, no, no. Sabine and I will be staying at Mount Sion for the foreseeable future," Brixton said. "If you allow, Mistress Anne, we will use Sabine's room at Friendship Estate as the need arises. We both have estates to run, and we do not intend to shirk our responsibilities in any way."

Anne and Margaret looked at each other. "Then it's settled. Brixton's arrangement works well for all of us," Anne deferred.

— 173 —

"Harry is passed out drunk on the bedroom floor, hugging a bottle of rum," Declan said, as he came back into the room. "Nana went to turn his head, so he doesn't choke on his vomit. Liam, she says you are to start without her. She knows the story, she said."

Liam nodded as all eyes turned to him. Dexter and Sabine sat forward. "Mistress Anne, Richard, and Nana were here the night Dexter was born. As soon as Mags realized Brixton was coming, they sent for Lyndon Holborn. Richard, maybe you should take it from here," Liam offered.

Richard took the floor. "Margaret was pacing, holding Dexter in her arms. She explained what she wanted to do. Dexter would be named the 7th Duke of Ergill. I would sign the birth paper, along with Margaret. I also prepared the gratuitous manumission, the official document that freed Dexter from slavery, declaring him white by law. It also avowed him to be Harry's legitimate firstborn son and rightful heir. Anne and Lyndon signed that document as the witnesses. As Margaret's contractions grew stronger, she had me draw up a title and deed giving Brixton Mount Sion. As the second son, that would be all he would get from his father's estate, but he would retain his title of Lord. I was so busy writing, Lyndon and Nana delivered Brixton as Anne held Dexter, nursing him. Sadly, Lyndon and Anne had just lost a child in stillbirth, so Anne was able to nurse Dexter along with Margaret, for the first three months of his life."

As Richard paused, Dexter looked at Anne and smiled. She reached out to him; Dexter took her hand and kissed it.

"We have no idea how they persuaded Harry to sign all the documents, but he did," Richard continued. Only Sabine saw the look that passed between Anne and Margaret, as Margaret's hand went to the amulet around her neck. Sabine understood immediately.

Chapter 12 | Lord Dunbarton

"Margaret sent the documents to Black River where they were registered. We all held our breaths, but when she got them back, the papers were sent to Lyndon for safekeeping," Richard said.

"Wait a minute. Do I have a birth paper?" Brixton asked, intrigued by the story. "Don't I need a birth paper to marry?" he asked.

"You do have a birth paper, but it is a Scottish one. Liam got it for you. It does say you were born in Jamaica, but your birth was never registered in Jamaica," Declan explained. "I handed it to the Vicar myself."

Liam picked it up from there. "When I arrived in Jamaica and saw your mother, I nearly killed Harry. But when I walked into her room and saw you both, one at each breast. Smiling, she invited me to meet her sons. She explained to me what she was doing, and I told her I would support her in any way. I never married, and I never had a son so that Dexter would one day become Chief. We knew he would need all the support we could muster for him."

Dexter went to his uncle's side. "I never regretted it for a moment," Liam said, turning to look at Dexter. "Mags wrote me letters telling me of the fine man you were growing into, how much everyone loved you, and how you were growing into the man she hoped you would be. When I saw that for myself, I knew I had done the right thing by you," Liam explained, emotion in his voice.

"Lyndon found Enos Knowles," Margaret added.

"Mas Lyndon knew Enos Knowles before I recommended him to Mas Lyndon?" Dexter asked. "Neither one ever let on," Dexter said, looking bemused.

"Well, when Lyndon met Enos, he wasn't a King's Counsel, but Liam supported his advancement. We needed a King's Counsel, and Lyndon made sure to find one sympathetic to our cause," Margaret said. "Enos Knowles, along with Declan when he took over from Liam, have been preparing for Dexter's return to England. His birth paper is registered as the 7th Duke of Ergill, along with his free paper and a letter from Harry, naming Dexter as his true heir. There is no chance of a challenge to Dexter's claim. Enos made sure of that. He has also worked to build support for Dexter in the Privy Council and with the court."

"How?" Sabine asked.

Anne and Margaret looked at each other. "That is where Lyndon came in. He made sure Dexter's claim was accepted based on the English law of Primogeniture by funding the campaign to gain support in the House of Lords," Anne said. "Sabine, he wanted to make sure you inherited everything he had built for you. He and Enos petitioned the Privy Council to give you legal rights based on Absolute Primogeniture, using Dexter's case as precedent."

"But that has yet to be ratified by the Privy Council," Dexter said. "Mr. Knowles was on his way to present those arguments."

"Yes, he is," Liam said. "But it will not be alone. He will need the voice of an ally in the House of Lords. He will need someone to make those same arguments to bolster his petitions. Who better than the man who wrote the arguments?"

Dexter sat back in his chair; doubt plagued him. "The love in this room is the foundation I am built on. Now you want me to leave the people that made me?" he asked, dread in his eyes.

"Yu ave to go! Because the foundation *yu* will build will be the foundation for a new world. A new place fe all a we, where love, peace, and acceptance will be de good instead of de bad," Nana said from the door.

Dexter went to her, sunk to his knees, and buried his face in her skirts, as he had done when he was a little boy. "I know yu fraid, and I know yu scared. Yu is a black bwoy going into a white man's world to challenge everyting dem feel belong to dem," Nana said, pulling him to his feet and drying his tears. "But look around dis room, Dex," Nana said, turning him around to look at everyone. "Look at all dese people who love yu, of every color, who believe in yu. Look at what yu have already built here in dis room, just by being yu."

Dexter stood and turned to his brother. "I can't do this without you!"

"You won't!" Brixton promised, walking toward his brother, Sabine following on his heels.

"Dex, anyone who meets you cannot help but respect and admire you as we do," Sabine said, voicing her support.

"And pray tell, where in this new world do I fit in?" Harry asked from the shadows.

"Nowhere," Brixton said, stepping in front of Dexter, shielding him from their father.

"You protect my own son from me?" Harry asked, sneering at Brixton.

"I have, all my life," Brixton snarled as Harry advanced into the room.

"So, my son. This son," he said, pointing at Dexter, "is now the rightful Duke of Ergill, the legitimate Lord Dunbarton with a seat in the House of Lords, and I, the man who bore him, cannot even return to England. Is that the way of it?"

"What you did to Cotton? What you did to me? You can take no credit for what has happened here!" Margaret shrieked at him.

"Oh, but I can, Margaret!" he shouted. "Like it or not, I am their father, and should their enemies come to my door, asking how this came to be, I would relish telling my side of this story. Witchcraft, magic. You will burn at the stake, you vengeful witch!"

Brixton advanced on his father. "Let me kill him now, Dex. It will be my first act of fealty to you."

Dexter stepped in front of Brixton and put a hand to his chest to stop his advance. Turning to Harry, he asked, "What do you want?"

"Everything you have," Harry snarled at him.

Dexter turned to Harry, facing him. "To take what I have, you would have to earn it. You would have to suffer being kicked, beaten, degraded, berated, and ignored every day of your life by your own father. To take what I have earned, you would have to live with the knowledge that you were born out of pure evil and hatred, knowing my mother's only act of defiance was living long enough to give birth to me. Yet understanding my history, suffering through all you have thrown at me, I cannot hate you. I love you, because you are my father. To take what I have, you would have to love Harry. And you are incapable of that, so you will never be able to take anything away from me."

Harry stared at Dexter, his eyes wide in fright. "My Lord," he whined.

"That is correct; I am your Lord, and I will decide your fate. I have two options. I have the one you, no doubt, would choose. To have my brother bear the guilt of killing his own father. Or, I can banish you and give my mother and my Nana the peace they so richly deserve," Dexter mused.

"There is a penal colony in French Guiana. I can get him to Haiti and have him transported from there. He would not be a threat to anyone from that remote territory," Anne offered.

Dexter looked from his father to his brother and back to his father. "He will be banished. Mistress Anne, please make the arrangements. Until then, Declan, make sure he is locked in his room, feed adequately, and provided with as many bottles of rum as he can drink."

"My Lord," Declan said as he grabbed Harry and shoved him toward his room. Harry's crying and blubbering did not stop until they heard the door firmly close, shutting him in.

Dexter turned to look at his brother. "Brix, if we want a better world, we must always face hatred and bigotry with mercy." Turning to face the others in the room, he asked, "Where happens now?"

"There is a ship bound for London in a month. Cabins are secured for you and Declan. Enos thought that Brixton might want to join you, so we booked another cabin before we left Spanish Town. Enos awaits your arrival in London," Liam revealed the final detail of the elaborate plan.

"So, I have a month to say goodbye to everything and everyone I have ever known?" Dexter asked softly.

"Dex, you are ready. We will always be with you. Our love will forever lift you up," his mother assured him, taking him in her arms.

"Well, this has certainly been another lively and entertaining evening," Brixton said, lightening the mood. "Sabine and I will be retiring for the evening. It has been a very long day," Brixton yawned, a mischievous smile on his face.

"Dear God Brix, please be discreet. Remember you are not legally wed yet, and that ceremony will stay all the gossiping tongues your sudden love affair will surely provoke," Dexter whispered.

"No promises, Dex, no promises," he said as he picked a giggling Sabine up and carried her out of the room.

"I can't help him, Mother," he said, laughingly, knowing his mother had heard their exchange.

"You never could, my darling," Margaret smiled.

"Dat bwoy don't tek nothing serious," Nana muttered as she left the room.

Sabine turned in the saddle, so she was facing Brixton. She kissed and teased him as he pushed the horse to go faster.

"Take me to our hill," she whispered. "I want you to make love to me where we will build our home."

By the time they rode to the top, they were both in a frenzy. Brixton jumped from the horse, Sabine, in his arms. Walking backward, locked in a kiss, they tripped over a rock and fell to the ground. Brixton broke the kiss to lift Sabine's dress.

"What the hell are you wearing under here?" he asked, pulling her to her feet.

Sabine laughed. "It is a French petticoat; it ties in the front."

"How do you pee in this thing?" he asked, looking under her skirt.

"There is a flap in the back. You unhook the flap. Help me take the dress off and," Sabine said.

"To hell with that! Turn around," Brixton said. As she did, he felt for the hook. Sabine squirmed at his touch. "Ah, got it, bend over. Now spread your legs a bit."

"What? Why? Ohhh!" Sabine exclaimed as Brixton entered her from behind. Brixton grabbed her breasts, caressing her nipples, as Sabine dissolved in pleasure, Brixton not far behind. Falling to the ground, Brixton held her in his arms. "How many different ways are there to make love?" Sabine asked, trying to catch her breath.

Brixton laughed. "Hundreds, and we will explore every one of them together," he promised.

Later that evening, they were back in the cave, getting ready for bed. Sabine was thoughtful. "Have you ever been to England, Brix?" she asked.

"No, I can't say that I have. I've never had the desire to go. Everything I want and need is right here in Jamaica," Brixton said, grabbing her around the waist and pulling her onto the bed with him.

"I've never been to England, only to Haiti, to visit my mother's family there," Sabine said, settling next to him.

"What is Haiti like?" Brixton asked.

"The Haitian fight for freedom is brutal, and it is bloody. I don't want to see that happen here. To answer your question, Haiti is loud; it's contentious. White, black, and everyone in between, trying to work together to build a society. There are lessons to be learned, I guess. What to do and what not to do," Sabine answered.

"Well, we can't be gone longer than two months, three at the most. Tomorrow I meet with Dex to find out what he wants to be done with Bellevue Estate, it does belong to him now, but Mother, Nana, and Uncle Liam will be living there. I have to find a way to make more money out of it. And we need to decide what to do with Mount Sion," Brixton said.

"What about Friendship Estate," Sabine asked cautiously.

"What about it? Friendship Estate belongs to you; I have no say in anything there. I will be happy to give advice, if asked and if I can, but that is your purview, not mine," Brixton said. Then he realized what she was really asking and sat up, looking down at her. "Sabine, I married you because I don't want to live without you. The only thing I have to offer is Mount Sion and my name. You married way below your station, my love," Brixton said, leaning down to kiss her.

Sabine smiled at him. "What are your plans for Mount Sion?"

Brixton lay back, one hand behind his head, the other absently caressing her shoulder. "Your father said I should grow coffee on the mountainside. Keep livestock on the low-lying lands and keep the area from the hill to the beach clear, so hurricanes would never erode the property. I believe that is what we should do, but I don't have enough coffee beans to plant, not to mention the English are not coffee lovers, so coffee does not necessarily pay the bills."

Sabine sat up, got out of bed, and started pacing. Brixton turned to look at her but was instantly distracted by her nakedness. "Coffee is not a cash crop in England, but it is in America. My father brought a man from America to Friendship Estate once. Oh,

I wish I could remember his name, but he wanted to buy coffee and export it to America. Papa took him around the island for a week. I remember him saying they found the best coffee beans from a purveyor in Mandeville, who told Papa they got the seeds from the Cockpit Country. The man from America was quite taken with the flavor of the beans. I remember Papa saying that Mount Sion would be the perfect place to grow those beans because of the river that runs through the mountains. Brix! That must be the river that feeds this waterfall," she said, pointing to the cascading waters behind her.

Brix just sat there, looking at her. A silly smile on his face.

"Brix? Did you hear anything I said?" she laughed, jumping on the bed next to him.

"My love, you are quite distracting, walking up and down, stark naked with your perfect breasts, just begging to be kissed and touched," he said, reaching out and grabbing her breasts. "But, yes, I heard everything you said, and it makes perfect sense. Your father always told me that Jamaica's future lay with America and the other Caribbean islands, not Britain. It is much easier to transport coffee to America than it is to Britain. I know the name of the man you are referring to. His name is Craig Holt. Your father introduced us. We have been selling him our coffee, but not in the quantity he wants, so England is still my biggest buyer. I don't have the money or the workforce to plant on Mount Sion yet."

"But I do, Brix," Sabine said softly.

"No, Sabine," Brix said, sitting up. Sabine grabbed his hands, holding them in hers.

"Brix, I know what you will say, but I love Mount Sion as much as you do. I always have. If we are going to build our life here, please let me be your equal - in everything we do," Sabine begged.

Brixton looked at her. She was his wife. She would bear his children, and they would make a life together on Mount Sion.

Everything he did from now on would be for her and the family they would create. Brixton pulled her to him and kissed her, turning her so she lay beneath him.

"We will build Mount Sion together," he said. "Tomorrow, I will bring the plans your father and I drew up for our home. I want you to approve them so I can start building," he said, gently pushing her legs open with his knee.

Ignoring his overtures, she asked, "Brix? Did you say you were still Lord Dunbarton?"

"Hmmm," he said as his kisses moved to her neck.

"So that makes me Lady Dunbarton?" she asked.

"It does, yes," Brixton said as he moved to her shoulders.

"So, I will be in London as Lady Dunbarton, correct?" Sabine asked. Brixton smiled; he knew where she was going with this.

"You will, my love. You will be the Lady of Ergill, seeing as Dexter has no wife. You will be a peer of the realm, so please use it to put anyone you wish to, in their place," Brixton said.

She smiled at him, reaching between them to pull him into her.

"And Sabine? Feel free to buy as many of those French petticoats as you wish," Brix said as they began to move in unison.

THE NEXT MORNING, they rode to Friendship Estate. Anne and Richard were just finishing breakfast in the dining room.

"I can't stay, I'm afraid. I have to meet Dexter and Uncle Liam for breakfast. We have a lot of decisions to make," Brixton said, leaning down to kiss Anne on the cheek.

"I wanted to ask if you were happy with the way things turned out?" Anne asked, concerned.

"How could I not be? I got the girl; Dex got the hard work," Brixton said, grabbing a johnnycake.

Sabine slapped at his hand. "Be serious, Brix. That is her anxious voice."

"Things worked out exactly as they should," Brixton said. "I am a child of Jamaica, Mistress Anne. Dexter outgrew this island when we were twelve. He was always destined for bigger and better things than Jamaica could offer him."

Bending down to kiss his wife goodbye, he said. "I will see you later."

"Join us for dinner, won't you?" Anne asked him.

"You will have to check with my wife, Madame," Brix said as he disappeared down the hallway.

"Well?" Anne said.

"Well, what?" Sabine responded, pouring herself a cup of tea.

"Sabine!" Anne said.

"Mother, if I had known how delightful sex was, I would never have held it against you and Richard for indulging," Sabine said as she grabbed a johnnycake and stuffed it in her mouth.

"Dear God!" Richard said.

"That's my girl," said Anne, satisfied with Sabine's answer.

Brixton rode up to the back veranda of the Bellevue Greathouse as Declan came out with an unconscious Harry over his shoulder. Dexter and Liam were waiting by a donkey cart.

"Ah, Brixton. Good to see you, man. Mind if I take your horse? My arse cannot take the splintered wood on that blasted cart," Declan said as he dumped Harry into the back of the cart and tied him to the floor.

"Be my guest," Brixton said, following him, holding the horse's reins. "Where are you off to?"

"North Coast, dropping this piece of garbage off to catch a boat for Haiti," Declan answered, pointing at Harry.

"Thanks for taking out the trash. How long will you be gone?" Brixton asked.

Declan laughed, clapping Brixton on the back. "Don't worry! I'll be back long before you wed that little lass again!"

Chapter 12 | Lord Dunbarton

Brixton stood with Dexter and Liam as Declan led the way down the lane. "Good riddance," Brixton said, kicking the dirt behind the cart as it left.

"Come, you must be famished after the excitement of the last few nights," Dexter said, as Liam started to laugh.

"One of Nana's big breakfasts would be greatly appreciated, yes," Brixton said.

As they helped themselves to ackee and saltfish, boiled bananas, callaloo, and breadfruit, the three men sat at the table—Dexter at the head, Brixton to his right, and Liam on his left. Brixton wasted no time, stuffing the food into his mouth.

"All our lives, Brixton and I have discussed what we would do with this property. Now, we are in a position to make our dreams a reality," Dexter said, as Liam nodded. Brixton stopped eating and looked at his brother.

"Dex, this estate belongs to you, man. I have Mount Sion, which is all I ever need. It will be my honor to work and preserve this property for you and your children to come, but I don't begrudge you full ownership," Brixton said.

"I know, Brix. I know, but we always said we would build this place together, and now, I am leaving you," Dexter said.

"But you are leaving, to make it better," Brixton said.

"Brix, just hear me out. We talked about freeing every person on the estate. I still want to do that, but this place is barely making enough to feed us as it is. I want to tear down the slave quarters; I want to build new row houses so the people on this estate will have pride of ownership in knowing they are working for themselves to better the lives of generations to come. I want to build a school," Dexter said.

"Those are all things we said we would do, brother," Brixton said.

"But it takes money, Brix and money is the one thing we don't have," Dexter said.

"I may have an idea," Brixton said. "Last night Sabine and I spoke, and we are going to build Mount Sion. As I build our home, we will plant the mountainside with coffee beans. I will grow livestock on the low lands. We can sell all the coffee to Craig Holt in America, through his purveyors in Mandeville. If we do that, we can get twice what we get selling it to England. With what we grow on the two estates, we should be able to meet Craig's minimums for purchase."

Liam sat back and said nothing. Dexter did not realize he was a rich man. Without missing the money, he could fund both estates and the changes they wanted to make. But Liam decided to stay quiet and see how the brothers worked together to figure this out.

"We don't have the time it will take to put that all in place. I leave in a month. The Mandeville purveyors get the seeds we buy to plant on Bellevue Estate from the Cockpit Country. We don't even know if they can supply the number of coffee plants you need to seed Mount Sion," Dexter said, and both men fell silent. Liam watched them as they struggled to come up with a solution.

"If I may?" Liam said. Dexter and Brixton turned their attention to him. "How difficult would it be to buy the beans directly from the existing growers in the Cockpit Country?"

"I don't know, we have only bought coffee seeds from them, through purveyors. We know nothing about their coffee bean production, but it is a good question. What do you have in mind, Uncle Liam?" Brixton asked.

"Maybe it would be a good idea for you and Dexter to take a look at what they are doing in those mountains. If they are willing to sell the beans to you, you have a sorting house and a processing factory already in place here. You could buy all they have to sell, then resell them to your Craig Holt. That should give you the cash flow you need," Liam said.

"That's a great idea," Dexter said, "The problem is, we don't have the money to buy the beans."

"I do," Liam said softly. As both men started to protest, Liam held up his hand to stop them. "Lords, with your permission, I would like to spend the rest of my days here. I understand now why your mother loves it as she does. I don't want to be a burden to you; I can pay my way."

"No, Uncle Liam! You have more than paid your way already. All that you have sacrificed for us," Brixton said.

"I have sacrificed nothing that was not worthy of the sacrifice. You owe me nothing; you never will. Allow me to partner with you in this, and you will give my life meaning again. I do not want to sit here and wither. I want to die, knowing I have been in service of a greater good," Liam said.

Dexter and Brixton didn't know what to say. It would take them three days to ride to Cockpit Country and put together the plan Liam suggested - if they could. The Maroons controlled that area; it was their stronghold. No outsider was allowed on their mountain, so no one had any idea of how they grew coffee or conducted their business. They did know that Craig Holt's Mandeville purveyors would be at Bellevue Estate in three weeks to buy all they had harvested before the storm. It was processed and waiting for their inspection in the factory storerooms on the Estate. They didn't have time to waste.

"Do you think Sabine can live without you for three days?" Dexter asked.

"I am pretty sure she can. Me, not so much," Brixton said.

"What do you say? One more adventure for the Dunbarton brothers before we start our lives as responsible men?" Dexter asked, smiling at the prospect.

"Well, when you put it that way, how can I say no? I'll talk to Sabine tonight. We can leave in the morning," Brixton said.

That was the first of many decisions that day. Pronouncing everyone on the estate free was one thing, but all the free papers had to be drawn up, signed, and then sent to Black River to be notarized. Both Brixton and Dexter distrusted the legal entities in Black River, so they decided to have them all finalized in Spanish Town at Enos Knowles' law firm. Margaret and Liam set to work preparing the free papers. Dexter and Brixton decided that each person of age who chose to stay and work on the estate would be given a new home with furnishings, replacing the current wattle and daub homes they lived in. The new homes would come with a plot of land behind each house large enough to grow crops and any small livestock they wished to consume or sell at the market in Black River.

All in all, each adult would get a quarter acre of land on Bellevue Estate to call their own. Marriages would be sanctioned and legal. It would be a requirement for children to go to school at Friendship Estate, where Mas Lyndon has established a school for freeholders' years before. Each person would continue to receive food and clothing rations from the estate in addition to the money they would now be earning for their labor.

The hardest part of the day was figuring out a living wage for each position on the estate. Slaves did it all, but freeholders specialized. They were encouraged to have a trade to improve their earnings and security, increasing their feeling of self-worth. Dex said this would put them on the path to self-actualization, thus fulfilling their God-given potential.

"You know, like what you have been doing for me all our lives," Dex said, smiling at his brother.

But Brixton had had enough. They had been stuck indoors all day, and he was ready for the day to end. "Dex, Friendship Estate has been doing this for years, man. Let's not reinvent the wheel; we can ask Sabine what she does. I also need to find out from her what our contribution to the school will be now that we are sending our children there. Come back to Friendship with me for dinner, and we will figure it out there. I'm not good at thinking this much," Brixton said, getting up stretch.

"Many hands are willing to accomplish the task, Dexter," Margaret said, kissing Dexter on the forehead. "You don't have to do it all in one day. I know your impending departure is pushing you, but you have one chance to do this right. We are all here to help and support you. Go with Brix, have dinner at Friendship Estate, and we will start again tomorrow."

"Thank you, Mother," Brixton said, anxious to get outdoors and eager to return to Sabine.

"Married life suits you," Dexter said as they rode along the beach.

"I have to admit, I do enjoy it," Brixton smiled at his brother.

"What's it like?" Dexter asked softly.

"What's what, like?" Brixton looked curiously at his brother, not sure what answer Dexter was looking for.

"I am asking what it's like to love a woman the way you love Sabine?" Dexter asked, turning to look at him.

"Oh, I see," Brixton paused before he answered, searching his heart for the right words. "When she looks at me, with love and desire in her eyes, it is like a punch in the gut. It takes my breath away. When I hold her in my arms, I feel complete. When we talk about our future together, I have hope, and when I make love to her, I know I will never feel as loved and secure as I do when I am with her," Brixton said.

Dexter nodded his head and smiled at his brother. "I am happy for you, Brix," Dexter said.

"You will find a love like that, Dexter. You're too good a man not to," Brixton said.

"I hope so, brother. I hope so," Dexter said as he kicked his horse into a gallop.

Anne was happy to see Dexter, welcoming him in by taking him in her arms to hug him. "Welcome, my Lord," she whispered.

"Thank you, Princess," he said, kissing her on the hand.

Brixton kissed Sabine. She could tell he was exhausted. "I can see you have had a busy day, my love," she whispered.

Brixton smiled weakly as he pulled the chair out for her to take a seat. Dexter did the same for Anne. Richard waited until the ladies were seated before he sat, along with Brixton and Dexter.

Richard broke the silence. "A lot to do before you depart, Dex?" he asked.

"Yes, sir. Today we started all the freehold papers. We worked out what each person would get, but we are not sure how to pay them based on their skill set," Dexter said.

"I can help you with that," Sabine said. "I have a schedule of every job on Friendship Estate and the value of it. You are welcome to it if you wish. I review it annually, and based on how well the Estate does, I increase it incrementally."

"That is exactly what we need. Thank you, Sabine," Dexter said.

"With your permission, Mistress Anne, we would like to start sending our children to the school you have here on the Estate. We are more than willing to help with the expenses," Brixton said.

"I am so pleased to hear that. Let's see how it goes for the rest of the year. If we need more help, I will let you know what funds are required," Anne said. "How does that sound?"

Dexter and Brixton looked at each. "That's fair," Dexter agreed.

"Sabine, tomorrow, the dressmaker will be here to work on your wedding dress," Anne said. "She will also be putting together your trousseau for your trip to London. Brixton, she can make your wedding suit. I am sure both you and Dexter will need a new wardrobe for London."

"We can't tomorrow," Brixton interjected. "Dex and I have to travel to the Cockpit Country on business," he looked at Sabine, watching for her reaction to the news.

"What business? If I may ask?" Richard said.

"Liam wants to buy coffee beans from the growers in the Cockpit Country. He feels we will have enough to satisfy Craig Holt's demands for our coffee. We are going to see what they have to offer. We know nothing about their setup, so we will do some investigating," Brixton answered.

"How long will you be gone?" Sabine asked, noticing Brixton's worried gaze.

"I wanted to discuss it with you first. We will be gone for three days," Brixton said.

"Brix, it's fine. I understand how business works," Sabine said, smiling at him. Brixton visibly relaxed.

"I think I can help you with that," Richard said. "I was with Lyndon and Craig when they met with the purveyors in Mandeville, who buy coffee in that region. It's mostly small farmers that grow the beans. As you know, the Maroons control everything in the Cockpit Country. It is a very closed society. You are going to have to deal with their government if you want to do business with anyone up there," Richard finished.

"We understand. What Liam is suggesting is not going to be easy to accomplish," Brixton said.

"No, but if Liam is interested in going into the coffee business, I would be interested in partnering with him," Richard offered.

"I'll mention it to him, Doctor Richard. I think if the growers see the person buying their beans as vested in the area, they might come together and sell just to us," Dexter thought out loud.

"You boys must be exhausted," Anne said. "Why don't you spend the night here? Tomorrow Sabine and I will get you packed for your trip. You can leave tomorrow morning bright and early."

"That would be wonderful, Mistress Anne. I don't think I can keep my eyes open another minute," Brixton said, yawning loudly.

"Mistress Anne, about our wardrobe. We have a tailor in England already working on what we will need there, according to Declan. But we will need new clothes for the wedding and to travel in. Nana knows our sizes better than we do. Honestly, she would be more helpful to a seamstress and tailor that we would. Brixton wouldn't be able to stand still long enough to take proper measurements, anyway. I will make sure everyone is paid, including Sabine's trousseau. She is our responsibility now," Dexter offered, smiling in Sabine's direction.

"Consider it done," Anne said. "Sabine, show Dexter to the guest room, then take your husband to bed before he falls asleep in his soup bowl," Anne said, remaining seated as they each kissed her goodnight.

Dexter was asleep as soon as his head hit the pillow. Sabine helped Brixton to undress and helped him to bed.

"Come here, wife, I am not that tired," he grinned at her.

"Why don't I show you something my mother told me about today. It's how the French make love," Sabine teased as she leaned down to take him in her hands. Smiling at him, she covered him with her lips.

Brixton's entire body jerked in response. "Your mother told you about this? Today?" he asked, shocked but quickly succumbing to the sensation. As Brixton shuddered, Sabine sat back, a satisfied smile on her face.

Brixton took her in his arms, just as sleep started to overcome him. "When I get back from the Cockpit Country, remind me to teach *you* something, also inspired by the French," he promised as he kissed her goodnight. He was snoring before she settled in beside him.

CHAPTER 13

Cockpit Country

Dexter was already at breakfast when Brixton and Sabine came down the following morning. Brixton had begged Sabine to stay in bed with him a little longer, but she reminded him that his brother was waiting. With a groan, Brixton got out of bed and dressed. Richard was explaining to Dexter his observations of his time spent with Lyndon and Craig Holt.

"Craig Holt did say the Jamaican coffee bean is the best in the Americas," Richard concluded as Sabine and Brixton walked in. Brixton held the seat for Sabine as Anne entered behind them. Brixton stepped to Anne's side to pull her chair out.

"I'm sorry, mother, I should have come down earlier to help you get them ready to leave," Sabine said, shooting Brixton a stern look.

"No need, darling, no need. I know what it's like to be a new bride," Anne said, looking at Richard, who smiled back at her.

"Brix, eat. I want to be on the road before the sun gets too hot," Dexter said, finishing his coffee.

"Dex, I just sat down," Brixton complained.

Sabine cut the johnnycakes on his plate, buttered them, and stuffed them with ham. She handed two to him. "Here, take these.

You can eat them as you ride out," she offered as she ushered him out of the dining room behind Dexter.

Sabine held his horse as Brixton swung into the saddle. As he bent to kiss her goodbye, she whispered, "I will be right here, ready and waiting for you to whisk me off to Mount Sion upon your return."

Brixton smiled at her, kissing her wildly as she pulled away and hit the horse on its rump to move it on its way. "Our honeymoon is far from over, wifey," he yelled as he looked back at her.

"How can it be over before it has officially begun. Keep your voice down, idiot," Dexter cautioned as they rode through the gates of Friendship Estate and on to the main road.

They were halfway to Black River before seeing the bodies waiting for the black undertakers to collect them. Brixton looked away. Hunted down by Maroon bounty hunters, these runaways were hung on the gates to discourage other slaves of like mind from fleeing.

"This island is a powder keg, begging for a spark," Brixton said, recalling Sabine's cautionary tale about Haiti's deadly fight for freedom and independence.

"I agree, but it will not help either side of the abolition argument if the islands disintegrate into open rebellion. When your hand is in the lion's mouth, you need to withdraw it slowly," Dexter said, his eyes following a woman and two children crying at the feet of one of the bodies, clearly mourning the loss of a loved one. Dexter looked away; they would be flogged for that love if the master or overseer of the plantation saw them in their grief.

"What kind of world will I bring my child into, Dex?" Brixton asked.

Dexter turned to look at Brixton. "Please tell me Sabine is not pregnant already," he said, trying to do the math.

"No, nothing like that. Sabine assures me she will not get pregnant until we are both ready. Another lesson from her mother, I expect," Brixton answered, shifting in his saddle as he remembered last night's lesson. "I do worry about that, Dex. It is not just about us anymore; it is not just the two of us against the world. We are responsible for a lot of people now."

"Believe me. I am aware," Dexter said solemnly. They rode on in silence, trying not to keep track of the dead they passed, resulting from the floggings and hangings as plantation owners fought to crush any thought of rebellion against their rule.

They pushed all day, bedding down for the night at the foot of the mountains. If they left before dawn the next morning, they would arrive in the heart of the Cockpit Country as the sun peaked in the sky.

"Brix?" Dexter asked.

"Hmmm?" Brixton responded, ready to go to sleep.

"When these plantation owners find out what we have done at Bellevue Estate and who I am, there will be hell to pay. Two of the largest estates on the island will be freeholds, and a black man is now a Duke. After what we witnessed today…" Dex did not finish his thought.

"We are buying time at this point," Brixton said. "That is why we are not using those gossiping midwives in Black River to set up the freeholds. You will have accomplished what you need to in London long before word gets back to this small island. By then, the writing will be on the wall."

"If I can, I will leverage my position to buy as much land in Jamaica as we can," Dexter said, sitting up. "If a plantation owner wants to leave because he disagrees with the abolition of slavery, I want you to have the money to buy him out. Get rid of the old guard so we can appoint a new one."

Brixton looked at him. Dexter could see his new world laid out in front of him. He rolled over. "Then I suggest you find a rich woman in London who shares your vision and marry her. Buying an entire island is not cheap," Brix said yawning.

THEY BEGAN THE next day filled with hope and brimming with determination. By afternoon they were in despair. No one would speak to them.

"We are being followed," Brixton told Dexter as they watched a group of workers run out of the field they were planting and away from the approaching men. "Now what?" Brixton asked.

Dexter stopped his horse, indicating that Brixton should do the same. Within minutes they were surrounded by warriors, cutlasses aimed at their hearts. Dexter and Brixton raised their hands in supplication. One of the men pointed with his cutlass, indicating they were to follow him, with their hands raised. Brixton looked at Dexter, who nodded slightly. They pressed their knees to their horses, prodding them to walk forward.

They followed for miles, deeper and deeper into the dense foliage. Without warning, they came upon a clearing. Wattle and daub houses stood in formation, surrounding a larger building, two stories high, made of wood and cut stone.

A man was waiting for them as they made their way to the center building, still on horseback and surrounded by warriors. "Welcome to the town of Accompong, my Lord," the man said, addressing Brixton.

Brixton looked around, not daring to lower his hands. It was Dexter who greeted the man on their behalf. A beautiful woman of the darkest ebony Brixton and Dexter had ever seen stepped out of the building in front of them. All the men bowed as she stopped at the steps, looking down at the scene before her. Her skin glistened in the sun. She had the bearing of a queen.

"Welcome to Accompong. I am Queen Nandi," she announced in a melodic voice.

Chapter 13 | Cockpit Country

"Nandi?" Dexter asked. "Like the infamous Queen of the Zulu Kingdom in Africa?"

She looked surprised that he knew that. "I am her great-granddaughter."

"Then it is a privilege to meet you," Brixton said as both men jumped from their horses, stepped back, and bowed deeply.

Shocked at the brother's reaction to her, she lost her composure for a moment. Never had a white man bowed to her. "Forgive me," she smiled, and Dexter nearly forgot to breathe. "Join me, won't you?" she invited.

"We would be honored," Dexter said. She clicked her tongue, and servants appeared to take their horses and show them into the building. They had to climb steep flights of stairs to access the main structure that stood on stilts. Guard towers stood at the four corners of the network of rooms built high off the ground. The view from the wrap-around balcony gave Dexter the feeling of being in the canopy of the trees surrounding them. He looked around discreetly. The structure was designed to spot an invasion coming; as they walked further through the rooms, he realized it was fortified enough to repel an attack. Queen Nandi led them to a rooftop garden at the back of the edifice. Behind them, the imposing mountain stood guard.

"To what do we owe the pleasure of your visit?" she asked as they sat. She was poise and elegance itself as she leaned forward to pour them glasses of sugar water laced with lime. The water was cool and sweet.

"We were hoping to meet with some of the coffee farmers in the area to ask if they would be willing to sell their coffee beans to us," Brixton said. "An opportunity has presented itself. We grow coffee on our estate in St. Elizabeth, Bellevue Estate, but we cannot supply the demand we have encountered.

"The Bellevue Estate? Are you Lord Dunbarton?" Nandi asked, turning to Brixton.

"Well, I am *a* Lord Dunbarton, not *the* Lord Dunbarton," Brixton answered.

"Brix," Dexter cautioned.

"Brother, she is a queen," Brixton said, explaining his candor.

"Brother?" Nandi asked in surprise. She turned to Dexter. "A white man calls you, brother?"

"He is my brother," Dexter said defensively.

Nandi sat back and looked at Dexter carefully. He was the first to look away. "So, he is, so he is. I apologize if I offended you, Lord Dunbarton," she said, her eyes never leaving Dexter.

Brixton looked at Dexter and then back at Queen Nandi before speaking. "I was hoping to speak to some of the growers, get an idea of how they grow such wonderful beans, maybe get a few pointers. I have some land that I would like to cultivate," Brixton stopped speaking when he realized neither Dexter nor Queen Nandi was listening to him, but he was mistaken.

"I will be happy to arrange that in the morning. Tonight, I would ask that you join me for dinner. I think we should get to know each other a little better before discussing business," Nandi said, turning her eyes from Dexter to Brixton and smiling.

Dexter nodded slightly, and Brixton accepted her invitation. With another click of her tongue, servants arrived to show them to their rooms and draw a bath for them. They joined Nandi for dinner later that night. With her was a man she introduced as an expert in growing coffee. "This is Bene. He runs the coffee production in the area for us. He will be happy to share his knowledge with you, Lord Brixton."

Brixton shook the man's hand as they sat across from each other to eat. Dexter sat next to Queen Nandi.

"We may have gotten off on the wrong foot today. I am sorry for that. Maybe when Bene and Lord Brixton are out tomorrow, we may spend some time getting to know one another," Nandi said to Dexter.

Dexter nodded but said nothing. Dinner with Queen Nandi was an event in and of itself. As they ate, Queen Nandi explained some of the Maroon traditions they were experiencing. Dexter was fascinated with the food. The meat was delicious and spiced to perfection.

"We call it jerk seasoning. We rub the wild hogs with a hot spice mixture, and then we slow cook the meat over pimento wood. It gives it a deep flavor," Queen Nandi explained. Dexter thought it was the most delicious thing he had ever eaten. As dinner was cleared away, drummers set up in the open courtyard in front of the building. The rhythmic drum beats were hypnotic. Dexter watched as the women began to dance, dipping and swaying to the beat of the drums. When Queen Nandi started to dance, Dexter was transfixed. She moved with a liquid motion that was almost spellbinding. All too soon, it was over, and servants came to collect them, showing them to their rooms. Finding sleep difficult, Dexter awoke in the middle of the night. He opened the door to his room, hoping to get a breath of fresh air. He stopped as he noticed the burly Maroon at his door, armed with a fierce-looking cutlass. Dexter nodded to the man, who nodded back. Dexter closed the door, returning to his bed, worry furrowing his brow.

When Dexter was ushered in to see Queen Nandi the next morning, she was drinking bush tea in her rooftop garden, attended by a servant. With a click of her tongue, bush tea accompanied with johnnycakes and guava jam were put in front of him.

"I know who you are, Lord Dunbarton, 7th Duke of Ergill. I knew from the minute I heard you were on my mountain. Your brother. He is the one my people refer to as the White Spirit?" At Dexter's affirmative nod, she continued. "And now you are here on my mountain. Why?"

Dexter looked around him before answering. "Are you the one responsible for the growers not speaking with us? Is it fair to say you control the sale of all the coffee beans in the area?"

Nandi smiled; her teeth were brilliantly white against her dark skin. Dexter was sure he had never seen a more beautiful woman in his life. "Neither one of us will get answers if we are both only asking questions." Dexter said nothing. So, she continued. "The Maroon government controls production. We buy and sell as a collective."

"And you set the price?" Dexter asked.

"I do," she answered, smiling as she realized Dexter understood there was no 'we.' "As is my right as queen."

"And your people?" Dexter asked.

"Ahh, you want to know if I am a fair queen or if I keep the wealth for myself?" Nandi asked, smiling.

Again, Dexter said nothing.

"Everyone living on this mountain lives on Maroon land. I am their Queen. My job is to serve the people I rule. Their children go to a school that I have built. They learn about their African and European history, a curriculum I have created. I may be a descendent of African royalty, but I am a born Jamaican. If the stories about you are true, Lord Dunbarton, it appears we have more in common than not. Like you, I am a nationalist, and my nationality is Jamaican."

"A born Jamaican who captures her own people and turns them over to their masters," Dexter countered.

Queen Nandi sat back, looking at him. Her head turned to the side as she regarded him. "My ancestors fought the English, valiantly. Their freedom was hard-won, and at a price I am no longer willing to pay."

"My brother and I help runaways, especially ones sorely used by their masters. I have encountered your slave trackers. They give no quarter," Dexter said, not ready to concede.

"The masters fear rebellion. Their apprehension is palpable. I don't want them on my mountain. I don't want my people enslaved again. I do what I need to do to protect my people and our sanctity," Queen Nandi answered.

"At the expense of other Jamaicans," Dexter hissed. "We cannot win the fight against slavery if we are not united in its defeat," Dexter said, looking at her.

"Are you telling me this as a black man or as an English Duke of untold privilege?" Queen Nandi asked.

"You seem to understand privilege," Dexter said, looking around him.

"I understand what it is to be a Queen. I understand the heavy burden of ruling men. I understand the fear of having to make the best decisions to protect my people. I understand our freedom comes at the expense of others, for now," Queen Nandi said. "I know who you are. I know who your brother is. I know what you believe and what you are willing to fight for. If you are the one to bring freedom to all, then I will support you in any way I can."

Dexter crossed his legs in front of him and sat back, looking at her. She was incredible, as intelligent as she was beautiful. "Bellevue Estate is willing to buy everything you can produce. We will take care of the processing, sale, and shipment of the coffee beans to America. We will underwrite all the risks, and you won't have strangers parading up and down your mountain," Dexter offered, his eyes piercing.

Nandi cast her eyes down. "I think you and I will be able to come to a suitable arrangement," she clicked her tongue, and the servants melted away. Lust in a man's eyes was something she was very familiar with.

Dexter stood up and walked to her. "Then I do have one more question. May a lowly Duke kiss a Queen?"

Queen Nandi stood up, taking his hand and leading him to the bed under an eve overlooking the garden. With a shrug of her shoulders, her dress fell to the floor. She was naked underneath the ornate dress. "He may," she said, pulling him to her.

When Brixton and Bene arrived that afternoon, they found Dexter and Queen Nandi waiting for them in the rooftop garden. Brixton had spent a productive day with Bene and realized that the mountainside on Mount Sion would provide excellent aeration for his coffee beans. The water from the river running through Mount Sion was as cold and crisp as the water Bene had him taste as they walked through the coffee fields in the Cockpit Country.

"The water is pure and sweet because the limestone filters it as it flows through. It should be the same for you on your mountain. The limestone in your caves filter your water, too," Bene said knowingly. At Brixton's surprised face, Bene smiled. "Yu tink yu is the first person to find them caves? The Maroons have been traveling through them for generations," Bene explained.

Brixton realized that what Bene had forgotten about the cultivation of coffee beans, Brixton would never live long enough to learn. "Bene, I cannot thank you enough for today. What I have learned from you is invaluable," Brixton gushed.

"It's a pleasure, me Lawd," he said. "When yu ready fe plant pon your mountain, send fe me. I will mek sure yu get de best seeds I can find fe yu."

"Thank you, Bene, I would appreciate that," Brixton said, startled by the offer.

"I have to tek care of yu, Mas Brix," Bene said, stepping away. "Yu Nana is me blood, she would skin me alive if I don't tek care of yu," Bene said before turning to leave. Dexter and Brixton looked at each other in shock. But it did explain why they were granted an audience with the mysterious Queen Nandi.

"Dex," Brixton said as he sat down, taking the glass, Queen Nandi offered him. "I can only hope your day was as productive as mine was," he said, enjoying a long drink of the sugar water.

"It certainly was," Queen Nandi answered with a smile. "Both productive and pleasurable. Lord Dunbarton has made an offer I cannot refuse. In fact, I have accepted it wholeheartedly, and several times today," she laughed as Dexter smiled at her.

Brixton looked at Dexter. *What the hell is she talking about?* he asked with his eyes. Dexter ignored him. They spoke of their plans through dinner, and it was well into the night before they said their goodbyes.

"My Lords, you have a long ride ahead of you in the morning. We shan't detain you any longer. Dexter, it has been a distinct pleasure to make your acquaintance. I hope to do so again," Nandi said as Dexter kissed her hand goodnight. Turning to Brixton, "I don't believe I will be here to say goodbye to you in the morning, but you will find your horses and provisions ready for your trip when you wake. Safe travels," she said as Brixton took her hand and kissed it.

When Brixton and Dexter returned to their rooms, they met on the veranda and shared the events of the day. "Well, as we suspected, she runs everything! She controls all the growers, and she controls the sale price for all the beans," Dexter said.

"And Bene knows everything there is to know about growing and handling beans. Were you able to make a deal with her?" Brixton asked.

"Oh yes, we came to an arrangement. It would seem our causes align. Our mountain Queen has created a free town up here. The Maroons live on this mountain building a life for themselves from her sale of coffee beans," Dexter explained.

Brixton nodded, impressed. "A job well done, brother. But what did she mean she accepted your offer several times?" Brixton asked, perplexed. Dexter looked at Brixton, and Brixton immediately understood what had transpired between Dexter and Queen Nandi.

Dexter leaned against the railing, his arms crossed in front of him. He was in a contemplative mood. "You have to admire a woman like that. She has used her intelligence and her beauty to leverage every man she has ever met. She is a strong, independent woman with a phenomenal sense of self. She uses her strength to bend anyone to her will, and she gets what she wants. But unlike most men, secure in their superiority, she uses her advantage to better the lives of those she serves. She is a queen in every sense of the word, born to rule, duty-bound to be selfless. She is fascinating. I have never met anyone quite like her."

"Yes, you have! You've never made love to her, but you do love her,' Brixton said.

Dexter smiled as he looked at Brixton. "And who would that be, brother?"

"Nana," Brixton answered simply.

The brothers slept fitfully that night, Dexter anxious to put the hopes and dreams of his youth into motion before his departure. Brixton was eager to get back to Sabine. They left at dawn the next morning. Escorted through the Cockpit Country by a cadre of Queen Nandi's warriors and taking hidden trails and paths, they cut their homeward journey down significantly.

They rode hard, stopping to rest for short periods only. They made it back to Friendship Estate in the wee hours of the following morning. Everyone was asleep as they crept into the Greathouse. Dexter bid his brother good night and went into the guest room as Brixton softly opened the door to Sabine's room. She was asleep, her back to him. Silently he undressed and climbed into bed beside her.

Sabine awoke slowly, savoring the delicious sensation traveling through her body. Brixton's hand was between her legs, and she moved to accommodate the other hand as it caressed her breasts, her back still to him. She opened her legs as she rolled onto her stomach to accommodate the urgency of his passion as she savored the building of her own. She grabbed his hand as their completion became one.

Brixton and Sabine were late for breakfast the next morning. As they entered the dining room, Dexter was sitting with Anne and Richard and a surprise guest, Liam. They were all laughing at a joke Brixton and Sabine had missed.

"Ah, there you are," Anne said as Dexter, Liam, and Richard rose, waiting for Sabine to sit. Brixton held her chair as she sat, the men following her lead.

"I was just saying, I didn't think we would see you until at least lunchtime. Sabine, you will be happy to know, Brixton did nothing but pine away for you the entire time we were gone. Hence the reason I had to apologize to Mistress Anne for our unannounced arrival in the dead of night," Dexter said, flicking his napkin at Brixton.

"From what Brixton tells me, you had a successful trip," Sabine said, looking pointedly at Dexter, whose mouth flew open as he realized what Brixton had told Sabine.

"It was interesting," Brixton said under his breath, looking at his brother sheepishly. "I'll give it that."

"Tell us," Liam said. "We are anxious to hear your thoughts."

Brixton looked at Dexter, who turned to look at Richard and Liam seated next to each other. "The good news is that the small producers are willing to sell to us."

"I'm glad to hear that," Richard said. "Liam and I have been discussing the idea you have for the sale of coffee to Craig Holt. An exclusive contract would seem to benefit what you are working towards." Brixton and Dexter nodded in agreement.

"Richard and I have formed a partnership," Liam began as the brothers looked at each other in surprise. "Between the two of us, we have the capital we need to broker an exclusive deal with Craig

Holt and buy all the coffee beans the Cockpit Country can produce. We will utilize the sorting house and processing factory at Bellevue Estate and split the profits with the Estate if the arrangement suits you?"

Again, Dexter and Brixton looked at each other. It took a moment for the news to sink in, then Brixton dissolved in laughter. "Well, if that is the case, we need to fill you in on what is happening on that mountain," Brixton said, trying to control his laughter. "Dexter is in a better position than I to tell you about Queen Nandi and her co-op of coffee bean growers. You will need to know exactly whose kingdom you are walking into," Brixton said.

Dexter shot Brixton a humorless look before answering his uncle. "Yes, Uncle Liam, that arrangement and division of profits will suit us perfectly."

"Wonderful!" Liam said excitedly. "Between your sale of the existing coffee beans at Bellevue Estate and splitting the profits processing the Cockpit Country coffee, you should have the money you need to enact the changes you want to make at Bellevue Estate. It seems you can leave Jamaica, Dexter, knowing that you have solved that problem."

"Yes, Uncle Liam," Dexter said, smiling broadly. "It seems I can, thanks to you and Dr. Richard."

"Sabine, you have a wedding dress fitting, go and get ready. I will leave you men to your plans," Anne proclaimed as she stood. The men rose as the ladies took their leave, then sat back down to finish their discussions.

As she supervised the dressmaker fitting Sabine's dress from her position facing the door, Anne saw the door open and Brixton sneak in, hiding behind Sabine's privacy screen. She lowered her head to hide her smile. Dexter had told her of Brixton's wish to spend the week before their wedding at Mount Sion. Brixton wanted time with Sabine before they traveled to London, and before they started their life together, full of the new responsibilities they would have. Change was not easy for Brixton, Dexter had explained. He needed this time with Sabine for them to find their level.

"Water always finds its level, Mistress Anne," Dexter said. "And Brixton and Sabine have been through some hurricanes in the last few weeks; they need time for the two of them to get to know each other and figure out how they are going to move forward together."

Anne had looked at Richard. Yes, she did understand the need for time to find a level. "Madam, I think that is enough for today," Anne declared. "I don't believe you will need any more fittings with Sabine; you should be able to finish the dress without her, non?" Anne asked the dressmaker in French.

"Bien sûr que oui. This dress will be ready for her on the wedding day," the dressmaker said, gathering her things.

"Bon. Sabine, we are finished with the fittings. Get dressed, and I will meet you downstairs," Anne said. She left the room, the dressmaker following behind.

Sabine walked to her privacy screen, in her underwear. Brixton grabbed her around the waist, surprising her with his kiss.

"Dear God, Brixton. You are going to be the death of me," she said when they came up for air.

"I see you are wearing my favorite petticoat; please wear it on the day we marry again," Brixton said.

Sabine laughed, "Is that your plan? To keep me naked and in our bed for the rest of our lives?"

"It's not a bad way to live our lives. I don't think I will ever tire of making love to you," Brixton said thoughtfully.

"Nor I, you, my love," Sabine said, hugging him to her.

Brixton savored the feel of her in his arms. "Did you ever think you would say that?" he asked, waiting for her reaction.

Tears sprang to Sabine's eyes. So much had happened in such a short space of time. Her life had changed in ways she could not have imagined. "If I think about what I have lost, what I have gained, my head spins. I need time," Sabine said.

"To reconcile it all?" Brixton asked. Sabine nodded, not looking at him. "Then time we will have. You and I are disappearing to Mount Sion for the next week. It is all arranged. We are going to take the time we need to get to know each other and to plan the life we are going to build together."

Sabine didn't argue; it was what she had hoped for. She reached up to kiss Brixton. "Thank you."

"Pack lightly; nothing at all will be fine," Brixton said, kissing the tip of her nose. "I will meet you downstairs," he said, leaving the room.

Sabine threw a few items of clothes and toiletries into a small valise and skipped down the stairs. Brixton was in the dining room, speaking to Dexter. Richard, Liam, and Anne waited patiently.

"I will make sure a basket of food and water is left for you each day. If you need anything else, just leave a note on the hitching post. I promise you will not be disturbed, brother," Dexter promised.

Brixton put his forehead to Dexter's. "You are the best of me, brother."

"As you are the best of me, brother," Dexter said, holding Brixton's head to his.

"Please come back the night before your wedding," Anne begged as she kissed her daughter.

"We will, Mother, I promise," Sabine said, smiling.

Brixton and Sabine rode to the cave. As they approached the grotto with the waterfall and pool, he lifted her into his arms. "I pray this is the first of many thresholds I will carry you over," he said as he carried her to their bed.

"Do you want to make love to me now, Brixton?" she asked.

"I do," he said, desire burning in his eyes. "But first, I want to tell you about my day with Bene the Maroon. I learned so much from him, but most importantly, I learned how perfect Mount Sion will be for growing coffee beans," Brixton said, pacing the floor as Sabine sat on the bed listening to him.

CHAPTER 14

The Wedding

The young man ran into the dining room and whispered in Anne's ear. With a smile, she excused herself, closing the dining-room door behind her as they left the room. She greeted Sabine and Brixton at the back door.

"The Vicar is here, quite anxious to speak to you two. It seems he wants to ensure that you are willingly betrothed," Anne said quickly.

"But we are not betrothed," Sabine whispered, giggling. Based on the last week, she most definitely was not betrothed but a very happily married woman.

Anne looked at her daughter, clearly not amused. "Sabine, as far as anyone who does not reside on either the Friendship or Bellevue Estates are concerned, you are most definitely betrothed, at least until tomorrow afternoon."

Both Sabine and Brixton looked suitably chastised.

"Brixton, take this coat and join us for dinner. Sabine, I have said that you are napping. Go upstairs, change, and join us for dinner as quickly as you can. I will not allow any gossip surrounding this marriage. Do you both understand me?" Anne said.

"That is her anxious voice, right?" Brixton asked, handing Sabine her valise.

"Mixed with her 'don't cross me, or there will be consequences,' voice," Sabine said, reaching up to kiss Brixton quickly. Brixton put the coat on and followed Anne into the dining room.

"Ahh, the happy groom is here," Anne said sunnily as she walked into the room, followed by Brixton. The Vicar was seated at the foot of the table. To his right was Margaret, who sat next to Liam and Declan. Anne sat at the head of the table with Richard to her right. To her left sat Dexter. Brixton sat next to Dexter, nodding at the men and greeting his mother by name.

The Vicar was about to say something when Sabine rushed into the room, breathless. "I am sorry to be late, Mother. I was so tired from all the preparations; I seem to have lost track of time," she said as she came to stand behind Brixton, awkwardly kissing him on the head and then patting it.

Brixton reached behind his chair and pushed her skirt up, putting his hand on her leg. She jumped at his touch, her eyes wide with surprise. All eyes turned to her as she again patted Brixton on the head, trying to look anywhere but at the Vicar as Brixton slowly caressed her leg.

"Dear God," Dexter exclaimed in exasperation, witnessing Brixton's playful prank.

"Dear God, what?" The Vicar asked, looking at Dexter.

"Dear God," Dexter began looking at Brixton, who just smiled at him. Brixton was enjoying himself immensely. "Dear God, we pray for the everlasting happiness and prosperity of the joyous couple," Dexter said uncomfortably.

"What a wonderful idea," said the Vicar. "It looks like they need all the help they can get," the Vicar muttered dryly, misunderstanding the awkward exchange. "Shall we pray?" He turned to take Margaret's hand as Brixton stood to help Sabine sit, his hand brushing against her breast. Dexter rolled his eyes, pulling his brother's coat, forcing him into his chair.

Chapter 14 | The Wedding

The dinner was spent convincing the Vicar that Sabine did indeed want to marry Brixton.

"I pray your love is real. I do not want to be party to a young woman forced to marry against her will. I do not believe in such a thing," the Vicar said, looking at them both.

"Where was he when I was getting married?" Margaret asked Liam under her breath. He patted her hand gently in response.

"No, Vicar," Sabine said, realizing he was serious. "I very much want to marry Brixton.

Dexter made a point of rolling his eyes at Declan, who caught on and rolled his back at Dexter. Brixton looked at both of them, frowning. The Vicar noticed and sat up in his chair.

"I can guarantee to you, Vicar," Brixton said, kicking Dexter under the table. "I am very much in love with Sabine as she is with me."

"Yes, Vicar. I was there when Brixton realized how in love he was with the young lass. As he told me, and if I remember his words exactly, 'it cut like a knife,' he said," Declan interjected. Brixton and Sabine looked shocked as Dexter stifled a laugh with a cough.

"Well, maybe you should think about it a little more, perhaps some counseling with me before you commit?" The Vicar asked

"No!" Everyone at the table shouted simultaneously, startling the Vicar, who dropped his silverware. It clanged loudly on his plate.

"I can assure you, Vicar," Margaret said, placing a hand on his. "Having been in an unhappy marriage myself, I would never subject my beloved son to such an arrangement."

The Vicar looked at Margaret. He had heard the rumors that her husband could never return to England. Why, only this evening, Dr. Chapman had whispered to him that the vile man had fled the island to parts unknown, for fear of being turned over to the authorities. He had always despised Harrington Dunbarton.

No loss there, he said to himself as he patted Margaret's hand in return.

Everyone turned to Anne as she explained the sleeping arrangements. The Vicar would sleep in Lyndon's room, which was now a guest room.

"Declan, Dexter, and Brixton," she said, looking pointedly at Brixton. "Will be in the guest room across the hall from Sabine's room. Margaret, you will be in the guest room next to them and Liam in the last room at the top of the stairway."

As everyone drifted off to bed, Sabine came to kiss Brixton goodnight, under the ever-watchful eye of the Vicar. "I will be up later to take you to France, my love," Brixton whispered as she kissed his cheek. Her cheeks were bright pink as she bid the Vicar goodnight.

Declan and Dexter filled Brixton in on the events of the past week. Declan had happily put a very drunk Harry on the supply boat to Haiti. He was no longer anyone's problem but his own. Dexter told Brixton that all the free papers were completed, and they would gather everyone before they left the island to let them know of the changes on the Estate. Liam would supervise the building of the new homes for those who wished to stay and oversee the construction of Brixton's house on Mount Sion. Craig Holt's Mandeville coffee bean purveyors would arrive within the next three days. Liam and Richard had prepared a contract and were ready to offer them all the coffee beans they wanted in exchange for an exclusive agreement. On Dexter's urging, Richard and Liam traveled to the Cockpit Country, paying a visit to Queen Nandi, introducing themselves as the men who would be the face of their business dealings until Brixton returned from England.

Dexter had willingly accompanied them to make the introductions. Liam understood the burdens that awaited Dexter in England. He recognized what drove Dexter to seek out the comfort of Queen

Chapter 14 | The Wedding

Nandi's arms. So, he said nothing, not begrudging the young man his solace. They had arrived back at Friendship Estate just last evening. All told, it had been a productive week for everyone.

The three men climbed the stairs to their room, still in conversation. Declan opened the door to their assigned room and went inside. Dexter was following until he noticed Brixton moving toward Sabine's door.

"Where the hell are you going?" Dexter asked.

"To spend the night with my wife. You don't think Mistress Anne was serious about the bedding arrangements, did you?" Brixton asked.

"She most certainly was!" Dexter whispered furiously. "The Vicar is just down the hall. Are you crazy?"

Before he could answer, the door handle to Sabine's room was yanked out of his hand, and the door opened. Nana stood at the door, tapping her foot impatiently.

"Brixton Dunbarton, wherever yu loss yu damned mind, I suggest yu tek de time to find it before yu tek another step to dis door," Nana said.

Brixton looked behind Nana to see Sabine standing there, with her hands open as if saying, *I have no idea what to do.* Brixton looked back and forth between Nana and Sabine as the door at the end of the hall opened, and the Vicar advanced. Brixton jumped back to stand next to Dexter in front of the entrance to their room.

"Brixton, Dexter," the Vicar said, looking at them and then turning to look at the open door to Sabine's room. Sabine lunged over the bed and out of sight.

"Good evening, Vicar," Nana smiled sweetly.

"Nana," the Vicar said.

"Just going over a few details before tomorrow wid de bwoys. Yu have a good night, sah. Big day tomorrow," Nana said, as sweet as sugar. They waited for the Vicar to go downstairs. Then hurricane Nana started to blow.

"But Nana," Brixton whined, realizing he would not be spending the night with his wife.

"But Nana, what? Get yurself inna dat room, before I cut it off," she warned Brixton, pointing to the door behind him.

She turned toward Sabine, out of hiding and peeking around the bedpost now that the Vicar was gone. "As for yu, likkle she-devil. I gwen sleep right next to yu with one eye open, and before your eye close tonight, we gwen have a likkle talk," Nana slammed the door in Brixton's face. The last thing he saw was the terrified look on Sabine's face.

"A wha de backside?" Brixton exclaimed in patois as he turned toward Dexter. Declan came out from behind the door where he had been hiding.

"How can one little old woman be so frightening," Declan asked, quite seriously.

"You have no idea," Dexter said as he pushed Brixton into the room and closed the door behind them.

Brixton awoke in a foul mood. It wasn't until Dexter reminded him that after today, no one could stop him from sleeping in Sabine's bed that he brightened a bit. He even managed to smile at Nana as he walked her to her seat in the corner where she could watch the ceremony. As Sabine walked toward him, he again thought she was floating. If possible, she looked even more beautiful than she did the first time he married her. Lost in each other, they stumbled over the Vicar's vows but managed to get them out. As Brixton kissed his wife, the Vicar realized it was not the first kiss they had shared and was oddly comforted by the realization.

Dexter was standing with Brixton when they were approached by three of the larger plantation owners invited to the wedding. Lame James, their old teacher, had been a proponent of old English

Chapter 14 | The Wedding

words and forced the boys to learn them as punishment. They had discovered some favorites they still used to characterize people they found dreadful and vile. Brixton and Dexter had nicknamed these three, Skelm, Nitheful, and Mixship. Brixton accepted their congratulations politely.

"With this marriage, Lord Dunbarton, you now become the largest landowner in two parishes," Nitheful said.

"Really? And here I was thinking I was just marrying the woman I love," Brixton said dryly to Dexter, who smiled.

"You know, Lord Dunbarton, should you want the appointment of Custos for St. Elizabeth, we would certainly support your bid," Mixship added.

"You want me to be the King's representative in the parish? To act as Chief Magistrate?" Brixton asked, shocked at the suggestion.

"We do, sir. We feel our interests align perfectly, and you will ensure that the status quo remains," Skelm said.

Brixton handed Dexter his drink and stood in front of the man, staring down at him. "And what in our past dealings would ever make you think I am interested in maintaining the status quo? Oh, that's right; we have had no past dealings, so you have no idea what my thoughts are on the status quo, but I certainly know where you stand," Brixton said as he stepped away from the man, taking his drink from Dexter.

"But Lord Dunbarton," Nitheful said, trying to be ingratiating.

"If you are serious about nominating someone for Custos of this parish who knows how it operates and what is best for the parish, then you should be speaking to my wife, sirs," Brixton said, his temper barely in check.

"Your wife?" Skelm asked, "Surely you jest, sir. A woman as Custos, how absurd," the man laughed.

Brixton turned to the man as Dexter took his arm. Declan walked quickly toward them. "It is because of my wife that this estate has not only flourished but prospered. Everything that you admire and envy about Friendship Estate is my wife's doing. By all means, if you want to maintain the status quo, then find a patsy of your choosing, but if you want to progress and if you want advancement, not only for this parish but for Jamaica, then you should be speaking to my wife and not to me. Enjoy your evening, gentlemen," Brixton said tightly as he walked away.

Dexter and Declan followed as he found Sabine surrounded by a group of young ladies, anxious to find out how she had landed the handsome Brixton Dunbarton without any of them knowing she had set her sights on him.

"Excuse me ladies, pardon me," he said sweetly as he waded through them to get to his wife. "Meet me upstairs. It is time I took you to France," Brixton whispered. Sabine's eyes grew wide, and she held on to the chair next to her. Turning to Brixton, she smiled and nodded slightly. He took her hand to kiss it, licking the inside of her wrist. She nearly fell.

"Enjoy the celebration, gentlemen. I certainly plan to," he said to Dexter and Declan as he left the room. He took the steps to Sabine's room two at a time. Sabine followed shortly after.

A very agitated Margaret and Anne found Dexter and Declan conversing with Liam a short time later.

"Where have those two disappeared to?" Anne asked through her teeth as she smiled at people stopping to congratulate her.

"Honestly, they can't keep their hands off each other for one blasted afternoon?" Margaret asked, equally upset. "Dexter?"

"I will find them, Mother," Dexter said, knowing exactly where they were.

"Tell them to make an appearance for the toasts and to cut the cake. They can be as busy as bunnies after that, for all I care," Anne said, still smiling at guests.

Dexter put his drink down with a sigh, trying not to be annoyed by Declan and Liam's laughter as he made his way upstairs.

Chapter 14 | The Wedding

Turning the handle to Sabine's door, he realized they had not even bothered to lock the door. He marched in to find Sabine in the throes of passion, with half of Brixton's body sticking out from under her skirts as she lay on the bed.

"Sweet Lord," Dexter said, exasperated.

"Dexter!" Sabine said, kicking at Brixton, who came out from under her skirts.

"Dex? What the hell? We are officially married now," Brixton began.

"But not quite finished with the official duties of the wedding. You still have the toasts and the wedding cake. Mother and Mistress Anne are beside themselves," Dexter explained.

"Well, you will just have to do those things without us," Brixton said, climbing back under Sabine's skirts.

"Why don't I go get Nana. Maybe she can get through to you," Dexter said, turning to leave.

"No, no! We're coming!" Sabine said, kicking Brixton off the bed.

Brixton helped Sabine to her feet. Taking his drink from the bedside table, he swallowed half the rum in the glass. "Dex, you do not fight fair, man. You do not fight fair."

"One more hour, Brixton, then you can stay in this room until we leave for England," Dexter promised.

Dexter ushered a reluctant Brixton down the stairs. Brixton was even less amused to find Liam and Declan bent over with laughter. A slow smile was spreading across Dexter's lips until he looked across the room, then it faded from his face. He tapped Brixton on the shoulder, pointing his finger in the direction he was looking in. There in plain sight stood Harry's sleazy solicitors. Dexter explained who the two men were to Liam and Declan, saying it was time the four of them went to welcome these particular guests. Surrounding the men, Brixton and Dexter waited for them to speak.

"Brixton, they said awkwardly, nodding to the men in turn, except Dexter.

"Brixton, we wanted to congratulate you on your marriage. It is a very advantageous union," the senior partner said, smiling salaciously.

"Why are you here?" Brixton asked, none too kindly.

"Well, we were invited," his little lackey whimpered.

"Not by me, nor any member of my family," Brixton snapped.

"We wanted to make sure you received the last statement we sent to Bellevue Estate. Your father seems to have left the island, owing us money. We want to be paid," the senior partner said.

"You want to be paid for preparing a fraudulent document, trying to steal land owned by a Princess of Navarre?" Brixton asked.

"Won't the crown be pleased to get a document like that?" Liam asked. "The Kingdom of Navarre is a great friend and ally to King George. What do you think he would do to these unscrupulous characters should he get a hold of that document, Declan?"

"I would guess they would meet the same fate Harry did, Liam," Declan answered, not taking his eyes off the two solicitors.

"It was Harry's idea," the little one whined. "He wanted the land and the women for himself."

Brixton reached for the man's throat, but Dexter stopped him, taking charge of the situation much to the solicitors' surprise. "You will be paid the full amount of the invoice," Dexter said, moving to the senior partner, so they stood nose to nose. "But for the rest of your life, you will be looking over your shoulder. You will jump out of your skin with fright from the slightest sound. The document you prepared is safely in our possession. Should you come within sight of Mistress Anne or Lady Sabine Dunbarton, you will find yourselves at the end of a hang man's noose because of it. It is in your best interest to disappear as quickly and as thoroughly as Harry did," Dexter said, never raising his voice. The two men stared at Dexter in shock, petrified by his words and the authority in them. Then, they turned and bolted out the door.

Dexter, Brixton, Liam, and Declan followed the two men as they scurried down the steps, not even bothering to find their carriage and leaving their bewildered wives behind. The four men watched as they ran through Friendship Estate's gates and disappeared from view.

"Dex?" Declan asked. "I thought you burned that document."

Brixton clapped Declan on the shoulder. "Oh, he did, I watched him do it, but those two bilge rats don't need to know that," he said as they all dissolved in laughter.

Sabine found them then, grabbing Brixton's hand, she pulled him inside. "There you are. Can we please get these formalities over with so we can go back to what we were doing?" she asked through gritted teeth. "I was quite enjoying France," she muttered as she pushed through the crowd, Brixton in tow.

"Duty calls, gents, duty calls," he smiled back at them as he allowed Sabine to pull him along.

CHAPTER 15

Leaving Jamaica

Later that night, as they lay in bed, Brixton told Sabine about his conversation with Skelm, Nitheful, and Mixship. She laughed at the names Brixton and Dexter had given the men.

"They're not that bad, Brixton. They are good planters. They know the land, respect it, and know how to utilize it."

"You see, right there," Brixton said, sitting up and looking at her. "That is why you are better suited for Custos than any man in this parish. You understand this island, you love it, and it loves you right back. Look at how you have made your estate profitable. That is the kind of management this entire island needs!"

Sabine sat up and looked at him. "What I have done? What do you know about what I have done at Friendship Estate?" She asked.

"Lady Dunbarton, your father was your most ardent supporter. He never ceased singing your praises," Brixton said gently. "He turned Friendship Estate over to you on your seventeenth birthday. It has grown and prospered under your management. No one can take that away from you."

"Brix, you know so much about me, and I feel I am just now getting to know you," Sabine said.

"This is all you will ever need to know about me," he said, pulling her under him. "You earned my respect long before I gave you my heart," he leaned in to kiss her.

The next afternoon, they rode over to Bellevue Estate. Margaret had insisted they come for dinner, and Nana had promised to cook Brixton's favorite meal.

"Likkle she-devil. If yu gwen tek care of my Brix, yu need to know how fe feed him," She said before dissolving into tears.

Sabine went to her and kissed her forehead. "Nana, he will always be your Brix. I will never be able to compete with you, and I don't want to. I know I can never provide him with the love and security a lifetime with you has. You made him into the man I love Nana; I owe you a debt I will never be able to repay."

Nana stopped crying and hugged Sabine back, "Well, maybe yu not such a likkle she-devil, after all," she acknowledged grudgingly.

"Her diplomacy skills are even better than her, well other skills," Brixton whispered to Dexter in awe.

Dexter ignored the inference. "If she gets Nana to forgive her cutting you, she is possibly the best diplomat I have ever seen," Dexter said.

Declan laughed, "She will be running King George's court in no time."

Dinner was a lively affair. The burden of the last few weeks seemed to dissolve as years of preparation fell into place. The trials of England and what they would face there were before them, but until then, Brixton and Dexter delighted in their change of fortunes.

"When do we tell everyone on Bellevue Estate what has happened, who Dexter is, and what my role on the estate will be moving forward?" Brixton asked, realizing just how much had changed in such a short time.

Chapter 15 | Leaving Jamaica

"We haven't had a crop-over festival," Margaret said. Crop over was a time of celebration on every estate. The crops were harvested, and time stood still for a few days until the cycle began again. "We could have a celebration and let everyone know that night," Margaret offered.

"But how do you explain to four generations of people who have known nothing but subjugation and oppression that they are now free to determine the direction of their lives? Nothing to date has prepared them for that responsibility," Dexter said.

The table fell silent as everyone around it contemplated this dilemma—most not really understanding what the difficulty actually involved.

"This will be my obligation, won't it?" Brixton asked. He looked at Dexter, who nodded. Sabine took his hand. "All my life, we have talked about this, Dex and I. We wanted freedom for everyone on this estate. Not only freedom from bondage but freedom from fear for Mother and Nana. Freedom for us to live together as Jamaicans and build our future on this island. Now that the time is here, I realize it is not going to be easy."

"Change never is," Liam said. "Change for the better, change for the worse; change is never an easy pill to swallow. There will be those that fight against it, both black and white, both for the same reason. They are secure in the present circumstance. To see change for the better, well, many do not have the gift of foresight and are unwilling to look beyond how things are to what they can be."

"What do I say, Uncle Liam?" Brixton asked.

"I have no idea, Brix," Liam responded honestly. "I don't have a lifetime of vested interest in the dream that you have made a reality. I do know that love and purpose will guide you. Listen to your heart; it will give you the words."

Brixton thought about that in the days that followed. He went about his work as he always had, but with a new sense of purpose, a new determination. He and Sabine sat with Liam, going over the plans for their home on Mount Sion. Sabine made no modifications. Her father had thought of every detail, down to the nursery off the master bedroom. There were no separate bedrooms for Sabine and Brixton. They would share the same room, the same bed, and they would begin their family there.

Brixton awoke early the morning of the crop-over festival. He and Sabine had spent the night in their grotto on Mount Sion. Brixton sat up, watching Sabine as she slept. Brixton missed Lyndon, missed his council during a time like this. But he understood that Lyndon's death had been the catalyst for change not only for himself and Dexter but for Sabine as well. He moved a lock of hair away from Sabine's face. He never dreamt he could love anyone the way he loved her. He understood love; he loved his brother, his mother, his Nana. But the love he felt for Sabine was primordial, almost elemental in its purity and strength. She was the air he breathed, the foundation he was built on, the fire in his blood, and the water that nurtured his soul.

Sabine opened her eyes. Brixton was staring at her. She smiled at him, and he smiled back. "Still worried about what you are going to say tonight?" She asked, reaching for his hand.

"Not so much worried as I am nervous. I want to say the right thing," Brixton said.

Sabine sat up so she could sit across from Brixton, still holding his hand. They just sat and looked at each other. "Brix, you have been so many things to the people of Bellevue Estate, protector, provider, master. You have worked side by side with them your entire life. You have not asked anything of a man, woman, or child on that estate that you have not done yourself."

"But I have failed, Sabine. So many times, I failed to protect them from my father, to provide them with the security they needed, including my mother and Nana," Brixton said, anguish in his voice.

Chapter 15 | Leaving Jamaica

"Every failure was a lesson. Every failure showed you what not to do. Your lessons did not come from books, Brixton, not like Dexter's. You learned from experience, and it is that experience that will show you the way forward," Sabine said earnestly.

Brixton looked at her, surprise on his face. "That's something your father would have said. He is on my mind today. I miss him," Brixton said sighing. "But if he hadn't left us, we wouldn't have found our way to each other, and that is a gift I would have killed him myself to take," he looked away from Sabine. "Still, I could use his council now."

"When I doubted myself," Sabine began, waiting until his eyes met hers, "he would tell me to believe in my purpose and trust my instincts. If he were here today, he would tell you the same thing," Sabine said softly.

They arrived just as the festival was beginning. The drums beat as dancers leaped around the bonfire in the middle of the slave quarter compound, buildings that would soon be destroyed, replaced by sturdier homes for those who wished to stay. He kissed Sabine's hand as Nana pulled her away and into a small group of women, including Nana's daughter and granddaughter, back from Friendship Estate. Beyond the fire, he could see Liam, Dexter, Declan, and Richard deep in conversation. Craig Holt's purveyors had come and gone, pleased with what they had found and even happier with the contract Richard and Liam has presented them with. Dealing with Queen Nandi and traipsing up and down the Cockpit Country was a job they were delighted to relinquish. It would be up to Brixton to honor that contract, and he would need the people dancing around him to accomplish that task.

It took a moment for him to realize that someone was tugging on his hand. He looked down at the little girl who was pulling on him and recognized Pearl, the young girl who had come to tell him his father was looking for him. It seemed like a lifetime ago.

"Pearly? Wha appen to you? Why yu not dancing wid everybody?" Brixton asked, dropping to his knees in front of her. Big tears fell from her eyes.

"Mas Brix, me fraid sa. Me no wan no one fe see me," She said.

"Why likkle pickney? Why yu a hide from everybody?"

"Yu papa say when me get titty dem he gwen tek me and hurt me how me see him hurt me madder," she said, starting to cry harder. She lifted her thread worn dress to show Brixton. "Look sa, me ave titty dem," she said, dissolving in tears.

Brixton looked at the crying girl. He knew what he was going to say. He picked her up and carried her to the front of the fire, indicating that the drummers were to stop. It was time for the Master to speak. He spoke in patois so everyone would understand what he was saying.

"Another crop over, another year, but this year is different. There have been many changes on the estate in the last few weeks. Some of you may have noticed, some may not if it has not directly affected your life. I understand that. My brother Dexter, you all know him," Brixton began.

Dexter came to stand beside Brixton, and Brixton put his arm around him. "This is my brother," he said with feeling, hugging Dexter to him. "My older brother, who has loved me, protected me, and watched over me my entire life. Every critical life lesson I have learned has been taught to me by this man. My brother will be crossing the sea soon; he will be taking his place as Master in a world of Masters. He is one of us, but he will go on a difficult journey to show Masters that you can be a Master no matter the color of your skin." Brixton stopped talking as the exclamations of wonder grew around him. Those who understood what he was saying whispered it to those who did not. Soon, they quieted, waiting for him to continue.

Chapter 15 | Leaving Jamaica

He held Pearly in front of him so that she could hear his words clearly. "My father is gone. He will never return to this property. He will never hurt anyone here again. No one has the right to come on to this property and hurt you ever again," he stressed, looking directly at Pearly. "If they try, they will answer to me."

"My wife and I..." he paused, Pearly still in his arms as Sabine came to his side. "Some of you know my wife. All of you know what she has done at Friendship Estate. Everyone who lives there is free; they all live together to create a society and build a life together as one. Dexter owns Bellevue Estate. A black man owns the land we stand on," Brixton said, pointing to the ground. "Land that he and I, his white brother, will share with you as he crosses the sea to make this world a better place for all of us." Brixton looked around at the faces in front of him, hanging on his every word.

"If you decide to stay here, to make your home here, work with me to build a life for all of us, then we will share all we have with you, including the land. There will be no more slave quarters! Each man, each woman, each family will have a home of their own, land they can grow provisions on. Your children will go to school, and you will be paid wages for the work you do on this estate and on behalf of this estate. There will be no slave and no master. We will work together for the betterment of all." Brixton concluded his speech, and you could hear a pin drop.

Finally, Pearly turned Brixton's face, so he was looking at her. "Mas Brix?" she asked. "A yu gewn give me, me free paper, sa?" she wondered, and Brixton nodded at her, smiling. "A yu gwen send me a school and build a new home for me and me madder?" Again, Brixton nodded at her and smiled. "A yu gwen tek care of me, till me grow?" she asked.

Brixton put her down, then knelt in front of her, "I will take care of you until you can take care of yourself, and then maybe one day, if I did my job correctly, you will find it in your heart to take care of me if I need it," Brixton said.

Pearly put her arms around Brixton, a big smile on her face, and kissed him on the cheek. "I will always tek care of yu, Mas Brix," Brixton smiled at her and hugged her to him.

Everyone was talking at once as they understood what this meant. Dexter, Sabine, and Brixton were overwhelmed with people coming up to them, thanking them. All three answered questions and explained how the free papers would be distributed and when. Each day a work schedule would be posted at the kitchen door of the Greathouse. Those who could read would learn their assignments for the day and week ahead, those who could not read would go to Nana, and she would let them know what to do.

Within a week, Nana and Margaret added reading lessons to the schedule, so inundated with questions, they felt it necessary to start remedial adult literacy classes immediately. Not one person opted to leave Bellevue Estate and strike out on their own. Brixton was both heartened and saddened by that. Encouraged that everyone wanted to be a part of the new world they would build together. Saddened because he realized everyone on the Estate understood that they wouldn't find a better place for themselves in the old world if they left.

Two days after crop over, Sabine, Brixton, Dexter, and Declan left Bellevue Estate for Spanish Town. Nana and Margaret were awash in a flood of tears as they gathered to see them off. Pearly was so anxiety-ridden about Brixton's departure, he had to give her one of his shirts to keep her company while he was away.

"Mas Brix," she cried, clinging to him. "Yu promise yu coming back?"

"Yes, Pearly," he promised, trying to untangle himself from her gently. "I will be back in time for Christmas."

Chapter 15 | Leaving Jamaica

"I gwen ask the White Spirit to watch over yu," She cried as Nana forcibly pulled the child off of Brixton.

"Thank you, Pearly," he said, kissing the child on the cheek while dodging her outstretched arms. "I am sure your prayers will keep me safe and sound."

Sabine stifled a laugh as Dexter shook his head, smiling. But it was Declan who was in an uproar. "Sweet baby Jesus, Sabine, how much luggage does one woman need? We can barely fit in the carriage," he complained. "I am quite sure it is going to take us a week to get to Spanish Town, as loaded down as we are."

"Whatever do you mean, Declan?" She asked innocently. "This is just for my first week in London until I can get the new trousseau Dexter and Brixton promised me."

At Declan's stricken face, Dexter and Brixton laughed out loud.

"Ah, Sabine?" Brixton whispered conspiratorially.

"Yes, Brixton," she whispered back, "the French petticoats are at the top of the trunk that will be in our cabin," she said.

"Thank you," Brixton said, relaxing against the carriage as Sabine rolled her eyes and settled into his arms.

They arrived in Spanish Town the day before they were to set sail from Passage Fort. Declan was in a tailspin. There were provisions to secure, and he only had one day to do it all, thanks to Sabine's luggage.

"The ship will probably sink from all the weight of your blasted luggage anyway," he said irritably to Sabine.

"Declan," Sabine said, taking charge. "Calm down. I have already brought many of the provisions we need in what you claim is my excessive luggage. Anything else we may want, I can get from the Friendship Estate purveyors who are right around the corner. I will take care of the additional provisions. You and Brixton can go down to the ship and start loading the luggage."

At Declan's loud harrumph, Brixton clapped him on the back, leading him off to do Sabine's bidding. Sabine had noticed that Dexter had gone directly into Enos Knowles' home, where they would spend the night. She found him in the study, a book already in his hand.

"Dex?" she asked.

"Thank you for all your help. Sabine. This trip will need a woman's touch, and I am glad you are here with us."

"A woman's touch? How so?" Sabine asked, sitting in the chair next to his.

"Declan advises me that London deals are made during the endless dinner parties and balls hosted each night by anyone with an agenda to promote," Dexter said. "I expect we will have to participate in those functions to push our agenda, and I have no idea how to throw a party."

Sabine laughed. "I wouldn't worry about that, Dex. Between Declan and I, we can figure it out. Your job will be making sure Brixton doesn't offend anyone with his crass manners or frighten the daylights out of an unsuspecting victim with his boisterous pranks! Who do you think has the harder task?" she asked, playfully, her head to one side.

Dexter smiled but said nothing. Sabine could tell the realities of what he faced in London were now setting in. She was so glad they would be with him for the first few months to help him settle in. Changing the minds of people who had held dominion over others for profit was difficult enough. But to move their hearts to effect a change that would alter how people saw each other would be a much more challenging feat to accomplish. Sabine did not envy him the job.

"Wait until you see the ship, Dex!" Brixton bounded into the room, full of excitement. "It's called the Boston, and it's a merchant vessel they have turned into a passenger and a cargo ship. There are only six-passenger cabins in all. We have four of them."

"Four? Why four?" Sabine asked.

"One for you and Brixton, one for Dexter, one for me, and one for your luggage and provisions, Lady," Declan said sarcastically.

"In any case," Brixton went on, full of boyish excitement. "It is beautiful. We are going to have so much fun on this ship, Dex!"

Dexter brightened at Brixton's depiction of the ship. As Brixton pulled him aside, describing the vessel and what it could do, Dexter listened, transfixed. Sabine could see how deeply rooted their relationship was, how much they loved and respected each other. When Brixton was with Dexter, she saw the boy in him and how they had grown up together as brothers. It was beautiful to witness, especially being an only child.

"We set sail tomorrow at noon!" Brixton concluded.

Sabine smiled as they turned to look at her. "I'm sure you boys will make the month-long voyage incredibly enjoyable," she said, rising to her feet. It would probably be best if they had an early dinner and retired for the night, although she was sure Brixton and Dexter would be too excited to get much sleep.

"That's the McKenzie in them," Declan said, following her to the kitchen.

"Excuse me?" she asked, turning to Declan.

"I was just a young lad in short pants when Mags married Harry. I remember how my mother cried; Liam was terrifying in his anger over the match. It was a hard time for our family. My mother wanted us always to stay together; she said our strength came not only from our love of each other but from the bond we shared in sticking together," Declan said.

"You think I'm worried that Brixton will want to stay in London?" Sabine asked, turning to face him. "He won't, Declan! He will want to come back here to enact the change his brother is fighting for. No matter the distance between them or the time that separates them, their bond is forged in more than blood."

Declan smiled and looked at her. "Yes, it is. I saw it with Liam and Mags. What makes me happy for Brixton is you have recognized it, and you don't resent it."

Sabine smiled back at Declan. "I could never resent it. Brix's dedication to Dexter is one of the reasons I love him. When Brix loves, it's for life. I'm counting on that."

"Brix is lucky to have you, lass. They both are," Declan said. "England will be hard for them. Dexter will definitely be looked down upon as a colonial, but you and Brixton will be as well."

"Wonderful," Sabine said, taking his arm. "Another tie that binds," she chirped as they headed toward the kitchen together.

The next day, Brixton and Dexter could not wait to board the Boston. They scurried about as the ship got underway, hindering progress in their excitement. They were soon asked to stay on the upper deck and enjoy the view of the island as they sailed out of the Passage Fort harbor. For the first two weeks, it was smooth sailing. Brixton and Dexter, not used to sitting around, made themselves useful in helping out on the deck. They waved to Sabine as they hung over the ship's side, cleaning the windows to the cabin where she was organizing her dresses and accessories. They were both happy and carefree for the time being. Declan and Sabine decided to give them that time together.

But, as they left the Caribbean Sea's calm waters and sailed into the Atlantic, the weather worsened. For two days, Brixton nursed Sabine as the rough seas plagued her with seasickness so severe that Dexter asked the ship's doctor to look at her. The doctor examined her as Dexter and Brixton looked on anxiously.

"Is she with child?" The doctor asked Brixton.

Brixton looked at Sabine for the answer; she shook her head.

"No," Brixton answered.

"She doesn't have her sea legs yet," the doctor said dismissively. "Once she does, she will be fine. Just keep feeding her warm broth and hard biscuits until she can keep them down."

Sabine rolled over and threw up on his shoes. Brixton rushed to her side as Dexter saw the man out.

"Well, he was of no help," Dexter said dryly.

"Brix, I am no longer enjoying this sea voyage," Sabine said as she lay back in his arms.

"Neither am I. Neither am I," Brixton said sympathetically.

Another wave of nausea hit and she threw up. Brixton held her hair back and stroked it comfortingly.

"Sweet Jesus," she said, lying back. "I must look like death warmed over."

"You will always be the most beautiful woman I have ever seen, my love," Brixton said as he spooned some broth into her.

Sabine smiled at him. *God, he is gorgeous*, she thought to herself. By the time they docked in London, ten days later, Sabine and Brixton learned how to use the ship's rocking to their advantage.

CHAPTER 16

London Town

Enos Knowles met them at the London docks. He had been staying at the Dunbarton home in London for most of his time in England. At Declan's request, he had traveled to the Dunbarton lands outside of London to make sure the castle there was ready to welcome Dexter in the weeks to follow.

"Well, well, Sabine Holborn. I must say I am very surprised to see you in London, my dear," Enos said, taking her hand and helping her down the gangway to a waiting carriage.

"Lady Sabine Dunbarton, Mr. Knowles," Dexter corrected.

"I beg your pardon?" Enos asked, not quite sure what he had just heard.

Brixton arrived with Sabine's valise. "Sabine is my wife, sir."

Enos stopped abruptly and turned to look at them both. Brixton smiled at his wife, and Enos noticed Sabine's smile in return. Enos nodded, his head down as emotion overtook him. "Your father would be very pleased with this union. Your marriage to Brixton was his fondest wish," Enos said, kissing Sabine's hand and hugging it to him.

"So, we have come to find out, Mr. Knowles," Sabine responded.

Dexter, Sabine, Brixton, and Enos Knowles settled into one carriage as Declan followed in another with the luggage. Brixton and Dexter were practically hanging out of the carriage windows as they took in all the new sights and sounds.

"Dear me!" Sabine exclaimed. "Is it always so loud and crowded?" she asked Enos.

"Welcome to London, my dear," Enos responded. "By the way, Sabine, do you remember Lady Georgina Collins?" As Sabine shook her head no, Enos continued. "Your mother sent me to London with a letter of introduction to her. They spent time together in Haiti. Both your mother and the Lady assure me that you have met," Enos stopped, hoping he had jogged her memory, but he could see Sabine was still at a loss.

"If you remember your family history, the third house of Bourbon ascended to the throne of Navarre in 1555. From there, they took the French throne in 1589. Lady Georgina is a minor member of the Bourbon dynasty, hence a distant cousin to your mother. She has lived in London all her life, married quite well, in fact. The lady is a favorite of the King and has a great deal of power and influence in his court. She has been busy making the Dunbarton home in London ready for Dexter's arrival. She is an avid supporter of our cause," Enos finished.

"I'm sorry, Mr. Knowles," Sabine said, "her name does not ring a bell. But if she has been as helpful as you say, I will be more than happy to make her acquaintance again."

"I dear say, she will be more than anxious to hear how you and Brixton came to be married. A lot seems to have happened in Jamaica in the weeks I have been away," Enos said.

Dexter and Brixton turned their attention to Enos and filled him in on all that had transpired since his departure. They were just concluding the tale when they arrived at the gates of the townhouse.

Chapter 16 | London Town

"Brixton and I delivered all the free papers to your law firm the morning we left for England. Your assistant assured me that once they were all notarized, he would send them to Bellevue Estate," Dexter explained.

The carriage drew to a halt in front of the most towering gates Dexter, Brixton, or Sabine had ever seen. A tall wraparound wall hid the house and grounds from view, but once through the gates, they could see the house, three stories high with windows along every floor and a myriad of chimneys jutting out of the roof. As the carriages pulled through the gates and circled the courtyard, the mansion came into full view, surrounded by manicured lawns and pretty gardens.

"Welcome to the Dunbarton townhouse," Declan said, opening the carriage door.

The three of them stepped down from the carriage, mouths agape as they looked around them.

"Harry walked away from this?" Dexter asked, astonished.

"No, Harry walked away from a crumbling decay of a residence. Liam and then I came in and rebuilt the place. We built this new portico that leads to a grand entrance hall. You will find two dining rooms, several drawing rooms, and a grand ballroom on the ground floor. A crystal staircase, the only one in London, leads to the fifteen bedrooms on the second floor. The third floor is where your servants live. There is a staircase that runs from the top floor to the bottom for them. On the roof, there is a small hidden garden with a plunge pool," Declan answered proudly, winking at Brixton and Sabine. "Thanks to the Romans, you even have indoor plumbing for baths and washing up."

Dexter looked at Declan. "Where did you get the money to do all of that?"

Enos took Dexter's arm. "When you have settled in, it may be a good time for Declan and I to go over your holdings, Dexter.

Thanks to Liam and Declan's management of your assets, you are a vastly wealthy man."

Brixton dropped Sabine's valise and swept her into his arms. "This is one threshold I will relish carrying you over," he said as he ran past Dexter with Sabine in his arms. As they entered the building, they stopped wide-eyed, staring at the enormous entranceway with its gilded ceilings, rich tapestries, and opulent furnishings.

"Well, that is quite an entrance," a musical voice said. Sabine and Brixton turned in the direction of the sound. In front of them was the most divine creature they had ever seen. Immaculately dressed, not a hair out of place, and skin so perfect, they were unsure if she was real or the most exquisite porcelain doll ever created.

"Ah, Lady Collins, allow me to introduce you to Declan McKenzie, Lord Brixton Dunbarton, and his wife, Lady Sabine Dunbarton, nee Holborn, your distant cousin, I believe," Enos said. The vision drifted toward them, her hand outstretched. Declan bent to kiss it. Brixton followed his lead and did the same. She assessed each man quickly, deciding she liked what she saw. When she came to Sabine, she stopped, her head cocked.

"Oui, I can see Anne in your eyes and the shape of your mouth. I think you are more beautiful, though," she said. Sabine, unsure what to do, curtsied and was rewarded with a laugh that sounded like the tinkling of bells. "I see we have some work to do with you before we let you loose in polite society," she said as she took Sabine's hand in hers and squeezed it gently. The Lady stood back, looking around. Her eyes found Dexter, and she glided toward him. "Mon Dieu, you are even more stunning than Enos said you were. You will be a grand success with all the ladies at court. Un Duc riche et beau. Qui peut résister à un tel homme," she said to herself, putting her hand out for Dexter to kiss.

Chapter 16 | London Town

"What did she say?" Brixton whispered to Sabine.

"A Duke with wealth and beauty. Who can resist such a man?" Sabine whispered back.

"You must be exhausted from your travels," Lady Collins said. "Why don't we enjoy a light repast in the drawing-room? The groomsmen will unload your luggage. Duke Dexter Dunbarton, your butler will see to the unpacking of your clothes. The tailor delivered your new wardrobe yesterday, along with Lord Brixton Dunbarton's. His butler will take care of his needs and Lady Dunbarton; your maids will do the same for you," she turned to smile at them all. "By the time you are ready to nap, all will be taken care of," she said as she led the way down a grand hallway. "After your nap, we will meet for tea and discuss your plans for the rest of the week."

"We have plans for the week?" Brixton whispered to Dexter as he took Sabine's hand and followed. Dexter shrugged in response; he had no idea what was happening.

"Mon Duc, why don't you walk with me so I may admire all your magnificent artwork?" The lady asked, turning slightly to look at Dexter out of the corner of her eye. As Dexter hurried to catch up with her, she placed her hand lightly on his arm.

"Madame, merci pour tout ce que vous avez fait pour aider notre cause." Dexter said, turning to her.

"You speak French?" Lady Collins asked.

Dexter smiled at her. "Hablo español con fluidez también."

"My, my, you are a delight, mon Duc," she teased, flirting outrageously.

Brixton looked at Sabine, his eyebrows raised. She swatted his arm. "It's called flirting," she whispered.

"I am well aware of what it is called. And what it can lead to," he whispered back.

Sabine was thoughtful. "He might as well practice his diplomacy skills on a receptive audience," she said quietly.

"Do you remember her, Sabine?" Brixton asked, wondering how anyone could forget meeting this creature.

"I can't say that I do. The last time I visited Haiti was two years ago before Papa died. I can honestly say I don't remember meeting her," Sabine said.

They had arrived at a small drawing-room, at least that is how Lady Collins described it. The room was the size of the entire ground floor of the Bellevue Greathouse in Jamaica. A small buffet was set up in the corner of the room. The room exuded comfort and warmth. A large settee dominated the center of the room. Surrounding the settee was a cluster of antique high back chairs, all with the Dunbarton family's crest engraved into the wood. The furniture was covered in luxurious, plush fabrics with Victorian, gilded tables scattered between the chairs. A large fireplace dominated the back wall. Lady Collins sat on the settee, gesturing for Sabine to join her, as the men sat in the chairs around them. Brixton was glancing at the buffet; he was quite hungry. With a slight nod of her head, servants appeared from nowhere with plates for each of them.

"Lady Collins, you don't seem surprised to see me here," Sabine began.

"My dear," the Lady answered. "A Lady never shows surprise; she adapts. I am curious to hear about your recent marriage. As the Lady of this Manor, you will have certain responsibilities that I will be happy to help you with. First and foremost, we must get you a fitting wardrobe for all the activities and festivities you will not only be attending but hosting," she looked at Sabine, who was decidedly overwhelmed. "You don't remember me, do you?" Lady Collins asked quietly.

Sabine's cheeks colored in embarrassment. "I am embarrassed to say I don't, my Lady,"

"The last time I saw you, you were fifteen, you taught me how to play jacks during a hurricane," Lady Collins said, taking a small bite of her cake.

Chapter 16 | London Town

The memory returned to Sabine, but the girl she played jacks with was not the vision that sat in front of her now. Sabine's eyes widened, and she took a deep breath.

"Ah, I see you remember me. The caterpillar you knew became a beautiful butterfly, thanks to your mother," Lady Collins said, and the bells tinkled as the Lady laughed.

Sabine turned to look at her, her eyes narrowed. Her mother had taught her some of her magic, but Sabine could not remember any magic spell that would transform the girl she played jacks with into the magnificent woman in front of her.

Lady Collins seemed to read her thoughts. "No, no magic, just the best advice one woman could give another. She told me that men are drawn to two things. One is a woman who commands respect, and two, a woman who wields more power than they will ever know. Master that, and you will control every man you meet."

"My mother told you that?" Sabine asked. It seemed very uncharacteristic of her mother, but her mother did command respect, and she wielded power like no other woman she had ever met, until now.

"She did," Lady Collins said. "And it changed the trajectory of my life."

They turned to follow Enos' conversation. He was explaining to Dexter and Brixton where the fight for the abolition of slavery stood in England. Supporters grew each day, but the small faction still to be swayed held most of the power to make it happen.

"That reminds me," Lady Collins interjected. "Two nights from today, you are all invited to a soiree at William Wilberforce's home."

"*The* William Wilberforce?" Declan asked.

"Who is William Wilberforce?" Brixton asked.

"William Wilberforce is a prominent member of the British Parliament. He headed the parliamentary campaign against the British slave trade and now supports the crusade for abolishing slavery. His voice is a champion for our cause. I sent him the arguments you prepared for me, Dexter. He was quite taken with them," Enos explained.

"Yes, he was. Hence the invitation," Lady Collins said, smiling.

"I have many of the recent papers he has written in support of abolition. I will make sure you get them, Dexter," Enos said.

"I would appreciate that, sir. I would like to know more of the gentleman's mind before I meet him," Dexter said.

"Wonderful, why don't we retire for the afternoon and meet back here for drinks before dinner," Lady Collins said, rising. "Sabine, I will show you to your rooms. Declan, I'm sure you will show the gentlemen to theirs." Her tone brooking no argument as she grabbed Sabine's hand and walked out of the room.

"What now?" Dexter asked, looking at Brixton.

"Why don't I show you to your rooms? Dexter, Enos, and I do have things we need to discuss with you and Brixton," Declan said as they followed the ladies out.

Declan led the way, and they started up the crystal staircase. "There are two master suites, one on each corner of the building. One for you, Dexter, and one for you, Brixton. They are identical," he said as he stopped in front of two massive doors. Declan tapped lightly, and Dexter's butler opened the doors to his suite. As Declan made the introductions, Dexter and Brixton looked around.

Again, the furnishings were lavish and opulent. Dark wood complemented with deep reds, blues, and greens seeming to mimic Jamaica's vibrant colors. They walked into a small sitting area with a sofa and chairs scattered around it. On the left was the door that led to Dexter's study. A large mahogany desk commanded the center of the room. Two walls were covered with bookshelves that went from floor to ceiling. Dexter's eyes lit up as he saw them. The door to the right led to Dexter's bedroom, where a massive four-poster bed with heavy curtains dominated the room. His dressing room was behind a door to the left of the bed. To the right of the bed was another door, closed to him. Dexter walked toward it.

"Where does this door lead to?" he asked.

"That door leads to what will be your wife's bedroom. It also has a dressing room, a little larger than yours, and a sitting room," Declan explained.

"My wife will not share my bedroom, my bed?" Dexter asked.

"It's not really done like that here, Dex," Declan started to explain.

"My wife is not sleeping in another room," Brixton exploded. "Where is my suite Declan?" Declan left to show him where he would be staying.

"This must be quite overwhelming for you," Enos said as they walked to Dexter's study.

"I'm trying not to let it overwhelm me. I do love this room," he said as he ran his hand along the books.

"Liam and I spent a lot of time in this room discussing your future," Enos said.

Dexter walked slowly to the desk, running his hand along the beautiful wood. He pulled out the chair and sat down. He turned to look at Enos, nodding that he should continue.

"After Liam visited your mother in Jamaica, he devoted his life to the cause she had laid out for you," Enos said. "As you know, he never married. He spent his time rebuilding the Dunbartons' reputation. Then he rebuilt this house and the castle in the country. He is quite an adept architect. Then he set about building your fortune. The books are there on the desk. You can go through them at your leisure. While Brixton is here, you might want to set aside a month to visit your lands here in England and in Scotland. They are magnificent and worth the visit."

"Did my uncle know the love of a woman?" Dexter asked, haunted by all Liam had sacrificed for him.

"He did," Declan said from the door, coming to sit in the chair across from Dexter.

"Your lands are on the English coast, and the Barbary pirates plagued them. We fought a great battle against them. They had pillaged villages up and down the coast. We caught them on the beach, ready to depart. Our army killed them all. On our way back, we found a young girl; she must have been around sixteen, maybe seventeen years of age. The pirates had savaged her, and the village healer said that she would never be able to bear children if she lived. Liam took her with us and nursed her back to health himself. He taught her to read and write, and they spent a great deal of time together. She was a comfort to Liam. I think Liam fell in love with her the minute he saw her, but as she grew, her love for him did as well. They could never marry, and she understood, but they loved each other. It was enough for both of them," Declan said.

"What happened to her?" Dexter asked.

"She died of consumption," Declan said, sadly.

"How did he convince you, your clan, to follow him in Mother's quest?" Dexter asked.

"So, you have seen them?" Declan asked.

"Hard to miss the fierce men with flaming red hair posted on the turrets and railings along the roof, armed with muskets and crossbows. Brixton noticed them patrolling the grounds as well. They look battle-ready," Dexter said.

"They are battle-hardened and battle-ready. They will follow their chief. It is the clan way,' Declan said.

"Even if their chief is a black man?" Dexter asked.

"The Scots know oppression; they know tyranny. All they need is someone to show them the way, and they will fight against the cruelty of one man against the other, to the death. It doesn't matter what the color of your skin is, Dex; all that matters is that you are worthy of leading them," Declan said.

"Am I? Am I worthy of leading them?" Dexter asked.

Declan looked at Enos before answering. "From what I have seen of you, Dex, I would follow you off the white cliffs of Dover if you ordered it."

Dexter nodded. "I assume these are maps of the lands under my portfolio," he said, pointing to maps laid out on the desk in front of him. "Show me what I need to know, and then we can go over the books."

Brixton found Lady Collins and Sabine sitting in Sabine's dressing room.

"Brixton!" Sabine exclaimed. "It's all so beautiful, isn't it?

"Not if you are sleeping in another room, it's not!" Brixton exclaimed.

"Of course, she sleeps in another room. Doesn't she?" Lady Collins asked, seeing the anger on Brixton's face.

"Madame, from the night we married, my wife has lain by my side every night and woken with me every morning. That is not going to change. And while we are at it, why do I have to take a nap every afternoon? During the afternoon, where I come from, there is work to be done," Brixton said, his displeasure evident in his voice.

Lady Collins leaned back on the sofa, looking at Brixton through hooded eyes. "His passion must be a delight to you, my dear," she said to Sabine

"Brix, you don't need to get so upset," Sabine said, running to his side. "Nothing will keep me from your bed," she whispered, trying to calm him down. Only Lady Collins's laughter stopped him from kissing her.

"We nap in the afternoon because it is considered rude to leave a party until after breakfast is served. No man, no matter how virile he is, can function with only a few hours of sleep each night," she said, caressing Brixton's cheek as she sashayed out of the room.

"I can't decide whether I like her or not," Brixton said, sweeping Sabine into his arms. "Where is our bedroom?" He asked. Sabine pointed the way, and they ended up in her bedroom.

"It is smaller than your bedroom, but it is more private. What do you think?" Sabine asked as he deposited her on the bed.

"It has a big beautiful bed. Works for me," Brixton said as he sat on the bed to take off his boots.

"She's not that bad," Sabine said, lying on her side to look at Brixton. He knew who she was referring to.

"Do you remember meeting her?" he asked, removing his shirt.

"Well, I did once she reminded me of when I met her. She certainly did not look like that when I knew her. She was plain and very timid," Sabine said, pulling off her dress.

"Not words I would use to describe her now," Brixton said, losing interest in the conversation as Sabine turned toward him. As Brixton looked into her eyes, he realized he was wrong in what he had said to Nana that fateful night he thought he lost Sabine forever. Sabine was not a few moments of comfort to him. She was his shelter amid the English storm they now found themselves thrust into.

Later as Sabine rested, he dressed and went in search of his brother. He found him in his office, surrounded by ledgers with Enos and Declan standing over him.

"Brix," Dexter said as he noticed Brixton standing at the entrance to the study. "Come in, come in." He motioned for Brix to sit across from him.

"So, all told, you have around a million-pound sterling in assets, three hundred thousand in working capital, and half a million in reserve," Declan finished.

"That's what you are worth, Dex?" Brixton asked, shocked.

"Well, between the Dunbarton holdings and the McKenzie holdings, roughly, yes," Declan said.

"Still happy with your lot in life, Brixton?" Enos asked.

"All I have ever wanted in my life is Mount Sion, a wife who loves me, peace and security for my mother and Nana, and for my brother to have what he so richly deserves. Yes, sir. I am more than happy with my lot in life," Brixton answered confidently.

"Now, the work begins. You will meet some wonderful people at the Wilberforce soiree. All people who support the abolition of slavery," Enos said.

"What about colonial rights?" Brixton asked. "The fight to free the colonies from imperial rule has just begun. The West Indies cannot wage war as the American colony has; we would be decimated."

"One fight at a time. Once slavery is abolished, we can work on gaining more freedoms for the islands of the West Indies," Enos said. "We have to begin toppling the dominoes in order and one at a time. Tomorrow, you will make your first appearance at the House of Lords to claim your seat, Dexter. Brixton and Declan will be with you and your bodyguards. We don't expect trouble, I have laid the groundwork, but a show of force will dampen the dust. In a few weeks, you will make your presentation to a joint session of Parliament and the House of Lords. It is there you will set your agenda."

"And in the meantime?" Dexter asked.

"In the meantime, you will attend as many festivities as you can. Throw a few of your own and get to know your friends and your enemies. You will need to know them both by name," Enos elucidated.

Brixton and Dexter looked at each other. Declan and Enos saw it was time to leave them alone. The brothers sat in contemplative silence for a few minutes after the men departed.

"We are no longer big fish in a small pond, brother, now we are the small fish in a much larger pond," Brixton said.

"I can't do this without you," Dexter said.

"You won't," Brixton answered.

"After my presentation, I would like to travel to our lands in England and Scotland. I would like you to see them," Dexter stated. "You will never want for money again, Brix."

"Dex, let's cross that bridge when we come to it. My intention has never been to make my home here. As for money, I have all that I need, and if I need more, I will earn it by my own hand. You have worked for all of this, Dex; it was not given to you only by birthright. You deserve it!" Brixton stressed.

Dexter came from around the desk and hugged Brixton. "You are the best of me, brother."

"As you are the best of me, brother," Brixton replied, hugging him back. Once they had parted, Brixton asked, "So what do you think of Lady Collins?"

"I don't think I would find the comfort in her I did with Queen Nandi," Dexter said, smiling gloomily. "So, I plan to walk a wide birth of Lady Collins, but Enos assures me that her assistance has been invaluable."

"As do I brother, as do I, but she will have our appreciation for all she has done for us," Brixton said.

"Come, show me your rooms," Dexter said as they walked out.

"I haven't seen my rooms yet," Brixton said as Dexter led the way out of his study and down the grand hallway. They walked toward Brixton's suite of rooms, and as if by magic, the large double doors opened.

"Good afternoon Lord Dunbarton," a middle-aged man said, bowing to Brixton. "My name is John. I am your butler."

"Oh, thank you, John, my name is Brixton, and this is my brother Dexter," Brixton said, walking into the sitting room.

"Duke," John said, bowing to Dexter.

Chapter 16 | London Town

"I don't think I will ever get used to this," Dexter said under his breath. They followed John as he showed them around the rooms.

"Lord Dunbarton, I have laid out your evening wear for dinner. You may freshen up here," he said, pointing to a washstand. "Let me know when you are ready to dress, and I will help you," John said.

"I see you have met John," Sabine said, walking into the room in her petticoat, while pinning her hair into a messy pile on top of her head.

Dexter and Brixton were both used to seeing women parade around in a petticoat or swimming shift. Considering the climate they came from, negligible clothing was a common sight. But, this was all too much for John, who sniffed in disapproval, looking away.

"If that will be all my Lords?" John asked.

"It will, John, thank you," Sabine said, ice in her tone.

As John left in a huff, Brixton turned to his wife. "I see *you* have met John."

"The man is insufferable. I came in here looking for you, and he practically threw me out of the room," Sabine said.

"Were you naked?" Brixton asked, already knowing the answer and understanding what angered her.

"Of course, I was naked," she stopped short, looking at Dexter, who stood smiling at them. "I didn't expect to confront a perfect stranger in your room," she said defensively.

"It won't happen again, Sabine," Dexter assured her. "Just tell him when he has access to the rooms, and I am sure he will honor your wishes."

"Thank you, Dex," Sabine said, as she looked closely at him. "How are you holding up? I know how overwhelming this is for me; how much more is it for you?"

"It's a lot to take in," Dex said, looking around. "But I am so glad you are both here to go through this with me. It makes it a lot easier to handle knowing I am not the only one out of his depth."

They sat in the little sitting-room and talked until John made another appearance with Sabine's maid and Dexter's butler in tow. "Lord Dunbarton, it is time to dress for dinner," he said. "And Lady," looking at Sabine down his nose, "your maid is here to collect you," he said dismissively.

Looking down her nose at John, Sabine sniffed, purposefully walking past John to use the secret door between her and Brixton's room to go to her rooms, her bewildered maid following closely behind.

"John, before you go and get yourself killed, I think you need to understand the pecking order in my little hen coop. As of now, you are most definitely at the bottom of that order," Brixton began as he explained that he and Sabine valued their privacy and did not need to be waited on hand and foot.

As John was helping Brixton dress, Brixton asked, "John, tell me about the secret garden on the roof, the one with the plunge pool. How would I get to it from my rooms?"

As John explained where the secret garden was and showed him the hidden staircase from his room that would take him to the roof, Brixton had a favor to ask. "While we are at dinner, would you please take two large towels up and leave them by the pool. After that, you and Lady Dunbarton's maid can take the rest of the night off. Oh, and John, I won't be sleeping in this bed," Brixton informed the bemused man.

Brixton waited for Sabine in his little sitting-room after he finished dressing. Despite the awkwardness of their introduction, it did not take long for Brixton to realize that John was a wealth of information. Brixton had no idea how to function in British high

Chapter 16 | London Town

society, and John was a willing teacher. Surprisingly, the butler was nonjudgmental, which made it easier for Brixton to ask him for help.

When she walked in, Brixton could not move.

"Well, don't just sit there with your mouth open, say something," Sabine asked nervously.

"Every time I think you could not possibly look more beautiful, you surprise me!" Brixton assured her.

"So, you think I look beautiful, nipped, tucked, powered, and plucked like a Christmas turkey?" Sabine asked, the uncomfortable corset cinched so tight she dared not take a breath. She had no idea how she was going to sit down for dinner.

"I think you are most beautiful lying naked in my arms, rosy and tousled from our lovemaking. But this is a distant second," he said, taking her arm.

Despite her discomfort, she smiled. They were directed to a parlor where Dexter, Lady Collins, Declan, and Enos were deep in conversation. Lady Collins was tutoring Dexter on the names and distinguishing features of Lords sympathetic to their cause.

"These men will be the first to approach you tomorrow. If you can, try and greet them by name. Your enemies will not be so welcoming. Lord Kavendish is your most fervent detractor. He has a coven of lesser Lords that do his bidding. He is who you must flatter and coerce to your side," Lady Collins was saying.

All the men turned as Sabine and Brixton walked in

"Sabine," Dexter exclaimed. "You are a vision to behold!"

"Agreed, agreed," Declan and Enos chimed in.

The dinner captain opened the door to the left at that precise moment, announcing that dinner was served.

"May I have the honor of escorting you into dinner?" Enos asked Sabine, who graciously gave him her arm.

Lady Collins put her arm on Dexter's, and he smiled cautiously at her.

"Dexter," she whispered. "I will be more than happy to join you in your rooms tonight to go over the names again." Dexter looked pleadingly at Brixton.

Brixton took the lady's hand and placed it on his arm. "Lady Collins, will we have the happy occasion of meeting Lord Collins anytime soon? He is as welcome here as you are, Milady," Brixton said, smiling sweetly.

Lady Collins's smile was not as saccharine when she started to walk, the Dunbarton brothers on either side of her. "Sadly, my Lord husband prefers his estates in the country; he very rarely, if ever, comes to London."

Brixton and Dexter did not hear her response. They walked into the most beautiful dining room they had ever seen, in hues of yellows and golds. The table seated sixteen people comfortably and was dominated by a heavy mahogany table. It was engraved with palm trees, pineapples, and hummingbirds, or doctor birds as they were called in Jamaica. As they approached the table, Brixton noticed place cards with their names on them. *Thank you, John*, he thought to himself.

Dexter was at the head of the table, Brixton to his right and Sabine next to him. Enos was seated next to her. On his left sat Declan and Lady Collins. Declan held out Lady Collin's chair and waited for her to sit. Brixton and Dexter ran their hands along the table.

"Do you recognize the table?" Declan asked.

Both men nodded, "I feel like I should, but I don't know from where," Dexter said, bemused.

Declan laughed. "It is made from mahogany trees from both the Bellevue Estate and Mount Sion. Your mother commissioned it after you were born, and Liam brought it back with him. It is your mother's gift to you, Dexter. Is it the wood that is familiar to you?"

Brixton was overcome with emotion and could not speak as Dexter shook his head. "No, it is our mother's touch that is familiar to us," Dexter answered softly.

"There is a much larger dining room at the end of the hallway. It is the formal dining room and flanked by two parlors. That table seats fifty; that is where you will host your candlelight suppers," Lady Collins said, drawing them out of their reverie. "Tomorrow is a big day for you, Dexter. Then you will meet William Wilberforce; he will be your greatest ally."

"Enos has given me some of his recent papers. I will read them tonight," Dexter said, the dinner captain placing his napkin in his lap, indicating that dinner be served. "What do Brixton and I need to know about tomorrow?" he asked, turning to Declan.

Declan, Enos, and Lady Collins spent the remainder of the dinner preparing Dexter for the ceremony tomorrow. It was surprisingly easy, considering the formality that was the hallmark of English aristocracy tradition. After dinner, they retreated to the parlor for after-dinner aperitifs and dessert. Dexter had a private word with Declan as they were leaving the dining room.

"Well, if you will excuse me, I have some reading to do, and I would like to be fresh for tomorrow. Thank you all for a lovely dinner," Dexter said. His butler appeared at his arm. To a chorus of goodnights, Dexter departed.

"I'm afraid Sabine and I will be retiring as well. It has been an overwhelming day, to say the least," Brixton said. He looked toward the closed dining room door, his mother's gift still on his mind. John waited outside to escort them.

"All is ready as you requested, my Lord," John whispered conspiratorially.

"Lady Collins, I cannot thank you enough for all you have done for the Dunbarton family," Declan said. "I am so interested in hearing about your connection with Sabine. This family history is fascinating to me, isn't it to you, Enos?" He and Enos settled back, intent on keeping Lady Collins away from Dexter.

"Dear God, Brixton! Please get me out of this corset before I faint dead away," Sabine pleaded. The panic in her voice was real, so Brixton pushed her into the bedroom. John had closed the large doors behind them and was long gone.

"What do I do?" Brixton asked, looking at the puzzle of a dress in front of him.

Sabine turned her back to him, grabbing one of the posts of the bed for support. "Undo the lacings of the dress, get that off me first," Sabine said breathlessly. Brixton worked furiously, tearing at the lacings. "Now, unlace the corset, don't pull on the lacings, please," she begged.

Brixton untied the laces and started unraveling them from the hooks as fast as he could. "I forbid you from wearing this torture contraption ever again. Your French petticoats are fine," Brixton snarled.

"Tell that to my very English maid," Sabine gasped. As Brixton undid the final hook, Sabine took a deep breath and collapsed to her knees.

Brixton took her in his arms and said. "I'll do one better; I'll have John tell her," they both dissolved in laughter as Sabine caught her breath. After a few minutes, Brixton asked her if she was feeling better. She nodded yes, and he pulled her to her feet. "Then let's get you out of the rest of your clothes. I have a surprise for you," Brixton said, his eyes twinkling as he pulled at her remaining garments.

When they were both naked, he took her hand and led her up the back staircase that John had shown him. Quietly, he opened the door and stood back. The moon was high in the sky, shimmering behind a fog that seemed always to shroud London. The city lay below them, lights flickering all around.

Chapter 16 | London Town

"It's not our grotto, but it is the best I could do," Brixton said, taking her hand and leading her into the pool. The water was soothing, heated from pipes below it, feeding warm water into the shallow pool. He sat down in the water, Sabine's legs wrapped around his waist, both lost in their kiss.

"Hmm, Brixton," Sabine said, breaking their kiss. "There are two rather large men trying desperately not to look in our direction," she said, sinking, so the water covered her.

"Goddamnit, I forgot about them! Stay here; I'll be right back," Brixton said, grabbing a towel to cover himself as he walked toward the men.

Brixton spoke briefly to the men, who disappeared after handing Brixton something he placed behind a small bush before climbing back into the pool.

"Is Dexter in that much danger, Brix?" Sabine asked quietly.

"Declan is just overly cautious, Sabine. It is nothing to worry about," Brixton said.

"Is that why you hid a pistol behind that bush?" Sabine asked, turning her back to him and holding on to the side of the pool, looking out over the city.

"Sabine," Brixton said, splashing behind her to take her in his arms, but she did not move. He covered her arms with his and put his head next to hers. They looked at the view below. "I don't like London," Brixton said.

"Neither do I. Have you noticed there are no stars in the sky?" Sabine said, looking heavenward.

"I have; the glow from all the lamps below hides them," Brixton said.

"Standing on the beach on Mount Sion, the stars are so many, they kiss the sea's horizon," Sabine said softly.

Brixton's arms tightened around her. "I miss our beach, I miss our cave, and I miss our home, my love," he sighed.

Both lost in their thoughts of home, Sabine folded back into Brixton's arms as they floated in the water. "We don't belong here," Sabine said eventually.

"No, we don't," Brixton said, kissing her neck. She moved her head to give him access. Then she turned to face him and deepened their kiss. For the moment, London, Jamaica, all their worries were forgotten as they lost themselves in the pleasure of each other.

The next morning, John was waiting as Brixton stumbled into his room from Sabine's bedroom. "Did you enjoy your evening, my Lord?" John asked.

"I did," Brixton said, surprised to see John there. Like Dexter, he was not sure he would ever get used to the intensely personal level of service English servants provided. "Thank you?" he asked, baffled.

John suppressed a smile. "Your clothes are laid out for you. I was able to find what you requested, two in fact. You may wash…"

"Yes, I know I may wash over there, thank you, John," Brixton interrupted him. He walked over to the washstand and started shaving.

"Breakfast is in the upstairs parlor today. You and the Duke will be leaving within the hour," John said as he turned to depart.

"Ah, one more thing, actually two more things," Brixton said, stopping John's departure. "About my wife's corsets, please inform her dressing maid that she will not be wearing them, ever again. The French petticoats will suffice nicely," Brixton turned to him to see if he understood.

Without a word, John nodded. "And the other thing, my Lord?"

"Where is the upstairs parlor?" Brixton asked. Brixton finished dressing and looked at what he had asked John to secure for him the night before. He carefully loaded two small pistols, putting one in his shirt pocket and the other in his jacket pocket. He followed

Chapter 16 | London Town

John as he made his way to the breakfast parlor. Sabine was there, deep in conversation with Lady Collins. He went to her and kissed her. Declan and Enos were enjoying breakfast. Brixton made his way to Declan.

"Good morning," Brixton said, addressing both men. "How many men are we taking with us today?" he asked Declan, his voice lowered.

"Twelve, all on horseback, all armed, following the carriage. Four will escort us in and be by our side at all times," Declan answered.

"I will be to Dexter's right at all times," Brixton said.

"Agreed," Declan replied, looking sharply at Brixton.

Brixton looked back at him, "At all times, Dec." Brixton's tone broached no disagreement.

Sabine turned to look at Brixton; she recognized his tone. He smiled tightly at her.

"Brixton's devotion to Dexter is very touching," Lady Collins said quietly.

"Brixton has been protecting Dexter all his life. I don't expect that will ever change, nor would I want it to," Sabine responded, not taking her eyes off of Brixton.

Dexter walked into the room, and everyone turned to bow to him. Brixton walked to his brother. Dexter looked at him and smiled. "Are you ready, brother?"

"Always. And you, brother, are you ready?" Brixton asked, smiling mischievously at Dexter.

"Always. Let's go," Dexter said, waving to Sabine and Lady Collins as they departed, Brixton behind him to his right and Declan on his left, in step with Brixton.

Lady Collins watched them leave. Then turning to Sabine, she said, "Why don't we find the dress you will wear tomorrow night? I understand Brixton has said you are not to wear corsets, just your French petticoats." She put an arm around Sabine's waist, and they left, walking toward her dressing room. "I have a fondness for French petticoats myself," she said, smiling saucily at Sabine.

The Dunbarton carriage was beautiful, covered in deep maroon with gilded gold edges. The Dunbarton crest prominently displayed so no one glancing at it could miss who was traveling within its elegant confines. Dexter and Brixton sat across from Declan and Enos.

"This is your writ of summons. It has King George's seal on it. You will present it to the Lord Chancellor. The Reading Clerk of the House will then read the patent and the writ to the entire body. At that time, you will take the Oath of Allegiance and sign it," Enos instructed, handing Dexter a leather binding with the documents inside.

The House of Lords, simply referred to as the Lords, was the British Parliament's upper house. It was housed in an imposing room with tall stained-glass windows and ancient tapestries depicting the grand body's history and tradition whose members came from the King's peerage. The House of Lords was created to keep a check on the House of Commons. While they could not prevent the passage of bills, their power was strong enough to delay measures put forth by the House of Commons and force them to reconsider their decisions. But their primary function was to act in the King's best interest.

Dexter, Brixton, Declan, and Enos were met by Lord Denby, the Gentleman Usher of the Black Rod, and Lord Braemar, the Garter Principal King of Arms.

"Welcome Lord Dunbarton, 7th Duke of Ergill. It is a distinct pleasure to meet you, my Lord," Lord Denby said as he and Lord Braemar bowed to Dexter.

"We are ardent admirers of you, my Lord," Lord Braemar continued. "It is our honor to welcome you to this chamber."

Dexter looked at Enos, who turned to the two men. "Lord Denby, Lord Braemar," he said, bowing to each man so Dexter

Chapter 16 | London Town

would know who they were. "Lord Dunbarton is honored that two dear friends and supporters such as yourself will be presiding over this ceremony."

"Indeed, I am, my Lords. The honor of meeting you is all mine," Dexter said graciously, bowing to the men.

"Shall we begin?" Lord Denby asked. "My Lord Duke, you will follow Lord Braemar in the procession. He will present your papers to the Lord Chancellor." Lord Denby paused as Dexter handed Lord Braemar the leather document holder. "Your brother, Lord Brixton Dunbarton, will follow you, as your junior supporter. Then Declan McKenzie will fall in behind Brixton as your senior supporter. You will kneel before the Lord Chancellor as your writ of summons is presented to the entire chamber. Then all three of you will bow to the Lord Chancellor. After bowing to the Lord Chancellor, Lord Braemar and I will introduce you, along with your supporters, to the body as you follow the Lord Chancellor out of the chamber." Lord Denby finished.

"Then what?" Brixton asked.

"Then we celebrate," Lord Braemar said with great anticipation.

"Lord Dunbarton will be hosting the celebration in the dining room off the library," Declan whispered to Brixton.

"Make sure there is a lot of rum. I will need it," Brixton whispered back.

"Dexter, there will be men in that room who are not happy at your appointment," Enos said. Brixton and Declan moved toward Dexter. "But there are those that support you in that room as well, find comfort in them, lean on them to bolster you."

"How will I know the difference?" Dexter asked.

"They will be obvious to you, my Lord," Lord Denby said. "They will hang back, and they will refuse to shake your hand."

"But they will be quick to eat your food and drink your wine," Lord Braemar added.

"Lord Braemar and I will be the first to shake your hands after the Lord Chancellor. But first, we would like to hug you as a brother peer to the realm, with your permission," Lord Denby offered deep emotion in his voice.

Dexter nodded, not trusting himself to speak as the men enveloped him in a hug. They lined up without a word as two page boys opened the large doors in front of them. There was no turning back now. The ceremony proceeded as planned. Brixton knew who Dexter's detractors were just by looking at them. He recognized the tilt of the head, the thinning of the lips, and the narrowing of the eyes as he passed by. He made a mental note of their faces. As they left the chamber, the Lord Chancellor and the Lords Denby and Braemar led them to the House Library to wait as the Lords made their way to the dining room.

"Lord Dunbarton," the Lord Chancellor said, taking Dexter's hand. "I cannot tell you what an honor it was for me to welcome you to this esteemed body today. I have read your papers. You are a very impressive young man."

"Thank you, Lord Chancellor," Dexter said. He was distracted by the library. "There must be a thousand books in this room," he said under his breath.

"A lover of books, are you?" the Lord Chancellor asked. "This library boasts the most extensive collection of historical, legal, and philosophical manuscripts gathered anywhere in the world. Let me show you some of my favorites," he said as he led Dexter off.

Declan, Brixton and Lord Braemar huddled in a corner as Enos Knowles and Lord Denby headed off to the dining room. Lord Braemar was not much older than Declan and Brixton. He was a handsome man, but from his tanned face and weather-beaten hands, it was apparent he loved to spend time outdoors. His lands bordered Scotland, so he and Declan were friends and spent a lot of time in each other's company.

Chapter 16 | London Town

"Don't worry, the English stiff upper lip, along with our code of polite behavior, will not allow any member of this chamber to be overtly rude, but Lord Kavendish and his minions are here, in their numbers," Lord Braemar said.

"Probably best to walk a wide berth of them, Brix," Declan cautioned.

"I have no intention of leaving Dexter's side, but if anyone is impolite, I will consider it an insult," Brixton said tersely. The anxiety of worrying about his brother's safety was evident in the tautness of his face and his body's rigidity.

"Oh, I like this one! I can tell we are going to be fast friends," Lord Braemar said, smiling. "We will have to drink and make merry at William's home tomorrow night. Today is a day for vigilance."

The Lord Chancellor escorted Dexter from the library to the dining room where the welcome celebration awaited his arrival, Brixton and Declan, one step behind them. The factions had taken to their corners. Lord Kavendish was at one side of the room flanked by the Lords that shared his position. Brixton was happy to see that he did not command the majority. Liam and Declan had been successful in their campaign, and Dexter's welcome was genuine and heartfelt from most of the Lords in the room. After three hours of greetings, handshakes, and welcome toasts, the Dunbarton brothers had enough. Thankfully, the Lords had motions to address, and Dexter was not expected to take his place until the next session in a week. Emotionally drained and physically exhausted from constantly being on guard, Dexter, Brixton and Declan relaxed against the carriage's plush seats.

"Well, that went better than expected," Enos said.

"What did you expect?" Dexter asked.

"For us to be met at the door by Lord Kavendish and tossed out on our collective ears," Enos said, releasing a nervous breath.

"No," Declan said. "A warm wind is blowing a revolution through this land. The aristocracy realizes they have to give the common man a say, or they will be lost. The voice of change now belongs to that man."

"William Wilberforce," Dexter said.

Declan simply nodded his head.

"Well, I am certainly looking forward to meeting him," Brixton said.

They arrived at the house, Dexter's butler met him and escorted him to his room. Before he left, Dexter turned to the men with him. "Thank you for being at my side today. I will probably never be able to articulate the range of emotions I experienced today, but the security I felt in knowing how much you believe in me guided me. I would love it if we could have dinner together in the upstairs parlor. I have had enough of pomp and ceremony for one day; I need the intimacy of my island home tonight."

Brixton understood what Dexter meant. He had felt it, too; they were far away from everything they had ever known. "Consider it done," he said. "And Dex, if it needs saying, I am so proud of you."

Sabine's dressing room was in upheaval. Lady Collins did not see anything suitable in Sabine's wardrobe. She immediately sent for her dressmaker, who had arrived with carriages full of fabrics and accessories. Brixton couldn't enter the dressing room because the floor was littered with bolts of cloth and trimmings of every shape, size, and color.

"Sabine, are you in here?" he asked irritably.

Both Sabine and Lady Collins popped their heads out from behind the dressing wall, where Sabine was trying on a dress that would be repurposed for dinner tomorrow night.

"Brixton, you are back," she said, trying to wriggle out of her dress.

Chapter 16 | London Town

Lady Collins took one look at Brixton's haggard face and jumped into action. "Madam, I think you have all you need to finish this dress for tomorrow. When you come back with it, we will finalize whatever else Lady Dunbarton will need." Turning to Sabine. "Go to your husband; he looks like he needs your comfort. I will finish up here," she said, smiling gently at Sabine.

Sabine went to Brixton; he looked drained. She took his hand. "Come and tell me all about it," she said as they turned toward Brixton's rooms.

CHAPTER 17

William Wilberforce

"Why can't I just watch what Declan does and follow him? We have been at this for hours," Brixton complained to John. They were in his sitting room as John showed him which fork to use for each dinner course.

"My Lord, it is elementary," John said, not the least bit ruffled by Brixton's outburst. "The table will always be set for the number of courses served for dinner, start from the outside, and work your way toward the plate to know what cutlery to use for each course."

"Why didn't you just say that in the first place?" Brixton asked. "That seems easy enough."

"Now, about the wine glasses..." John started.

"Sweet Lord, deliver me!" Brixton exclaimed.

John gave up, trying not to let his irritation show on his face. "The same thing, work from the outside in. If you drop your napkin, do not bend to pick it up, your waiter will do that. Look to the host. When he starts eating, you begin."

"You couldn't have said that three hours ago?" Brixton asked angrily.

"I thought it best you learned from a visual display," John said, slightly hurt by Brixton's outbursts.

Brixton softened. "You do set an elegant table, John. Thank you for taking the time to help me," he said, sitting down. "Let's go over it one more time."

Sabine's day was not going any better. She and Brixton were roused from their bed in the early hours of the morning. John walked into Sabine's room, gingerly covered their nakedness with the bedsheet, then unceremoniously opened the curtains, allowing daylight to flood the room. He handed them their robes and told them it was time to get up. Lady Collins and the dressmaker were waiting for Sabine, and Brixton would spend the morning with him.

By the time Sabine met Brixton for lunch in his sitting room at the table John had set up, they had both had enough for the day.

"If one more person tells me what I have to do today," Sabine started as she sat down.

"Don't start. I am right there with you," Brixton said.

"Oh, stop acting like spoiled brats," Lady Collins chastised as she sat and placed her napkin on her lap. John appeared at her side with a plate of food. "This evening is not about you. It is about putting your best foot forward for Dexter. He needs your support, Brixton. He does not need to worry about whether you are using the correct knife to cut your filet mignon," she said, looking at Brixton. "Or whether or not you are dressed like the Lady you are," she said, turning to Sabine.

Both looked down at their plates and started eating without another word. They had not seen Dexter all day, but Brixton had described to Sabine the weight of the burden he felt yesterday. They both surmised that the pressure was much more taxing for Dexter.

"Take your afternoon nap, do what you need to, and take the edge off," Lady Collins instructed. "Just remember, you are here for Dexter."

Chapter 17 | William Wilberforce

That evening, as they waited for Dexter to appear, they gathered in the foyer. Sabine was breathtaking in a crushed silk dress of the faintest green; emeralds sparkled at her throat. Brixton was handsome in a coat of forest green, with dark britches and black boots, polished to a high shine.

"They do make a stunning couple, don' they?" Enos whispered to Lady Collins.

"They do. They are a formidable team as well. We need to find that for Dexter," Lady Collins replied, pulling on her gloves.

Dexter appeared, and they all bowed to him. He was in a coat of dark maroon, complimented with tan britches and black boots. The Lords Dunbarton did catch the eye. No one could take that away from them. Years of living on an island in the Caribbean and working the land had given them lean, muscular bodies that exuded strength. Living outdoors gave them a healthy glow with hair bleached by the Jamaican sun. They were a breath of fresh air in the fetid halls of English privilege.

William Wilberforce was a serious man, but with a gleam in his eye. He was charming and witty but understood his audience and spoke eloquently. His hair was graying on the top of his head and at the sides. Below that was a mane of thick, brown hair. He reminded Dexter of an aging lion he had once seen a drawing of in a book. He greeted the Dunbartons and escorted them into his home, where the festivities were in full swing.

"I am honored to welcome you to my home, Lord Dunbarton. Please allow me to introduce you and your family to my guests," he declared to a hushed crowd as he bowed low to Dexter and then to Brixton.

They were ushered into various rooms, separated by those who wished to greet them first and make themselves known. Two hours later, Declan found Sabine, Brixton, and Dexter huddled in a corner by the garden, trying to catch their breath and compose themselves. Lady Collins made her way to them.

"I don't know how I will keep all these names straight," Dexter said, running his hand through his hair. "I mean, I am honored by the welcome, but this is too much to take in during one evening."

"That is why you will host your own functions, at least once a week for the next few weeks," Declan advised. "Enos, Lady Collins, and I have set the guest lists, and we will prepare you for each event. For now, just concentrate on who you want to get to know."

Dexter stood straight up as if a puppeteer had pulled his strings. "I would like to get to know her," he said, pointing to a woman who had just walked into the garden. Her gown was as white as snow, with a red sash across the front ending in a bow at her waist. Her chestnut hair was long. It floated around her exquisite face, framing it.

"You have excellent taste, my Lord," Lady Collins said. "That is Lilliana De Castille, a Princess of Spain. She is an emissary for the Spanish court. Many believe her to be a spy. She certainly has the intelligence for espionage, but no one has ever caught her performing her undercover reconnaissance, such is her skill."

"She is quite possibly the most beautiful woman I have ever seen. Is she married?" Dexter asked.

"She is not, she has turned down many suitors, and it has fallen to King George to find her a match, but she is very strong-willed and has refused everyone he has put in front of her," Lady Collins answered.

"She can do that? She has the power to defy a King?" Sabine asked.

"It would appear that she does since she is not married," Lady Collins said dryly. "But she is not in the good graces of His Majesty. It is best if I introduce her to Sabine, she can invite the princess over for tea, and we will arrange a discreet introduction."

Dexter nodded his agreement, not taking his eyes off of Lilliana. Lady Collins grabbed Sabine's arm and pointed her in the direction of the Princess.

"Lord Dunbarton! There you are," William Wilberforce said, coming to Dexter's side. "I was wondering if you would join us in the parlor. A few of us would like to discuss the papers you submitted to Parliament. They are most intriguing," he said, pulling on Dexter's arm and leading him away, Brixton and Declan following close behind. Dexter pulled his gaze away from Lilliana and followed Mr. Wilberforce.

"The sugar estate owners in the Caribbean are invested in maintaining the institution of slavery. Why Lord Kavindish's youngest brother has a large plantation on the island of Antigua, he is so wealthy; he subsidizes Lord Kavindish's dwindling estate outside of London," Mr. Wilberforce said as they sat in a parlor with ten other men Dexter had met at the beginning of the evening.

"Many absentee estate owners in England, in fact, in every country that has colonies, feel that it is free labor that drives profits, but in essence, that is not true," Dexter began. "The most profitable estate in Jamaica is Friendship Estate; it is now the largest estate on the island because of the four estates that now encompass it. Slaves have been free there for over ten years, a woman runs it, and it has grown exponentially every year," Dexter stood to face his audience.

"Years ago, the Lords of England, the sole landowners, realized that their people were more productive and invested if they had a stake in the land. In time, your serfs worked to become freemen through their own enterprise and became what you are today, commoners," he said, pointing to William Wilberforce. "Friendship Estate is built on the premise that free men work together for the good of all. Each has a place on the estate, a purpose, and that purpose gives them the respect, the self-esteem we all need to achieve our greatest desire, the freedom to be the best that we can be," Dexter stopped speaking as heads nodded in agreement all around him.

"If these Lords are losing their lands to debt collectors and taxes, it is because they do not understand how to make their lands profitable. Generations of privilege have stripped from them the drive to succeed, the need to care for others as they care for themselves. It has nothing to do with the institution of slavery but all to do with their own inadequacies." Dexter concluded.

"That is not a message they will receive willingly," Lord Braemar said from the back of the room.

"But it is a message that will come crashing through their fortified doors and steal their precious way of life, if not heeded," said Brixton forcefully.

"Time stands still for no man, nor will the force of progress that is in the very nature of a man, no matter his color or creed," added Dexter.

"By God, you are just what we have been praying for, my Duke," Lord Denby said as the room erupted in applause. "Yours will be the voice that tears down the barriers to freedom, and they will see you coming, sir. They cannot help but see you coming."

"Your presentation to the joint session of the House of Lords and the Parliament must be the hammer that brings down the blocks of slavery once and for all," William Wilberforce said quietly to Dexter.

"Then I pray I find the words," Dexter said, looking nervously at Brixton. "It is time we left, Brix." It was close to one in the morning.

As Brixton searched for Sabine and Lady Collins, Dexter tried to move toward the front door, Declan and Enos in tow.

"You will forgive me, Mr. Wilberforce," Dexter said, turning to his host. "I am a mere farmer. I'm afraid I am not used to keeping such late hours into the night."

"Of course, I do understand what it is to be a working man," William laughed with Dexter.

"I would appreciate your friendship, sir, and to that end, I would invite you and your family to dine with us in two nights hence. I would like to reciprocate not only your generosity of spirit but also your kindness to my family," Dexter said, taking the man's hand with feeling.

"It would be my honor, my Lord," William said, squeezing Dexter's hand in a firm handshake.

Sabine moved toward the door, deep in conversation with Lilliana De Castille. Dexter could not take his eyes off her.

"It would seem we are all departing now," she said, her voice beautifully accented with her Spanish tongue.

"Parecería así, sí," Dexter answered.

Lilliana's eyes flew open in surprise, and her mouth spread slowly into a smile. Dexter watched her every move.

"Lady Dunbarton, it would be my pleasure to attend you tomorrow for tea," she said, never taking her eyes from Dexter's face. She smiled again and walked out, as her carriage came forward to collect her.

"Well, it seems it has been a successful evening for all," Lady Collins said as she settled into the Dunbarton carriage. "William Wilberforce is quite taken with you, young man," she said, pointing her fan at Dexter. "I will make sure you give him a dinner he will never forget," she added, closing her eyes and resting her head against the fabric.

Brixton and Dexter looked at each other. Then at Declan, who raised his hands unknowingly. They would all love to have her powers of knowing what was going to occur before she was advised of it.

As Sabine settled into his arms that night, Brixton told her of Dexter's meeting with the men in the parlor. Then she told him about her encounter with Princess Lilliana.

"She is nobody's fool. She didn't accept my invitation until after her encounter with Dexter. If she has an agenda, she hides it well," Sabine said.

"Don't get caught up in the Palace intrigue, my love. If you like her as a friend, treat her as such. I am sure it is hard to find a true friend among the vipers at King George's court," Brixton said, kissing her.

"I will say, you Dunbarton men do have a type," Sabine said.

"We do?" Brixton asked, kissing her breast. "Do tell," he encouraged.

"You like a woman who is fierce, yet compassionate—one who loves unconditionally while being uncompromising. One who is a true partner, but who feels free to challenge," she said. As Brixton moved down her body with his kisses, it was getting harder to concentrate on what she was saying. "A woman who is strong where you are weak, but weak where you are strong," she breathed, arching her back to receive him, as Brixton positioned himself above her.

Brixton started to move inside her, "She must also be beautiful, inside and out. And very, very passionate!" he said throatily, as they both gave in to their hunger for each other.

It was Lady Collins who came to their room to wake them in the late morning. She took a moment to appreciate Brixton's naked body. He really was a fine specimen of a man, and she wondered what it would be like to have him make love to her. She dismissed the thought and moved toward the curtains. He was devoted to Sabine as she was to him, *but he would make for a rather amusing challenge*, she thought as she pulled open the curtains and stood by the bed.

"John, I would so appreciate it if you did not wake us up so harshly in the morning," Brixton said, stretching.

"I will be sure to advise John of your wishes," Lady Collins said.

Brixton sat up straightaway, reaching for the bedsheet to cover himself. Sabine sat up, rubbing her eyes. They both gaped at Lady Collins, surprised to see her in their bedchamber.

"Lady Collins?" Sabine asked as Brixton tried to cover her with the bedsheet.

"You have a lot to do today, my Lady," Lady Collins said, looking around for Sabine's robe. "It is not every day a princess comes for tea, and there are specific protocols that must be adhered to." She handed Sabine her robe. She did not look for Brixton's.

Sabine threw the robe around her and handed Brixton his robe. He turned his back to Lady Collins and put it on, tying it firmly in front of him.

"And this could not wait until breakfast?" Brixton muttered under his breath.

Lady Collins ignored him. "You will meet her at the bottom of the stairs as her carriage arrives. Then you will escort her to the parlor for tea," Lady Collins was saying to Sabine. "Now, this tea is obviously an excuse for her to meet Dexter. Brixton, that is where you come in."

Brixton turned around to face her. It was apparent the unbearable woman was not leaving the room. He looked at her, his head to one side, his face showing that her antics did not amuse him. Again, she ignored him.

"You and Dexter will casually walk by the parlor. Sabine will notice and invite you in. Then she will introduce you both to the Princess. Sabine, make sure you introduce your husband first," Lady Collins said.

"Why?" Sabine asked. "Dexter is always introduced before Brixton."

"Because she is an unwed Princess. Dexter is an unmarried Duke. He is not allowed to be alone with her at any time. You and Brixton are there to chaperone them," Lady Collins said, beginning to lose her patience.

"Then how do they get to know each other?" Brixton asked through his teeth.

Lady Collins turned to Brixton, "Where did Dexter learn to speak Spanish fluently?" she asked. "I trust you do not know how to speak Spanish. You barely speak English."

Brixton shook his head, conceding defeat. He would not win against this woman, he decided. "Mistress Anne, Sabine's mother, tried valiantly to teach Dexter and me French. Dexter took to foreign languages like a duck to water. I was bored half to tears, but I did learn enough to impress the ladies," Sabine gave him a sharp look, but he continued. "Mistress Anne found a Spaniard who was living in Spanish Town, no doubt through Enos. She had him teach Dexter Spanish."

"Interesting," Lady Collins said. "Tell Dexter to speak to her only in Spanish. I will make sure her ladies in waiting are kept busy. They want privacy to get to know each other? Then they shall have it, speaking her native tongue."

Brixton nodded. It wasn't a bad plan. "Well, if you will excuse me, I think that is my cue to leave." He walked over to Sabine, kissed her, then left in search of John.

"Make sure you pass by precisely at 4:30 pm, Brixton." Lady Collins said after him. He waved to indicate he had heard her. "That will give you enough time to welcome her and make her feel comfortable and for me to get rid of her ladies in waiting," she said to Sabine.

Taking Sabine's hand, she led her into the dressing room. John was waiting for Brixton in his chambers. "I am going to presume you could not stop her?" Brixton asked.

"Your presumption is correct," John said dryly.

"She is the most insufferable woman," Brixton started.

"That is one way of looking at her," John said as he poured Brixton's coffee. Brixton looked at him. "Lady Collins is a very well connected lady. It is because of her efforts and her belief in your brother that England has a black man as the 7th Duke of Ergill."

"Tell me," Brixton said, sitting forward.

"I was born a servant. I never expected to be anything more than a servant. But, when Lady Collins hired me, hired all of us, she told us that we would be part of a greater effort to change the hearts and minds of Lords and Commoners alike. She made me believe I had a role to play in changing the world, but when I met you and your brother," John stopped as he tried to control his emotions. "When I saw the measure of the men you both are, I realized I want to be a *part* of the new world you are creating."

"You are John," Brixton assured him. "You are invaluable to me. I may not always show it, but I value your guidance, and I respect your expertise."

John turned away to collect himself. He never dreamed he would hear those words from a Lord. Turning back to Brixton, he said, "That is not to say she won't have a go at you, whether for her own amusement or to teach you a lesson. She is not one to be trifled with, my Lord," he cautioned.

"I am beginning to understand that. Now, what do I need to know about attending an English tea party?" Brixton asked.

Sabine and Lady Collins met Princess Lilliana as her carriage came to a stop at the foot of the stairs. Four ladies in waiting attended her. Lady Collins knew their names and titles, greeting each by name. As Lady Collins escorted them in, Sabine and Lilliana followed behind. They dutifully listened as Lady Collins told them about the Dunbarton home's history and paused at paintings or trinkets she wanted them to make a note of. Sabine understood that this was all part of the process of getting to know the Dunbarton family. Her ladies in waiting would assess the family and advise the Princess if it was a friendship worth pursuing. However, Sabine suspected that the Princess would draw her own conclusions and make her own decision.

At precisely 4:20 pm, Lady Collins invited the ladies in waiting out to take a tour of the gardens. A tea service was set up out there, and Lady Collins assured Sabine that Dexter would have a full uninterrupted hour with Lilliana. At 4:30 pm, Brixton and Dexter walked by the parlor door, pretending to be deep in conversation.

"My Lord Husband, please come in and meet my new friend," Sabine said a little too loudly. She looked at Lilliana, embarrassment coloring her cheeks.

"My Lady Wife, how delightful to see you," Brixton said stiffly. He moved to kiss her cheek, but she pushed her hand in his face, reminding him that he was to kiss it. Dexter watched the awkward pantomime with amusement.

"Princess, may I present my husband, Lord Brixton Dunbarton," Sabine said as Brixton bowed to the Princess. "And my brother-in-law, Lord Dexter Dunbarton, the 7th Duke of Ergill." Dexter bowed low and took Lilliana's hand to kiss it. A very bold move. Brixton and Sabine exchanged nervous glances.

"It is an honor to meet you, Princess," Dexter said in Spanish.

"As it is you, my Lord," Lilliana answered in Spanish.

As Sabine led Brixton over to the tea service to be out of earshot, he asked. "So, how is it going?"

"How the hell do I know? You just got here, remember?" Sabine whispered furiously.

"All this formality, it is more than I can handle," Brixton said cantankerously. They turned to see the Princess invite Dexter to sit next to her on the settee. Sabine and Brixton sat across from each other on two chairs positioned away from the couple.

"I am delighted to see you again," Dexter said in Spanish. He was in awe of her beauty, but it was her eyes that drew his attention. They were emerald green and flashed with intelligence.

"That is a very audacious statement, my Lord. We have only just met," Lilliana said, putting the teacup to her lips.

"I'm not one for pretenses, Princess," Dexter said

"So, I have heard," Lilliana said, looking at him.

Dexter sat back and looked at her. A smile formed on his lips, and she watched as it broadened across his face. Her breath caught in her throat. "For you, I am an open book, ask me anything you like," he offered.

"I despise slavery. It is a scourge on the world and prevents humanity from moving forward. Would you allow me to read the papers you have written on the subject?" Lilliana asked.

"If it pleases you, I will recite them to you word for word. Will you stay for supper tonight so we may discuss your thoughts on humanity's scourge?" Dexter asked. "I value your thoughts on the matter." Then it was he who watched the small smile that started on her lips and spread across her face.

"I would like that very much," Lilliana responded.

Lilliana stayed for supper that night and for most nights afterward. As Lilliana and Dexter spent more time together, fewer ladies in waiting attended the visits until it was left to Sabine and Brixton to act as chaperones. They realized that when the two started speaking Spanish, they wanted to be alone.

Dexter came to rely on Lilliana's knowledge of the members of King George's court and sought her advice on how to press his agenda with them. Lilliana became a fixture at his side during the many dinners and festivities they both hosted and attended in the time leading up to Dexter's presentation. Dexter's self-assurance bloomed under Lilliana's gentle guidance. Her belief in him and her unwavering support in his destiny buoyed his confidence in himself.

A few days before his presentation, the Dunbartons hosted a garden party. The weather was still warm, so Lilliana advised Dexter to host a less formal event giving them a chance to meet with some parliamentarians who were still firmly in favor of slavery, hoping to change their minds. Towards the end of the evening, Lady Collins, Lilliana, and Sabine sat on a garden bench. Lady Collins could see Brixton and Dexter making their way toward them. As they came within earshot, she turned to Sabine, whose back was to the advancing men.

"Sabine, you have only been with your husband. My darling, that simply will not do! You must have an affair," she said, looking around for a potential candidate. "How about Lord Braemar? I can tell you from experience he is a wonderful lover." Lady Collins watched Brixton and Dexter, who had halted their advance, shocked at her words. Brixton crossed his arms in front of him.

Sabine turned to Lady Collins. "My Lady, would he keep my father alive so I could have one more dinner with him? Would Lord Braemar run across a moonlit beach to tell me of his love after I cut him with a knife, then make love to me under an enchanted waterfall? Would he hold my hair as I vomited from seasickness, all the while telling me I am the most beautiful woman in the world? Would he make my blood boil just from looking at me and smiling? I have had all of that and more, my dear friend, so I know no man will ever make me feel the way Brixton Dunbarton does."

Brixton had resumed walking as soon as Sabine started to speak, a smug smile on his face. He snuck up behind Sabine, startling Lilliana, as he whispered in Sabine's ear. "Time for me to take you to France, wifey."

Sabine did not turn around, but continued to look at Lady Collins. "The sound of his voice in my ear still sends a thrill through my spine," she said as she turned to kiss Brixton. He picked her up, his mouth firmly fixed on hers, and headed inside.

Dexter sat down next to Lilliana and took her hand. He studied Lady Collins. "Did that go as you had planned?" he asked, irritated by how she had tried to humiliate his brother.

"It did," she said, turning to Dexter and Lilliana. "What Sabine and Brixton have is what I want for you, Dexter. You will need that intensity of love and commitment if you are to survive your calling. If Lilliana is the one to give it to you, then you need to decide soon. The King is losing patience with you, Lilliana. If Dexter is who you want, time is no longer on your side." Lady Collins walked off, leaving them alone.

"Would you come with me?" Dexter asked Lilliana. "I want to show you something." As she nodded, he helped her to her feet, still holding her hand. They took the back stairs to the roof, Dexter leading the way to the secret garden and pool.

Lilliana looked around; the little garden was delightful, and the view of the city below intoxicating. She smiled at Dexter as she dashed around, going from one discovery to another.

"If you would like to remove your clothes and go swimming, I will look the other way," Dexter offered, turning his back to her.

Lilliana went to him, turning him around to face her. "Since we met, we have been together every day, for most of each day. You have never tried to kiss me, never gone beyond holding my hand, yet I know you have grown to love me," she said, her hand moving to caress his face.

"I would never do anything you do not wish me to," Dexter said, covering her hand with his.

"I know, but you have never asked me what I want," she said softly.

"Lilliana, you are one of the most extraordinary women I have ever met. Your advice, your wisdom, I have come to count on it.

I do love you. Maybe I have from the moment I saw you! I know I have never wanted another woman the way I want you. But, if you feel the same way, you will have to tell me. I could not survive your rejection," Dexter said, lowering his eyes.

Lilliana took Dexter's head in her hands, raising it so he would meet her eyes. Then she kissed him. It was like butterflies' wings fluttering against his lips. When she pulled back, she smiled at him. "This is the first time I have ever kissed a man."

"Would you like me to show you how?" Dexter asked, his voice rough with emotion.

She answered him by moving her lips to his. Dexter kissed her with all the tenderness and love he felt in his heart. She moved into his arms, and he deepened the kiss.

It was Dexter who pulled away first. "What do you want, Lilliana?"

"I want you, Dexter! With everything I am, I love you," she answered immediately.

Dexter had never been with a woman as innocent as Lilliana nor with one who had so much to lose. There was no guarantee the King would allow their marriage, and the weight of that realization gave him pause. He wanted her to feel the depth of the desire he felt for her, but he could not taint her reputation. "I want to show you love. I want you to feel passion," Dexter said, looking into her eyes for her reaction. "Will you trust me to give you that gift tonight?" Dexter asked.

Lilliana smiled at Dexter and nodded. Her faith in him absolute.

Slowly he undressed her, turning her back to him as he disrobed. He lifted her into his arms and waded into the pool. He kissed her as his hands explored her body. When she was panting and arching toward him, he moved his hands between her legs. Dexter's watched with hooded eyes as the pleasure of their intimacy played across her face. Her eyes wide as the ecstasy of it moved her to tears. Dexter held her gently as they floated in the water, enjoying the shared moment of wonder.

That was how Brixton and Sabine found them. After enjoying their own lovemaking, they had come to the roof for a swim.

"Now I know we have to go back to Jamaica. Our beach is never this crowded," Brixton said, amused.

Dexter smiled at Brixton as Lilliana shrunk into Dexter's arms, this familiarity new to her.

"I'm glad to see you have found each other. I was wondering how much longer you would both be able to hold out," Sabine said with a laugh.

Brixton and Sabine sat on the nearby bench. "I guess you will need these," Brixton said, putting the towels they had brought on the edge of the pool, hiding Lilliana from view as he looked away.

Neither Dexter nor Lilliana made a move to leave the warmth of the water.

"We will have to make do with our bed tonight," Brixton said, standing up and reaching for Sabine's hand, but Dexter's words stopped him.

"What can I say to make them understand?" Dexter asked, his greatest fear finding a voice. Lilliana put her arms around him and lay her head on his shoulder. She understood what he was asking.

"You should tell them the story you told me," Brixton said, sitting back down.

"What story?" Dexter asked.

Brixton looked down; this memory was a painful one. "The story you told me when we were children. I was angry with Nana and called her a darkie. You took me aside and told me a story. In that story, you taught me the lesson that has guided my life."

"You were only a small boy. You remember that?" Dexter asked incredulously.

"As were you, when you told it to me. But it changed my perspective, making me reject everything my father tried to teach me. Tell that story Dexter, and you will change their minds," Brixton advised his brother earnestly.

Dexter thought about what Brixton said as he absently brushed his lips across Lilliana's forehead. Looking at her, he smiled. "I would very much like to marry you if you will have me."

"Voy a," Lilliana answered, giggling happily.

"Then I am sure Lady Collins is already making plans," Sabine said.

"Lady Collins? How would she know? We have only just decided," Lilliana asked, surprised.

"Don't ask me how, but the Lady knows all and long before we do," Brixton said wryly.

"I would like to marry you before my presentation to Parliament. It will give me strength, knowing that you are mine. Do you mind marrying so quickly?" Dexter asked Lilliana.

"I would marry you tonight if only to experience such pleasure again," Lilliana whispered into Dexter's ear, sending a thrill through him. "But we need the king's permission," Lilliana said aloud.

"Leave it to me, brother. You made it possible for me to marry the woman I love; I will do the same for you," Brixton promised as he stood up.

"Will you be back from France in time, Brixton?" Lilliana asked.

"Back from France? I'm not going to France," Brixton replied.

"I heard you tell Sabine you were taking her to France," Lilliana said, puzzled.

Brixton started to laugh as Sabine smiled and took his hand, ready to leave them. "I will leave it to Dexter to explain that turn of phrase to you, my dear."

As they started down the steps, Brixton looked back; Dexter had lifted Lilliana onto the side of the pool.

The next morning, Brixton met John in his rooms, much to the man's surprise. The first thing Brixton did was send John to advise Dexter's butler to leave breakfast in Dexter's sitting room and not go into the bedroom under any circumstance.

"No one is to go into that bedroom," Brixton commanded. He knew his brother would never compromise Lilliana's reputation, but if they slept in each other's arms, he would not allow anyone to find out about their night together. "Then collect Lady Collins and come back here, please," he asked as Sabine walked in. "It seems we have a wedding to plan."

By noon a plan had taken shape. Lady Collins left, on her way to King George's court. Brixton and John sat down to make a guest list. It would be a small intimate wedding with a celebration dinner to follow.

"Sabine, it is probably best if you go and collect our guest. John advises me her ladies in waiting are beginning to rouse," Brixton whispered.

"Here, my Lady," John said, handing her a dress. "Just in case a fresh change of clothes is warranted," he handed her the dress, not looking at her. Brixton and Sabine exchanged a surprised look.

Sabine snuck through the rooms that would soon be Lilliana's and found Lilliana asleep in Dexter's arms.

"Lilly, Lilly," she said, shaking her. "You have to leave now, Princessa." Lilliana and Dexter awoke with a start then settled back into each other's arms, smiling.

"Lilly?" Dexter asked.

"A nickname Sabine gave me," she answered.

"I like it," he said, pulling her close.

"Then it is yours, but not now!" Sabine said, pulling␃Lilliana away from him and out of bed. "Put this dress on. The story is that you slept in my room last night because Brixton and I argued. Brixton will go to his grave swearing he spent the night here with you, Dex," Sabine said, exasperated. "Stop staring at her like a lovesick puppy and get up. Your breakfast is outside, and Brixton will meet you in your study.

Dexter sighed and jumped out of bed. Lilliana stopped as she turned to admire his body. "Oh, for God's sake!" Sabine exclaimed, pulling at Lilliana's arm. "I am well aware of how intoxicating a Dunbarton man is, but you will have plenty of time to enjoy him once you are married. Trust me; they don't tire easily," she said, pulling Lilliana behind her.

It took Dexter a while to get control of himself. As promised, he had not deflowered her, but when she had insisted on touching him, he was undone. The memory of it had him in the toilet closet for nearly twenty minutes. When he finally met Brixton in his study, Brixton recognized the problem.

Smiling broadly, he asked. "Had a hard night, did you?" Not the least bit sympathetic.

Dexter said nothing in response. John was with Brixton. "Where are we with the planning?" Dexter asked brusquely.

John answered him. "Lady Collins has gone to the Palace. King George has to give his permission for the marriage to take place. Since he has not yet met you, that might present a complication."

At Dexter's sudden look of concern, John continued hurriedly. "But I have all the faith in the world in Lady Collins. Many at court have met you, my Duke; they like you. His Majesty can call on any number of people for a character reference."

"Let's assume King George gives his permission," Brixton said, trying to move John along.

"Then he will set the wedding date and time," Dexter groaned as Brixton gave John a stern look. "But, Lord Dunbarton can say they want an intimate setting, and you would then get married in a small chapel at the Palace. The King will attend, and then, you're married, my Lord," John completed his dissertation of the required protocol.

"I don't want her to leave this house, Brix," Dexter said, starting to pace. "I'm afraid they may not let her come back."

"We can always say she is staying in Sabine's room because we are still at odds," Brixton offered.

At John's loud snort, they both turned to him. He looked back at both men, embarrassed by his outburst. "No one is going to believe *you* are sleeping away from your wife, my Lord."

"There will be no need for that!" Lady Collins said, sweeping into the room. "The King will approve the marriage as long as the Princessa tells him she wants to marry you. Dexter, she does want to marry you?" the Lady asked, looking directly at Dexter.

"After what I witnessed last night, she definitely wants to marry him," Brixton said. Dexter turned, giving him a stern look.

"I will forget I heard that," Lady Collins said through gritted teeth. "As far as the King is concerned, you are doing him a favor by marrying her, so he will agree and want it done immediately." Lady Collins said.

"Done!" Dexter said. "When do we meet with him?"

"This evening, we are all going to Court for an audience with the King. Pray, he is in a good mood, and it all goes well."

Telling the Princess's ladies in waiting did not go as smoothly. Dexter and Brixton could hear the exclamations and cries from the study. Cautiously they stepped into the hallway. Lilliana and her ladies had been given four rooms to share. All the rooms in the Manor opened out onto the same grand hallway. It was there that Lilliana was holding court, facing her ladies in waiting. She looked furious. Dexter was about to go to her side, but Brixton stopped him. She spoke in Spanish, so Dexter translated.

"I am a Princess of Castille, an emissary of Spain!" she said. Her voice authoritative, but she was not shouting. "My ladies in waiting do not command me. I command them! Each of you has come to me, pushing your choice of a husband on me. Do you think I do not know that they bribe you to do that? Do you think I do not know your loyalty is for sale? Well, my loyalty is not for sale! My love is not for sale! I will marry the man I choose, and no man, woman, or King will tell me otherwise," she turned toward Dexter's rooms and marched toward them.

Brixton and Dexter stood to the side, arms crossed in front of them, watching the firestorm brewing. "Isn't she magnificent?" Dexter asked.

"Dexter, you had better get your bride under control. If she greets the King with that attitude," Lady Collins cautioned.

Dexter turned to her. "Do you think I can control that? I would sooner try to turn the tides with my bare hands," he said.

Lady Collins came right up to Dexter, pointing a finger in his face. "Do whatever you must to put that temper of hers in check, or you can both forget about this marriage," Lady Collins warned.

Lilliana was approaching Dexter's door. She turned to look at him, and he rushed forward to open the door. She stepped inside as he followed, closing the door behind them.

Lady Collins took charge. She packed up Lilliana's ladies in waiting, and she and John shipped them off to the Palace. As Dexter did his best to calm Lilliana down, his butler prepared the rooms next to his for the new bride, moving her things from the guest room to her new chambers. Sabine sent her maids to attend Lilliana. When Brixton offered to help Sabine dress, Lady Collins instructed one of the maids to stay in Sabine's employ for the time being. *The concept of time means nothing to these Colonials,* she thought to herself.

When the rooms were ready, Sabine and Brixton knocked on Dexter's bedroom door. Dexter opened the door to them as Brixton informed him of the arrangements and told him the rooms were ready for Lilliana. It would soon be time for them to go to court. Sabine went to Lilliana's side. She was looking out the window.

"How is she?" Brixton asked.

"She goes from being resigned to being outraged. She chafes under the restraints of being a Princess. Maybe I should have waited," Dexter said.

"Waited for what, my love?" Lilliana said, turning to face him.

"Waited to court you according to the protocol, waited to let your guardians get to know me better, pandered to your ladies in waiting—anything to make this easier for you. I would never want to cause you pain, Lilly," Dexter said as she walked into his arms.

"Dexter, you and I were born to destiny. There is very little we control in our lives, yet much is expected of us. Is it wrong to find comfort and strength in each other so that we may accomplish what providence has laid out for us?" Lilliana asked.

"No, it is not wrong. I will do my best to explain that to the King," Dexter said.

"It is not for you to explain, mi amor. I am a Princess; I am the only one who can sway a King. I am not a damsel in distress, Dexter. You will never have to slay a dragon for me. I wield my own sword," Lilliana said forcefully.

"I have never had to fight a battle on my own; I have always had my brother, my mother, my Nana, and countless other people. It pains me to hear you feel you are alone in your battles. While I know you are capable of winning your wars, as my wife, you will no longer have to face an enemy alone. My resources are yours to command as you do my heart." Gently, Dexter placed his forehead against hers. Neither saying a word, but each drawing strength from the other. Brixton and Sabine stepped out of the room, giving them their privacy.

Dexter refused the maid's help. He and Lilliana helped each other to dress. She left her hair down as he liked it. Together they met Brixton, Sabine, Enos, Declan, and Lady Collins downstairs in the foyer. As they approached, Lady Collins noted that it was the 7th Duke of Ergill and the Princess of Castile whom she curtsied to. Dexter and Lilliana were in full control of their emotions and knew what they had to accomplish at court.

They were led into a small antechamber deep in the heart of the palace. Dexter had yet to be presented to the court of King George. The King could only invite him, and to date, no such invitation had been forthcoming. Lady Collins accompanied Lilliana as she met with the King. Dexter paced as they waited. After countless minutes, Brixton started to walk with him. Enos, Sabine, and Declan sat, watching them.

Lady Collins emerged first, her face betraying nothing. But when Dexter saw Lilliana's face, he ran to her, taking her in his arms, swinging her around. Her laughter released the tension in the room.

"We can get married tonight, right now, if you wish. The King will attend but only on the parapet. You have yet to meet him officially," Lilliana was saying.

"I didn't hear anything past we can get married tonight," Dexter said, kissing her.

"Sabine, would you act as my maid of honor?" Lilliana asked. Sabine nodded yes, grabbing Brixton's arm. "Mr. Knowles, I would be grateful if you would walk me down the aisle. I know how much you mean to Dexter, and I think he would appreciate your being a part of our wedding."

"It would be my privilege, Princessa," he said, bowing to her.

"Lady Collins," Lilliana said, turning to her. "You acted as a mother who loved her child in there, and I will forever be thankful to you for your words. Would you stand in for my mother?" Lilliana asked.

With tears in her eyes, Lady Collins bowed to Lilliana.

"Deja vu," muttered Declan. "Lead the way, Lady Collins," Declan said.

It was a small chapel at the very end of the palace keep. The King's private chapel, they later learned. A tiny prie-dieu for two stood below the altar. They turned and bowed to the king as he entered the upper chamber, hidden in the shadows. The service took no more than ten minutes. Dexter kissed his bride, and they turned to bow as the King left. They had been inside the palace walls for less than an hour, but their lives had changed forever.

Declan, knowing the Dunbarton brothers as he did, had the foresight to bring two carriages. Dexter and Lilliana were dispatched in one; the other followed with everyone else. The second carriage took the long way back, and by the time they returned to the Manor, Dexter and Lilliana had retired for the evening.

"Did you tell him that the celebration dinner is tomorrow night?" Declan asked Brixton.

"I did, but who knows if he heard me. I will have John leave a note with their breakfast," Brixton said.

Dexter and Lilliana were half an hour late for dinner the following night. All the guests had arrived, and Sabine was practically sitting on Lady Collins to stop her from storming their rooms. Brixton had warned anyone that if they went near the bedroom, he would shoot them. William Wilberforce had everyone's attention. He remembered what it was like to be a newlywed and was only too happy to distract the small gathering when Declan pressed him into action.

John came to tell Brixton that the happy couple was outside. He and Sabine casually left the room. They walked out to find Lilliana trying to fix Dexter's coat as he tried to adjust her dress and smooth her hair.

"Sweet Mother!" Brixton said under his breath. "Come here, Dexter, let me help you."

Sabine went to help Lilliana. "Did you enjoy your wedding night?" Sabine asked as she straightened her dress.

"The only bad thing is that I was pulled away from it," Lilliana said loud enough for Brixton and Dexter to hear. Brixton smiled at Dexter. "You were right, Sabine; Dunbarton men do not tire easily," Lilliana said breathlessly, as Dexter smiled back at Brixton.

Brixton took Sabine's hand and walked ahead of Dexter and Lilliana. "Dear guests, it is my pleasure to introduce to you the 7th Duke of Ergill and his wife, Princess Lilliana, formally of Castille, now of the house of Dunbarton," Brixton announced formally.

After dinner, the entire party met back in the parlor for after-dinner drinks. It was clear that Dexter and Lilliana were ready to resume their wedding celebration on their own. William Wilberforce announced his departure, indicating it was time for the others to leave. Dexter thanked him.

"Do you know what you will say during your presentation to the joint session of Parliament and the House of Lords, the day after tomorrow?" William asked.

Dexter looked around the room. He looked at Enos, talking to Lady Collins, Declan working the room on his behalf, a worthy advocate. Then he looked at Brixton and Sabine, gracious and kind to everyone who spoke to them, but never more than an arm's length away from each other. Then he looked at his wife; she turned as if sensing his eyes. Smiling at him, she walked over to take his arm.

Turning to William, he said. "Yes, sir, I know exactly what I am going to say."

CHAPTER 18

The House of Lords

On the day of Dexter's presentation, the Lords Dunbarton and their wives met for breakfast. Just as dawn was breaking over the horizon, the foursome sat in their secret garden, sipping coffee and watching the sunrise.

"Are you ready?" Brixton asked Dexter, who was sitting next to him, Lilliana on his lap.

"He is ready," Lilliana said confidently, kissing his cheek. Dexter smiled at her before replying.

"You will be by my side?" Dexter asked.

"Always," Brixton promised.

"Then, I am ready," Dexter said, smiling at them.

The carriage arrived at the Parliament building. Westminster Hall was one of the oldest buildings within the Palace of Westminster. It had played a central role in Britain's governance for over nine hundred years. The building was designed to exude power and majesty. Its opulence and grandeur intimidated anyone who walked through the doors. Sabine and Lilliana, being women, were not allowed on the Parliamentary floor. They would be able to watch the proceedings from the royal balcony overlooking the large room where the country's government decided Britain's fate along with her vast array of colonies. Lilliana led Sabine to two seats in the middle of the box. Dexter would be able to raise his eyes and see her sitting in front of him.

They watched as the procession of Lords and Parliamentarians took their seats. Every seat was full; guests crowded the hallways and back areas. Dexter's speech was the highlight of the Parliamentary session for the year. Dexter took his seat directly in front of the podium, looking resplendent in his tricorn hat and robes. Brixton sat next to him, Declan and Enos behind him. As the Lord Chancellor introduced the day's session and outlined the order of events, a gentleman and lady quietly entered a secret chamber through a hidden passage. Out of sight, but not out of hearing, they sat quietly.

"My Lords," Dexter started, looking up at the balcony and seeing Lillianna's face. She smiled her encouragement. "My Ladies," he continued, nodding his head to her. "Allow me to tell you a story. Listen to my voice and envisage my words as if you are seeing it for yourself." Dexter's voice was melodic and sing-songy, entrancing as only a Jamaican accent can be. The lady in hiding placed the palm of her hand over the man's eyes, forcing them closed as he took her hand.

"Imagine yourself living your life, loving the people always around you. Picture yourself going about your daily duties. Suddenly, you are ripped from the ones you love, from the only home you have ever known. Then you are yoked to people you have never met and forced to walk for days half-starved and sleep-deprived until you reach a body of water with no end. The terror you feel is paralyzing. You are loaded like cattle onto boats, the likes of which you have never seen, by strangers from a nightmare.

You don't know if they are men or evil spirits come not only for your life but for your very soul. They shout at you in a language you do not understand, but you feel the bite of their whips and

Chapter 18 | The House of Lords

the sting of their chains. They force you into the bowel of their ship, where the water slaps at the boards in a terrifying crescendo. They lay you down in a coffin, others above and below you. You cannot move. You defecate where you lay and the smell coupled with the fear makes the air too fetid to breathe. You volunteer to carry the dead; they die every day and night."

"You throw the bodies overboard so you can get a breath of fresh air and steal a potato peal fallen from the garbage or snag a crumb of bread brushed from the mouth of your captures in haste."

"You endure months in the coffin because your will to live is stronger than your prayer for death. Finally, you land in an unknown land with people you have yet to know, but with whom you have been caged, your feeling of isolation is complete."

"You are sold into a life of sunup to sundown back-breaking toil. You learn to live on garbage and forget the taste of your grandmother's cooking as you forget what she looks like. You will never know love again. You cannot forge bonds because those you may care for will be sold, raped or even murdered on another man's whim. You realize that an evil spirit did not take you, nor an enemy's spell or even an evil God, but mere men who feel they are worth more than you, simply because of the color of their skin. They mangle your spirit as they try to turn you into a beast of burden, but never break your will as you pray that one day they will see. They will see what you have refused to relinquish to the inequalities you have endured. They will see what you have found the fortitude to hold on to, they will see that you are a man!"

The gentleman in hiding still had his eyes closed. A single tear ran down his cheek. Then the voice telling the story changed. It had the same melodic cadence, but another man now took the floor, continuing the account.

"Then, one day, you look up from your toils as you bake in the hot sun, and you see your face in another. You recognize him because you know him only as a brother," Brixton said, his voice breaking as he ended the story.

The hidden man's eyes flew open. He looked out from behind his hiding place. He saw the Dunbarton brothers, arm in arm. One black and the other white. Raised from birth to love each other, their respect and admiration for each other grew as they did.

"Are their feelings for each other genuine, Georgie?"

Lady Collins squeezed the hand holding hers and kissed it. "They are, my King. They are deeply devoted to one another, from birth."

Dexter and Brixton heard the sharp intakes of breath. Tears in many of the eyes of the men around them. They looked up toward the balcony, searching for their wives' faces. They found them. Through tears, Sabine and Lilliana smiled at their husbands.

William Wilberforce was the first to get to Dexter and Brixton. Tears streaming down his face, his hands applauding them. "That was amazing! That was beautiful, Dexter, Brixton," he said, taking both man's hands in his.

Lord Braemar and Lord Denby were close behind. "Simply breathtaking. No one could have made this argument better than you two," Lord Denby said.

"You have lived your words, there is no greater testimonial than that," added Lord Braemar.

"Everyone is asking for copies of your papers," Enos said breathlessly. "Declan is taking my original copies, the ones you wrote, to the Parliamentary printers as we speak!" Enos hugged Dexter. "I am at a loss for words, Dex. Brilliant does not suffice."

It took them another forty-five minutes to get through the crowd of well-wishers and others asking questions. Lord Kavendish stopped them as they were about to make their escape.

"I was not expecting such a moving argument," he said.

Chapter 18 | The House of Lords

"Lord Kavendish, I understand your motivations for wanting to keep the status quo, but I can assure you, the wave of change crashing on our shores will not affect your profits if you enact the right changes at the right time," Dexter offered.

"I would like to meet with you both to hear your ideas," he said, shaking both men's hands. Lord Kavendish smiled, releasing Dexter's hand. "Well done, my Lord. Well done," he said.

The young page opened a door, motioning for the brothers to go inside. Sabine and Lilliana turned toward the door. Brixton and Dexter rushed in, falling into their arms. The ladies hugged their husbands to them.

"Oh, my darling," Lilliana said to Dexter in Spanish. "I have never heard a more poignant presentation."

"You did it, Brix. You caught lightning in a bottle," Sabine whispered. The emotional toll on their husbands was enormous. The women held them as the enormity of what they had done ceased to overwhelm them.

"What now?" Brixton asked. He turned in Sabine's arms to face Dexter.

"We write papers; we formulate plans. I would like to use what Sabine has done at Friendship Estate, what you are doing at Bellevue Estate to create a blueprint for what should happen after slavery. Abolishing slavery is not the end; it is the beginning, as we well know," Dexter said.

"We can do that," Sabine said, looking at Brixton.

"Then I want to visit our lands. Brixton, I want us to travel around England, Scotland, and learn our history," Dexter said.

Brixton looked at Dexter. "That is not my history, brother; it is yours. It will be your children's. Sabine and I have our history on a tiny island in the Caribbean. That is where we will build our lives, write our own story with our children. We will help you see this through, but Dex, we have to go home," Brixton said.

Dexter nodded; he understood what Brixton was telling him.

Declan and Enos came through the door, stopping as they saw the brothers in front of them, happily ensconced in the arms of their wives. They closed the door softly behind them. Brixton and Dexter went to them, hugging each in turn.

"This is your victory, Enos, and definitely yours, Declan," Dexter announced triumphantly.

"We haven't won the war, but this battle may soon be over. It will take years to go through Parliament, but if the House of Lords backs the abolition of slavery, today is the day that made that possible," Enos announced jubilantly.

"Dinner invitations are pouring in, as are requests for you to speak at auxiliaries and address board meetings. It is truly remarkable what you have accomplished here," Declan was elated.

"I don't know about you, but I would like to go home. I would like to spend the rest of the day in my wife's arms," Dexter said, exhaustion in his voice.

"As would I, brother, as would I," Brixton added.

"I think you two have earned at least that," Enos said, smiling broadly.

They arrived home to find the Dunbarton Manor's entire staff, including their burly Scottish bodyguards, lined up along the carriageway. The sound of applause brought the brothers to the windows of their carriage. John was unabashedly wiping tears from his eyes as he greeted the foursome at the bottom of the stairs that led into the Manor.

"News travels fast," Brixton said, taking his outstretched hand.

"Indeed, it does, my Lord. Indeed, it does," John said. Dexter and Brixton walked along the line of people, greeting each person and thanking them for their support.

"Your dinners will be served in your sitting rooms. I took the liberty of informing the staff that you would be in your rooms for the rest of the day and evening," John whispered to Dexter and Brixton.

"As you should, John," Dexter said. "I am sure that falls under the duties of the Head of Household, doesn't it, Brixton?"

"My Lord?" John asked, confused.

"You are now the Head of the Dunbarton household, John. You are in charge of all of this now," Brixton said, pointing to the house and grounds.

"My Lords!" John said, overcome.

"Well deserved, John, and well earned, taking care of this one," Dexter said, clapping his brother on his back. "Please be sure to open the wine cellars to everyone tonight."

"Breakfast in the upstairs parlor tomorrow, my Lords?" John asked.

Dexter closed the bedroom door behind him, taking Lilliana into his arms. "Let me help you to undress, my love." Taking her dress off, he stopped and looked closely at what she was wearing. "What is this?" he asked.

"Oh, it's a French petticoat. Sabine gave it to me. It is so much more comfortable than a corset, and look," she said, turning her back to him. "It has a little flap back here," she said, turning her head to look at him over her shoulder.

"I see that!" Dexter said. "Let me show you the delight of it." He smiled, advancing toward her.

Brixton was more reflective. He and Sabine undressed but lay on the bed, her head on his shoulder. "Today was hard for you, wasn't it?" she asked.

"I will never forget the day Dexter told me that story. I remember going to Nana and crying myself hoarse in her arms. She wanted to beat Dexter for upsetting me so badly, but I told her I would take the beating for him. She called my mother in and made me tell her that. I was standing in front of Dexter, shielding him.

They just looked at me, then turned around and walked out of the room. Today, I understood the look they had on their faces," Brixton said, his voice raw with emotion.

"What was it, my love," Sabine asked, raising on her elbow to look into his eyes.

"Pride, they were proud of me for recognizing him as my brother," Brixton said.

THE DAYS THAT followed were filled with events. At times, they had to divide and conquer, each of the four attending functions separately but spreading the message of freedom to anyone willing to give them an ear.

They did come together for one evening when the Lords Dunbarton and their wives entertained Lord Kavendish and his retinue for dinner. They had prepared for this meeting, and each knew the role they had to play.

"Talk of the "Abstract of the Slave Law," proposed by the Jamaican House of Assembly, desirous of permitting slaves the same rights only God-fearing Englishmen now possess, is already causing great consternation among proprietors in the colonies. By including hefty fines for non-compliance by overseers and owners, the devaluation of property in the colonies has begun," Lord Kavendish said. "Why a property in your very parish of St. Elizabeth, valued ten years ago at sixty-four thousand pounds currency, was last year valued at six thousand pounds. Advertised for sale in Jamaica and at the Auction market here in London, no purchaser came forward. Due to ill health, the poor owner was forced to sell for seventeen hundred pounds, roughly one pound per acre."

"We have heard of a house with land adjoining in Black River bought only a few years earlier for eighteen hundred pounds by the very solicitor firm that occupied it. Said property just sold for three hundred and fifty pounds! The end of slavery may well be the end of prosperity in the colonies," one of his minions chimed in.

Dexter and Brixton looked at each other surreptitiously. They knew who those solicitors were. That sale was not due to the end of slavery but to Harry's solicitor's own avidity. But the gentlemen's point was well taken. There would be an economic cost to the end of slavery that would have to be borne by all. However, if done fairly, it might be mitigated.

"That slavery is a curse, none will deny, nor would any mortal, possessing a spark of humanity, degrade himself by advocating the policy, or its continuance. But the British House of Assembly has pandered so efficiently to the voices of the abolitionist movement that no thought has been given to the proprietors pertaining to their welfare, livelihood, and safety," another added.

"We are, in effect, persecuting one to affect the other," Lord Kavendish said. "Allow me to read from a letter my brother sent me from his plantation in the colonies, and I quote, "if Emancipation alone is the object required, then why did Britain, as our motherland, commit the wrong of establishing colonial slavery in the first place? Should that nation not redeem the wrong instead of throwing the onus on individuals' shoulders, who merely acted as tools by which said evil was performed? It is manifestly unjust to fix the burden upon those who happened to be in possession of slave property, either by inheritance or purchase. We obtained our property under the express sanction of British law, which is now neither repealed nor obsolete, but by indirect and covert means, having the effect of gradually deteriorating the planter's property and dragging it piecemeal from its lawful owner." Lord Kavendish looked up from the letter in his hand.

"My Lords," Dexter replied. "The action need not be characterized so dismally. The aspiration is to avoid creating a deep wound that will fester and grow into resentment and divide," he said, smiling placatingly

But, Lord Kavendish had more to add. "And as a loyal British subject, should I not demand that the slave mongers in Africa also bear some of the burdens of repealing the evil that they, too, have promoted?" he asked, looking at the four seated in front of him. They had retired to the parlor after dinner, enjoying aperitifs as their discussion intensified.

"Britain cannot hold Africa accountable; each nation on that continent holds its own sovereignty. If any autonomous nation, involved in slavery, undertakes to right this wrong, it will be their conscience that compels them," Lilliana explained. "We can only hope to lead the way with our acts of contrition."

"We understand the principal tie that binds master and servant together, and we cannot snap that bond rendering the relationship more precarious and less advantageous to either party. To do that would bring ruin to Jamaica for generations to come while destroying a relationship that is needed for Jamaica to grow and progress," Brixton jumped in.

"Then, what is your solution?" Lord Kavendish asked.

"We propose to fix a specific date for slavery to cease, possibly allowing two years to elapse before the end of slavery commences. We recommend that all slaves are valued and the full value awarded to the proprietor of every Plantation, Estate, and Penn," Sabine answered. "Instead of framing it as an unremitted loss in punishment of the heinous crime the master has involuntarily committed in having inherited from his ancestors or purchased from his neighbors, property that is now deemed illegal, we recommend that the sum paid be adequate enough to cover the deficiency of labor needed to cultivate the lands." Sabine paused as Brixton leaned forward in his seat.

"Those funds would be used to hire these laborers back, with the desired effect of destroying the stigma of working in the fields as an onerous and demeaning task," he said, completing Sabine's thought, as she nodded her head in encouragement and support.

"Within the plans we are suggesting, we will create free towns, funded by British coffers overflowing with taxes already earned from the colonies and slavery," Sabine emphasized. It was important that these English Lords, who had no vested interest in the colonies besides a modest stipend, understand that their personal property and wealth in England would not be affected. "Enabling former slaves to feel and consider themselves free and independent beings, which they can never do under the present system of being bound to reside on the properties they work with owners feeling compelled to feed, lodge, and clothe them," Sabine said, underscoring her message.

"His own home in the free towns would become a preferable habitation to the 'home in sufferance,' at the property he will no longer belong to except as a hired laborer," Brixton added, remembering the sadness he felt at the realization that nobody left Bellevue Estate when given their freedom because they knew they wouldn't find a better place for themselves if they did.

Dexter had the final word. "The boon of freedom, so long desired, would now be obtained. All restless and jealous feelings would naturally subside, replaced with ambition and a desire to obtain the same standing as many in Jamaica have already achieved by good conduct, undeviating integrity, and the love of those who bore them, regardless of race." Dexter rose to stand behind Brixton and Sabine, who were sitting together on a small settee. Lilliana joined him, and the four looked at the men gathered in front of them. "And in realizing their true potential, we will find the best in all of us," Dexter said, as Brixton nodded in agreement.

Lord Kavendish stood, taking Dexter's hand in his. "So, I see my Lord. So, I see," he said, then turned to shake Brixton's hand.

To his credit, Lord Kavendish approached the dinner with an open mind and a willing heart.

LATER THAT WEEK, they were all sitting down to dinner when Lady Collins breezed in, handed Dexter a packet, and sat down.

"Lady Collins! Where have you been? We have missed you," Sabine said, excited to see her friend.

"Not all of us," Brixton said under his breath.

"Lady Collins, this has the seal of the King on it. Where did you get this?" Dexter asked, opening it.

"To answer your question Dexter, from the King. To answer your question, Sabine, I have been working on this family's behalf, and Brixton, since you did not ask a question, I have no comment," Lady Collins said, taking a sip of wine.

As Dexter went through the documents, his eyes widened, and his mouth fell open. "Dear Lord above!" he exclaimed, looking at Lady Collins.

"Never underestimate the power of a woman or the influence she brings to bear on a belief she holds dear," Lady Collins said.

"Dex, what is it?" Lilliana asked as his face grew pale.

"The Parliament has ratified Sabine's right to own Friendship Estate based on Absolute Primogeniture. The King has appointed her the Governor-General of Jamaica. Enos, you have been appointed the Magistrate General of the British colonies in the Caribbean, based in Jamaica," Dexter said.

"What?" Sabine and Enos exclaimed.

Brixton sat back in his chair as a smile spread across his face. He looked at Lady Collins, nodding to her. She smiled and nodded back, raising her wine glass to him.

"Here are your papers," Dexter said, getting up to hand them the documents.

"There is more," Lady Collins said.

Dexter took out the last document, read it, and then handed it to Lilliana to read. His hand over his mouth.

Lilliana read it and looked at Lady Collins, "Now I understand what you meant when you spoke to the King on my behalf."

"What did Lady Collins say to the King?" Declan asked.

Looking at Dexter, she said. "She told him that you had moved the heart of a Princess, and given a chance, you would move the heart of a King. It appears you have moved the heart of a King, mi amor."

"King George has directed his Parliament to draft the decree for the abolition of slavery. He has appointed Dexter his voice in this matter and given him full authority to act on his behalf," Lady Collins said, sitting back.

"We also have an invitation to court. The Dunbarton family is invited back to court, all of us," Dexter said, throwing the invitation on the table.

Declan clapped his hands, got up, and started pacing. "I wish Liam were here to see this!" he said.

Dexter looked at Brixton. "Brix! You, Sabine, and Enos leave for Jamaica in a month, on the King's own frigate. It seems you will be able to tell Uncle Liam yourself."

Brixton looked around the room before he spoke. "Then, we shall enjoy the next month to the fullest," Brixton said, rising to hug his brother. "You have fulfilled your destiny, Dex. Now it is time for me to fulfill mine," he whispered.

ON THE MORNING of Sabine and Brixton's departure from London, they met in the secret garden. The air was crisp, hinting that fall would soon become winter. Sabine sat on Brixton's lap, wrapped in blankets. Dexter and Lilly shared a blanket, locked in each other's arms.

"I can't wait to see the Jamaican sun again," Brixton complained, snuggling into his blanket.

"You will be home for Christmas, as you promised," Dexter noted.

"Christmas in Jamaica!" Brixton smiled at the thought. "I cannot imagine anywhere in the world will offer a better Christmas than Jamaica does," Brixton declared.

"I will accept that challenge, Brixton," Lilly said, looking at Sabine. "Dexter and I will meet you in Jamaica next Christmas. That is a promise," she said, smiling at Dexter.

"You want to spend next Christmas in Jamaica?" Dexter asked her.

"I do. I want to see the island that bore you, made you the man I fell in love with," she said with feeling. "Besides, the Spanish perfected Christmas, I doubt Jamaica will rival the Christmas I will give you, but I am willing to give Brixton the benefit of the doubt until I can judge for myself," she teased, smiling at Sabine over Dexter's head.

Lady Collins had declined the invitation to see them off. Brixton asked John to convey a message to her. "Please let the Lady know she is always welcome in any Dunbarton home she may wish to visit."

Declan, Dexter, and Lilliana accompanied Brixton, Sabine, and Enos to the docks.

"Seeing as you are the only passengers on this ship, you might not sink it with all your luggage, Sabine," Declan said dryly.

Lilliana and Sabine hugged each other. "Thank you for everything," Lilliana said.

"Thank you for making it easier for Brixton to leave Dexter," Sabine responded.

"Brixton, I expect as beautiful a handfasting ceremony as you had," Lilliana said. Sabine had told Lilliana about their handfasting ceremony, and she had asked Dexter if they could do that for the family when they went to Jamaica. Dexter had quickly agreed; it would be the best way to introduce his new wife to everyone on the estate. He and Lilliana had written a personal letter to Liam, asking if he would preside over it.

Sabine, Lilliana, Declan, and Enos walked toward the ship, giving the brothers time to say goodbye.

"This is the longest we will ever be away from each other," Dexter said, hugging Brixton to him. "But I am confident I am leaving you in good hands."

Brixton hugged him back. "I, too, am confident I am leaving you in good hands. You are the best of me, brother," Brixton said, the words catching in his throat.

"As you are the best of me, brother," Dexter said, tears in his eyes.

Sailing home seemed to take a lot less than getting to England had. Sabine and Enos filled their days with learning about the new positions they would hold, their duties to the King, and how much autonomy each had to enact the changes they wanted to make. Including moving Jamaica's capital from Spanish Town to Kingston. The decision was easy to make because Kingston was home to the best natural harbor in the Caribbean. The area had served as the commercial capital of Jamaica since 1703, while Spanish Town served as the political capital. Sabine realized that both industries had to work in tandem and nearby for Jamaica to grow. Liam would oversee the building of the Governor General's mansion that Sabine asked Enos to move into. She would not leave her beloved Friendship Estate, and she knew Brixton would never leave Mount Sion.

Sabine and Brixton talked late into the night of their plans for Mount Sion and what they hoped to build there. Their excitement grew as they sailed past the harbor of Port Royal. The ship glided on the cerulean waters, so close to land, the Captain joked they could chuck a biscuit ashore. Sabine and Enos roamed the deck as they viewed the picturesque sandy beaches dotted with majestic coconut trees skirting the shore in neat rows, seeming to salute as they sailed by.

Brixton joined them as they sailed past the Kingston wharf, crowded with barrels of rum, hogsheads of sugar, rough-hewn crocus bags of coffee and ginger, loads of pimento, legs of mahogany, and immense piles of logwood and lignum vitae, all awaiting shipment back to England.

"You are perfectly correct, Sabine," Enos said, turning to her. "Kingston is the perfect location for Jamaica's capital."

Sabine nodded. The surrounding mountains' welcome safety, coupled with the harbor's busy scene, was enough to drive away any doubts she may have had. She could envision Kingston become an expansive city with streets inclining gradually to the harbor, in her mind's eye.

As they sailed along the island's shoreline, Sabine and Brixton marveled at the beauty of every turn, one captivating tableau after another. Brixton held Sabine as they cruised past the bays and ports of Salt River, Old Harbour, Alligator Pond, Great and Little Pedro, as recognizable to each of them as their lover's face. This time, they sailed into the Black River Harbor.

They disembarked quickly, anxious to get home, riding out of Black River as the carriages followed behind. With whoops and hollers, Brixton raced his horse through the gates of Bellevue Estate as the sun began its descent into the sea. He came to a screeching halt in front of the back veranda, rushing into the Greathouse, searching for his mother and Nana. Pearly heard him first. She jumped into his arms, her screams of joy drawing everyone to them.

Pearly covered Brixton's face with kisses as he hugged her to him. When he saw his mother and Nana coming down the passageway, he moved Pearly to his back and opened his arms.

Chapter 18 | The House of Lords

"Brixton! You're home," his mother exclaimed, running to him. He embraced her, then Nana, hugging them close.

"Where that likkle she-devil wife of yours?" Nana asked.

"She will be over shortly. We stopped at Friendship Estate first because of the carriages. I stopped long enough to pay my respects to Mistress Anne and Doctor Richard, but I had to see you. I have missed you both so much," Brixton exclaimed.

Brixton noticed Liam, standing back and watching the reunion. He let the ladies go and walked toward him. "Uncle Liam, I have carried these with me, close to my heart, because I wanted to be able to give them to you the minute I saw you," Brixton said, extracting envelopes tied with ribbon from his jacket and handing them to Liam. "Open the top one first."

Liam took the small bundle from him and untied the ribbon. First was the invitation from the King for the Dunbarton brothers to join him at court. Liam looked at it and started to laugh, tears running down his face.

"Liam? What is it?" Margaret asked, concerned.

"It is our fondest wish, Mags. Your sons have realized our dream," he said, handing the invitation to Margaret, who read it, then passed it to Nana.

"There are letters there from Declan and from Dexter," Brixton said quietly.

"Dexter?" Mags said. "Tell me of my son, Brix," she begged.

"I have letters for both of you from Dex," Brixton stated, handing them each a small bundle of letters. "And from his wife."

"His wife?" Mags and Nana asked in unison.

"Yes," Brixton said, laughing. "She is a force of nature, Mother. Beautiful, smart, and the perfect match for Dexter. She is also a Princess of Castille."

"Dexter marry a Princess?" Nana asked.

Margaret started to laugh. "Imagine that Liam, both my sons, married Princesses. We never dreamt of that," she said, shaking her head.

"There is so much to tell you," Brixton proclaimed.

Nana quickly fixed Brixton a heaping bowl of stewed peas and rice, which he ate with unabashed delight. Anne and Richard arrived with Sabine not long after Brixton had his reunion with his mother and Nana. Sabine and Brixton sat for hours that evening. They told their eager audience everything, starting with the Dunbarton townhouse in London.

"Mother, it is magnificent. You and Nana have to go and visit Dexter and Lilly. Dexter is missing your cooking, Nana. Lilly had the purveyors scouring London for the hottest peppers they could find because Dexter says English food is bland," Brixton said to Nana's delight.

"Tell us about your visit to court," Anne beseeched.

"It was a delight, Mother. Lady Collins arranged it all," Sabine said.

"By the way, thank you for that introduction," Brixton said sarcastically.

Anne laughed. "Yes, she is an acquired taste, but she has grown from a hapless girl into a formidable woman. I knew she would be an asset to you."

"She was," Brixton agreed. "Both a valuable asset and an acquired taste."

"She dressed me in a gown of yellow as bright as the sun—Topaz jewels at my throat, with a tiara to match. Lilly was in blue, the color of the Caribbean Sea, with a dazzling sapphire choker and tiara," Sabine began.

"They were beautiful; the entire court stopped as they walked in," Brixton added proudly.

"She wanted to make sure our Jamaican heritage was on full display," Sabine said, going on to describe the night's events and the King's devoted attention to them. "The King made it known the Dunbarton brothers were a favorite of his and most welcome at court," Sabine concluded, smiling with pride as she looked at Brixton.

"Declan said your presentation to the Parliament was a grand success, but he says you are to tell us what transpired," Liam said to Brixton, he had read Declan's letter.

Sabine and Brixton looked at each other. As Brixton took her hand, Sabine started to speak. "I have been granted ownership of Friendship Estate based on Absolute Primogeniture," Sabine said excitedly as they all gasped in delight. "But that is not all. The King appointed me the Governor-General of Jamaica. Enos Knowles is the Magistrate General for all British colonies in the Caribbean." Sabine finished to the shocked faces all around.

"One of her tasks is to ready Jamaica for the abolition of slavery," Brixton said. "The King has abolished slavery in Britain and her colonies. He has appointed Dexter his voice in this undertaking."

"How yu do all dat, Brix?" Nana asked, unable to take it all in.

Brixton went to Nana and kneeled in front of her. He took her hand in his. "By telling them the story Dexter told me when we were just little boys. You wanted to beat Dexter for upsetting me, but I suspect you and Mother wanted to teach me a lesson. And in doing so, you built a bond so strong, it tore through the hearts of men and broke the back of slavery."

Nana clasped Brixton to her. "My golden bwoy! My golden bwoy," Nana wept as she hugged him.

Margaret took Liam's hand in hers as Richard leaned down and kissed Anne. All they had suffered, all that they had endured, and now the two knights they had sent into battle had not only won the war but had conquered hearts in the process.

"Sabine, Brixton," Liam said. "You must be anxious to see the progress on your home."

"We are, Uncle Liam," Brixton said. "But tonight, Sabine and I would like to spend the night at Mount Sion. Tomorrow we will meet and go over all that needs to be done on the estates. I expect it will take a few days for Sabine and I to get back into the swing of things, but we are ready."

Margaret and Anne were reluctant to let their children out of their sight, but they understood how much the grotto meant to them, so they were not surprised they wanted their first night back to be spent in their little sanctuary.

"The more things change, the more they remain the same," Brixton said. They were swimming in the phosphorous pool in the grotto.

"What?" Sabine asked.

"Something, your father said to me once," Brixton replied, swimming to her. "I never understood what he meant, but I think I do now. This cave, our cave. This island, our home will remain constant even as changes happen all around us to make it better."

"That does sound like something Papa would say," Sabine said, nuzzling his neck.

"Do you think the pain of his loss will ever go away?" Brixton asked her.

"It will lessen. In time you will think of him and smile instead of feeling the sharp sting of loss," Sabine said.

"When will that be?" Brixton asked.

"When we can make do with only the love he left behind," she said, leaning her head against his.

WEEKS TURNING INTO months as Sabine and Brixton worked to prepare Jamaica for the end of slavery. Sabine invited Queen Nandi to visit them at Friendship Estate. She was only too happy to oblige, arriving with Bene and the seeds he had promised Brixton for Mount Sion. King George had offered repatriation to

Chapter 18 | The House of Lords

Africa for anyone who wanted to return. While Queen Nandi was proud of her African heritage, she could no more identify with Africa than Brixton could with England. She was happy to stay in Jamaica, to build a nation with an equal and fair say in the island's future for her people.

"Out of these many, one people will emerge," she said to Sabine, who promptly appointed her Jamaica's first Prime Minister, a post that would be ratified by Dexter on his return visit to Jamaica later that year. Brixton took Queen Nandi aside and told her of Dexter's marriage to Lilliana.

"Dexter is very much in love with her," Brixton explained.

"Is she a compliment to him? His equal?" Queen Nandi asked.

"In every way," Brixton assured her.

"Then I am happy for him. Destiny is never kind to those it calls to serve. Their path is not an easy one. If they are committed to walking it together, they will be better for it."

"They are devoted to each other," Brixton said confidently.

Queen Nandi smiled sadly as Sabine looked on. Sabine's heart went out to her. She had watched Dexter struggle until Lilliana's love helped him find his footing. She could only admire the strength of will this regal woman exhibited. Queen Nandi had hacked and fought to forge a path for her people, and she had done it all by herself.

Now Sabine was asking her to forge a new path for the entire island of Jamaica. Queen Nandi did not disappoint. Together they created the Commonwealth of Caribbean Islands. The organization worked on behalf of the islands to negotiate prices to sell goods and services to the British Empire and beyond. With the help of Enos Knowles, they also created a Caribbean Court of Appeals, replacing the Privy Council.

Before they knew it, a year had passed. Sabine and Brixton were on their way to Kingston to collect Dexter and Lilly. Their house on Mount Sion was finished, and they would be hosting their first Christmas dinner there. Dexter and Lilly would stay with them as their guests.

Margaret and Nana were beside themselves with excitement. Not only for Dexter's homecoming but to welcome his new wife. Margaret, Nana, Liam, Anne, and Richard waited on the Bellevue Greathouse's front steps as the carriage carrying Sabine and Lilly arrived. Brixton and Dexter rode before them on horseback, the children of the estate running beside the carriage, trying to catch a glimpse of Dexter's bride.

Dexter ran up the steps to greet them as Brixton helped Sabine and Lilly from the carriage. Smiling, Dexter returned to take his wife's hand, escorting her up the steps.

"Mother, Nana, I would like you to meet Lilliana De Castille, Princess of Spain, and my wife," Dexter said, standing back.

Margaret and Nana curtsied to Lilly, who laughed and embraced them. "It is I who should be curtsying to you," she said. "I will forever be in your debt for raising the man who is now my beloved husband."

Nana and Margaret were instantly charmed. "Well, there goes my spot as the favorite daughter-in-law," Sabine said, deprecatingly.

Brixton looked at Sabine as a smile played on his lips. "My darling, Nana still refers to you as my she-devil wife. I am not sure you were ever in the running."

Christmas was a festive affair as Brixton proudly showed Lilliana all the Jamaican traditions. He took her to the Christmas Markets, where Jamaicans from all walks of life came to celebrate the story of Christmas with outdoor concerts and plays and to shop for Christmas ornaments and presents. The costumed Junkanoo dancers also came out to perform for children, scaring them, then rewarding them with candy and treats. Lilly was particularly taken with the Junkanoo dancers, so Brixton invited them to Mount Sion.

Chapter 18 | The House of Lords

As they sat down for Christmas dinner, Brixton looked down the table to Sabine sitting at the other end. She smiled at him, and he lifted his wine glass in a special toast to his wife.

"If I may, Brixton," Dexter asked, standing. "Lilly and I have one more gift for our hosts." They had all exchanged gifts before dinner, so this was unexpected. Lilly stood, taking her husband's arm. "Sabine, Brixton, if you would join us, please," Dexter invited.

Lilly handed Dexter a leather document holder. "Lilly and I want you to have this," Dexter said, giving the holder to Brixton.

"What is it, Brix?" Margaret asked as Sabine put her hand over her mouth in surprise.

"It's the deed to Bellevue Estate," Brixton answered softly.

"You wanted nothing in England or Scotland, so Lilly and I thought you should at least have this. You have more than earned it," Dexter said as Brixton hugged him.

"Thank you, Dex," Brixton said. "You are the best of me, brother."

"As you are of me, brother," Dexter replied fondly.

THE NEXT DAY was the handfasting ceremony for Dexter and Lilly. The foursome decided to go for an early morning swim before the heat of the day was upon them. Sabine introduced Lilly to a swim shift, a long muslin dress that clung to the skin when wet but made moving arms and legs in the water easier. Dexter and Lilly were sitting on the beach as Brixton helped Sabine out of the water. He drew her to him, as his hand fell to her stomach, caressing it.

"Dexter, look!" Lilly exclaimed.

"Look at what?" he asked lazily.

"Look at Sabine's stomach," she urged, jumping to her feet. A small, discernable bump was just beginning to appear.

"When were you going to tell us?" Lilly asked, running to Sabine and hugging her.

"After the ceremony tonight, we wanted this time to be about you and Dexter, but we did plan to tell you tonight," Brixton said as he lay down on the towel next to Dexter. Sabine and Lilly sank to the sand, talking excitedly.

"I am so happy for you, my sister," Lilly said. "May I?" Lilly asked, her hand moving toward Sabine's stomach.

Sabine placed Lilly's hand on her stomach. "Sometimes, he moves. It feels like butterflies racing."

"He?" Lilly asked, looking at Sabine, who nodded, smiling. "I am dying to get pregnant," she said. "I so want to give him a child," Lilly said, looking wistfully at Dexter.

"Then that will be my gift to you," Sabine whispered as Lilly turned to look at her. "Tonight, after your ceremony, I will ask my mother to give you a blessing. I promise you will leave Jamaica with a baby in your belly," Sabine said.

"Now, I am even happier that you have Bellevue Estate along with Mount Sion," Dexter said to Brixton.

"There will always be a Dunbarton in Jamaica, Dex. Whether living in the Greathouse at Mount Sion or in a simple cottage at Treasure Beach. A Dunbarton will always call Jamaica home with roots buried so deep in the island soil that it will bind us to her shores forever," Brixton said, looking out at the Caribbean Sea. The bright Jamaican sun kissed its surface, making it sparkle and shimmer before him.

IN FULFILLING a destiny born of hate and degradation but nurtured by love, loyalty, and dedication, two young men changed the course of history. Their devotion to each other and the island that bore them prevented future generations of Jamaicans from suffering under the stunted economic growth of oppressive taxation resulting from the brutal response to rebellions that shook the foundations of a society in its infancy. There was no destruction of the Jamaican psyche to create deep resentment between the races, ignoring their shared heritage and culture, unable to work together to create a society of equals.

British subjects did not lose their West Indian relatives. The British King formed a Commonwealth of Nations, rooted in brotherhood. Much admired for this 'symbol of their free association,' the member nations willingly accepted the King as their monarch. All because two men, endowed with love strong enough to move the heart of a king, made him recognize the benefit of representation, the promotion of democracy, and the individual pursuit of equality with opposition to racism.

Two brothers stood together against deprivation, and promoted the creation of a culture based on friendship, loyalty, along with the shared desire for freedom and peace.

If only...

THE END

Acknowledgements

I want to thank my brother, Andrew Finlason, for bringing the seed of this story to my imagination and for his unwavering commitment to editing this book. His love of Jamaica, born of his dedication to learning our history, was instrumental in crafting this story.

To my great, great, great, great grandfather, Bernard Martin Senior, who wrote a book in 1835 that scholars selected as one of the most culturally significant records of this period in Jamaica's history.

To my Uncle Howard Finlason, whose enthusiasm for my writing is inspiring. He always seems to merge his comments with my father's voice in his reviews of my writing. He is the Brixton to my father's Dexter.

To my beloved cousin, Anna Henriques, the bond we have shared since birth goes far beyond the ties of blood and friendship.

To George Graham, a renowned journalist as well as a fellow Jamaican author. His input was invaluable, as were his editorial comments and corrections. He is truly a kindred spirit.

To my "editing team" of Aurora and Joel Ehrman, whose attention to detail far exceeds mine. Their friendship is the stuff legends are made of.

I grew up listening to "Rivers of Babylon" sung by Boney M. The song left an indelible mark on me.

Author Bio

I was born in Mandeville, Jamaica, in 1967, the beginning of a turbulent time in Jamaica's history. The island had just gained independence from Britain, with the colonial class and color divisions still firmly in place. The economy was in free fall as communism and capitalism battled for supremacy by destabilizing the government, encouraging violence, and exerting tactical financial control. I came of age during these times. My playground extended from Mandeville to the beaches and small villages of the South Coast and the island's capital, Kingston.

Eight generations of my family are buried on the island. Roots so deep in the Jamaican soil that they will bind my heart and soul forever to my island in the sun, no matter how far afield I may go. Even though I have lived in the United States for decades, Jamaica still holds my navel string, a pull deep in my soul that begins as a low drumbeat growing stronger and louder until I visit her shores.

I now live in Orlando with my husband of twenty-four years... who still says I am his most expensive souvenir.